Dear Reader,

I'm thrilled to present *The Darkest Pleasure,* the third installment of my brand-new paranormal trilogy, Lords of the Underworld, which began with *The Darkest Night* and continued with *The Darkest Kiss.* In a remote fortress in Budapest, six immortal warriors—each more dangerously seductive than the last—are bound by an ancient curse none has been able to break. When a powerful enemy returns, they will travel the world in search of a sacred relic of the gods—one that threatens to destroy them all.

Join me on a journey through this darkly sensual world, where the line between good and evil blurs and true love is put to the ultimate test. And stay tuned for further adventures from the Lords of the Underworld as the stakes get higher, the quest more dangerous and the romance hotter!

Wishing you all the best,

Gena Showalter

Other sexy, steamy reads from

Gena Showalter

and HQN Books

Catch a Mate
The Nymph King
Playing with Fire
Animal Instincts
Jewel of Atlantis
Heart of the Dragon
The Pleasure Slave
The Stone Prince

**And don't miss
the first two installments
of the enthralling
Lords of the Underworld trilogy:**

The Darkest Night
The Darkest Kiss

Available now!

Gena Showalter

THE
DARKEST
PLEASURE

HQN™

ISBN 13: 978-0-373-77310-7
ISBN-10:   0-373-77310-2

THE DARKEST PLEASURE

This edition published by arrangement with Harlequin Books S.A.

® and TM are trademarks of the publisher. Trademarks indicated with
® are registered in the United States Patent and Trademark Office, the
Canadian Trade Marks Office and in other countries.

www.HQNBooks.com

Printed in U.S.A.

This first Lords of the Underworld trilogy could not have been possible without the following amazing, wonderful, kick-ass people
(whom I adore):

Donna Hayes
Loriana Sacilotto
Dianne Moggy
Randall Toye
Tracy Farrell
Margo Lipschultz
Keyren Gerlach
Kathleen Oudit
Juliana Kolesova
Diana Wong
Stacy Widdrington
Marianna Ricciuto
Pat Muir-Rand
Melissa Caraway
Kristin Foti
Kim Elliott
Vicki So
Josh Hilburt
Nancy Fischer
Sally Noonan
Brian McGroarty
The Harlequin Sales Group
Deidre Knight
Patricia Rouse
Susan Grimshaw
Kathy Baker
Max Showalter
Matt Showalter
Roy Showalter
Destinee Showalter
Sheila Fields
Jill Monroe

To Kemmie Tolbert, an amazing woman who loves books as much as I do

CHAPTER ONE

REYES STOOD on the roof of his Budapest fortress, five stories up, his feet balanced precariously on the highest ledge. Above him, moonlight seeped red and yellow from the sky, blood mixed with fickle gold, dark mixed with light, wounds freshly cut in the endless expanse of black velvet.

He gazed down at the gloomy, waiting void beneath him, the taunting ground opening its arms as if begging to embrace him. *Thousands of years, and I'm still reduced to* this.

Frigid wind blustered, ruffling his hair in every direction, tickling his bare chest, the hated butterfly etched up onto his neck and the remembered lifeblood splattered there. Not his blood, though. No, not his, but his friend's. Every stroke of hair against that phantom evidence of life and death was like kindling thrown into the fire of his blazing guilt.

So many times he'd come here, wishing for things that could never be. So many times he'd prayed for absolution, relief from his daily torment and the demon inside him responsible…relief from his utter dependence on self-mutilation.

His prayers had never been answered. *Would* never be answered. This was what he was, what he would always be. And his agony would only increase. Once an immortal warrior to the gods, he was now a Lord of the Underworld, possessed by one of the many spirits formerly locked inside *dimOuniak*. From favor to dishonor, beloved to despised. From happiness to constant misery.

He ground his teeth. Mortals knew *dimOuniak* as Pandora's box; he knew it as the source of his eternal downfall. He and his friends had defiantly opened it all those centuries ago; now he and his friends *were* the box, each holding a demon inside himself.

Jump, his demon beseeched.

His demon: Pain. His constant companion. The tempting whisper in the back of his mind, the dark entity that craved unspeakable evil. The supernatural force he battled every damned minute of every damned day.

Jump.

"Not yet." A few more seconds of anticipation, of knowing most of his bones would shatter on contact. He grinned at the thought. The razor-sharp bone shards would cut his injured, swollen organs and those organs would burst like water balloons; his skin would rip from the excess fluid and this time the lifeblood that drained would be his own. Agony, such blissful agony, would consume him.

For a little while, anyway.

Slowly his smile faded. Within days—hours, if he failed to hurt himself badly enough—his body would heal itself, totally and completely. He would wake up, whole again, Pain once more a commanding force inside his mind, too loud to be denied. But oh, for those few blessed ticks of the clock before his bones began to realign, before his organs began to weave back together and his skin to reconnect, before blood once more pumped through his veins, he would experience nirvana. The ultimate paradise. Rapture of the sweetest kind. He would writhe in the exquisite pleasure the pain brought with it—his *only* source of pleasure. The demon would purr with utter contentment, so drunk on the sensation it was unable to speak, and Reyes would experience such blissful peace.

For a little while. Always, only, a little while.

"I do not need another reminder about how fleeting my

peace is," he muttered to drown the depressing thought. He knew how quickly time passed. A year sometimes felt like nothing more than a day. A day sometimes felt like nothing more than a minute.

And yet, both were sometimes infinite to him. Just one of the many contradictions of life as a Lord of the Underworld.

Jump, Pain said. Then, more insistently, *Jump! Jump!*

"I told you. Just a few seconds more." Once again Reyes glanced at the ground. Jagged rocks winked in that bleeding moonlight, the clear puddles surrounding them rippling in the wind. Mist rose like ghostly fingers, summoning him closer, wonderfully closer. "Plunging a blade into your enemy's throat kills him, yes," he told the demon, "but then it's over, done, and you have nothing left to anticipate."

Jump! A snarled command, impatient and needy, a child throwing a tantrum.

"Soon."

Jumpjumpjump!

Yes, sometimes demons really were like whiny human children. Reyes shoved a hand through his tangled hair, a few strands ripping from his scalp. He knew of only one way to shut his other half up. Obedience. Why he'd even tried to resist and savor the moment, he didn't know.

Jump!

"Maybe this time you'll be sent back to hell," he muttered. A man could wish, anyway. Finally, he splayed his arms. Closed his eyes. Leaned…

"Come down from there," he heard a voice say from behind him.

Reyes's eyelids popped open at the unwelcome intrusion, and he stiffened. He rebalanced but didn't turn. He knew why Lucien was here, and he was too ashamed to face his friend. While the warrior understood what he dealt with because of his demon, there would be no understanding what he'd done.

"That's the plan, coming down. Leave and I'll see that it gets done."

"You know what I meant." There was no hint of laughter in Lucien's voice. "I need to talk to you."

The dewy scent of roses suddenly saturated the air, thick and lush and so unexpected in the late-winter night that Reyes would have sworn he'd been transported to a spring meadow. A human would have found the aroma hypnotic, lulling, almost drugging, and would have done anything the warrior asked. Reyes merely found it annoying. After thousands of years together, Lucien should have known the fragrance held no power over him.

"We'll talk tomorrow," he said tightly.

Jump!

"We'll talk now. Afterward, you may do whatever you please."

After Reyes admitted his newest crime? No, thanks. Guilt, shame and grief might bring emotional pain, but none would soothe his demon in any way. Only physical suffering offered relief, which was why Reyes had always guarded his emotional well-being so diligently.

Yes, and you've done such a great job at it.

He ran his tongue over his teeth, unsure who had whispered that sarcastic little gem. Himself or Pain. "I'm in a bad place right now, Lucien."

"As are the others. As am I."

"You, at least, have a woman to comfort you."

"You have friends. You have me." Lucien, keeper of the demon of Death, was tasked with escorting human souls to the hereafter, whether the hereafter was heaven or the deepest fires of hell. He was stoic, ever calm—most of the time. He'd become their leader, the man every warrior residing in this Budapest fortress turned to for guidance and aid. "Talk to me."

Reyes didn't like to deny his friend, but he told himself it was better that Lucien did not learn the terrible thing he'd done.

Even as Reyes thought it, he recognized the lie for what it was: a shameful lack of courage on his part. "Lucien," he began, only to stop. Growl.

"The tracking dye has worn off and no one knows where Aeron is," Lucien said. "No one knows what he's doing, if he's the one who slaughtered those humans in the States. Maddox said he called you right after Aeron escaped the dungeon. Then Sabin told me you left Rome and the Temple of the Unspoken Ones in a hurry. Want to tell me where you went?"

"No." Truth. He didn't. "But you may rest assured Aeron is no longer able to slaughter humans."

There was a pause, the rose scent intensifying.

"How do you know for sure?" The question possessed a bite.

Reyes shrugged.

"Why don't I tell you what I think happened?" Where Lucien's tone had been sharp before, it was now threaded with expectation. And fear? "You went after Aeron, hoping to protect the girl."

The girl. Aeron had kidnapped *the girl*. Aeron had been ordered by the new gods, the Titans, to murder *the girl*. Reyes had taken one look at *the girl* and allowed her to invade his most private thoughts, color his every action and reduce him to a lovesick fool.

With only a glance she had changed his life, and not for the better. And yet, the fact that Lucien refused to say her name pissed Reyes off royally. Reyes desired that girl more than he desired a hammer to the skull. For Pain, that was saying something.

"Well?" Lucien prompted.

"You're right," Reyes said through tight lips. Why not admit it? he suddenly thought. His emotions were in turmoil and remaining quiet had only roused them further. More than that, his friends could not hate him any more than he hated himself. "I went after Aeron."

The admission hung in the air, as heavy as shackles, and he paused.

"You found him."

"I found him." Reyes squared his shoulders. "I also... destroyed him."

Rocks crumbled under Lucien's boots as he stalked forward. "You *killed* him?"

"Worse." Still, Reyes did not turn. He peered down longingly at the still-waiting ground. "I buried him."

The pounding of footsteps ceased abruptly. "You buried him but did not kill him?" Confusion drifted from Lucien's voice. "I do not understand."

"He was about to kill Danika. I could see the torment in his eyes and knew he did not want to do it. I cut him down to slow him and he *thanked* me, Lucien. Thanked me. He begged me to stop him permanently. He begged me to take his head. But I couldn't do it. I raised my sword, but I just couldn't do it. So I had Kane collect Maddox's chains and bring them to me. Since Maddox no longer needs them, I used them to lock Aeron underground."

Reyes had once been forced to shackle Maddox to a bed every night, cursed to stab his friend in the stomach six hated times, knowing the warrior would awaken in the morning and Reyes would have to kill him all over again. *Some friend I am.*

After hundreds of years, Maddox had come to accept the curse. Restraining him, however, had been a necessity. As the keeper of Violence, Maddox tended to attack without warning. Even his friends. And as strong as the warrior was, he would have rent man-made metal in seconds. So they'd commandeered links forged by the gods, links no one, not even an immortal, could open without the proper key.

Like Maddox, Aeron had been—was—helpless against them. In the beginning, Reyes had resisted using them on his friend, not wanting to take even more of the warrior's freedom. Sadly, as with Maddox, employing them had become a necessity.

"Where is Aeron, Reyes?" Underneath the question was a command laced with the authority of a man used to getting what he wanted, when he wanted. A man who ensured there were severe consequences for any type of delay.

Reyes wasn't frightened. He simply hated to disappoint this warrior he loved like a brother. "That, I will not tell you. Aeron doesn't wish to be freed." *And even if he did, I do not think I would free him.*

There lay the crux of Reyes's guilt.

Another pause slithered between them, this one strained and expectant. "I can find him on my own. You know I can."

"You have already tried and failed or you would not be here." Reyes knew that Lucien could flash into the spirit world and follow a person's unique psychic trail. Sometimes, though, the trail faded or became tainted.

Reyes suspected Aeron's was tainted, as the warrior was not the man he used to be.

"You're right. His trail ends in New York," Lucien admitted darkly. "I could continue my search, but that would take time. And time is something none of us can spare right now. Already two weeks have passed."

How well Reyes knew that, for he'd felt every day of those weeks like a noose tightening around his neck, one worry stacking upon another. Hunters, their greatest enemy, were even now searching for Pandora's box, hoping to use it to suck the demons out of each and every warrior, destroying man and locking away beast.

If the warriors wished to survive, they had to find the box first.

Chaotic as life now was, Reyes was not ready to end his permanently.

"Tell me where he is," Lucien said, "and I'll bring him to the fortress. I'll bolt him inside the dungeon."

Reyes snorted. "He escaped once. He could escape again. Even from Maddox's chains, I'm thinking. His bloodlust gives him a strength I've never encountered before. Better he stay where he is."

"He's your friend. He's one of us."

"He's warped now, and you know it. Most of the time, he is not aware of his own actions. He would kill *you* if given the chance."

"Reyes—"

"He'll destroy her, Lucien."

Her. Danika Ford. *The girl.* Reyes had seen her only a few times, talked to her even less, but still, he craved her with every ounce of his being. Something he didn't understand. He was dark, she was light. He was anguish, she was innocence. He was wrong for her in every way, and yet, when she looked at him, his entire world felt right.

He knew beyond any doubt that the next time Aeron reached her, the warrior would savagely murder her. There would be no stopping him. Not again. Aeron had been ordered to kill Danika—and her mother and her sister and her grandmother—and was as helpless against the gods and their powers as everyone else. He would do it.

Reyes's temper flared and he had to glance at the rocks below to calm himself. Aeron had resisted the gods' dark task at first. He was— No. He *had been* a good man. But with every day that had passed, his demon had grown stronger, louder inside his head, until finally it overtook his mind. Now Aeron *was* the demon inside him. He was Wrath. He obeyed. He slew. Until those four women were destroyed, he would live only to hunt and kill.

Except, inside Danika's temporary apartment those fourteen days, four hours and fifty-six minutes ago, there had been a small part of Aeron that had known the crimes he committed. A small part that hated who and what he had become and desired death above all things. Desired an end to the torment. Why else would Aeron have asked Reyes to kill him?

And I refused him. Reyes couldn't bring himself to hurt another warrior. Not again. Still. What kind of monster left his friend to suffer? A friend who had fought for him, killed for him? Loved him?

There had to be a way to save both Aeron and Danika, he thought for what, the thousandth time? He'd spent countless hours pondering, but still did not see a solution.

"Do you know where the girl is?" Lucien demanded, cutting into his musings.

"No, I do not." Truth. "Aeron found her, I found Aeron, and that's when we fought. She ran. I didn't follow her afterward. She could be anywhere by now." Best that way. He knew it, but he was still desperate to know her location, what she was doing…if she lived.

"Lucien, man, what's taking so damn long?"

At the second intrusion, Reyes finally turned. Paris, keeper of Promiscuity, now stood beside Lucien. Both men were facing him, eyes narrowed. Beams of crimson moonlight fell around them but not *on* them, as if those colored rays were afraid to touch the evil that even hell itself had been unable to contain.

Immortal that he was, Reyes saw them clearly, gaze cutting expertly through the darkness.

Paris was tall, the tallest of the group, with multicolored hair, pale otherworldly skin and eyes so pure a blue not even the most fanciful poetry would do them justice. Human women found him mesmerizing, irresistible, constantly throwing themselves at him and begging for a single touch. A heated kiss.

Lucien, though mated now, was not so lucky. Human women stayed far away from him. His face was hideously scarred, grotesque even, giving him the appearance of a bedtime monster found only in fairy tales. Didn't help that he had mismatched eyes—a brown one that saw the natural world and a blue one that saw the spiritual world—and both promised death would soon come knocking.

Both men were corded with the kind of muscle mass only hours of daily physical exertion could provide. They were loaded down with weapons and ready to fight at any moment of any day. They had to be.

"I don't recall deciding to throw a party up here," Reyes said.

"Well, old age will wipe your memory like that," Paris replied. "Remember, we need to discuss our next plan of action? Among other things."

He sighed. The warriors did what they wanted, when they wanted, and no biting remark would stop them. He knew that firsthand, because he was the exact same way. "Why aren't you out researching Hydra's hiding places?"

Lush lips better suited for a woman thinned into a mulish line. Paris's eyes flashed the kind of agony Reyes usually saw staring back at him from his own mirror, replaced all too soon by the warrior's usual irreverence.

"Well?" Reyes prompted when there was no answer.

Finally his friend said, "Even immortals need coffee breaks."

There was obviously more to the story than that, but Reyes didn't press. *I am not the only man with secrets.* Several weeks ago the warriors had split up to search for Hydra, a cranky half snake, half woman…*thing* who was guarding some of King Titan's favorite "toys." Those toys—weapons, really—were supposed to lead them to Pandora's box. So far, they'd only managed to snag one. The Cage of Compulsion. They had only the barest of clues about the locations of the others.

"Yes, but when faced with extinction, coffee breaks lose their importance. And yes, I realize I need to do more for our cause. I will. After."

Paris shrugged. "I'm doing what I can. The U.S. is a huge damn place and studying it from afar is almost as difficult as navigating its lands amidst all those people." Each of the warriors had traveled to different countries to ferret out clues about the box, had no success and had quickly returned to learn what they could from here. Without switching his attention from Reyes, Paris asked Lucien, "Did he tell you where Aeron is or what?"

One of Lucien's black brows arched toward his hairline. "No. He didn't."

"Told you he'd be difficult." Paris frowned. "He hasn't been himself for weeks."

Reyes could say the same about Paris, he realized as he noticed lines of fatigue and stress around the usually optimistic man's eyes. Perhaps he *should* press Paris for answers. Clearly, something had happened to his friend. Something major.

"We're running out of time, Reyes." Accusation coated Paris's words. "Cooperate. Help us."

"Hunters are more determined than ever to end us," Lucien added. "Humans have discovered the Unspoken Ones' temple, limiting our access yet increasing that of the Hunters. We've only found one artifact out of four, but all are supposedly needed to locate the box."

Reyes arched a brow, mimicking Lucien's earlier expression. "You think Aeron can help with any of that?"

"No, but we do not need discord among us. Nor do we need the distraction of worrying about him."

"You can stop worrying," Reyes said. "He doesn't want to be found. He hates who and what he is and he hates us seeing him like that. I swear to you, he's content where he is or I would not have left him."

The door to the roof burst open and Sabin, keeper of Doubt himself, stalked through, dark hair dancing in the breeze.

"For fuck's sake," the man said, throwing up his arms. "What the hell's going on?" He spotted Reyes and comprehension instantly dawned. He rolled his eyes. "Damn, Pain, you sure know how to spoil a meeting."

"Why aren't you researching Rome?" Reyes asked him. Had everyone stopped working in the half hour he'd been on the roof?

Gideon, keeper of Lies, was close at Sabin's heels and prevented the warrior from answering with a sober, "My, my, how fun this looks."

In Gideon speak, "fun" meant boring. The man couldn't utter a single truth without experiencing debilitating pain. *Pain, exactly what I need.* If only Reyes simply had to lie to receive it, how easy life would have been.

"Shouldn't you be helping Paris research the States?" Reyes demanded. He didn't bother waiting for an answer. "This is starting to feel like a damned circus. Can't a man do a little sulking and self-mutilation in private?"

"No," Paris said, "he can't. Stop stalling, and stop changing the subject. Give us the answers we want or, I swear to the gods, I'm coming up there and laying a big wet one right on your mouth. My boy is hungry and looking to feed. He thinks you'll do just fine."

Reyes didn't doubt Promiscuity wanted to bed him, but he knew Paris, and knew the warrior preferred women.

Get rid of them. Reyes studied his newest guests. Gideon was dressed entirely in black, with hair dyed electric blue, eyebrows pierced in several places, the silver studs gleaming, and charcoal-rimmed eyelashes. Humans found him cut-your-heart-out scary.

Sabin wore all black, as well, but his brown hair, brown eyes and square, guileless face didn't make him look as if he would kill anyone who approached him—and laugh while doing it.

Both men were stubborn to their very cores.

"I need time to think," Reyes said, hoping to play on their sympathy.

"There's nothing to think about," Sabin replied. "You will do what's right because you're an honorable warrior."

Aren't you? Perhaps you are as weak as the human girl you desire. Why else would you hurt those who love you like this?

Ouch, he thought, cringing. He *was* weak. He was— "Sabin,"

Reyes growled as realization set in. "Stop sending doubts into my mind. I have enough of my own."

The warrior shrugged sheepishly, not even trying to deny it. "Sorry."

"Since our meeting is clearly *not* canceled," Gideon said, "I'm *not* heading into the city, *not* visiting Club Destiny, and *not* screwing a few screams of pleasure out of a human female." He disappeared behind the door a second later, shaking his head in exasperation.

"Don't cancel the meeting," Reyes told the others. "Just… start without me." He glanced over his shoulder, his gaze starting in the sky and falling slowly. Night's sinister canvas still waited, beckoning him to finally leap. "I'll be down in a few."

Paris's lips twitched. "Down. Funny. Maybe I'll meet you down there and we can play Hide-the-Pancreas again. Forcing you to completely regenerate rather than simply heal always amuses me."

Even Lucien grinned at that.

"Oh, oh, I wanna play! Can I hide his liver this time?"

At the sound of Anya's sultry voice, Reyes stifled a groan.

The white-haired goddess of Anarchy rushed through the doorway and threw herself into Lucien's now-open arms, her strawberry fragrance drifting on the ever-increasing wind. The pair cooed and cuddled like lovesick idiots for an eternity, lost in each other, the world around them forgotten.

It had taken Reyes a while to warm to the woman. She belonged in Olympus, home to the very beings he reviled—strike one. She left chaos in her wake, something as natural to her as breathing—strike two. But in the end, she had aided every warrior here, and had blessed Lucien with a happiness Reyes could only imagine.

Sabin coughed.

Paris whistled, though the sound of it was strained.

A pang of envy tightened Reyes's chest, squeezing at the heart that would soon stop beating. The heart he wished he did not possess. Without one, he would not have wanted Danika even though he knew he couldn't have her.

Didn't matter, he supposed. She would never want him in return. Most women did not appreciate his particular brand of pleasure and sweet, angelic Danika would hate it more than most. Even being near him had terrified her.

Perhaps, though, he could have won her over, seduced her, softened her toward him. Perhaps…but he refused to even try. The women he bedded always succumbed to his demon, became drunk on it, addicted to its predilections. They developed their own need for pain, lashing out and hurting everyone around them.

"Someone gather the others," Reyes said, sarcasm dripping from the words and hopefully hiding his inner agony. "We'll make this a reunion." What was Danika doing right this second? Who was she with? A man? Was she cuddling against him as Anya was cuddling against Lucien? Was she dead, buried as Aeron was buried? His hands curled into fists, his nails elongating into claws, slicing skin and stinging beautifully.

"You can shut it, Painie," Anya said, facing him. She burrowed her head in the hollow of Lucien's neck, blue eyes peeking through thick strands of pale hair. "You're wasting Lucien's time, and that seriously irritates me."

Bad things happened when Anya was irritated. Wars, natural disasters. Reyes's weapons left in the rain to rust. "He and I have already spoken. He has the information he desired."

"Not all of it," Lucien said.

"Tell him or I'll push you," Anya said. "And then I swear to the gods—bastards that they are!—that while you're recovering and unable to stop me I'll find your little girlfriend and mail you one of her fingers."

Just the thought caused a red haze to curtain his eyes.

Danika...hurting... *Do not react. Do not allow fury to swamp you.* "You will not touch her."

"Watch your tone," Lucien told him, tightening his grip on his woman.

"You don't even know where she is," Reyes said more calmly, marveling at how protective the once stolid Lucien was.

Anya smiled a secret smile.

"Anya," he warned.

"What?" she asked, all innocence.

"Aeron needs to be with us," Lucien said.

"Aeron is no longer up for discussion," Reyes growled. "You weren't there. You didn't see the torment in his eyes. You didn't hear the pleading in his tone. I did what I had to do, and I'd do it again." He spun away from his friends. Glanced down. The puddles were now undulating fiercely against the jagged rocks lining the ground. They were still beckoning.

Deliverance, they whispered.

Just for a little while....

"Reyes," Lucien called.

Reyes jumped.

CHAPTER TWO

"Order's up."

Danika Ford caught the two steaming plates that slid across the silver warmer. One a greasy hamburger, hold the onions. The other a chili dog with extra cheese. Both were overflowing with heart-attack-in-the-making fries and wafting delicious scents to her nose, making her mouth water and her stomach rumble.

Last thing she'd eaten had been a bologna sandwich before bed last night. The bread had been crusty and the meat ripe. Sadly, she would have paid good money for another crusty, overripe sandwich just then. If she'd had any money, that is.

Three more hours till her shift ended, *then* she could eat again. Three feet-throbbing, backbreaking, limb-shaking hours. She wouldn't last. *Don't be a princess. Chin up. Game on. You're a Ford. Built for strength and all that jazz.*

Despite the pep talk, her gaze fell to the plates. She swiped her tongue over her lips. Maybe a nibble. What could it hurt? No one would know.

Her arm rose before she could stop it, her fingers reached...

"I think she's stealing one of my fries," she heard a man whisper.

Another whispered back, "What'd you expect from someone like her?"

Danika froze. For a moment, her appetite was forgotten and a million emotions swept through her. Sadness, frustration and embarrassment were the front-runners. *This is what my life has become.* From sheltered daughter to woman-on-the-run in a single bleak night. From well-respected artist to take-whatever's-dished waitress.

"Like to say I'm surprised, but…"

"Check your wallet when we leave."

Embarrassment edged ahead of the other two. She didn't have to see the men to know they were watching her with hard, judging eyes. Three times they'd come to eat at Enrique's and all three times they'd given her self-esteem a good workout. It was weird, too. They never said anything harsh, always smiled and thanked her when she brought them something, but they just couldn't mask the distaste shining in their eyes.

She'd dubbed them the Bird Brothers, so badly did she want to flip them off.

Don't bring attention to yourself, her common sense piped up. These days, it was the only rule she lived by.

"I better not catch you trying to sneak food again," her boss snapped. Enrique was the owner, as well as the short-order cook. "Now, hurry up. Their food's getting cold."

"Actually, it's too hot. They might burn themselves and sue." The plates were obscenely warm against her cold skin—skin she hadn't been able to warm in weeks. Even now, in the heat of the diner, she wore a sweater she'd purchased for $3.99 at the thrift shop down the street. But to her consternation, the burn from the plates never seeped inside her.

Surely *something* good would happen to her soon. Weren't good and evil supposed to balance each other out? Once, she had thought so. Had believed happiness waited around every corner. Sadly, Danika now knew better.

Behind her, past the wall of windows that provided a mocking view into the pulsing heart of L.A.'s nightlife, cars whizzed and people strolled, carefree and laughing. *Not too long ago, that was me.*

Danika had taken the job here, working as many hours as

possible, because Enrique paid her under the table, no social security number required. Cash, no taxes deducted. She could disappear at a moment's notice.

Was her mother living like this? Her sister? Her granny—if she was still alive?

Two months ago, the four of them had decided to take an extended vacation in Budapest, her grandpa's favorite city. *Magical,* he'd always said. After he died, they'd gone to celebrate his memory and finally say goodbye.

Biggest. Mistake. Ever.

They'd soon found themselves kidnapped and locked away. By monsters. Real, honest-to-God monsters. Creatures the Boogeyman probably searched his closet for before daring to go to bed. Creatures who sometimes looked human and sometimes *didn't.* Every so often, Danika had caught a glimpse of fangs, claws and skeletal faces underneath their human personas.

In a moment of luck, she and her family had been rescued. But she'd been captured again, only to be released unharmed. Unharmed but warned: *Run, hide. You'll be hunted soon. If you're found, you and your family are dead.*

So each of them had run. They'd split up, hoping they would be harder to find that way. They'd hidden, shadows their new best friends. Danika had first traveled to New York, the city that never slept, trying to lose herself in the crowds. Somehow, the monsters had found her. Again. But once more she'd managed to escape them, hitching nonstop to L.A., each day making just enough money to survive and pay for self-defense lessons.

In the beginning, she and her family had maintained contact every day by calling and leaving disposable cell-phone numbers with trusted friends. Then Danika's grandmother had gone silent. No more calls.

Had she been found by the monsters? Killed?

Last time Danika had heard from her, her granny had arrived in a small town in Oklahoma. She had friends there, had known better than to travel anywhere familiar, but at her age had probably grown weary of running. Yet even those friends had not heard from her in weeks; Grandma Mallory had gone to the market and simply never returned.

Thinking about her beloved grandmother and the pain the woman might have endured caused grief and sorrow to well up inside Danika's chest. She couldn't call her mom or her sister and ask if they'd heard anything. They, too, had stopped checking in. For everyone's safety, her mom had said during their last conversation. Calls could be traced, cell phones confiscated and used against them.

Her eyes burned and her chin trembled. No. *No! What are you doing?* She couldn't think about her family now. "What if" would paralyze her.

"You're wasting time," Enrique said, tugging her from her dark musings. "Shake your ass like I told you. Your customers are waiting and if they send back their food 'cause it's cold, you're going to pay for it."

She wanted to throw the plates at him, but "No attention!" was screaming inside her head, so she just smiled and pivoted on her heels, ratty sneakers squeaking. Chin high, back straight, she marched toward the table with dread congealing in her stomach. Both men watched her with those hard eyes. They were clearly middle-class with their inexpensive clothes and average haircuts. Tanned and buff as they were, they could have been construction workers. If so, they hadn't come straight from a job. They were clean, their jeans and T-shirts unstained.

One had a toothpick sticking out from between his teeth and was rolling it from one side of his mouth to the other, the motions faster and faster the closer she came. Her hands were shaking from fatigue, but she managed to set the plates in front of each man without accidentally dumping the food in their laps. A lock of inky hair escaped her ponytail and fell down her temple.

Hands finally free, she hooked the strands behind her ear.

BB—before Budapest—she'd had long blond hair. AB—after Budapest—she'd chopped it to shoulder length and dyed it black to alter her appearance. Another crime to lay at the monsters' door.

"Sorry about the fry." Despite their clear disdain for her, these men were good tippers. "I wasn't trying to eat it, just to keep it on the plate." *Liar.* God, she never used to lie.

"Don't worry about it," Bird One said, unable to mask the slight twinge of irritation in his voice.

Don't send the food back. Please don't send the food back. She couldn't afford the cut in her pay. "Can I get you anything else?" Their cups were almost full, so she left them in place.

"We're fine," Bird Two replied. Again, polite enough words but uttered in an unmistakably waspish tone. He waved one of the paper napkins and settled it on his lap.

She caught a glimpse of a small figure eight tattooed on the inside of his wrist. Surprising. Had anyone asked her to bet, she would have put big money on a dark-haired female with a bloody hatchet coming out of her back.

"Well, holler if you need anything." She forced herself to smile, knowing she probably resembled a feral wolf. "I hope you enjoy your meal." Just as she was about to move away—

"When do you take a break?" Two asked abruptly.

Uh, what now? He wanted to know when she went on break? Why? She doubted he'd asked for romantic reasons, since he was still watching her with mild distaste. "I, uh, don't."

He popped a fry in his mouth, chewed, then licked his grease-smeared lips. "How about taking one tonight?"

"Sorry. Can't." *Keep smiling.* "I have other tables." She should have added: Maybe next time. Encouragement might have softened him at tip time. But the words clumped together in her throat, forming a hard knot. *Go, go, go.*

Pivot. They disappeared from view. Her smile—gone. Six quick strides and she reached Gilly, the only other waitress on duty tonight, who stood in front of the drink counter, filling three plastic cups with different sodas. Though Danika should've been checking on the patrons she'd used as an excuse only seconds before, she needed a moment to fortify her composure.

"God save me," she muttered. She flattened her hands on the bar and leaned forward, cocking her hip. Thankfully, a half wall blocked her from the customers' view.

"He won't." Gilly, a sixteen-year-old runaway—eighteen if anyone asked—flashed Danika a tired grimace of sympathy. They'd both been working fourteen-hour days. "He's already given up on us, I think."

Such pessimism seemed wrong in someone so young. "I refuse to believe that." Lying must have become second nature to her. Danika wasn't sure God cared anymore, either. "Something wonderful could be days away." *Yeah. Right.*

"Well, my something wonderful was that the Bird Brothers sat in your section again."

"Who are you kidding? They smile at you as if you're the Sugar Plum Fairy and they smirk at me as if I'm the Wicked Witch of the West. I have no idea what I did to them or why they keep coming back for more of me." Second time they'd come in, she'd feared they meant to pull her back into the nightmare she'd just escaped. But they'd never revealed a monstrous side, so she'd eventually relaxed.

Gilly laughed. "Want me to shank them for you?"

"Now, Gilly, that would be a travesty. Shanking's a felony and cuffs are so not a good look for you."

The girl's smile slowly melted away. "Don't I know it," she muttered.

Part of Danika wanted to tell her to go home; life with her mom couldn't be this bad. The other part admitted that life with Gilly's mom could indeed be much, much worse. The terrible things Danika had seen on these darkened streets, even in the short time she'd been here…women with deadened eyes sell-ing their bodies. Beatings. Drug overdoses. Whatever Gilly's mother had done to drive the teenager to the streets had to have been severe.

Once, Danika had been able to delude herself into thinking the world was a safe and magnificent place, full of possibilities. Now, her eyes had been opened.

"Are you going to class in the morning?" she asked, propelling them into a safer conversation. She'd only worked here a week, but every day of that week she and Gilly had taken self-defense lessons, learning how to kick, hit and yes, kill with lethal precision. Besides her family, those lessons were the only thing Danika lived for anymore.

She would never be helpless again.

Gilly sighed and faced her. Danika thought again that she looked too young and fresh to be leading such a life of drudgery. Dark, chin-length hair, as straight as a pin. Big brown eyes. Honey-kissed skin. Average height, curvy body. She was innocence mixed with haunted sensuality. Right now, she was the only friend Danika had.

"My feet will loathe me forever, but yeah. I'm going. You?"

"Absolutely." Friends weren't something she could afford these days, but Danika had taken one look at the sad, brave girl and felt an instant kinship with her.

"Maybe we'll overpower the instructor again. Now, *that* was fun."

A chuckle escaped her, the first in what seemed forever. "Maybe."

A bell rang, hacking through the cackle of voices that echoed across the diner. Another order was up. Neither of them moved, however.

"Gotta tell you," Gilly said, anchoring her hand on her hip. "When Charles told us to come at him, rage, like, took me over. I could have killed him and giggled about it later."

"Me, too." Sadly, those words were not a lie.

Picture me as your enemy and show me what you've learned so far. Attack me, Charles had said, and both of them had.

He'd needed fifty-nine stitches before the night had ended. Fortunately, he'd been a good sport about it.

Dark fury had consumed Danika as images of Aeron, Lucien and Reyes—she gulped. *Reyes!*—had fluttered through her mind. Her kidnappers, her tormentors. Men she should hate with every fiber of her being. *Did* hate. Except for one. Reyes. *Stupid girl.*

Him, she dreamed about constantly. Waking, sleeping, didn't matter. He was always on her mind, as if he'd been branded there.

Sometimes he even defeated the creatures in her nightmares. He would attack them, they would fight violently, and blood would flow in rivers. Always afterward, he would come to Danika, injured and hurting. Without hesitation, she would take him in her arms. He would kiss her everywhere—slow, so slow—laving his tongue over her hollows and planes, each lick another brand.

Every nighttime second spent with him caused her to crave more and more and more, until he was all she wanted, all she needed. He became more important to her than air. He was like a drug, the worst kind of addiction.

What's wrong with me? He'd kidnapped her for no reason, held her family hostage. He didn't deserve her desire! Why did she crave him so desperately? He was handsome, dangerously so, but other men were handsome, too. He was strong, but he would use that strength against her. He was intelligent, but he didn't exude any sort of humor. He never smiled. Yet she had never wanted a man the way she wanted Reyes.

Like Gilly, he had dark hair, dark eyes and honey-kissed skin. Honey mixed with melted chocolate. He also possessed that same haunted sensuality, as if he'd seen the most painful side of love and was marked forevermore.

The differences ended there, however. Reyes was tall and

stacked with a warrior's muscle. He wore more knives than he did clothing, strapping them behind his head, on his wrists, ankles and thighs and hanging them at his waist. Every time she'd seen him, he'd been covered in combat wounds, cuts up and down his arms and legs, bruises on his face. He was a soldier to the bone.

They all were, those self-proclaimed "Lords of the Underworld."

Lords of Nightmares, *she* called them, for of all the frightening dreams she'd had in her life, none came close to the reality of these men.

Aeron had black gossamer wings and could fly like a bird— or a malevolent dragon of lore. Lucien had multicolored eyes that swirled hypnotically just before he disappeared as if he'd never existed. The scent of roses always drifted from him, insidiously sweet.

What magical ability Reyes possessed, she didn't know.

All she knew was that he'd saved her once. Had fought his fellow soldier for her. Why? she'd wondered so many times since. Why had he hurt his friend rather than her? Why had he looked at her as if she were his only reason for breathing? Why had he then set her free, again?

Does it matter? He's one of them. He's a monster. Don't forget.

Another *ding* sounded, slicing through her thoughts. "Girls!" Enrique shouted.

Gilly moaned.

Danika massaged the back of her neck. Reprieve over. She straightened. From the corner of her eye, she saw one of her customers wave his arm in a bid for her attention. To Gilly, she said, "I'll be at your place about…four-thirty tomorrow morning? Sound good?"

"Make it five. Yep, I'll be tired but ready." Gilly turned and gathered the drinks.

Danika moved off. Ten minutes of napkin and straw duty,

coffee pouring and fetching for the Bird Brothers followed. Kept her mind off Reyes, at least.

Twice, Bird One dropped his fork and needed her to fetch him a new one. Once, Bird Two needed a refill. Once he needed a clean napkin. When she tried to leave after the last delivery, Two grabbed her wrist to stop her, his touch sharpening her nerves to razor points.

She didn't rebuke him—*every penny counts, every damn penny counts*—but politely asked what he needed and tugged free.

"We'd like to talk to you," he said, reaching for her once more.

She stepped backward. If he touched her again, she just might snap. No longer were strangers allowed to put their hands on her. Not for any reason. "About what?"

A mother and young son strolled inside, the bell above the door tinkling to announce their arrival.

"About what?" she repeated.

"About a job. Money."

Her eyes widened. Dear God. They thought she was a hooker? So that was what they'd meant by "someone like her." Funny that they looked at her with disdain and yet were willing to buy her services. "No, thank you. I'm happy where I am, doing what I do." Well, not really *happy*, but they didn't need to know that.

"Danika," Enrique called. "Got people waiting."

The men glanced at the entrance and frowned. "Later," Two said.

How about never? Seriously. A hooker? Closer to the door than Gilly, Danika gathered two menus and ushered the new arrivals to a table. They were a little unkempt, thin, clothing stained and wrinkled. They would not be good tippers, but the smile she gave them was genuine, if a bit envious.

She missed her mother like crazy.

"What can I get you to drink?"

"Water," they said in unison.

There was a wistful gaze in the boy's blue eyes as he stared at the soda resting on the table a few feet away from him, condensation running down the plastic. Danika's head tilted to the side, her artist's eye seeing the heart-wrenching possibilities of a portrait. Human desires were always simplified when all but the bare essentials were taken away.

You're not going to paint anymore, remember?

It was too much of a luxury in this die-any-moment world. Besides, she had to *feel* to paint. Not just happiness, either. For her, painting required a wide spectrum of emotion. Fury, sadness, bliss. Hate, love, sorrow. Without them, she simply mixed colors and splattered them on a canvas. But with them, she would lose the edge she needed to stay alive.

Tamping down the sadness she couldn't afford, she handed the pair their menus. "I'll be back in a moment with your drinks, and then I'll take your order."

"Thank you," the mother said.

On the way to the fountain, Bird Two grabbed her arm again, fingers locked in a tight grip. Danika stiffened, sparks of fury so hot under her skin she suddenly felt wrapped in flames. She couldn't fight the emotion, couldn't tamp it down as easily as she had the sadness. The ice she'd imagined coating her skin all these weeks melted.

"What time do you get off?"

"I don't."

"We're asking for your own good. The world is a bad, bad place and unless you're one of the bad guys, you shouldn't be out there alone."

"Grab me again," she said through clenched teeth, ignoring his feigned concern, "and you'll regret it. I'm not a hooker, and I'm not looking to make any money. Okay?"

As both gaped at her, she ripped free. She stalked away from them before she did something stupid. At the station in back, she filled the mother and son's drink order, her hands shaking. Her heartbeat nearly cracked her ribs. *You have to calm down.* Deep breath in, deep breath out. *That's the way.* Finally her muscles released their vise-grip on her bones.

She steered clear of the Bird Brothers on her way back to the table, remaining completely out of reach. When the mother realized she'd brought the boy a Coke, she opened her mouth to protest but Danika stopped her with a raised hand—a still-shaking hand, she realized with surprise. Hadn't calmed from Two's touch, then. Another deep breath in, another deep breath out.

"On the house," she whispered. Enrique gave nothing away, not even to his waitresses, and would deduct the dollar ninety-seven from Danika's pay if he heard. "If it's okay that he has it, that is."

The boy's expression lit with happiness. "It's okay, right, Mom? Please, please, please."

The mother gave Danika a grateful smile. "It's okay. Thank you."

"My pleasure. Know what you want to order?" She withdrew the pad and pencil from her apron. Her hand had stopped shaking, but the muscles were so rigid she accidentally snapped the pencil in two. "Oops. Sorry." More carefully, she dug out the spare.

The pair placed their order, and as she wrote she scanned the diner. Another family had just walked in. She gave them only a cursory inspection. Less and less, she jumped when people entered. First few days here, she'd expected Reyes to stalk through the door, throw her over his shoulder and steal into the night with her.

Gilly motioned the family to the only other available booth, her gaze catching Danika's. They shared a tired smile. Danika's felt brittle, her nervous system clearly still raw from Two's touch. *You know you can't react like this. You have to be prepared, ready for anything.*

"Did you get that?" the woman asked her.

She returned her attention to her customer. "Yes. Two hamburgers, one plain, one with everything, both with fries."

The woman nodded. "Great. Thanks."

"I'll get this turned in. Shouldn't take too long to get it cooked." Danika tore the page from her pad and marched toward Enrique.

Bird One grabbed her this time. "Look. We don't think you're a prostitute. We just want to talk to you. Bad things are headed your way."

Before she could stop it, instinct took over. In her mind, she saw her sister's panicked face the night they'd been snatched from their hotel room and carted to that fortress, prisoners of the monsters. She heard her mother's voice in her head: *Your grandmother might be dead. Might have been murdered.*

Red clouded her vision and fury returned full force, morphing her from woman to berserker. *Attack! Never helpless again!* She slammed her free hand into the man's nose. Cartilage broke on contact, and blood poured onto his shirt, his plate. He howled in pain, tenting his hands over his face.

In the wake of that howl, there was a heavy silence. Then someone dropped a cup. *Clang, splash.* Liquid gurgled over the tiled floor. Someone cursed. All of the sounds boomed like thunder, piercing her mind and jerking her out of the vengeful haze.

Danika's mouth fell open.

Two gasped, his eyes widening. He jumped up, breath sawing in and out. "What the fuck do you think you're doing, bitch?"

"I—I—" A tremor rolled through her entire body. She stood frozen, fighting panic. She'd just brought attention to herself. A lot of it, and none of it good. "I—I told you guys not to touch me."

"You assaulted him!" Looming menacingly, the uninjured man settled his hands atop her shoulders and shoved her backward.

She could have stopped him from pushing her, could have

shoved her pencil in his jugular before stumbling away. She didn't. Mortification blended with regret and both tumbled through her, overshadowing any lingering hint of fury. *Where's your numbness now?*

"You know what?" he said, snarling at her. "You're just like them. 'She might be innocent,' I was told, 'so be careful with her. Be gentle.' I didn't believe it, not for a second, but I obeyed. Shouldn't have. You just proved how despicable you really are. Maybe you're a whore after all—*their* whore."

You're just like them, he had said. Just like who? "I'm sorry. I didn't mean—I—" There was nothing she could say to make this better. Clearing her throat, she smoothed the wrinkles from her sweater. Blood must have splattered her palm because streaks of crimson appeared everywhere her hands touched. "I'm truly sorry."

"Someone call 9-1-1, for fuck's sake!"

Oh, God. She was going to have to run again, when she'd only just settled in. If this made the papers… *Oh, God,* she thought again. Her heart once more began slamming against her ribs.

Enrique stomped out of the kitchen, double doors swinging behind him. He was a big man, both tall and overweight, and utterly imposing. His thinning hair fell into his narrowed eyes as he barked, "You, little girl, are fired. And that's the least of your problems. Go to the back and wait 'til the cops get here."

Of course she was fired. And deep down, she knew he was going to stiff her for today's work. "I'll go," she lied, "just as soon as you pay me. You owe me for—"

"You'll march back there now! You're scaring the customers."

Danika's gaze moved through the diner and landed on the mother and son. The woman had one arm locked protectively around the boy while the other pushed away the Coke Danika had given him. Both were staring at her in fear. *Me? But I was merely defending myself.*

Her eyes moved away, and Gilly came into focus. Concern radiated from the girl's face as she approached, obviously meaning to support Danika. She'd lose her job and today's pay, as well, and Danika couldn't allow that.

"I'll wait for the police at my apartment," she lied.

"No, you won't," Enrique said. "You'll—"

Turning, she marched from the diner, head high, shoulders squared. Thankfully, no one tried to stop her, not even Bird Two. The night was warm, lit with neon signs and crowded. She felt as if she were spotlighted in the glare and everyone she passed was staring at her.

God, what was she going to do?

She quickened her pace, almost running. She had forty dollars in her pocket. Enough for a bus ticket somewhere. Where should she go? Georgia, maybe. The peach state was a good distance away. More importantly, she would pass through Oklahoma. She could search for her grandmother.

The thought had barely registered before something slammed into her back, propelling her into a darkened alley. She hit the pavement with so much force, oxygen whooshed from her lungs. Rocks cut past her thin sweater and T-shirt and into her skin. Her jaw cracked against the concrete. Bright white stars glittered behind her lids.

"Demon bitch!" a man growled at her temple, spittle spraying into her hair. Bird Two. Hadn't let her escape, after all. "Did you really think I'd let you run again? You're ours and, baby, you're going to suffer just like your friends. I'm not allowed to kill them, but you…you'll beg for it."

Instinct once again kicked into gear. *Don't scream, just fight. Don't react, just strike.* The words had been drilled into her mind and now seemed as much a part of her as her arm or leg. When her assailant grabbed her by the hair, lifting her, she spun of her own accord. Her scalp stung as the hairs ripped free, but that didn't slow her as she jabbed her arm forward to cut off his airway and buy herself enough time to slip free while he gasped for breath. *Contact.*

There was a grunt, a wail. His hold on her loosened.

Warm liquid ran down her fingers, pooling in her knuckles. What the—realization clattered through her. She'd still been gripping the pencil and she'd shoved the tip deep into his jugular—just as she'd stopped herself from doing in the diner.

"Oh, my God. Oh, my God!" Dazed, she scrambled to her feet. She swayed and had to grab on to his shoulders to stay upright. Horror nearly drowned her as the man fell to his knees, gurgling.

Moonlight seeped past the buildings surrounding him, high-lighting his pale, pain-filled, *shocked* features. He tried to speak, but no sound emerged.

"I'm sorry!" She splayed her fingers, releasing him completely. She held up her hands, palms out, and the blood poured down her arms. Panic blended with her horror. There was no precious numbness to be found. Not now.

One step, two, she backed away. Oh, God. Oh, God. *Murderer,* her mind screamed. *You're a murderer.* The metallic scent of his blood blended with the aromas of urine and body odor.

Two slumped, collapsed onto the concrete. His head was turned and his eyes seemed to focus on her as his chest stilled. Oh, God. Bile rose in her throat. *You had to do it. He would have killed you.*

Not knowing what else to do, Danika spun, ran and barreled through the people crowding the far side of the building. Those neon signs illuminated her every movement, and her raspy pants were like drumbeats in her ears. No one tried to stop her.

Two weeks ago in New York, one of her self-defense instructors had told her that she didn't have a killer instinct.

If only.

I'm as bad as the monsters.

CHAPTER THREE

"I KNOW WHERE your woman is."

Reyes straightened on the couch, the tip of the knife stilling inside his arm. He'd pushed it deep, so deep he'd sliced the vein in half. But the wound healed all too soon, sealing shut around the blade. Blood dried on his skin.

He'd jumped from the roof three days ago and was only now recovered enough to walk. Unfortunately. Pain was louder and more demanding than ever, wanting something more. What, Reyes didn't know. This cut hadn't helped in the least.

He ripped the weapon free, creating another injury. He licked his bottom lip, trying to savor the pain. This injury healed quickly, as well. *Not enough of a sting. Never enough.*

"Nothing to say to me?"

"You're as bad as Gideon." He glared over at Lucien, who stood in the doorway. The warrior's dark hair fell in waves to his shoulders and his mismatched eyes gleamed with expectation.

"As if I would lie."

They were alone in the entertainment room. Paris, who could usually be found there watching one of his fleshfests, was now in the city, keeping up his strength by bedding as many women as he could. Maddox and his woman, Ashlyn, were in their bedroom. As always.

Sabin and the other warriors were currently in the kitchen—they'd kicked Reyes out ages ago for bleeding on the table—outlining a plan to raid the Temple of the

Unspoken Ones in Rome without humans knowing they were there.

Reyes doubted the temple would lead the way to the All-Seeing Eye, the Cloak of Invisibility or the Paring Rod, whatever that was, but he was in the minority so he kept quiet. Still, he knew he was right. If there *were* something to be found amid the crumbling rock, moss and seashells, they would have found it by now. Besides, the Cage of Compulsion they'd discovered after searching the Temple of the All Gods hadn't helped them find the box in any way.

Yes, it was a nice weapon to own. Anyone locked inside that cage was magically compelled to do anything the owner commanded of them. But who were they supposed to lock inside it? What were they supposed to command that person to do? Until they learned the answers, he suspected Lucien and Anya would continue to play with it like naughty children.

"Reyes," Lucien said. "We were discussing Danika."

"No, we weren't." He wanted her purged from his mind, but he was beginning to suspect she was a permanent part of him now. Like his demon. Only worse. She had destroyed his precious sense of peace. Peace that had not returned, even while he was lying in bed, broken and throbbing in delicious agony.

"Shall I tell you what I know about her?" Lucien asked.

Do not take the bait. You're better off not knowing. Without Reyes providing a constant stream of tangible pain, his demon would spiral out of control, ravenous for *someone's* bodily suffering. His—others. It didn't matter. That's one of the reasons he'd sent Danika away. Were he to find her, he might one day hurt her irreparably.

"Tell me," he found himself commanding, his voice hoarse.

"Three days ago, she stabbed a man."

That sweet little angel, hurt a human? Reyes snorted. "Please. Now I'm sure you are lying."

"When I have never lied to you before?"

No, Lucien had never lied to him. Reyes gulped back a surge of bile, his next words emerging hard and strained. "How do you know she harmed a man?"

"More than harmed. She killed him. The victim lingered in the hospital for two days and only died this morning. When I was summoned to take his soul, I saw he bore the mark of a Hunter."

"What!" Reyes popped to his feet, fury washing through him. Hunters had found Danika? She'd been forced to slay one? In that moment, he no longer allowed himself the delusion of disbelief. Hunters hated him. They could have seen her here, at the fortress, followed her and tried to torture her for information about him.

His teeth gnashed together. *Damned Hunters!* They were so mindlessly fanatic they believed all of the world's evil stemmed from the demons inside the Lords. They were ruthless in their quest to destroy those spirits and the men who harbored them, and they would not hesitate to cut down anyone they considered a friend of the warriors.

Danika was not a friend, but they couldn't know that. Even now, they might be planning to use her as Bait, hoping to draw him out in the open by dangling her in his face.

This changed everything.

"Was she hurt? Did they touch her?" He palmed his second blade before he realized what he was doing: preparing for war.

Lucien continued his story as if Reyes had never spoken. "As I escorted the Hunter's soul to hell, I saw the last few acts of his life inside my mind."

"Was. She. Hurt?" The stilted question hissed out of his throat, from between his clenched teeth.

"Yes."

Pain prowled the corridors of his mind, sharpening its claws against the sides of his skull. "Is she—" Reyes pressed his lips together. He couldn't bring himself to say it. Could barely tolerate thinking it.

"No," Lucien answered anyway. "She is not dead."

Thank the gods. Relief gobbled up his fury, and his shoulders sagged. "Were any other Hunters involved?"

"Yes."

Again, Lucien did not elaborate.

"How many?"

"One. She broke his nose."

"On purpose?" he asked, shocked.

"Yes."

The Danika he remembered had been gentle, sweet. He was not sure what to think of this tigress, but he would stake his own life on the fact that she was tormented by her actions.

"Where is she?" He would go to her, check on her, find a way to protect her from future Hunter attacks, and then he would leave her. He would not allow himself to linger, would not even engage her in a conversation. But he had to see her, had to verify that she was alive and well.

Afterward he would find and savagely kill the other Hunter responsible for her pain. A broken nose wasn't nearly enough to satisfy his raging need for vengeance.

Lucien didn't answer him. "We're traveling to Rome in less than a week to search the temple again. We *need* those artifacts."

So that was the way they were going to play it, huh? "I know."

"I want Aeron brought here before we leave."

"You want to place the entire household in danger, then. You want to ignore Aeron's wishes to appease your own."

"He is one of us. He needs us now more than ever."

Reyes stalked forward, past Lucien and out of the room. Since Anya and Ashlyn had moved in, the old crumbling fortress had been transformed into a home. Flowers now overflowed from colorful vases. The walls had been lined with artwork Anya had stolen—mostly of naked men; she had a wicked sense of humor—and the furniture had been updated.

Haphazardly patched-together couches were out and plush leather was in. Intricately carved and polished chests, wire-rimmed benches and pillowed lounges filled the rooms and adorned the hallways. He'd been leery of the women at first. Now, he wasn't sure what he'd do without them. They were anchors amid a terrible storm.

His boots pounded the staircase, creating a wild *thump, thump* rhythm. He rounded the corner of the third floor—and stopped abruptly. Lucien waited at his bedroom door, expression determined.

All Death had to do was think of a location and he could flash there in an instant.

"I will not give up," Lucien said. "That should please you. I would not give up were the situation reversed and it was *your* life I fought for."

Scowling, Reyes propelled back into motion. He shouldered Lucien aside and shoved open his bedroom door. Inside, he marched straight to his favorite cache of weapons.

"The others feel as I do and are angry about your refusal to speak of Aeron. I have asked them for a few days to talk some sense into you. After that…"

After that they would be at his throat constantly. To them, he was choosing Danika over Aeron, and a warrior did not choose a woman over another warrior. Ever. Reyes did not point out that Maddox had chosen Ashlyn and Lucien had chosen Anya. He did not point out—again—that Aeron preferred death over the creature he'd become and would not be happy about returning to the fortress. It would do no good. Worse, part of him felt as Lucien did.

Reyes lifted his Sig Sauer, checked the twenty-round, chrome-plated magazine. Full. Checked the chamber. One already loaded. Good.

"Going to find her, guns blazing?"

"If necessary." Reyes pocketed three other rubber-floored

magazines and a box of .45s. There were daggers already strapped to his ankles and throwing stars attached to his belt.

"You don't know where to go."

"That won't stop me. I *will* find her."

Lucien sighed, loud and long. "I can flash you to her. You can be with her, *saving* her, in seconds."

Saving her. An admission of the danger she was in or a trick? He anchored the gun at his back and flattened his palms on the velvet-lined table, head bowed. For a long while he remained silent, weighing his options. Waste time searching for Danika or free Aeron, who could already taste her blood in his mouth?

Neither appealed to him.

Reyes sighed, the sound an echo of Lucien's. His king-size bed lay sprawled at his left side, spacious and rumpled. He'd imagined Danika there every night since meeting her, blond hair tumbling, naked body glistening with desire. Nipples pearled, desperate for his tongue. Legs spread, core wet.

Sometimes, though, the fantasy was replaced by his greatest fear, an image of blood and death. Danika's throat cut, her naked body painted crimson…motionless. The likelihood of that fear coming true would increase upon Aeron's release. *You knew you could not hold him prisoner forever. Release him, save her and then protect her.*

Protecting her would mean keeping her with him rather than walking away from her as planned. That would increase her contact with the death-hungry Aeron, but it would also increase her contact with *Reyes*. Dangerous though it was, the thought was as sultry and heady as a lover's caress might be—if Reyes had been able to find pleasure in softness.

To have Danika here…to hold her… Her angel face flashed through his mind. Wide green eyes that had looked at him with a range of emotions: fear, hope, hate—and desire? Small, pert nose. Lush pink lips that cursed him to everlasting hell while silently promising the sweetest rapture. Delicate body deliciously curved and ripe for a man's touch.

He closed his eyes, his nostrils suddenly filled with her scent. Stormy nights and innocence, sugar sweetness edged with something a little dark…perilous. His brow furrowed. Dark? Perilous? She had been neither of those things before.

"Give me your hand," Lucien said, suddenly in front of him, warm breath beating over Reyes's cheeks.

Reyes blinked in surprise as he faced his friend. He trusted this man, respected him, yet he had disappointed him over and over in the past few days. Though he didn't know what Lucien planned, he offered his hand without reservation.

Without dragging his swirling eyes from Reyes's gaze, Lucien wrapped his fingers around Reyes's.

At the moment of contact, a lightning spear slammed through his entire body. Every muscle he possessed clenched and unclenched as though hooked to a generator, volts of pure, electrical power pumping through his bloodstream. Heat slithered around him, a python holding on to a meal, tightening more and more until he could no longer breathe. Felt so good, the pain. He squeezed his lids shut, savoring. His demon purred.

His mind blackened for several heartbeats, a dark shroud covering every corner. Then pinpricks of light formed, growing… growing… An image winked into place, not yet cohesive. Just an outline. And then, suddenly, he could see Danika lying on a bed just as he'd imagined all these weeks. Except she wasn't a fair goddess spread and waiting for his pleasure. She was shackled to the bed, her once-pale hair cut and dyed.

She was trembling. Tear streaks had dried on her cheeks, and she'd nibbled on her lower lip so forcefully that tiny droplets of blood had beaded. In that moment, rage was like another demon inside him. Danika was a woman meant for pleasure and light, not darkness and fear.

"She does not look well." Lucien released him and stepped

away, taking the vision with him. "The longer she is with them, the more harm they can do to her. I followed the dead Hunter's body to a funeral home, stayed there in spirit form and watched as Hunters came to visit. They unknowingly led me straight to Danika. They know she killed their friend. Apparently they've had her since the night of the stabbing. They have her chained to a bed and have kept her asleep. She is unable to fight them like that, is helpless, vulnerable, a—"

"Yes!" Reyes's arm fell to his side. He was panting. "Yes," he repeated. He didn't have to think about what to do any longer. "Give me Danika and I will give you Aeron." Perhaps this was the answer to his torment. Save Danika, protect her and help restore Aeron to his former self, reminding the warrior of what he had once been. Though how he would accomplish the latter, he still didn't know. "But I will have your word that when he is brought here, he will be given the solitude he craves."

"You have it." Lucien nodded, grim. "Know that I do this partly because Anya thinks Danika can lead us to one of the artifacts. And doubt me not. When the girl is here, I *will* use her to find it."

"And doubt *me* not. I am not myself when I am with her and do not know how I will react if you willingly place her in harm's way." Already he felt feral with the thought. "Take me to her."

"First tell me you understand that we might save her now, only to lose her later. I will not have you blame me if—"

"She will not die." He wouldn't let her. "No more talking. Take me to her."

I FOUGHT FOR MY LIFE only to lose it like this? Danika laughed bitterly. She'd only just woken up, wasn't sure how much time had passed or what had been done to her. The thought made her gag.

After the…the…attack—*oh, God, don't think about it*— she had raced to her shabby apartment to gather her things. Mistake. She should have left the gun and clothing behind, but without the day's pay she'd known replacing them would have been too expensive. And since she hadn't yet mastered the ability to steal without getting caught, she'd felt she had no other recourse.

A group of strange men had been waiting for her, standing in the shadows next to the fire escape as though they'd known what route she most often took. As if they'd been watching her for days and knew her habits.

She could have fought one or two. Even three. But there had been six of them, all bearing the same figure-eight tattoo on their wrists as the man she'd—she'd—she couldn't even think the word now. They'd possessed the same tattoo as the man who'd died in that dirty alley. They'd overpowered her, knocked her out.

Never helpless again, huh?

When she'd first opened her eyes a little bit ago, her hope that the men were cops and she might make bail was completely dashed. Cops did not chain women to strange beds. Who were these men? What did they want with her?

Nothing good, that much was clear. Panic bloomed inside her chest, freezing her blood. Her ears rang with fear. Her jaw ached from the knock it had taken. Her strength was depleted, hunger gnawing at her. She had trouble drawing in a breath, her airways too constricted.

Don't make a sound. The chains were cold and heavy, abrading. She tugged at them as her wild gaze circled the room. It was nicely furnished with overstuffed chairs, colorful beaded pillows and a mahogany vanity that boasted a square, gilt-edged mirror.

Reyes's doing? she wondered, not knowing what to think about that. He had kept her in comfort, too.

No, not Reyes, she decided in the next instant. He wasn't the kind of man to send others to do his dirty work. He would have been there, would have subdued her himself. So who had taken her? she wondered again. Friends of the man she'd…hurt, obviously. Those tattoos…

Did the men mean to punish her for hurting him? Did they mean to rape her? Torture her? Oh, God. Did they think she was a hooker, too, and plan to sell her services?

Tears burned in her eyes. Right now she was alone. She continued to work at the chains, minute after minute dragging by. Sweat poured from her and soaked the sheets underneath her. The more she moved, the more her clothing pulled away from the metal bands, no longer acting as a block. Soon her skin was sliced and blood oozed from her wrists and ankles.

A knock sounded.

Her heart skipped a beat, and she pursed her lips to silence a whimper. She stilled. Should she pretend to be asleep?

The room's only door creaked open, revealing a tall, average-looking male. She couldn't force her eyelids to close. Could only stare at him, taking his measure. He wore a white button-down shirt and black slacks and looked to be in his late thirties. He had brown hair, which was combed from his face. His eyes were large, green like hers. He appeared very professional, very unmurderer-like. Calm, perhaps even friendly.

That didn't lessen her terror.

Danika swallowed the sudden lump in her throat. *Not a sound.* She bit the inside of her cheek until she tasted blood. *Don't reveal fear.* In, out, she breathed, slowly, each intake and exhalation precise.

"Good. You're awake." With barely a pause, the man added, "Relax, my dear. I have no plans to hurt you."

"Unchain me, then." The pleading quality of her voice stripped away every effort she'd made to appear strong.

"I'm sorry." He sounded genuinely upset. "The chains are a necessity."

"Just let me go and—"

He held up one hand, silencing her. "I'm afraid we don't have a lot of time. My name is Dean Stefano. My friends call me Stefano, so I hope that you will, as well. You are Danika Ford."

"Let me go. Please."

"I will, just not yet." His brows disappeared into his hairline. "Let's cut to the heart of the matter, shall we? What do you know about the Lords of the Underworld?"

The Lords? This was about her *other* kidnapping? A crazed laugh escaped her. What kind of shit had Reyes and company dragged her into?

"Tell me."

"Nothing," she said, because she didn't know what kind of answer Stefano wanted. "I know nothing about any Lords."

Irritation flickered in his eyes. "Lying will only get you in trouble, my dear. So let's try again. You stayed with a group of men in Budapest. Not just any men, but unquestionably the most violent men the world has ever seen. Yet they didn't harm you. And if they didn't harm you, that means they considered you a friend."

"They're monsters," she said, and prayed that was what he wanted to hear. "I hate them. I don't know why they kept me, and I don't know why they let me go. Amusement, maybe." Truth and hate blared from every syllable. "Let me go. Please. I didn't mean to hurt… It was an accident and I…" Tears once again stung her eyes.

Stefano sighed. "We kept you drugged while we decided what to do with you. Drugged yet safe. You took a strong soldier from us, Danika, one of our best. We miss Kevin terribly. His wife hasn't stopped crying since I told her of his demise; she refuses to eat and prays for death so that she can join him. You owe us now, don't you agree?"

As he'd probably hoped, his words filled her with white-hot guilt and that guilt cut deeper than the shackles. "Please. I just want to go home." Not that she had a home anymore. She laughed again, feeling a little crazed and a lot shaky. Dizzy. "Please."

Stefano's expression didn't soften. "The Lords—Maddox, Lucien, Reyes, Sabin, Gideon, they call themselves. Shall I go on? They are demons, created in the heavens yet spawned from hell itself. Did you know that?"

She blinked, breath congealing in her lungs. "D-demons?" A few months ago, she would have rolled her eyes at him. Now, she nodded. That explained so much. She'd seen her captors' faces morph into skeletal beings. She'd been flown through the city cradled in the arms of a winged man. She'd seen fangs elongate and claws sharpen. She'd heard growls and screams of pain and torture.

Demons. Like the ones in her dreams, her secret paintings. Had she somehow known, even as a little girl, that she'd end up in Budapest with Reyes and his friends? Then later, with this man? Had the nightmares she'd always battled been a means of preparing her for this?

"Yes. Oh, yes. You believe. You see the truth." Stefano stalked toward her, hate radiating from him. That hate transformed him from calm and friendly to menacing beast. "Death is a demon. Destruction is a demon. Disease is a demon. Every evil deed the world has ever known, every evil that has ever transpired, can be traced to their doorstep."

The closer he came to her, the more she shrank into the mattress. "Wh-what does this have to do with me?"

"So no one you've loved has died? Nothing you've owned has been destroyed? No one has ever lied to you? Sickness has never plagued you?"

"I—I—" She didn't know what to say.

"Still aren't convinced of their treachery? One of those demons seduced my wife. She was all that was pure and right and never would have betrayed me on her own. Yet somehow, some way, the very demon spawn who tricked her into bed convinced her that she was evil, that she needed to die. So she killed herself, and I was the one to find her body hanging from the rafters of our garage." Each word sharpened his voice. His jaw had become granite.

Danika knew the pain of discovering a loved one dead. She'd been the one to find her grandfather after his heart attack, and the image of his pale, lifeless body still haunted her, tainting the memories of the vital man he'd once been. "I'm so sorry for your loss."

Stefano gulped, seemed to gather his composure around himself. "That loss gave me a purpose in life—one I share with thousands of others around the globe. While the Lords are darkness, we are light, and we were not meant to endure the evil they have brought into this world. *Our* world," he added. He closed his eyes as if he could taste the delicious flavor of his hope. "Once we capture the Lords and contain their evil once and for all, things will be as they were always meant to be. Beautiful…peaceful. Perfect."

Keep him talking. Keep his thoughts off you. "Why capture? Why not kill them?"

Slowly his eyelids cracked open, the happy glaze already fading from his irises. He stared at her, seeming to probe her soul. The sensation was eerie. "Killing them frees the demons inside them, allowing those vile beasts to roam the earth crazed and unfettered. We need man and spirit bound together." He shrugged as if he didn't care, but his gaze razored. "Until we find the box, that is."

"Box?" Trying to appear relaxed, she wiggled her wrists against the chains. They were still too tight, but her skin was wet with sweat. If she could just slip free… She could, what? Run? *Demons* were chasing her family. Not humans. Would her loved ones ever truly be safe?

"Pandora's box," Stefano said, still watching her intently.

Her eyes widened, and she stilled. *Is this a dream, perhaps? Another nightmare?* "You're kidding, right?" Her grandmother used to tell her stories about Pandora and her infamous box. "That's a myth. A legend."

He crossed his arms over his chest, stretching the fabric of his shirt and defining the lean line of his muscles. Obviously he trained with weights and weapons, just like the Lords. "And demons do not walk the earth, I suppose?"

Her stomach tightened with dread.

"I'll tell you a story, all right? Listen closely."

He paused, waiting. She nodded, hoping that's what he desired. Obviously, it was. He said, "A few hundred years after the creation of the earth, a horde of demons escaped hell. They were the vilest creatures Hades and his brother Lucifer had ever spawned. They were uncontrollable, living nightmares. In a bid to save their world, the gods used the bones of the goddess of oppression to create a box. With cunning and precision they were able to capture the demons and lock them inside."

"I know the rest," Danika whispered, the tightening in her stomach becoming a sea of sickness.

Stefano arched a brow. "Tell me."

"The gods asked Pandora to guard the box."

He nodded. "Yes."

"Pandora opened it," she continued, because it was the most well-known version of the story. That wasn't what her grandmother had told her, however.

"No. That's where legend is wrong," Stefano traced a fingertip over the tattoo on his wrist. "Pandora was a warrior, the greatest female warrior of her time. The box was given to her for safekeeping. She wouldn't have opened it, even upon threat of death."

Another tug against the chains, this one weaker. Danika found herself suddenly fascinated, listening despite her desire to leave. Stefano had just confirmed what her grandmother had told her, a tale unlike the one the world believed. "And?"

"And the gods' elite soldiers were angry that they hadn't been chosen to guard it, their pride slighted. They decided to show the gods their mistake. While the one called Paris seduced Pandora, the others fought her guards. In the end, the soldiers won. Their leader, the one named Lucien, opened the box, releasing those vile demons upon the innocent world once more. Death and Darkness reigned."

Danika once again sagged into the mattress. She stared up at the ceiling, trying to imagine harsh, rugged Reyes as Stefano claimed he'd been. Prideful, jealous. When Danika had been with him, Reyes hadn't seemed to care what others thought of him. He'd barked orders and snapped commands. He'd been surly and brooding. "And?"

"The box disappeared. No one knew where it had been taken or who had taken it. Having no other alternative, the gods gathered the demons and placed them inside the warriors responsible for the travesty, then banished them to earth. Those men lost all threads of their humanity; they *became* their demons, bathing our world in blood. And they continue to be a blight upon us all. As long as they're roaming free, no one is safe." Stefano rubbed at his Adam's apple, his head tilting to the side, expression intense. "I asked you before, but I will ask you again. Can you imagine a world without rage, pain, lies and misery?"

"No." She couldn't. For the past two months, those were all she'd known. They'd been her only companions.

"The Lords killed your grandmother, Danika. Are you aware of that?"

"You don't know that for sure!" she yelled, the words leaving her on a burst. Tears filled her eyes again, but she suppressed them as she had before. "She could be alive."

"She's not."

"How do you know?" The question was panicked, hoarse. "You can't know unless you've…unless you've…"

"Seen her."

Oh, God, oh, God, oh, God. No. Goddamn it, no! "Have you?" She barely heard herself, but didn't have the strength to ask again.

"Yes and no," he admitted. "One of my men saw the creature Aeron carrying her limp body over his shoulder. The pair disappeared inside a building, or my agent would have followed." Stefano pinched the bridge of his nose in regret. "At first, we planned to watch you and wait for the Lords to come for you again. We assumed you meant to aid their cause, and we planned to capture all of you at the same time. But you continually ran as if you didn't want them to find you. That intrigued me."

Like she cared about his plans! *Was* her grandmother dead? A limp body did not a corpse make. Grandma Mallory could very well be alive, laughing, eating a bowl of her favorite soup. She pictured it and nearly cried out in longing, desperate for it to be true.

The image soon morphed, a dagger protruding from her grandmother's chest. *No. No!* She wanted to scream, to rail. *Emotion does you no good. You know that. You cannot wallow or you'll collapse.*

Hardly matters if I collapse, she thought, nearing hysteria. *Not like I can run now.*

"You can help us capture them, Danika. Ensure that they never do to others what they've done to you and me. You can punish them for hurting your loved one. Your family can finally stop running. You can all be together again."

Without Grandma Mallory?

This time, she couldn't stop the sob. Her chin trembled and her jaw ached. Warm tears flowed down her cheeks freely.

"Help me," Stefano added earnestly. "In return, I'll help you. I'll guard you and your family until every single one of the Lords is dead. Those demons will never hurt you again. You have my word of honor."

To know her family was safe and would remain safe... She wouldn't have cared about the terms of the deal even if she had to sign her soul over to the devil. The hope that Stefano could help her mother and sister was irresistible. The thought of revenge was overwhelming.

"What do I have to do?"

CHAPTER FOUR

ONE AT A TIME, Lucien flashed most of the warriors to an abandoned building. They were inside the fortress in Budapest one second, night all around them, and someplace sunny and warm the next.

Lucien flashed Reyes last. Last time he'd been transported like this, he'd vomited. This time, his concern for Danika overcame even the slightest bit of nausea.

Inhaling dust and crumbling plaster, Reyes opened his eyes. The silver stone of the fortress had disappeared, the comforts of hearth and home gone. Bare gray walls, cement floors and piles of lumber now greeted him. Several windows were cracked; black garbage bags had been taped to them but now fell halfway, as if bowing, allowing the men to peer into an unknown world of…silence and stillness, he realized, hearing nothing and seeing no one.

The others stalked the building, searching for a hidden enemy, blades and guns raised and ready for action. All but Anya, who'd come in place of Maddox, wore expressions of confusion. A few muttered, "Where are the Hunters?"

"Not here," Lucien answered.

"Where are we?" Reyes asked quietly. His own blades were pressed against his thighs. Urgency swam laps in his bloodstream.

"The States." Sabin closed his eyes and inhaled deeply. "L.A. is my guess. No place else has the stench of Hollywood."

"Correct," Lucien said with a grim nod.

"Hunters have a large faction here." There was relish in the undertones of Sabin's voice. "A faction I despise with every ounce of my being. The leader and I have history, and he despises me, too, so be ready for anything. He joined the Hunters after his wife and I…" He shrugged, some of his anticipation muted by sorrow. "We were together, but I'm not good for humans and things ended badly. Hunters recruited him, and he's been gunning for me ever since."

Sabin and his men had been battling Hunters far longer than Lucien and his group had. Paris, Maddox, Torin, Aeron and Reyes had split with Sabin, Strider, Gideon, Cameo, Amun and Kane several thousand years ago.

Their friend Baden, keeper of Distrust, had been brutally murdered by Hunters. After revenge had been meted out, half of the Lords had desired peace. What was better for a battered soul than a cessation of the constant struggle between good and evil, darkness and light? The other half had desired Hunter blood spilling into the streets of ancient Greece, crimson rivers of pain and terror.

Unable to come to terms, they'd gone their separate ways. Until Sabin brought the blood feud to Budapest, that is.

Though Reyes had walked away all those years ago, he would not, could not, do so now. He was involved, the illusion of peace forever shattered. Hunters had recently cut Torin's throat, attempting to weaken him and capture everyone else. Thankfully, those Hunters had failed.

Reyes would *not* fail in his mission.

Whatever he had to do to destroy his enemy, he would do. And if he had to destroy the gods who might very well support the Hunters' quest, eventually he would find a way to do that, too.

It was hard to know the gods' ultimate goal, however. Fickle and mysterious, they were like a puzzle missing several key pieces. While the silent Greeks had angered Reyes with their neglect, the cryptic Titans edged him toward a murderous rage.

They claimed to want harmony for the world, both in the heavens and below. They claimed to desire worship and adoration, freedom from death and destruction. And yet they had ordered Danika's execution. They'd even ordered Anya's execution, though they'd since changed their minds. And what they were doing to Aeron…

Do not venture down this path. Not here, not now. Already his nails were elongated, pinpricks pressing into his palms. Red spots winked over his vision, and the demon whispered seductively: *Cut yourself. Hurt.*

"No," he gritted out.

"This way," Lucien was saying, but he paused when Reyes spoke and peered at him quizzically. "Is something wrong?"

"No. I am fine." When Danika was safe and tucked in his bed, he would feed his demon. Until then, there would be no hurting himself. Blood loss ultimately would weaken him, and he needed to be at top strength for the coming combat.

But for every second he resisted, the demon would grow louder and louder. Reyes knew that well. He would become more and more distracted. That was the bane of his demon-curse. He needed to cut himself, but in the end he weakened like any other being when injured, albeit temporarily.

"What were you saying?" he asked Lucien.

Every gaze shifted to him.

Lucien rolled his eyes. "The girl is being held one street over. Innocents fill the area, so we will have to be careful."

He didn't care about innocents. Cold and callous of him, but then, he'd never been a soft, easy man. Well, that wasn't true. In the years before his pairing with Pain, he remembered laughing and joking with his friends. "How many Hunters are with her?" A muscle ticked in his jaw as he thought of the suffering she might even now be enduring.

Whatever was done to Danika, Reyes would retaliate a hundredfold when facing the Hunters. He might hate his demon for the torment he constantly endured, but he wouldn't hesitate to hand over the reins of control so that the creature could unleash its powers. Not today. Pain could look into a human's soul, find every vulnerability, even the tiniest chink, and systematically scrape each one with poisoned arrows until the human was screaming, writhing, clawing at his skin to stop the agony.

"Earlier today," Lucien said, "there were twenty-three in the building."

"They multiply like rabbits." Sabin grinned, and the sight of it was pure wickedness. "Could be a hundred more by now."

Lucien motioned to the far window, his dark hair swaying at his temples. "We have several hours until nightfall. I will flash to the building, remain in the spirit world and listen. Observe. We need to know what she's told them, and we need to know what they're planning."

All Reyes heard was "several hours." "We're supposed to stay here?" he growled. "Do nothing?"

"Yes." Lucien eyed him now, those mismatched orbs swirling once more. "If they are monitoring the area, I will disable their computers. Then, at dark, when humans are less likely to notice your height, your build and your weapons and send policemen after you, you will walk there. I'll be waiting for you in the shadows outside."

More inactivity. More waiting.

The knowledge was both emotionally and physically painful for him. Reyes wanted to lash out, punch something, and that he couldn't…the demon fed off that corporal agony and demanded more. Wanted control.

Soon, he promised.

This was one of the many reasons Reyes had sent Danika away and one of the few reasons he should not be here to rescue her. She roused him *and* the demon as surely as if she were rattling a stick against a hungry animal's cage.

If he gave his demon free rein as it craved, he would lose

control of his actions. What if he hurt Danika? What if he enjoyed hurting her? Smiled while beating her bones to powder? What if he killed her, the very act he'd locked his best friend away for even contemplating?

He wouldn't be able to live with himself, knowing he'd destroyed something so…precious. Yes, he realized then. She was precious to him. She was the angel to his demon, the good to his evil. The pleasure to his pain. And she was inside a Hunter stronghold, bound, helpless…suffering.

Once again red winked over his vision and rather than welcome it he now fought it. Damn this! There could be no giving over to his demon side, then, not even to battle the Hunters. Reyes would have to maintain command.

Someone slapped him on the back, jostling him from his musings. "Save it, my friend," a female said.

Calm, settle. Reyes turned his head and found himself staring down at Cameo, keeper of Misery and the only female Lord. He quickly looked away. With her long black hair, silver eyes and skin like peaches and cream, she was beauty incarnate. She was also a strong, fierce warrior despite her delectable little body. It was hard to face her, though, when all of the world's unhappiness seemed to seep from her pores and into his heart.

"We'll retrieve her safely," Cameo said, meaning to comfort him but only managing to make his chest ache. "Don't worry."

Gods, her voice. He tried not to cringe while the demon inside him sighed, liking the pain she unwittingly inflicted. Why couldn't Reyes have been attracted to *her?* Would have made his life easier.

You're hurting now only because the subject being discussed is Danika. Much as his demon enjoyed physical pain, Cameo represented an avalanche of emotional turmoil and dysfunction. So no, wanting her would not have been easier. Her tragic voice could drive any man to suicide and Reyes tried to kill himself enough already.

"Hunters once abducted a lover of mine," she said.

Reyes rubbed his chest. Someone had actually slept with her? "And you were able to save him?"

"Oh, no. He died horribly. They cut out his heart and mailed it to me."

Reyes blinked against a surge of panic, but didn't face her again. *That won't happen to Danika.* He scanned the building, breathing in and out, slowing his wild pulse, calming again. Lucien was already gone, and the others were sitting along the edges of the walls, polishing their weapons with lethal efficiency.

Finally, he trusted himself to speak without screaming. "That little story is supposed to soothe me?"

"Yes. They bested us once in this manner. We won't allow them to do so again."

Small comfort. Even now, a fist could be flying toward Danika's face, a foot toward her stomach. A whip arching toward her back. A knife sliding into her organs. She could be sobbing for him to save her. And here he was, close, but waiting, leaving her helpless.

The knowledge was intolerable.

He stalked away from Cameo. Back and forth he paced. Should he ignore Lucien's command and attack now? *Let him work. He knows what he's doing. He'll come for you if she's placed in any sort of danger.*

Even knowing that, time passed with agonizing slowness, every tick of the clock a torturous beat. Only when the sun began to wane, dulling from bright gold to hazy pink, from hazy pink to deep purple and finally blessed gray, did he relax.

"I've never seen you like this," Paris remarked. "Fidgety, distracted."

"Hopefully you won't see me like this again."

"I'm sending a prayer heavenward that *I* never look that way," Sabin muttered. "Not that it'll do any good. Still."

Strider grinned. "But you're so pretty when you're in love."

Sabin flipped him off.

Love? Was Reyes capable of such an emotion? "Night has fallen. Let's go." He pounded toward the front door.

Anya latched on to his arm, her fingernails digging into his bare flesh. "Hold it right there, sweetness. You don't know the way."

He barely managed to plant his feet into the concrete. "And you do?"

"Of course." Her nails sank deeper, cutting skin, and he nearly moaned at the heady sting. "Lucien tells me everything."

"Guide us, then, but do it now. I won't spend another second inside this building, and I *will* break into every shop, home and structure that I encounter if necessary."

"So impatient." She *tsked* under her tongue and released him. "I admire that in a man. Just…keep up with me. If you can."

With that, she claimed the lead. Everyone else filed out behind her. Overwarm, stuffy air became cool and fragrant, a mix of good and bad aromas: fresh flowers, car exhaust, baked breads and cloying perfume. Multihued lights pulsed from signs—Nude Dancers Here—and horns blared in a hurried symphony. Footsteps clomped in every direction, though nothing overshadowed the frantic dance of Reyes's heart.

At one time, he had dreamed of traveling, of seeing this new world he'd hidden from for hundreds of years, but he had been bound to Budapest by Maddox's curse. Now, he didn't care about the world around him. He just wanted to reach Danika.

Though he and the others remained in the shade as much as possible, humans did notice them. Some jumped out of their way, some stared. Most grinned, seemingly fascinated. Not the typical mortal reaction; even the Buda townspeople were more respectful than friendly. *Hollywood,* Sabin had said. Reyes realized these humans thought the men were part of a movie.

A few times, Paris stopped to steal a kiss from a willing

female. He was as helpless against his demon as Reyes was, so when Promiscuity wanted to play, Paris took time to play. Otherwise, he weakened unbearably. But for the first time in all their years together, Paris did not look as if he enjoyed the kissing.

Reyes didn't slow, didn't wait for his friend or ask him what was wrong. Urgency pounded through him, harder and more intense with every slap of his boots against concrete. Anya turned a corner, her long pale hair a beacon in the night. Down a dirty alley she escorted them, the scent of urine suddenly saturating the air.

When she turned the next corner, she tossed an anticipatory smile over her shoulder. "We're almost there."

Reyes palmed his gun and a knife. They were so familiar to him, so much a part of him, they were almost a natural extension of his hands. *Not much longer now and you'll see her.* Soon, very soon, the battle would begin.

He would not leave a single survivor.

Around him, he could feel the adrenaline surges of his friends. War was a part of them, infused in their every cell. They'd been made for it, after all.

The Greeks, their creators, had known the ease with which a heavenly being could be toppled, for they themselves had fought and imprisoned the Titans. In an effort to protect themselves from the same fate, the Greeks used the blood of the god of war to breed immortal warriors, and thereby an army of defenders.

After the *dimOuniak* tragedy, with Pandora slain, the box missing and the demons locked inside the warriors responsible, the gods had banished them to earth. New warriors had been recruited to take their place. Not that they'd done the Greeks any good in the end, Reyes thought with a satisfied smile.

"Just a bit more..." Anya breathed, excited. There was no better replacement for Maddox. Anya adored violence.

A large trash can burned ahead, the golden flames flickering, smoke billowing. Four men stood around it, one holding out a spoon, melting a small, solid mass into bubbling liquid. With his free hand, he used a syringe to suck that liquid up. The others awaited their turn.

Drugs. How Reyes wished they worked on him. But he'd tried all of them, from smoking to pills, drowning in liquids, injecting his veins with needles. Nothing had dulled his need for pain.

Anya stopped abruptly at the end of the alley. Lucien was there, stepping from the shadows. He and Anya shared a kiss, Lucien's arm automatically winding around her waist as it did every time they were together.

Reyes glanced away from them, the sight of their love too much to witness at the moment. *Who are you trying to fool? It's too much at* every *moment.*

The alley forked into three sections: left, straight and right. Five buildings glared at him in a half moon. He didn't need to ask which held Danika. Suddenly he could smell her thunderstorm scent. He could feel her fear all the way to the marrow of his bones, as if it pulsed from the redbrick shop in front of him.

A weapons store. How appropriate. And ironic. With all their talk of peace, the Hunters should have picked a church.

"There are private rooms above the public one. She is up there," Lucien said, his tone grim. "The men have been strangely silent, almost as if they knew I was there, waiting."

Bile rose in Reyes's throat. "Is she…still alive?" The words would barely form.

"Yes."

He gulped. Something about Lucien's inflection did not settle well inside him. "But?"

"She is still sleeping."

His fingers clenched around his weapons. "How many Hunters are in the building now?"

"Twelve. Several have already left."

"Their leader?"

"One of the absent."

Bastard. Reyes would find him, though. Soon. Once Danika was safe, there would be no stopping his wrath.

"There *is* a man who appears to be guarding her," Lucien said. "He has barely left her side. He's there now, watching her sleep."

"Has he…did he…touch her?"

"Not in anger."

Then in what? Lust? "Was she raped?" Reyes's teeth gnashed together with a dark need to strike.

"I do not know."

"He is mine." Despite the false calm in his voice, he left no doubt of his intention. "No one else even approaches him."

Lucien nodded. "Very well. The time for battle has arrived."

Ready, Reyes pushed past his friends and stalked to the building. When he entered, a bell tinkled merrily, announcing his presence. The human behind the counter was in the process of smiling—until he spotted Reyes's harsh countenance. The smile froze midway and hate filled the Hunter's eyes.

To Reyes's knowledge, they had never met, but they instantly recognized each other for what they were: enemies.

"Where is she?"

"You killed my son, demon."

"I've never met your son, Hunter."

"You're a cancer upon this earth, all of you, and you're responsible for *every* death. Not for much longer, though. Long live the Hunters!" As though he'd been expecting Reyes all along, the man lifted a semiautomatic with a silencer.

Reyes lifted his own gun. They fired at the same time. Reyes, to savage. The Hunter, to injure. Killing him would have freed his demon, and the Hunters would do anything to prevent that. The knowledge was as good as a weapon.

A bullet slammed into Reyes's shoulder, and he laughed at the wonderful sting. The Hunter's brains splattered onto the wall behind him; the man didn't laugh. Reyes felt a moment of sorrow, but reminded himself there could be no peace as long as Hunters lived to spread their hate.

One down. Eleven to go.

"Jeez. Try to save some for the rest of us," Sabin muttered, moving around Reyes, past the counter of guns to a door. He kicked it open, revealing a narrow staircase.

"Good job, Painie." Anya slapped him upside the head. "Now the others know we're here."

With that, she flew up the stairs, right behind Sabin.

Blood dripped from Reyes's wound as he climbed.

"May I join my dear wife and watch your destruction from above," a human shouted, but he was silenced as another muted gunshot sounded. There was a scream. A gurgle. A thump as a body hit the floor.

Footsteps. "See you in hell, demons," another human yelled, but he, too, was soon silenced.

"She's in the third room on the right," Lucien said, suddenly beside Reyes.

They reached the top and raced in different directions. Reyes encountered only one other Hunter before he reached Danika's room. That Hunter shot at him, too, nailing him in the stomach.

Reyes never paused, his adrenaline too high, his demon too happy.

Smiling, he reached the human and sliced his throat. Then he was in front of the bedroom door. He kicked it open, not bothering with the lock. Too time-consuming.

A *pop* and *whiz* crackled in his ears as another bullet hit him, this one in the thigh. His limbs trembled as weakness tried to set in, but he managed to remain upright. Blood poured, the demon sang and Reyes scanned the room, taking stock. Danika lay in bed, bound, motionless. A human stood at her side, trembling and pale as he aimed a gun at Reyes.

"I've waited for this moment a long time," that human said hoarsely. "Dreamed of it. Craved it. Now here you are."

Reyes zeroed in on the man's tattoo: the mark of infinity, symmetrical, black. "Here I am. Did you touch her?"

"As if you care what's been done to a human."

Another shot. Reyes leapt to the side. He would enjoy the pain, but didn't want to lose any more blood. The next five minutes were too important.

This blast sailed past him, and he raised his own gun. Aimed.

"Whatever you do to me, staying here, watching the woman, was worth it," the man said as Reyes squeezed the trigger. Another head shot. The Hunter collapsed onto the carpeted floor and didn't rise.

Reyes was at Danika's side in the next instant, snapping the bands apart and liberating her wrists and ankles. He gathered her sleeping form in his arms, his blood dripping onto her stained white shirt and too-pale face. Her dark hair was matted to her scalp and temples, her cheeks hollow—how much weight had she lost?—and her eyelashes cast ghostly shadows that blended with the bruises under her eyes before branching into menacing spikes. There was another bruise on her jaw.

"Danika." Her name was both a prayer and a curse.

She didn't stir.

Her arms hung limply at her sides, her head lolled. Awake, she would have shoved him away. He would rather that happen than this…inactivity. This nothingness.

Behind him, the sounds of battle ceased, replaced by the wail of sirens. He could hear his friends filling the doorway, shuffling inside the room. He didn't care. He tightened his hold on Danika—too long, it had been too long since he'd last seen and held her—resting her cheek against his neck.

Her skin was cold, so cold. Like ice. Her heartbeat was slow against his chest.

"Lucien?" The name croaked from his throat. Hot tears blurred his vision.

"I am here, my friend." A hand settled on his shoulder. "Somehow they knew we were coming and were prepared, but they have now been dispatched."

"Never mind that. Take us home."

CHAPTER FIVE

DANIKA HAD BEEN COLD for so long that the blazing-hot blanket draped over her shocked her out of the death-sleep. Her eyelids popped open, and a gasp shoved past her lips. Remnants of her nightmare refused to fade, however, preventing her from seeing what surrounded her. She saw only a darkness slashed with crimson, the night bleeding from lethal wounds. She heard swords clanking, demons laughing evilly and the whoosh of heads as they rolled.

Death, death, her every breath proclaimed.

Calm down, just calm down. This isn't real. You know better.

Her grandmother had once suffered from dreams like these. Dreams where demons ruled and evil reigned. Dreams that had driven the frail woman to try and kill herself at the age of sixty-five.

The dreams were not premonitions of the future, for they never came true. Until Reyes and his friends had entered her life, that is. But the dreams *were* real enough to terrify, so Danika understood her grandmother's pain.

Most of them were turbulent, screams and fatality infusing every macabre scene. All her life, that's how it had been. Bloody death. Used to be, she would awaken from those painful nights and paint what she'd seen in an attempt to draw the madness from her subconscious—and keep it out.

Once, before she'd known any better, she had shown her parents one of the paintings. They'd been so frightened and upset, looking at her as if she were one of the monsters she'd painted, that she had never let another person see them. Besides, *she* didn't even like to look at them.

On the opposite side of the spectrum, though, her dreams were sometimes utter serenity. Angels, their wings spread in white-feathered glory, would float through the bright azure skies. Their beauty always amazed her, and she would awaken smiling and full of verve rather than sweating and trembling as she was now.

"I'm here, angel, I'm here."

That deep, rich voice belonged in her nightmares *and* those angelic glimpses, both heaven and hell rolled into one mesmerizing seduction. As she lay there, the bad dream quieted and the darkness faded, light pushing its way into her mind.

A bedroom came into view, but it wasn't the one she remembered falling asleep in. Weapons adorned the walls, from throwing stars to swords to daggers. Even axes. There was a polished vanity, but no chair. The owner didn't sit there? Didn't study his reflection or brush his hair?

His? *How do you know this room belongs to a man?*

In and out she breathed, the familiar scent of sandalwood and pine filling her nose. Oh, she knew. A man, definitely, and one in particular. The knowledge rocked her to the core. *Maybe you're wrong. Please be wrong.*

The bed was swathed in black cotton; turning her head, Danika saw that she was draped by a half-clothed man. He possessed skin of chocolate and honey, taut muscle and ripped sinew. No hair marred his chest, but there was a menacing butterfly tattoo that stretched from one shoulder to the other and up his neck. *Menacing butterfly*—two words that could be used together to describe only one man.

Reyes.

"Oh, God." She bolted upright, dislodging him. Panting, she scrambled to the edge of the mattress, never turning her back to him. A snippet of her conversation with Stefano played through her mind.

"What if they try and kill me?" she'd demanded.

"They won't," he'd answered confidently.

"How do you know? You can't be sure."

"They are men. You are a woman. Think about it. Besides, they could have hurt you before, but didn't."

"They warned me to stay away from them."

"Why?"

"I don't know."

"Find out. Find out everything you can. Their weapons, their weaknesses, their plans, their likes and dislikes. You'll take a cell phone. It's small, easy to hide. I'll give you a day to settle in. After that, we'll talk every night if possible."

"What about you?" she'd asked, not wanting to consider the dangers of spying just yet. *"You're not a woman. By your rationale, they'll kill you if they find you here."*

"By the time they arrive, I'll be gone, watching from another location if I can. Others will be here to guard you, to make sure the Lords don't intend to harm you, so don't fret. These men are willing to give their lives to ensure the downfall of those demons. Don't let their sacrifice be for naught."

"What? Oh, hell no. I don't want anyone sacrificing anything."

"Would you feel better if I told you they'll run as soon as the Lords arrive?"

"Yes."

"Then they'll run."

Had they, though?

Slowly Reyes sat up, and their eyes met in a heated clash, his as dark as his skin. Turbulent. Hers, a little watery. His lips pulled in a tight frown. Her gaze dropped and she studied the rest of him. His nipples were hard enough to cut glass; three wounds were healing, one scabbing on his shoulder, one on his sternum and one marring his stomach.

"Where am I?" she asked, the words a mere whisper.

"My home."

"In Buda?"

"Yes."

Her eyelids narrowed, her mind a black hole that couldn't provide a single memory of being moved from one location to another. "How did I get here? How did you find me?"

He looked away, hiding his gaze under his lashes. "You know I am not human. Don't you?"

Knowledge she wished she didn't possess and a conversation it was best not to start. *Why, yes, Reyes, I do know you're a demon. Your greatest enemy gave me the scoop and now I'm here to help him destroy you.* "You came for me," she said, changing the subject. Part of her had hoped for just such a thing; part of her had feared it.

"Yes," he repeated.

"Why?" Without the heat of his gaze holding her captive, she was able to scan her own body. She was still clothed, thank God. Her sweater had been removed, but her white T-shirt was still stained with grease and now blood—hers, the man she'd hurt—her jeans ripped from her struggle with her assailant. She...smelled. How long had she been wearing these clothes?

Suddenly the bed bounced, and her eyes jerked back to Reyes. He had propped his back against the headboard, widening the distance between them. That should have pleased her. Yes, it should have.

"I have a feeling I will always come for you." His angry voice whipped through the silence, his accusing expression laying the blame at her feet.

Once again her eyelids narrowed to tiny slits. "Let me guess. You'll always come for me because you like hurting me. Well, why didn't you just kill me while I slept? I wouldn't have been able to fight. You could have cut my throat, quick, easy. That *is* what you ultimately plan to do, isn't it? Or have you changed your mind?"

A muscle ticked in his jaw. He remained silent.

"Have you captured the rest of my family?"

Again, no reply. Only that increasingly erratic tick.

"Answer me, damn you!" She slammed her fist into the mattress. The frustrated and panicked action offered no relief from the sudden horror in her chest. "Do you know where they are? If they're alive?"

Finally he deigned to speak again. "I have done nothing to them. You have my word."

"Liar!" She'd sprung across the bed before she even realized what she was doing, slapping his face, pounding her fists into his wounds to cause maximum pain. "You know something. You have to know something."

His eyes closed and a blissful smile lifted the corners of his lips.

Her fury intensified. "You think this is funny? Well, what about this?" Seething, not knowing where the desire came from, she launched forward and sank her teeth into his neck, incisors digging so deep she immediately tasted blood.

He moaned. His hands tangled in her hair, not jerking her away but urging her closer. She offered no resistance; she couldn't. Embers of her anger and helplessness were twisting, breaking apart and realigning into something infinitely sweeter. The heat of him...so good, so damn good. He burned her soul-deep, flames licking at her, consuming her. She liked it, liked hurting him, liked having her mouth on him, and the knowledge shamed her.

Between her legs, his shaft swelled and hardened. When he moaned a second time, it blended with the sound of hers. He arched into her—*yes, like that*—and she scraped her nails up his chest, to his nipples.

A harsh animal growl filled her ears as his hands settled on her waist, squeezing. His hips writhed against her. Again. She wanted him to do it again. But a moment later, he stilled.

"Stop, Danika. You have to stop."

No, she didn't want to stop. She wanted—*what the hell are you doing? Nibbling on the enemy?*

Her jaw went slack. Gasping for breath, she jolted backward. His arms fell to his sides, his features hard, tight. She wiped her mouth with the back of a shaky wrist. Her entire body was shaking. Her nipples were pearled and aching, her stomach clenched. A metallic tang coated her tongue.

Reyes shifted, covering his jean-clad, swollen cock with the sheet. His cheeks glowed a rosy pink shade. Was he embarrassed? Blood trickled from his neck and swirled down his chest like a tiny, winding river. As she watched, the blood dried and the bite marks partially healed, already scabbing.

Monster, she reminded herself. *He's a monster.*

Horror—at her feelings, her actions, and his—washed through her. Must have coated her expression, too, because he said, "Do not touch me again, and I will not touch you."

"Don't worry." A violent tremor overtook her, and she crossed her arms over her middle. She'd wanted to hurt him, had *liked* it even. *Seriously, what the hell is wrong with me?* "I won't come near you."

"Good." He paused, his eyes perusing her body. Checking for injuries or something more erotic? "What did those men do to you?" He sounded unemotional now, her answer clearly of no importance.

That nonchalance irritated her. She hated him, so why did she want him to care? "They—" A wave of dizziness suddenly attacked her. A groan pierced the air. Hers, she realized. Her eyelids closed, so heavy she could no longer hold them open. Her adrenaline had crashed, she supposed, draining her strength.

How long since she'd eaten? Stefano hadn't fed her, had only given her sips of water every few hours. And he'd injected her with something. Something that had spun her mind out of control, tossing it into the sky before dropping it into a churning ocean to be ripped into a thousand pieces.

"We can't make it too easy for them," Stefano had said. *"We knew the demon of Death would follow the trail we left him, and that he'd have no idea we were expecting him. We worked hard to make this abduction look real and I won't fail in that endeavor now. No food, no fresh clothes. We can drug you or we can beat you. Which do you prefer?"*

"Neither."

"Choose or I'll choose for you. Don't forget, Danika, you're doing this for your family."

"So much for my training," she'd laughed resentfully. *"Drug me. Again, apparently."*

"Danika, what did those men do to you?"

Present collided with past, tearing her from those surreal musings. *Stupid girl. Do* not *relax your guard in front of Reyes!*

She pried her eyelashes apart. The world around her was blurred, Reyes nothing more than a dark slash directly in front of her. His fingers were gripping her shoulders and urging her down…gently…softly. As her vision cleared, she saw that his usually harsh features now seemed almost tender with concern.

"No touching," she told him, the words slurred. Delicious heat once again enveloped her. Perhaps the demon blood she'd ingested was responsible. "We agreed."

"Shhh." His breath caressed her cheek, as warm as his touch. "Relax. We will talk later."

"Go to hell."

He had no trouble understanding her. "Didn't we once have this very conversation? I'm already there."

Fight this. Fight him! She tried, she really did, but a dark tunnel beckoned her, dragging her closer and closer to the edge. "Where is…my mom? My sister? Grandma?"

"I'm sure they are fine." Fingers brushed her brow, softly smoothing her hair behind her ears.

"I want…to see…them. I won't…sleep. Can't make me. Hungry."

"I'll feed you." A petal-soft press of…lips? Yes, lips against the corner of her mouth.

She inhaled deeply, suddenly drowning in the scent of man and spice and inexplicably happy for it. "Hate you," she said, wishing she meant it.

"I know." He whispered directly in her ear, his warm breath traveling inside. "Sleep now, angel. You are safe. I will allow nothing else to happen to you."

She sagged. The cool mattress pressed against her back. Flames on top, ice beneath. Unable to fight any longer, she fell into the tunnel. Oblivion claimed her.

SHE WAS HERE, IN HIS BED. *His bed.*

Waiting for her to awaken had been a lesson in self-control and Reyes had begun to grow fearful that she would sleep forever. Then she had pulled herself from slumber, those long lashes cracking open to reveal bright emerald eyes, and he'd gotten a *real* lesson in self-torture.

Pain didn't like that Reyes was in the process of tiptoeing from the room. *More, want more teeth and nails and hurt.* "No."

The demon roared inside his mind.

Reyes pressed onward, only throwing one backward glance over his shoulder. Danika's black locks were splayed over his pillow, her face where his often rested. That knowledge filled him with pride. Even now, she might be breathing in his scent, making his essence a part of her.

Or perhaps not.

Danika slept fitfully, eyes rolling behind her lids, body twisting, small moans of alarm escaping her. Did she dream of what the Hunters had done to her? What *had* they done? Torture her for answers? Rape?

She had not answered him when he'd asked, had told him

nothing, in fact. He hadn't pressed her, for her pulse had quickened at the base of her neck, her skin had lost any semblance of color and panic had glazed her lovely eyes.

Fists clenched, he pounded down the stairs and into the kitchen. *Soon.* He would see her again, talk to her again and learn the truth. He had to know. And perhaps by then he would forget the horror he'd seen in her expression when she realized he had enjoyed being bitten.

Gods, that bite. His heartbeat had yet to slow from the pleasure of it. He'd held Danika, her sharp little teeth in his neck. For a single moment, she'd responded to him sensually; she'd wanted him, had been unable to stop herself from grinding against his cock. Then he'd realized it wasn't him she desired but pain, the demon already clouding her judgment, and he had commanded her to stop. She'd wrenched away. The physical agony he'd experienced in that moment had been the worst of his life—and the best.

Pain wanted more.

Hands shaky, Reyes opened the refrigerator. Paris did the shopping, so Reyes never knew what he'd find. Today's selection was shaved meats and loaves of bread. A sandwich, then.

"Where is Aeron?" Lucien asked behind him. "I kept my part of our bargain. The time has come for you to keep yours."

Reyes didn't turn. "I will take you to him. In the morning."

"No. You will take me to him *now.*"

Reyes withdrew a package of turkey and a package of ham, looked from one to the other, then shrugged. He didn't know which Danika would prefer, so he would make her both. "Danika is weak and hungry. After I see to her needs, I will be at your disposal."

The usually calm Lucien uttered a low growl. "Every minute he is locked away is probably absolute agony. Our demons cannot stand to have their hosts restrained, and you know it. Wrath is likely screaming for release, even now."

"Need I remind you again that he begged for it? And what I know is that when Aeron is brought here, he will have to be…what? Locked away. What is the difference if the prison is somewhere else? Besides that, he does not want to be near us." Reyes tossed the packages onto the counter and grabbed one of the loaves of bread. Wheat.

Did she like wheat or white? After a moment's deliberation, he decided to use both. Just in case. He pinched the plastic covering the white and slid the loaf in front of him. "I'm only asking for one more night."

"What if he's dying? We are immortal, yes, but under the right circumstances we can die like any other living thing. Another fact you already know."

"He's not dying."

"How do you know?" Lucien insisted.

"Somehow I can feel his desperation burning inside of me every minute of every day. It is stronger with every second that passes, as I'm sure *he* is weaker against Wrath." Reyes drew in a breath, held…held…then slowly released it, letting his sudden burst of anger leave him, too. "Just a few more hours. That's all I ask. For me, for Danika. For him."

There was a heavy pause. He fit two slices of meat atop each slice of bread, smashed them together.

"Very well," Lucien said. "A few." His boots clomped as he strode away.

Reyes studied the sandwiches. "Not enough," he muttered. Humans needed variety. Isn't that what Paris always said about his lovers? Frowning, Reyes opened the refrigerator again and searched inside. His gaze landed on a bag of purple grapes. Yes, perfect. Last time Danika had stayed here, she'd plowed through a bowl of the fruit in minutes.

He withdrew the entire bag, washed the contents and spread them around the four sandwiches.

What would she like to drink? Back to the fridge he went.

He saw a bottle of wine, a pitcher of water and a carton of orange juice. He knew better than to give Danika wine. The wine here was laced with ambrosia stolen from the heavens and had once almost killed Maddox's human woman, Ashlyn.

Reyes scooted the chilled bottle aside and latched on to the juice. He poured every drop into a tall glass.

"Damn, boy. You feeding an army?"

Reyes tossed a quick glance over his shoulder. Sabin leaned against the door frame, thick arms crossed over his chest. He was as modern as Paris with his silly *Pirates of the Caribbean* shirt, but he lacked Paris's finesse. "She is hungry."

"I guessed. Tiny as she is, I don't think she'll be able to eat all that. Besides, she just spent three days with Hunters. You should starve her, question her about what went down, and only then, when you have answers, should you feed her." Arm outstretched to claim one of the squares, Sabin moved forward.

Reyes latched on to his friend's wrist and squeezed. "Make your own or lose the hand. And she is not in league with the Hunters."

Sabin arched a sandy brow, the picture of pique. "How do you know?"

He didn't have an answer, but he would not allow *anyone* to hurt her in any way. "Just stay away from her," he said, "and leave the food alone."

"Since when are you so giving?" Gideon asked at his other side, swiping a sandwich before Reyes could do anything about it.

"Giving" equaled *"stingy"* in Gideon's messed-up world.

"Back off," Reyes growled.

Both warriors chuckled.

"Yeah. Whatever," Sabin said, and grabbed a sandwich with his free arm.

Reyes ground his teeth together. *I will not pull a weapon on my friends. I will not pull a fucking weapon on my friends.*

"Oh, goodie! Food." Anya skipped into the room, Ashlyn at

her side, their arms linked. "I thought I smelled the sweet scent of culinary genius."

Red spotted Reyes's vision as he gathered the plate and the glass before the women could confiscate a single crumb or drop. "Danika's," he said tightly.

"But I really like turkey." Anya pouted up at him. She was tall for a woman, but even in four-inch heels she only reached Reyes's chin. "Besides, when I slap a sandwich together, it never tastes as good as when you do it. There's something so delicious about food prepared by a man."

"Not my problem." He tried to step around her, but she leapt in front of him, hands fisted on her hips. He sighed, knowing she would trip him if he attempted to pass her. "Lucien will cook something for you."

Another pouting frown. "He's out collecting souls."

"Paris, then."

"He's doing some chick in town, the nympho."

"Starve," Reyes told her unsympathetically.

"I'll make us something," Ashlyn offered, rubbing her slightly swollen belly. She was pregnant, just beginning to show. "While I do, I want to hear all about Danika."

Reyes wasn't sure how he felt about the coming birth. Would the baby be a demon? A human? He couldn't decide which would be worse. Constant inner torment or mortality? "She's well. Nothing more to say."

"Make me something, too," Sabin told Ashlyn. "I'm ninety-seven percent famished. That sandwich I stole only helped a little."

"I'm totally full," Gideon said, which meant he was on the verge of starvation. He wiped his hands to dislodge any remaining crumbs.

"Shame on you boys for making a pregnant woman do all the work," Anya scolded.

"Hey!" Sabin wagged a finger at the gorgeous goddess.

"You're letting a pregnant woman make your sandwich. How is that any different?"

"Pregnant or not, I'll let her make me one, too."

At the sound of that scratchy voice, everyone stilled. Turned. A collective gasp rang out. Then a collective, "Torin!"

Grinning, Ashlyn stepped toward the now-healed warrior, arms opening to hug him. Anya latched on to her shoulder and jerked her back.

"He's Disease, sweetness," the goddess said. "You can't touch him without getting sick, remember?"

"Oh, yeah." Ashlyn smiled at him. "I'm glad you're better."

Torin smiled in return, though his expression was tinted with sadness and yearning. "Me, too."

He looked just as Reyes remembered—before the man's neck had been cut from end to end by Hunters, that is. White hair, black brows and bright green eyes. Beautifully masculine and utterly eerie. He wore black gloves that stretched from fingertips to armpits, for he could not touch another living being skin to skin without infecting it with disease. Not even an immortal. The warriors would not become ill themselves if they touched him, but they *would* spread the disease to humans.

"How are you feeling?" Reyes asked him.

"Better." That green gaze lowered to the plate Reyes held. "Hungry."

"Back off," Reyes said. "I'm glad you're better, but not enough to share."

Torin's grin lost its edge of sadness. "You almost make me wish I were still bed-bound. You'd have to bring me food with a smile. Oh, guess what?" he said, pivoting toward Anya. "Your friend is climbing the hill. He keeps shouting that he wants to put you over his knee and spank you, so I decided not to kill him as Lucien instructed. Guy has a blade strapped to his left thigh, but that's the only weapon I detected. He should reach the door any—"

Knock. Knock.

Grinning, Anya clapped her hands. "William's here!"

"What is he doing here?" Reyes asked. "Lucien told him never to return or he'd kill him, and you hate him."

"Hate him? I adore him! Even made sure he'd come back by holding his favorite book hostage. And FYI, Lucien was only teasing about killing him. They're BFF's now, I swear." She bounded off, clapping happily.

"William!" the group in the kitchen heard a moment later.

"Where's my book, woman?"

"Where's my hug, you big teddy bear?"

"Is this the same William who drove Lucien crazy while Anya was recovering from the loss of her key?" Ashlyn asked, just as Maddox strode up behind her and enfolded her in his arms. "And what book?"

"The very same," Maddox said, nuzzling her cheek. "The book, I don't know. This William did not strike me as the intellectual type. What's a BFF?"

"A best friend forever."

Maddox frowned. "I did not get the impression the two were best friends forever or even temporarily. Someone should lock the man up until Lucien returns."

Ashlyn melted into her man. "Anya seems to like him. I say we leave him alone. The more, the merrier, right?"

Reyes rolled his eyes. Every day in the fortress was a party now, it seemed.

While Ashlyn and the men engaged in a heated discussion about who would cook what, as well as what they should do about the mysterious William, Reyes finally made his escape, careful to hold the plate straight and the glass of juice steady as he stalked from the kitchen.

I hate you, Danika had said.

I know, he'd told her, and he'd meant it. He'd once held her and her loved ones prisoner. He'd helped bring her to the

Hunters' attention. She had every reason to despise him. But now, he wanted to give her something good. Something she could smile about in the years to come. Even if it was only a simple meal.

Up the stairs he climbed, and still, he did not spill a drop. Most likely, she was still sleeping. He hated the thought of waking her, but knew it was for the best. The paleness of her skin and the shadows under her eyes concerned him. She needed sustenance.

While she's here, I'll see to her every need. She'll want for nothing.

He sailed into the bedroom, but stopped abruptly when he reached the edge of the bed. His mouth dried and the haze of red returned to coat his vision. The black sheets were rumpled. Empty.

Danika was gone.

CHAPTER SIX

AERON CROUCHED in his underground prison, fury flowing through his veins. Fury with himself, the gods, his demon. Reyes. *He should have killed me. Too late now. I want to live. I want to taste the death of those women.*

Darkness would have enveloped him completely, but he'd long since given over to his demon. His eyes glowed bright red, throwing crimson beams wherever he looked. Mud and rock surrounded him. He was buried so deep in the earth he could hear the screams of the damned, could smell the sulfur and rotting flesh wafting from hell's gates. He'd thought Lucien was the only warrior with access to the hereafter, but apparently Reyes had it, as well.

Wrath, his demonic companion, foamed at the mouth and chomped at the edges of Aeron's mind, desperate to escape this hated place. To act.

Too close to home, the demon shouted. *Won't go back.*

"No, you won't go back."

Aeron couldn't survive without his demon; they were now one being, two halves of a whole, incomplete without the other. No longer was Aeron ready to die. Craving his own demise had been a momentary burst of madness, surely. Now he knew, now he accepted. He couldn't allow himself to be killed until the blood of those four women stained his hands, coated his arms and filled his mouth.

Mallory, Tinka, Ginger and Danika.

He smiled, practically tasting their deaths already. *Cut their throats,* Cronus, the king of gods, had commanded him. *Do not leave their sides until their hearts stop and their lungs still.* Aeron thought he might have resisted at first—innocent, they were innocent—but he could not be certain. Allowing those women to live seemed…abhorrent.

"Soon," he promised himself. He trembled with anticipation.

He'd killed recently. He knew it, deep in his bones, but his memory was hazy. All his mind would provide was the image of an old woman splayed on the cold ground, blood crusted on her temples. There were tears in her eyes and cuts on her right arm.

"Don't hurt me," she begged. "Please, don't hurt me."

In one hand, Aeron clutched a dagger. His other hand was pure claw, sharp and lethal. He lunged forward—

And then, as always, the vision faded completely. What had happened after that? What had he done? He wasn't sure. His only certainty was that he would not have backed away from the kill. He would not have left her alive.

Want out. Want up! Want to stretch wings and fly.

"I know." Aeron jerked at his chains. They rattled and cut his already scabbed wrists, but they didn't budge. He bared his teeth in a scowl. Fucking Reyes.

Fucking Pain.

Aeron could not recall how Reyes had defeated him and carted him here, only that he had. A tortured "Forgive me" still rang in Aeron's ears.

They were the same words Aeron used to mutter as he stood on the outskirts of Budapest, watching the humans, amazed that they blithely went about their days unconcerned about their inherent weaknesses and the knowledge that they would soon die. Some by his hand.

Aeron had sometimes erupted into blood-rages, Wrath judging and executing those who deserved his particular brand of punishment. Rapists, molesters. Murderers. *Like me.* Some, though, did not deserve what he did to them. *Like the women.*

He frowned. The thought was out of place in the chaos of his mind, a notion he would have considered before the gods tasked him with the beautiful death of the Ford women.

Suddenly rocks crumbled, falling from the far cavern wall and disrupting his brooding. Aeron's attention whipped to it, eyelids slitting. There was a narrow hole in the center, a pair of glowing red eyes—demon eyes like Aeron's—pulsing through it.

Aeron growled a warning. He was chained and weaponless, but he was not helpless. He had teeth. He would eat his foe, if necessary.

More rocks fell, widening the hole. Then a bald, scaled head pushed through. Those bright red eyes looked right and left before landing on Aeron. Sharp, glistening fangs appeared in a feral smile.

"I sssmelled you, brother." The creature spoke with a lisp, forked tongue flickering. It sounded happy rather than menacing.

"I am not your brother."

Thin lips slithered into a pout. "But you Wrath."

Aeron's claws elongated to razor points. "Yes, I am." *You know him?* he asked his demon.

No.

There was a third tumble of rocks as scaled shoulders emerged, followed by a short scaly body.

"Come any closer and you will die."

"No, I won't. Me never die." The creature planted hoofed feet on the ground and stood. It was so short it couldn't have reached any higher than Aeron's navel. A tremble passed through its small body, scattering dust from its dull green scales.

"How can you be so sure?"

"We friendsss."

"I have no friends. Who are you? What are you doing here?"

"Massster used to call me Legion before he called me Ssstupid Idiot." It moved one step closer, humming with giddiness. Grinning, fangs making another appearance. "Want to play?"

Legion. Interesting. "One of a thousand what?"

"Minionsss." Another step.

Servants of hell, Wrath supplied with disgust. *Useless, disposable, unworthy. Eat him.*

Aeron drew his knees up to his chest, preparing to attack. "Stop." Now why had he said that? He *wanted* the thing to approach. Wanted to feast on it.

It obeyed, the pout returning to its lips. "But we friendsss now. Friendsss get to sssometimesss ssstand next to each other. I ssseen them do it."

He didn't bother reiterating that they weren't friends. "Why are you here, Legion?" Questions first, dinner second.

Anticipation brightened those crimson eyes. "Me want to play. Will you play with me? Pleassse, pleassse, pleassse."

"Play what?" Saliva dipped from the corner of Aeron's mouth, and he licked at it. The more he considered the option of eating his foe, the more he liked the thought of having the demon for a snack. Aeron had enough slack in his chains that he'd been able to catch and sustain himself on rats. The demon would make a tasty change. Mustard would have been nice, though. Fucking Reyes. "What game?"

"Catch the demon! Massster stopped playing with me. Kick me out of home." It looked down and punted a pebble with its hoof. "Me did a bad, bad thing and don't get to play with him no more."

"What bad thing?" He asked the question before he could stop himself.

Those fangs emerged, chewing away at that thin bottom lip. "Ate Massster'sss hand. Want to play?"

And perhaps lose one of *his* hands? He thought about it, shrugged. "We can play." Turnabout was only fair.

"Goody!" Claws clapped together in excitement, though the fiend remained a good distance away. "Can we change rule?"

There were rules? "What rule is that?"

"Winner never can beat me with ssstonesss."

"Agreed." Aeron would just bite him with teeth.

Laughing eerily, Legion leapt into the air. He bounded from one side of the cave to the other, a mere blur to Aeron's eyes. Twice he whizzed past, cackling happily, and twice Aeron reached out, the metal bonds cutting deeper. The creature arched just out of reach.

Aeron stilled and pondered his options. He had limited range of motion, and Legion moved too quickly to see. He'd have to wait, a spider weaving a web, using his other senses.

Determined, he closed his eyes, welcoming total darkness. He placed his hands on his upraised knees, hoping he was the picture of tranquility.

Legion's gleeful laughter echoed in his ears, closer…closer… Fingertips scraped his forehead, but Aeron didn't even twitch.

"Catch me, catch me, if you can."

Stones fell from the far wall a split second before the laughter increased in volume and a breeze ruffled the humid, ash-soaked air. Any moment…wait…wait for it… Something hot brushed his arm, and Aeron snapped his fingers closed.

A gasp, a squeal. Legion wiggled against his grip, laughter ceasing.

"I win." Aeron's teeth sharpened and he threw his head forward. Contact. Acid blood filled his mouth, burning, blistering.

"Ow!"

Coughing and spitting, Aeron released the demon. His eyelids popped open but soon narrowed to slits. *Why didn't you tell me he was poison?* he barked at Wrath.

Didn't know, was the pouting reply.

"You bit me." There was accusation in the creature's tone. Accusation and hurt. Tears filled those red eyes.

"You taste like bile, you disgusting maggot."

"But…but…you made me bleed." Legion rubbed at his neck, black blood seeping from between his scaled fingers. "You promisssed not to."

"I promised not to *beat* you." Something almost like… remorse? Yes, remorse sparked to life in Aeron's chest, over-shadowing his constant anger and overwhelming death-lust. "I—" What? Nearly gnawed you to bits but I'm sorry now? "I thought that's how the game was played."

"You thought wrong." Legion sniffed and turned away. He— no longer an "it" in his mind, Aeron realized—stalked to the corner and buried his face in the rock, sulking.

Dear gods. *How did I stumble into this situation?*

Minions are such babies, Wrath growled, as if *it* wasn't a baby.

"I didn't know the rules," Aeron said, shocked that he felt more like himself in that moment than he had in months and unsure of why.

Legion peeked over his shoulder, scales glistening like polished rubies in the red glow of Aeron's demonic irises. His scales had been green before, hadn't they? "If we going to be friendsss, you have to promissse not to bite anymore. My feel-ingsss got hurt, too."

Friends? "Legion, I do not wish to hurt your feelings, but—"

"Sssee!" Grinning again, the tiny demon spun and clapped his clawed hands. "You not wisssh to hurt me anymore. We friendsss already. What ssshould we do, what ssshould we do? Want to play another game?"

Aeron's head tilted to the side, and he eyed his new…friend thoughtfully. "I know another game we can play."

"Oh, what? What?" The clapping became happily frantic. "Me want to play. What'sss it called? Me win thisss time, I jusssst know it!"

"It's called break-the-chains."

PARIS LAY SPRAWLED beside the human woman on the rented bed. He'd been inside this room countless times before. A king-size mattress, white walls with classic paintings hanging strategically. A black desk, golden lamp. Number fourteen of the Boutique Hotel Zara. Only he'd been with a different woman each time.

He didn't know his companion's name, he mused, and he didn't care to know. She was a tourist, and he'd never see her again.

He never saw his bedmates again.

Usually he left immediately after the sex was finished. Lingering promoted feelings, and since he couldn't screw the same woman twice, feelings were nothing but a nuisance.

Tonight, however, he'd stayed. Now the woman was snoring softly at his side. His mind was restless, his body tense, but he didn't want to go home. Maddox had Ashlyn, Lucien had Anya and now Reyes had Danika. Seeing them together reminded Paris of the woman *he* wanted—the woman he had killed.

Sienna.

Adorably plain Sienna with her freckled skin, thick glasses and dark curly hair. Thin, too thin, with barely any curves, barely any breasts. Yet she'd snared him from the first. He'd desired her, romanced her as best as he was able and seduced her. And she'd quickly betrayed him. Had planned to betray him from the beginning.

She'd been a Hunter, his worst enemy, and she'd used his arousal against him, distracting him and drugging him, then leaving him for her coworkers to find. They had locked him up, chained him. Studied him. He'd almost died and they'd had to throw Sienna into the lion's den, so to speak, to keep him alive.

Promiscuity couldn't survive without sex. The longer Paris went without it, the weaker he became. Those Hunters hadn't wanted him dead. How, then, could they have studied his abilities? How, then, could they have used him to lure his friends into Hunter territory? More than that, to kill him was to unleash his demon onto the world, crazed and blood-hungry, insane without its host.

Hunters didn't want that. Oh, they wanted the demons sucked out, but not until they found Pandora's box. As yet, no one was close to finding it. Not even the Lords.

So they'd sent Sienna into his cell. She had ridden him hard, just right, just the way he liked, and he'd regained his strength—more than usual, in fact. For the first time since his bonding with Promiscuity, he'd gotten hard for the same woman twice.

Paris had decided to keep her. Punish her, yes, but keep her for the rest of her life all the same. Because for the briefest of moments, he'd thought he'd found a woman who could save him. He'd no longer cared that she was a Hunter and that she thought the world would be a better place without him and his friends in it. He'd only cared about finally, blessedly having the same woman over and over again. Savoring her, learning her. Maybe even loving her.

He'd foolishly assumed they were meant to be together, that the gods had at last decided to relieve his inner torment. He was tired of searching for a new woman every day, tired of making love without really loving, not remembering who he kissed and touched, never really discovering what they liked or didn't like because there were so many faces, bodies, preferences and requests swimming in his memories.

So he'd escaped that Hunter prison with Sienna at his side. Like an untrained soldier, he'd allowed her to be shot. Not once, not twice, but three times.

She'd died in his arms.

Should have protected her. Weeks had since passed, but Paris couldn't scrub her face from his mind. Could no longer get hard unless he thought of her.

She wanted me. She hadn't *wanted* to want him, but want him she had. She'd been dripping wet as she slid down his swollen shaft. Despite everything, ecstasy had glazed her eyes. Over and over she had moaned his name. *His* name. Not another man's.

Despite their differences, they could have been happy together.

"But no. I allowed her own people to snuff her out." He laughed bitterly. "Some warrior I am. My fault, all my fault."

"What's that?" his companion asked, her voice sleep-rich. She rolled toward him, hand flattening on his chest.

Shit. He hadn't meant to wake her. Didn't want to talk with her.

Paris threw his legs over the side of the bed and stood, dislodging her.

"Hmm," she said. "I like the view."

Motions clipped, he gathered his clothing from the floor. There were blades strapped on his arms and legs, and he didn't bother trying to hide them. They had turned the woman on.

She purred his name.

He ignored her and dressed.

"Come back to bed," she beseeched. "I want you again. I need you."

Similar words had been said to him a thousand times, would probably be said a thousand more by a thousand others. The thought made him cringe. "I need to go."

She huffed in disappointment. "Please stay. I need to start my day right, and having you inside me is oh, so right."

At the moment, he couldn't even remember what she looked like—and he'd been looking at her just seconds before. She wasn't Sienna, that much he knew. His cock was as limp as a wilted flower and would stay that way.

"Perhaps another time." It was a lie, but it was the kindest thing he could say.

The covers shifted. A little moan escaped her. She was probably fondling herself, seeking to tempt him or maybe find release. Either way, he didn't care. His body gave no reaction. *This is what my life will always be reduced to: fucking and leaving. I'm pathetic.*

He adored women. They were his life's blood and he'd always taken care to soothe their emotions, plump their self-esteem. More and more, he just didn't have the energy for it.

"Paris," she whispered, breathless. "Replace my fingers with yours. Please."

"Sounds as if you're doing a good job. The room's paid up for the rest of the night. I'll leave you to it."

"Leave?" She jolted up, reached for him and dragged a fingertip down his side. "Stay. I'm begging you."

"Forget me. I've already forgotten you." He strode out of the room, out of the hotel, and never looked back.

CHAPTER SEVEN

HAVING AWOKEN in Reyes's bed alone, another turbulent night-mare swirling in her mind, Danika had realized she couldn't do it. She couldn't stay here, no matter her purpose. Not with Reyes. Just being near him affected her in a thousand different ways, none of them good.

Every time she spied him, hate should have filled her. Hate and rage and violence. But every time she peered into the dark fathomless pools of knowledge and pain that were his eyes, she experienced…something else. She drowned, pieces of her dying then quickly reforming for him. *Him.* Not her family, not her own survival. Him.

How could she forget her purpose like that? How? Kid-napped all those weeks ago, and now bereft of even the miserly life she'd built, how could she still want to reach out to Reyes? To be held by him? Comforted? Even pleasured? How did he slip into her most private fantasies and rouse her animal needs?

Not knowing what else to do, she'd sprung from the bed and raced from the bedroom. She'd gotten pretty far, then back-tracked, fearing that a wrong turn could land her face-to-face with one of Reyes's friends. Her legs had finally given out, and she'd stopped here at the staircase.

She wrapped her arms around her middle, trying to conserve warmth. The cold had returned full force, and she shivered. Only one thing had managed to warm her: Reyes.

"Danika!"

Speak of the devil—or rather, demon. Reyes's voice echoed through the hallway behind her, panicked and as sharp as a razor. She propped her head against the stair railing, fatigue and dizziness swamping her. *I should run.* She remained in place. Like a fool, she was eager to see him.

"Danika!" He sounded closer.

She didn't waste her time responding. He would find her soon enough. No reason to help him.

"Dani—"

Her name trailed off as a gust of air brushed the back of her neck. He must have stopped abruptly. She couldn't see him, even peripherally, but she could feel his heat all the way to her bones. God, he was warm. Her shivers faded.

Then suddenly he was there, sitting beside her, his thigh brushing hers. Jolts of electricity shot through her veins, running the length of her entire body. She gulped.

For a long while, they simply sat in silence.

Finally, she glanced over at him. Her gaze traveled from his mud-coated boots to his ripped jeans. Up his powerful arms, which were resting on his thighs. Three deep grooves were etched into his skin. Blood had trickled and dried.

He was peering down at the steps, but he must have felt her gaze because he moved his arms behind his back and braced his weight on his elbows, placing his face out of sight.

"You hurt yourself again," she said, trying to tamp down a wave of concern.

"It's nothing."

"Nothing." She snorted. "You're the clumsiest man I've ever met. You're always scraped up and bleeding."

A pause, then, "Did you think to run from me?"

"Yes." There was no reason to deny it.

"Why?"

"As if you have to rack your brain for the answer."

"No, I mean, why did you stop?"

Afraid of the truth and too tired to weave a lie, she ignored the question entirely. "Why do you and your friends want to kill my family? You've never given me a reason. To my knowledge, we hadn't insulted you, trespassed or done anything to deserve…this."

He sighed heavily, wearily. "No, you did nothing wrong. And I do not want to kill you."

Whether he spoke true or not, she didn't know. Either way, she reacted. Her heart sped up as though it had just heard the starting shot of a race, beating so swiftly she feared it might burst out of her chest. His voice had been laced with a husky rasp, the words broken. A lump formed in her throat, and she had to swallow it to be able to speak. "That isn't what you said last time. Last time—"

"We will not speak of last time. It is over. Done."

"No. It's not done." Anger rose inside her, hot and hungry, giving her a flare of strength. She slammed a fist against her knee. Her leg bounced up in reflex. "It will never be done."

"Do not hurt yourself, Danika," Reyes said, sounding just as angry as she felt.

"Funny words coming from you. Last time you threatened me. Told me I would die if you found me. Well, you found me."

His head whipped to her, his eyes suddenly piercing all the way to her soul. Dark, sultry, the onyx orbs practically alive. "I said that, yes. I have since proven I cannot hurt you in any way."

True. Damn him. Everything inside her softened, and she couldn't stop it from happening. *Look away. He's dragging you under again, shifting your thinking. Ruining you.* She peered down at the bottom of the stairs. A lush red carpet waited, so thick her feet would never sink to the marbled floor below it. "Your friends still want me dead."

"Want?" He laughed, but it was not a pretty resonance. "No. No one wants you dead, but they will do what they must."

"And they *must* kill me?"

Now he remained silent.

"And you'll, what?" she insisted. "Let them?"

Another sigh, this one heartsick. "Have I hurt you, even once?"

No. "What do you know of my family, Reyes? My grandmother has been—" she nearly choked, did gag "—missing for over two weeks."

Reyes reached out, twined his fingers with hers.

Gasping, she jerked her hand away. "We agreed. No touching." His skin was too hot, and her body too responsive. With only that split-second contact, she'd felt seared to the bone. Her nipples were hard.

"I do not know about your grandmother, but I…I know someone who will."

Danika laughed, and like Reyes's, it was an ugly sound. "Yeah. Right."

"I spoke true. I would not lie to you about something like this."

The seriousness of his tone didn't convince her. The actual words convinced her. Three times she'd interacted with him, and not once had he lied or even stretched the truth. He was blunt, painfully so. Her stomach clenched in hope…in fear. What would she learn if she visited this nameless person? That her mother, sister and grandmother were healthy and whole or that they had suffered terribly before dying?

"Take me to this person." A command. She faced him, shifting her body until they were chest to chest. Their breath mingled, warm and minty. She inhaled deeply. So deeply she feared he became a part of her. *He's been a part of you since the beginning.*

No. I refuse to believe that.

"I will not take you to him, but I will question him for you."

"Hell, no." She wanted to grab Reyes's shoulders and shake him, but knew that touching him willingly would shatter her composure. "I'm going with you."

"I—" He massaged the back of his neck. "No."

"You won't talk me out of this and there'll be a fight if you try and force me to stay behind."

A long, tired sigh. "Very well. But first, you will eat. You can barely hold up your head." His gaze roved over her. To his credit, he didn't leer. His expression became guarded, revealing nothing of his emotions.

"I need to know what happened to them. I won't be able to keep down a single bite until I do."

He was shaking his head before the last word left her mouth. "This is non-negotiable. You will eat, shower and then we will go."

"Don't tell me what to do! I'm not the same girl I was the first time you abducted me. I will *not* meekly obey you."

"Is that the way you saw yourself before? Meek?"

She stared at him, incredulous. "Didn't you?"

"No. I saw a strong, proud woman who did whatever necessary to calm her family and keep them alive."

Don't react. Don't you dare react. "I was weak and afraid. Now I know how to defend myself." The fire in her tone practically dared him to find out firsthand. Stupid of her, since she currently possessed the strength of a newborn. But she wanted him to know there would be consequences for hurting her.

He nodded in understanding, but his pensive expression didn't change. "I heard about the human you killed."

Human, he'd said, the single word driving home their differences in a big way. Then there was a flash of black and red in her mind, a pained gasp in her ears, concrete burning her palms and knees, pencil snapping, a dying breath echoing, and she didn't care how different they were. She just wanted Reyes to pull her to safety.

"Danika."

Somehow, with only her name, his rough timbre *was* able to drag her from the mire of the hated memory. She gulped, shook her head. "I don't regret my actions." She only hoped the words were true. Right now, she was too numb to know for sure.

"I'm glad."

Of course he was—wait. *Did he say* glad? "Why?"

"He meant to hurt you. You did what was necessary to protect yourself. I only wish I had been there."

"Well, I didn't protect myself well enough," she said bitterly, then cursed. Bringing up the aftermath and her time with the Hunters wasn't a smart move. Besides, she had a job to do. "How did you hear about what happened? Is there a warrant out for my arrest or something?"

She'd spoken so quietly, *she* had to strain to hear herself, yet he answered without pause. "No warrant. No one knows. But what I am about to tell you, Danika, can never be repeated. You hate us. With reason. So arming you with this information is foolish of me. And yet, I want you to know why we've done the things we've done."

Suddenly she was terrified of breathing—of stopping him, of allowing him to continue. What dark secret was he about to reveal? He had to sacrifice virgins at every full moon? She was next? Well, news flash. She wasn't a virgin.

He inhaled deeply, slowly released every molecule. Looked away from her. "I told you the warriors here are not human. What I did not tell you is that every warrior here is possessed by a…a demon." There was shame in the word. "Lucien—do you remember him?—is possessed by the spirit of Death. When your human died, he was summoned."

I know, she almost told him, but managed to cut off the words. Except, Stefano had said the men had *become* the demons, not that they were simply *possessed* by them. Still, her shoulders sagged as relief pounded through her. Funny that she felt relief at his admission. She didn't have to hide her knowledge now.

What are you doing? her mind shouted. He didn't know that she knew, and she had to keep it that way. Relief would seem odd. So...how should she react to such an admission? Laughter? Screams?

"Demons," she said on a broken catch of breath. What else could she say?

"Yes."

"I—I suspected," she said, opting for a half truth. "Last time I was here, there were things I couldn't explain. Supernatural things."

He nodded, and her relief doubled. "I don't want you afraid of us," he said. "We are demons, yes, but we will not hurt you. Not any more than we already have," he added wryly.

It wasn't a promise of comfort, but she wanted to lean on him, anyway, maybe confess why she was here so he could solve the problem for her. *Stupid.* How gentle would Reyes be if he knew the truth? That she was here to learn everything she could about him so that the information could be used against him. *You're doing this for your family. Don't forget.* "I didn't see him that night."

Leaning on his elbows again, putting distance between them, Reyes eyed her quizzically. "Didn't see who?"

"Lucien. When that man died, I didn't see Lucien." Questions spun through her mind at the same speed Reyes's warmth abandoned her body, leaving her cold and shivering. "You said he was there, that he saw what I had done."

"The human did not die in the street, but in a hospital three days later. Had he died that night, though, you still would not have seen Lucien. He is able to remain in the spirit world, unseen as he does his duty."

She had to keep him talking. This was exactly the kind of information Stefano desired. Even as the thought filled her mind, there was a spark of guilt in her chest. Guilt? Why? Reyes and his horde deserved to be ratted out. "How is that possible? How does he remain in the spirit world? What does he see?"

"That is not for me to answer."

To press would have been suspicious. Right? Her mind simply wasn't functioning at optimum levels. "You said you are all possessed. Wh-what demon possesses you?"

He stiffened, his back going ramrod straight. "The men who attacked you, they were Hunters."

"Hunters," she repeated. Reyes had just ignored her question as she sometimes ignored his. Perhaps it was better that he didn't answer. Right now, she could almost pretend this was just another dream, her family was safe and the only thing concerning her was whether or not she would finish her next painting on time for her client. She could almost pretend Reyes was a normal man, here to romance her. Almost. "Ashlyn once mentioned them, but at the time we didn't know what they were."

"They are a league of men who want us dead. They think the world would be a better place without us."

"Would it?" she couldn't help but ask.

His eyes darkened. "As long as humans have free will, the world will never be perfect. We do not force them to do bad things. They do them of their own volition." Bitterness dripped from every growled word. "Hunters are disinclined to consider that truth, however. It is far easier simply to blame all their problems on that which they do not understand."

What he said made sense, but she didn't let it sway her. Too much was at stake. "Well, you *willingly* hunted my family. Why? Tell me this time. I deserve to know. Why did you hunt us? What does my family have to do with any of this? With you?"

"Danika—"

"I'm begging you. Tell me!"

He rubbed the spot just above his heart. "The gods ordered Aeron—you remember Aeron?"

She shuddered, even as her heart drummed excitedly at how close she was to getting answers. No way would she ever forget that man. Soon after her—first—kidnapping, Aeron had been chosen to take her into the city to gather medicine for Maddox's girlfriend—how any woman could be insane enough to get involved with one of these warriors, she didn't know, even though she'd later come to enjoy Ashlyn's company. He'd removed his shirt, revealing a body covered in violent tattoos, and she'd panicked, thinking he meant to rape her. Of course, she had resisted him every time he'd reached for her and he had nearly beaten her for it.

Reyes had calmed her—how, she still didn't know—and finally she'd allowed Aeron to gather her in his arms. Wings had sprung from his back and he'd flown her through Budapest. *Flown her.* Just to find her purse and bring Tylenol to the sick Ashlyn.

Danika recalled thinking how odd the men were, a strange combination of ancient and modern. They hadn't known anything about human medicines, yet they had a plasma-screen TV and an Xbox. They dressed like warriors of old, weapons strapped all over their bodies, yet one of them constantly partied at the local nightclub. They pampered Ashlyn but sought to destroy Danika. The contradictions had confused her. Still did.

"Yes, I remember Aeron," she finally said.

"The gods ordered him to slay you and your family."

Her eyes widened, disbelief storming through her. "You're lying. One, there are no *gods.* Two—"

"There are no demons, either, I'm sure."

Her mouth opened and closed as she tried to form a coherent answer. Stefano had used the same logic on her. She was sure the two wouldn't be pleased to know how closely their thoughts had aligned.

"There *are* gods, and they *do* want you dead. The sooner you start believing that, the sooner you can protect yourself."

"Fine. But why? I've done nothing wrong. My family has done nothing wrong."

"We do not know why. I had hoped you could solve this mystery for me."

"Sorry, but no." She laughed again, and this time the sound

was like broken glass being scraped on a chalkboard. "I used to go to church every Sunday. I always tried to be nice to the people in my life and I never purposely hurt anyone." A pause as the dying man's visage filled her head again. "I can't say that now, can I? Until I met you and your friends, I liked to think that I was a pretty decent human being."

"You are."

Her gaze narrowed on him. "You don't know anything about me, and I don't want you to. I want you to take me the fuck to see the man—" Realization slapped at her and her anger faded to shock. "It's Aeron, isn't it?"

Reyes nodded reluctantly.

She nearly vomited at the thought of facing the winged warrior again, but she repeated, "I want you to take me to see him."

Still, Reyes's features remained calm, collected. "I have a tray of food in my room. You know what you must first do."

Grrr! There would be no talking him around. Determination radiated from him. "Fine," she said, wasting no more time. "I'll eat." She gripped the banister and pulled herself up. Her knees quickly gave out.

Reyes's arm wound around her waist and held her in place. That arm was hot, like a brand.

She hissed at him. Hissing was safer than purring. "I said no touching."

He didn't move away from her, but swept her up, cradling her against the hardness of his chest. His heart pounded against her shoulder, strong and sure.

"Let me go." Her cheeks heated as the breathlessness of her tone registered. "Just let me go. Please."

"I am afraid I will never be able to let you go."

REYES CARRIED DANIKA back to his room and eased her onto the edge of the mattress, careful not to disturb the plates resting nearby. She refused to look at him as she scooted away.

She concentrated on the food, reaching out and grabbing one of the sandwiches. The turkey on wheat. She nibbled on it for a while, then popped several of the grapes into her mouth.

Her eyelids closed, ecstasy coating her expression.

He stepped away, palming a dagger then hiding his arms behind his back to sink the tip into his wrist. *Good, so damned good.* All the while, he watched her. She had not reacted to his demon confession as he'd feared. He'd expected terror, screams, even disbelief. Instead, she'd accepted everything, remained calm and hadn't demanded proof.

That meant she'd already known.

What else had the Hunters told her?

Much as she hated Reyes and his friends, Reyes had a sudden fear that the Hunters had convinced Danika to work with them as Bait. And if she *was* acting as Bait, that meant she'd allowed herself to be drugged. Probably so he wouldn't suspect what she was. It saddened him, that she might be pushed to such extremes.

Was her job to distract him and lead his enemy inside the fortress? Or was she simply to learn everything she could about him? Because of her earlier questions, he suspected the latter. She'd wanted to know about Lucien's abilities. She'd wanted to know about Reyes's demon. Would she relay everything he'd told her to the Hunters?

If something had happened to her family, she *would* betray him, no doubt about it. *Can you blame her?* No, he couldn't blame her, but neither could he suppress the hurt that came with the thought that she would turn—had turned—against him.

Maddox had nearly killed Ashlyn over these types of suspicions. And if the others thought, even for a moment, that Danika might be Bait, they would demand Reyes slay her immediately—or they would do it themselves.

Except for these past few months, he hadn't battled Hunters in thousands of years. Still, he remembered the beginning of their blood feud very well. The fights and the deaths, the screams and the destruction. Theirs, his. Every shadow had been suspect, every stranger a possible assassin.

Reyes hadn't lived in fear, for he'd been a warrior to the core even then. He'd been cocky and arrogant and sure of his success, in battle and with women. He'd killed without remorse, taken every woman who desired him, showing them the pleasure found in pain, totally unconcerned about the aftermath.

Some had beaten their next partner to powder, some had sought beatings for themselves. All had become shells of their former selves, as desperate for pain as he was.

He would not do that to Danika nor would he let his friends hurt her. No matter what her purpose was. He had worked too diligently to save her, needed her with him too badly, and did not think he could function any longer without her. He would either win her affections so that she would not betray him or stop her from contacting the Hunters.

Decided, he nodded. He just, he couldn't let her go. She…eased his torment, he realized. Every time he neared her, his need for pain slackened considerably. Not once had he felt compelled to jump from the fortress. Not once had he craved broken bones and shredded organs. A few cuts here and there seemed to be sustaining him. Amazing.

"Thank you. For the food," Danika offered grudgingly. She popped another grape into her mouth, chewed.

"My pleasure." Already her color was brighter, her limbs less shaky. Dirt still smudged her cheeks, but the blue veins he'd been able to see before were no longer visible. "When you are done, you will shower."

She tensed but didn't face him. "That will just waste time."

"Does not matter."

"Does Aeron refuse to speak with unclean women?" she snapped. "I didn't realize demons had such strict standards of personal hygiene."

"I want you comfortable," he said on a sigh. "I want you at

your best, your mind clear. You will need every ounce of your strength. A shower will help."

That mollified her. "Fine, but I'm not showering with you in the room."

"A pity," he muttered.

Finally her bright green gaze sharpened on him. "What was that?"

When she looked at him, no matter her expression, desire always pounded through him. Even now, his shaft swelled and his hands itched to touch her. *You can't. You know better.* "There are clothes in the dresser. Take anything you need."

Still watching him, she bit into a grape.

He hardened all the more, lengthened another inch. He could very easily imagine those sharp, white teeth sinking into him again. The pain…the pleasure…a mingling of rapture. His angel would transport him to heaven.

His angel? Such a dangerous thing to want, yet he couldn't help himself. Everything inside him screamed that she was his. That they were meant to be together.

He doubted she would agree, and that was for the best.

If she wanted him as he wanted her, how would he be able to deny her? How would he be able to stop himself from taking her? And if he took her, how could he live with himself, knowing he'd ruined her? The demon of Pain *would* corrupt her; she would live only to hurt.

Sadly, the dark musings failed to dampen his arousal.

"I shall return soon."

Danika's gaze landed between his legs, and she hastily looked away, cheeks burning bright. She choked on the grape. "Sure. Okay. Take all the time you want."

If she ever learned the extent of his need for agony and the fact that he lost all hold on sanity without it…if she ever passed that knowledge on to the Hunters… Bad news, all the way around.

He would have to be careful around her. Much as he desired

her, much as he wanted to ease the pain that had become her life, he had to be careful. It was strange, this desire to ease pain rather than cause it.

Sighing, he turned to go.

"Reyes," she called.

He stopped, faced her. "Yes."

"I know you," she said, suddenly sounding shy, "but I don't really know anything about you."

"And you wish to know more?"

Reluctantly, she nodded.

Was she truly curious or did she wish to know for the Hunters? He'd thought he had not cared about her purpose, but right then, he wanted *her* to be curious. He wanted her to *want* to learn about him. Because she cared.

"What would you like to know about me?"

She shrugged, traced a finger over the black comforter. Her cheeks heated to a pretty pink. "How long have you lived here? What are your hobbies? Do you have any children? What are your hopes and dreams?"

Innocent enough, he supposed. "I have lived here longer than you have been alive. I have one hobby. Weapons—making them, cleaning them, collecting them. I have no children." He'd always been afraid of hurting them. Worse, of outliving them because of their mortal half. He pitied Maddox, who might one day know that sorrow. "I dream of—" *You.* "I dream of peace, a life without pain."

"What—"

"I have answered enough questions to make you now feel more comfortable staying in my room. It is time for your shower. I'll return in half an hour. Be ready. We will learn what we can about your family."

"Twenty minutes." Their gazes met, locked. Hers was filled with determination and…hatred? Of him? Or Aeron? "Return in twenty."

He nodded, already missing her. "Until then."

CHAPTER EIGHT

REYES STRODE to Lucien's private hallway, careful to avoid the other warriors. He was too on edge, his body too hot. All of his strength had been required to leave Danika. Even now, water was probably sliding down her curves, pooling in her navel before dripping into the curls between her legs.

He wondered what she tasted like. Sweet, like the angel she appeared to be? Or wicked, like the devil in her eyes? His demon wondered, too, pacing the pathways of his mind, practically sobbing in curiosity.

"—put Willie in the bedroom next to ours," Anya was saying, her voice muffled through the door.

Reyes had to strain to hear, his demon growing louder with every second that passed. *Danika.*

"I don't want him here, woman," Lucien said. "He must leave."

"I put up with your friends every damn day," she pouted. "You can put up with mine for a week, at least."

"*Your* friend tried to kill you."

There was a whoosh, as if she'd tossed something in the air. "That's the past. I hardly remember what I did five minutes ago, much less a few weeks."

"You hate him."

"Who are you kidding? I love him. We have history. He was my first real friend back in our Olympus days."

"Woman. He also tried to kill me and I recall you swearing to punish him for the rest of his miserable life."

"How better to punish him than to have him close to me? Wait, that came out wrong. Look, everything turned out okay, so I'm willing to give him another chance."

Lucien gave a warning growl. "The warriors will kill him. You're lucky they have not done so already."

"Why would they want to slay the man who will divert my attention *away* from them?"

Twenty minutes, Reyes reminded himself, and then he could be with Danika again.

Danika. It was a pitiful whimper he could not blame on his demon.

Though he didn't want to interrupt the couple, he knocked on the door.

Their voices stopped abruptly. Footsteps pounded. A second later, the wood swung open and Lucien stood there, frowning at him. Anya peeked over his shoulder and grinned.

"Hey, Painie," she said. Her arms wound around Lucien's waist, her ice-blue nails rubbing the skin just above his heart. "What's happening?"

Jealousy was a hot poker inside him, and he hated himself for it.

Danika.

"I am ready to take you to Aeron," he said.

A LIFE WITHOUT PAIN.

Reyes's words continued to echo through Danika's mind after the door closed behind him. What had he meant by that?

She could have pondered it forever, but she doubted the answer would ever come to her.

Finally full and strengthened, and feeling, well, human again, she quickly rifled through Reyes's dresser, shocked to find women's clothing. In her size. What the hell? She lifted two shirts and held them out, studying them. They wouldn't fit the warrior's extra-large body, so that ruled out cross-dressing.

Either he had a girlfriend Danika's same height and weight—why did the thought cause her stomach to clench?—or he'd bought them specifically for Danika.

Since they were soft T-shirts, sweaters and faded jeans like those she'd brought with her on her vacation, she suspected the latter and gulped. Why had he done this?

Does the answer really matter?

Gulping again, she gathered a shirt and a pair of pants. Didn't dare glance at the underwear, just grabbed a bra and pair of panties amid the sea of colorful lace.

She rushed through a shower, the soap and shampoo reminding her of Reyes. Woodsy, sultry, enveloping her in a warm cocoon. *He's a demon. You can't forget.*

By the time a gentle knock sounded at the door, she was dressed in a gray tee, black sweater and stylishly ripped jeans, wet hair dripping down her back. Some of the dye had washed out, leaving her with a skunklike mane she did *not* want Reyes to see. Didn't matter what he thought of her, she supposed. Vanity was not something she could afford.

She patted her ankles to make sure the daggers she'd removed from the wall and hidden there were anchored solidly. They were. "Come in," she called. She braced her feet apart, preparing for war if Reyes had changed his mind about taking her to see Aeron.

The door creaked open and a woman stepped inside, surprising her. She gasped, drawing a honey-colored gaze to her. A second later, the woman was rushing forward with a delighted smile. "Danika!"

"Ashlyn." Smiling, too, for the first time in what felt like forever, Danika spread her arms and welcomed the best memory she had of this place: her friendship with Ashlyn. Having both been held in this fortress against their will, they'd bonded quickly and for good.

They embraced, both sighing happily. Danika had known she'd missed her friend, but she hadn't realized how much until now.

"I've thought about you every day," Ashlyn said, squeezing her tight. "What have you been doing with yourself? How are you?"

"Running. And honestly? I've been better. How are *you?*"

"Don't hate me, but I've been doing wonderfully, if truth be told." Pulling back, the sweet woman looked her up and down. Her smile faded into a frown of concern. "You've lost weight you couldn't afford to lose and there are circles under your eyes."

"And you look amazing. You're glowing. The men really *have* been treating you well."

"Like a queen." Ashlyn paused, studied her again. "Is there anything I can get you? Anything you need?"

"A ticket home. My family. Reyes's head on a platter. Other than that, no. Nothing."

Ashlyn's smile returned, and this time it was laced with feminine knowledge. "Reyes isn't so bad. He's intense, but sweet."

She intertwined their fingers and led Danika to the bed. "Listen, I don't want you worrying about anything while you're here. Things are different now. It's not an all-boys club anymore. Anya and Cameo moved in and are helping to keep the men in line. Have you met them? No? Well, you'll like them when you do. Together we'll find a way to save your family, I have no doubt about that. And the guys will help. They have hearts of gold, once you get to know them."

"I hate to break this to you, Ash, but they're demons. Real, honest-to-God demons from hell."

"Yes. I know."

Danika gaped at her, unsure she'd heard correctly. "You know? And you're staying with them anyway? Of your own free will?"

"Yes." Ashlyn looked at her through the thick shield of her lashes. "In fact, say hello to the next generation of demon. Maddox and I are having a baby." Practically purring with contentment, she rubbed her slightly bulging belly. "I can't wait!"

"Oh, Ash. Congratulations." Danika was genuinely happy

for her friend, and wanted only the best for her. "You're sure Maddox will…"

"He'll be an amazing father," Ashlyn said confidently.

If I don't help bring him down. She closed her eyes against the new complication. Hurting Maddox would hurt Ashlyn, one of the sweetest people she'd ever met. And what about the baby? What would Hunters do to the innocent child of a demon?

"What's wrong? The color in your cheeks is fading."

"Headache," she lied, rubbing her temples.

"Oh, you poor thing. You've been through a lot these past few months. This, however, I can fix. You once flew into town to get me some Tylenol, and now I get to do the same for you." Ashlyn gave her another tight squeeze. "Actually, there's some in the kitchen—Maddox stocks it by the truckload these days just in case—so I'll be right back."

The bed bounced and footsteps sounded. Hinges squeaked. *I'm in deep. So deep.* Destroying Ashlyn's life was not a possibility she'd considered, and the thought of doing so sickened her.

But Danika had no opportunity to think of a way to meet her objective *and* prevent Ashlyn's downfall. The bedroom door swung open a second time, slapping into the wall. Her eyelids pried apart as a warrior she didn't recognize stepped inside the bedroom. He was tall and muscled like all the others. Yet while they had appeared harsh, savage, he had an all-American face, square jaw and puppy-dog brown eyes.

She jumped to her feet, wet hair dripping down her arms. "Who are you? What do you want? Where's Reyes?"

"I'm Sabin," he said, and she'd never heard a more cocky man. He punted the door shut behind him but didn't move any closer to her. "I came to ask you some questions. And I don't have any clue where Reyes is."

"Well, you can leave." Her fingers itched to grab one of the daggers. *Steady, hold your ground.* No reason to reveal her secret. Not yet. *You've been trained. You know what to do if he attacks: go for the throat, eyes and groin.* In that order.

Rather than leave, Sabin pressed his back against the door and folded his massive arms over his middle. He was a hand-some man, in a rough sort of way. Women probably melted for him. She'd rather cut out his heart. "You're one of them."

He stepped toward her, caught himself and backed off. Why? "One of who?"

She was surprised by his calmness. His gaze was sharp enough to slice her in half. "The demons."

"Did Reyes tell you we were demons?"

"Yes."

Dark eyes gleamed with menace. "I doubt he'd be such a naughty boy. Want to know what I think? You recently spent some time with Hunters. I bet *they* told you."

"So?"

"So. Interesting that you don't have to ask me who and what the Hunters are, or what their purpose is."

Damn it! She raised her chin all the higher. "Again, Reyes told me." *And he told you never to repeat what he'd said.* Grr! *I will not feel guilty for ratting him out to his friend. And this demon will not make me feel guilty for having been kidnapped by Hunters.*

"What did they ask you to do to us, hmm? Tell me and I might let you live."

Her blood instantly chilled, ice chips crystallizing in her veins. Surely she paled. "They asked me to kill you," she said, sticking to the truth as much as possible. Less chance of slipping up that way.

His anger softened into surprise, as though he hadn't expected her to admit such a thing. "Do you plan to try?"

Her eyes narrowed to tiny slits. "Depends on what I learn about my family."

Expression unchanging, he withdrew a dagger and a rag

from his pocket. Slowly he began polishing the sharp sliver with practiced strokes. "I won't allow anyone to hurt my friends. Ever."

Acid burned in her chest. "And I won't allow anyone to hurt my family." *Please, let them be all right.* "Is the weapon supposed to scare me?" Well, it worked. Bastard. Not that she'd back down. "You'll have to try harder than that." *Please don't.*

"You're on their radar now, you know?" he said casually, as if she hadn't spoken. "The Hunters will never leave you alone. And if you betray them to help us, which I doubt you're willing to do, they'll hunt and torture you. If there's anything left of you after I'm done, that is."

"So I'm screwed either way?" She laughed, another of those ugly sounds. The happiness she'd felt at seeing Ashlyn already seemed a distant memory. "News flash. I had already figured that out, moron."

His lips twitched. In amusement? Irritation? "You should know that the Hunters' torturing will seem like child's play compared to what I'll do to you if you so much as *look* as if you're going to fight my friends. They aren't evil, they aren't the source of the world's problems and they deserve to be happy."

Something in his flat tone struck her. "And you don't?"

Again, he ignored her. Reyes and company were masters at evasion, she was coming to realize. They answered those questions they wanted to and discarded everything else as if it had never been uttered.

"You should know that my family means everything to me and I will decapitate any immortal who even *thinks* about hurting them."

"Spoken like a true Hunter," he said with a shake of his head. "Well, guess what. Cut off their heads and you can kiss your pretty world goodbye. Their demons will be loosed, a source of havoc unlike any you have ever seen."

"Saving my loved ones is worth any price."

"I feel the same about mine." There was another warning in his voice. "I protect mine, though."

My family is on the run because of me. The stray thought slithered through Danika's mind, and she blanched. Was she completely responsible? Maybe she could have done more, fought harder during the abduction.

If they die, it will be my fault.

Tears suddenly burned her eyes. Tears of shame and horror. She *was* responsible. She'd been so scared the night Lucien and Aeron had come to her hotel room, she had frozen. She hadn't screamed. She had let them bundle her up, gather her family and cart them here.

How could she have been so…passive?

Sabin gave her a look of total understanding. "Perhaps you'll take care of matters on your own, huh? Save me the trouble."

Meaning, perhaps she would kill herself. He didn't know her very well. Suicide would never be an option for Danika. Too vividly she recalled the strain her grandmother's attempt had placed on her family. She remembered her mother's tearstained face, remembered seeing her quietly sob in a darkened corner. She remembered the lies everyone had told her, shame whispering in their voices and glowing from their eyes. *Your grandmother had an accident. She's going away for a few months to recover.*

Behind closed doors, they'd said something else entirely. *Why would she do something like that? She has a great life, no reason to end it.*

Now that Danika thought about it, that was funny coming from her dad. He'd had a great life, but not long after her grandmother's breakdown, he'd packed up and moved on to a new one. God, where were these depressing thoughts coming from?

The door suddenly banged closed, jolting her. A scowling Reyes had entered the room, the scarred Lucien on his heels. Seeing her beautiful nemesis, her breath caught in her throat and her traitorous heart skipped a beat.

Enemy, she reminded herself. How many times would she be forced to do so? Why could her mind not get the message? She tried to look away from him, but her gaze snagged on an ugly cut decorating his cheek.

The two men must have fought. Both of them sported bruises on their faces, bleeding scratches and savaged lips. Mud streaked their skin. There were crimson splotches on Reyes's T-shirt, as though he'd taken the brunt of the beating.

I will not be concerned about Reyes.

They carried the scent of roses and...old eggs? Her nose wrinkled in distaste. Ugh.

Reyes spied Sabin and his scowl intensified. He glanced from the warrior to Danika, from Danika to the warrior. Fury blazed over his expression as he stalked to Sabin, his hands fisted. "What are you doing here?"

The two men faced off.

"Someone needed to question her," Sabin said, brows dancing into his hairline. "You refused to do it, so I got it done."

"You were not to come near her."

Their muscles bulged, their bodies tensed. If Danika hadn't been so torn between fear and disgust, she would have enjoyed the view.

"She's alive, isn't she? So what's the problem?"

Reyes licked his lips, the action somehow menacing. "Are you hurt?"

"I'm fine," Sabin said dryly. "Thanks for asking."

"Not you. Danika, are you hurt?" Reyes never removed his lethal attention from Sabin.

Physically? "I'm fine." Her throat constricted around the words.

Reyes shoved Sabin, and the warrior stumbled backward. "Don't come near her again."

Danika gasped, expecting the narrow-eyed man to launch himself at Reyes and for the two to roll on the ground in a bid for dominance. He didn't. He popped his jaw, ran his tongue over his teeth.

"I did you a favor, boy. You'd do better to thank me."

Danika stepped toward them. What she planned to do or say, she didn't know. In the end, she didn't have to think about it. Lucien moved in front of her, blocking her forward progress.

"Enough," he said to the men. "Sabin, get your team ready. We leave for Rome in the morning."

"This isn't over," Sabin said.

"I know." A weary sigh.

"Why did the plans change?" Reyes asked Lucien.

"Researching was getting us nowhere," his friend said. "We'll go back to the temple, see if we find anything there."

Anticipation sizzled and snapped along Reyes's olive skin. Truly flickering, making him look like a walking electrical socket. His dark hair even stood on end. Why anticipation? The thought of having her alone? Then Danika's eyes widened. Did it matter? The supernatural occurrences were stacking one on top of the other. Pretty soon, she might leave normalcy behind forever, unable to return.

When have you ever been normal?

When she was a child, the girls in her class had wanted to play Barbie. Danika had wanted to play angel. So many times she'd pretended to have wings, pretended to fly through the playground and battle evil. And yet, when evil truly did knock on her door, she hadn't battled. She'd curled into a fetal ball and cried for her mommy.

Never again.

"This isn't over," Sabin said again, and stalked from the room. The door slammed shut behind him.

Danika gulped. Alone with Reyes and Lucien. *Don't you dare lose your courage.* She raised her chin.

Slowly Reyes turned to face her. His dark eyes were haunted, his features strained. "You had tears in your eyes when I entered." A muscle ticked in his temple. "What did Sabin make you doubt?"

That ticking usually meant a storm brewed inside of him. She might not know much about him, as she'd told him earlier, but she did know that. "Doubt?"

Reyes nodded, the action clipped. "He made you doubt something about yourself."

"No. He warned me not to hurt you."

"He wouldn't have spoken the doubts aloud. You would have heard them in your mind."

"What are you talking about? The only thing I doubted was—" Dear God. She gasped. "That's his demon? That's his power? Making people doubt themselves and their actions? Making them feel terrible about what they've done or haven't done?"

Another nod.

All the grim thoughts that had snaked through her mind in Sabin's presence echoed once more. "That bastard! I'll kill him." Growling, she lunged for the door. She'd track him down and—

Reyes caught her by the arms and held her until she stilled. "What did he use against you?" He moved his hands up, slowly, gently, and cupped her cheeks.

A tremor slid down her spine. She couldn't pull away. He offered comfort from her shame, and she gladly accepted. His palms were warm, calloused with scabs, giving her exactly what she needed. "M-my family. My fault."

He shook his head violently. "Not your fault. The gods' fault, our fault, but never yours."

Tears again burned her eyes. That's all she seemed to do lately, start to cry then stop it from happening. "I didn't fight."

His grip tightened. Not hurting, but no longer gentle. "We are warriors. Immortal, no less. We have been trained to slay, to hurt. What could you have done against us?"

"More," she said simply. God, it felt good, being touched by him. Why had she ever thought to deny herself this bliss?

"Nothing would have changed."

"No way to know that now." How wonderful would it feel to burrow into the hollow of his neck? Inhale his scent? Remaining still proved one of the most difficult things she'd ever done. "Is there?"

His mouth curved in a gradual smile. "You are stubborn."

The sight of that smile nearly melted her bones. Every time she'd been with him, he'd frowned, he'd raged, he'd cursed, but he had never smiled. The glorious expression lit his entire face, softening his eyes to a warm honey.

Another shiver trekked down her spine, and she forced herself to rip away from him. No more stimuli. No more being near him, taking comfort when she knew better. Softening. Hungry. *You deny yourself the bliss because it could be your downfall,* she reminded herself.

If she had stayed close, she would have reached for him, perhaps fallen into the cradle of his body. Perhaps tangled her hands in his hair and kissed the breath right out of him.

His arms fell to his sides, and he sighed. Danika dug her nails into her palm to remind herself that this was reality. A reality fraught with pain, desperation. Determination. There was no time for romance. Especially with Reyes.

"Here's the Ty-lenol," Ashlyn stuttered, having walked into the room and spied them. Her palm was extended, two red-and-white pills resting in the center. In her other hand, she clutched a glass of water. "I'm sorry. I didn't mean to interrupt."

"You're fine," Lucien assured her as Reyes backed away from Danika.

Damn, she'd forgotten Lucien was still in the room. "Thank you for the pills," Danika told Ashlyn, glad for the reprieve. She closed the distance between them and took the offered items. Her head might not have been hurting earlier, but it was throbbing now. She tossed the medicine back with a single gulp of the water.

"Ashlyn," Reyes said. "Thank you for caring for my—for Danika."

"My pleasure." Ashlyn shifted her focus between the two warriors, as though she wondered what was going on but didn't want to be rude and ask. "I'm sorry I took so long. I ran into Maddox, and well… If there's anything else I can do…?"

Danika shook her head. Part of her wanted to glom onto her friend, leave this room and never look back. "I'm good."

"Sorry I'm late. Ashlyn tells me—" Another woman strolled into the room, tall, pale and utter perfection. She wore a short blue dress that veed low between her breasts and matching heels that laced up her calves. Her equally blue gaze performed a single sweep of the area, and she grinned. "Cool. A secret gathering. I'm Anya, by the way."

"Nice to meet you," Danika told her. Ashlyn had mentioned her, but not which warrior the woman belonged to. Whoever it was obviously treated her well. Never had Danika seen a happier female.

Lucien released a sigh. "What are you up to, Anya? You only grin like that when you have something planned."

Scarred Lucien was her man? Wow. A true beauty and the beast.

The gorgeous woman twirled a strand of her hair around her finger, throwing the warrior a come-and-get-me look. "Just wanted to do a little girl bonding, that's all." Those electric blues slid back to Danika. "These boys treating you well, sugar?"

"I—I—" Didn't know how to answer that. They were, with the exception of Sabin, but she didn't want to admit it. Every minute that passed, something new seemed to rise up and stop her from wanting to act against these men. These demons.

"They don't, you just tell little ol' Anya and I will personally cut out their hearts," Anya said. "That's a promise. Not that I can be trusted. Lying is a hobby of mine. Lucien, honey, you gonna be long? I wanna throw William a welcome-to-the-fortress party and I'd like your help picking the decorations."

Lucien closed his eyes and shook his head, as if he couldn't believe what he was hearing.

"I'm thinking masked ball with a creatures of the night theme."

Anya changed directions faster than Danika could keep up, but Ashlyn took everything in stride. "No party. Not with the box and the artifacts and Hunters and God knows what else hanging over our heads. Danika, you call me if you need anything, okay? Anything at all." With that, she dragged a protesting Anya from the room.

Such sweet women. Smart, too. So what were they doing with these warriors? *What am I doing with these warriors?* Danika sighed. What artifacts had Ashlyn meant? "I'm ready," she said, bringing everyone back to Topic One. "Where's Aeron?"

Reyes and Lucien shared a dark look.

"What?" she demanded.

Reyes faced her again, his expression blank. "Here," he said. "Aeron is here, in the fortress."

Anticipation rushed through her with dizzying speed. "Take me to him." She had to know. For better or worse, she had to know. "Right now. Please. I want to see him."

"He is chained, but you cannot go near him. In his case, chained does not mean helpless. Promise me you will remain at a distance."

At the moment, she would have promised him the moon and the sky. "I promise." But if Aeron refused to answer her questions, Danika thought she might leap at him and attack. Maybe even add a number two to her kill list. If only her former self-defense instructor could see her now.

Reyes glanced up at the ceiling, as if praying for guidance. Then, "Very well. Come. I hope you receive the answers you wish."

CHAPTER NINE

WHILE A WARRIOR FOR THE GODS, Reyes had battled heavenly creatures now only whispered about in books and fables. Cerberus—a three-headed dog thought to have stood watch at the gates of hell. Chimera—human/animal hybrids. Harpies— half woman, half demented bird. All had left him bleeding and in agony. Back then, pain had not been a pleasure.

His first few years in ancient Greece, the demon had churned inside him, pulling his strings, leading him to slaughter and maim. When the humans finally started fighting back, war had reigned, destruction in every corner. He'd lost limbs, regrown them only to lose them again, had nearly been decapitated several times. And yet he had never experienced fear as potent as this.

Danika would soon be face-to-face with Aeron. A man whose demon urged him to kill her with the same kind of relentless per- suasion that always plagued Reyes. A man who had clearly tried to gnaw his way through his own wrist to free himself of the chains that bound him. Thankfully, he'd only gotten through the first layer of muscle when Reyes and Lucien arrived.

But what if Aeron managed to slip free while Danika was nearby? What if his strength increased exponentially and he snapped his wrists off in a blink, launching forward, teeth bared— *Stop!*

Reyes wanted to sweep Danika up and carry her away from the fortress, but she wanted answers, so he would get them for her.

It was that simple. Her wants came before his own.

He descended a flight of stairs to the lowest level of the dungeon, Danika behind him and Lucien behind her. They journeyed from homey to slightly cared-for to completely neglected. The stone walls were crumbling and broken bits coated the floor, digging into the soles of his boots. Reyes could not even tell if he walked upon wood planks or marble, the rocks and dust were piled so high. His guilt returned, increased. *How can I treat my friend this way?*

So what that Aeron, the real Aeron, didn't want to kill the women. So what that Aeron yearned for death. The man didn't deserve to suffer like this, bound and locked away as if he were disposable. In a place Anya had proclaimed even gloomier than the godly prison Tartarus.

Damn the gods for reducing Aeron to a killer and Reyes to a jailer!

Thankfully, none of the other warriors were around. They were too busy packing and gathering supplies for the upcoming trip to Rome. A trip Reyes wasn't sure he would take. He wanted to find Pandora's box and defeat the Hunters once and for all, but he didn't want to cart Danika all over the world.

She might run again. He might not be able to find her. The Hunters might decide she was better off dead and come after her.

More and more, he was beginning to think his existence depended on hers. He didn't understand it, didn't like it, but there it was. He was still amazed that every time he neared her, he and the demon both calmed.

Danika coughed.

He rounded a corner, tossing a glance over his shoulder. She was waving a hand in front of her face. Dust sparkled around her hair like a halo. Some of her tresses had been washed of the dye, revealing a tantalizing glimpse of blond. First time he'd seen her, he remembered thinking her hair was like the sun, bright and radiant. "Want to return to my room?" he asked. "I would be very unhappy if you sickened."

She offered him an exaggerated frown, an expression of dry amusement. "I coughed. I'll live. Keep going."

A man's irritated grumblings echoed off the walls. "I don't want to play Wrists-and-Blood anymore. I told you, stop."

At least Aeron was not screaming.

Reyes turned another corner and barred cages came into view. He stopped abruptly, holding out his arm so that Danika would not pass him. For a split second, her breasts pushed into his forearm, soft and full, and her damp hair slapped at his skin.

He swallowed a curse; she stumbled backward as though she'd been shoved. His entire body suddenly felt engulfed by white-hot flames. Her scent filled his nose, thunderstorms and innocence.

"Stay here." The raspiness of his voice embarrassed him. He didn't mind if others—and even Danika herself—knew he desired her. There was no hiding that fact. What he did mind was anyone knowing the *intensity* of that desire. The knowledge could be used against him.

"Why can't I go farther?" she asked.

He was pleased to note her voice shook.

"I want to see him first, discover if his mood has changed since I left him." And check to see if his wrists had healed and were no longer in danger of detaching, but Reyes didn't add that part. "If he's relatively calm, you may approach the bars. You will not enter the cell at any time. Understand?"

"Yes."

"You may ask him questions, but do not insult him and incite his…wrath."

"Okay! I get it. Stay back, ask nicely. Just get on with it already."

He didn't. He remained in place. "When you see him, do not be afraid. I will not allow anything bad to happen to you."

"Yeah, and tomorrow I'll count to infinity. Twice. If you don't move this along, I'm going to snap."

Reyes peered over at Lucien, who was watching him with a hard expression. "Stay with her. Please."

At that, Danika growled. He didn't think she was angry that he wanted her guarded and didn't trust her to take care of herself. She truly had reached the breaking point and needed answers.

Lucien nodded.

Reyes pivoted away from them. More than he wanted to take his next breath, he wanted to look at Danika, to reassure her, comfort her. Hold her. But one glance at her, and he would not be able to stop himself from doing *all* of those things. He would not be able to leave her.

Fisting a blade in one hand and the cell key in the other, he unlocked the door. The hinges creaked as the metal parted. Creaked again as he closed the door. Aeron crouched against the far wall, steeped in shadows. He ceased mumbling the moment he spied Reyes.

Reyes studied his friend, hoping to find signs of the warrior he'd once been, not the monster he'd become. Eyes—still dilated and hungry. Teeth—still sharpened and bared. Still a monster, then, but also a man Reyes loved. The tattoos that covered Aeron from the top of his head to the bottom of his feet were familiar.

Reyes didn't know why Aeron had tattooed himself with colorful depictions of things he probably wished he'd never done: killing, mutilating, destroying. Reyes had never asked, and Aeron had never volunteered the information. Some things were simply too painful to talk about. *That* he knew very well.

"Leave," Aeron barked.

The command was not slurred or layered with the voice of his demon, and Reyes blinked in surprise. Had the warrior's bloodlust faded, even slightly?

"You are lucid now, I see." A glance at the bound man's wrists, and Reyes saw that they were mostly healed. "You were crazed when Lucien and I appeared in the cave. I'm sorry if I hurt you trying to get you here."

"Free me. I have a job to do."

"Two weeks ago, you were grateful to be restrained. You hated what you'd been ordered to do and begged me to kill you."

"Grateful no longer." Aeron shifted, his legs inching closer to his chest. "Those women need to die."

No, the bloodlust had not left him. "So they still live? All four?" Tension radiated from Danika and enveloped him. There was distance between them, yes, but still he felt that blistering tension.

Guilt flashed in Aeron's eyes. Guilt—both beautiful and terrible. Beautiful because it meant Aeron was still inside that mind, still fighting. Terrible because it probably meant one—or more—of the women were already dead.

Reyes's skin pulled tight against his bones, and he held back a disappointed groan. He'd desperately yearned for good news. Now, he could only pray there was a survivor. "Aeron. Tell me about the women."

Silence.

"Please," he said, ready to beg if necessary.

Again, silence.

No, not silence, he realized a moment later. In the background, there was a soft but menacing growl.

"Answer him!" Danika shouted.

Aeron stilled, even stopped breathing. His eyes glazed over, glowing with crimson rage that overshadowed any hint of guilt. Then, without warning, he sprang forward. His wings popped from the slits in his back, black gossamer that ripped away the remaining tatters of his shirt and expanded across the entire cell. Their razor-sharp points scratched at the walls.

Reyes held his ground. Aeron wanted to lash out, so he would allow Aeron to lash out at him. Better him than Danika.

The chain around Aeron's neck jerked taut, placing the warrior inches from Reyes's face. So close a sulfur-laced breeze caressed him. He'd been so near hell, he would reek of its scent for days. Reyes almost wished his demon had not remembered how to get there, allowing him to bury Aeron in the first place.

"Girl," Aeron shouted. His hands snaked around Reyes's neck and squeezed tight. "Want her."

"Mine," Reyes managed to push past his lips. "Tell me about her family."

"Die!"

"Tell me."

He heard Danika gasp. Thought he heard Lucien shout a terse warning.

"Tell me." The plea was barely audible. He dropped his knife, unwilling to use it on his friend to save himself, and clutched Aeron's wrists. If this was needed to get answers out of Aeron, this he would allow.

But all too soon, the feeling of Aeron's hands squeezing tighter and tighter, harder and harder, became too good. The pain was too intoxicating. His demon purred happily.

More.

"She must die," Aeron snarled.

"She's…innocent."

"Doesn't matter."

"Once it would have." Before Reyes could add anything else, his mind fogged, dizziness rushing through him like the ocean to the shore.

You have to protect Danika. As he pried Aeron's hands off him, his windpipe shattered, a thousand needle pricks in his throat. Oxygen could not get through. Blood laced with the bone shards and swept them into his stomach; along the way, they cut everything they encountered.

This was going to kill him. For a little while, anyway.

His eyes closed in bliss, but his mind screamed in denial.

"HELP HIM!" Danika shouted to Lucien. She gripped the prison's bars, cold all the way to her soul. Colder than ever before. Right now, she couldn't see Reyes. Not even a glimpse. Aeron, the bastard, had him wrapped in those lethal black wings. "Help him." None of her instructors had prepared her for demons attacking other demons, and she didn't know what to do. "Please."

"He'll survive." Lucien withdrew a gun from the waist of his pants, checked the magazine.

"No one could survive that," she said, eyeing the weapon. Her first thought was that he meant to shoot her. Her second, that he would have done so already if that had been his plan.

"Aeron, let him go," Lucien called.

"No!" the warrior roared.

A moment passed. Lucien stiffened, muttered, "What *is* that thing?" and withdrew a bullet from his pocket. He slid the lethal ball into the gun's chamber.

Danika was shaking violently, couldn't stop. "What if you accidentally hit Reyes?" She wanted Reyes…what? Alive, yes. Unhurt, definitely. He had protected her two weeks ago, had taken the brunt of Aeron's rage today, and now she would protect him. At the moment, he was her only lifeline. At least, that's what she told herself. That had to be the reason he suddenly mattered to her.

"As I said, he'll survive."

Would he, though? He was immortal, he was a demon, but was he completely immune to strangulation and bullets? Every time she'd seen Reyes, he'd been cut and bleeding. Clearly, he could be injured. And what if Aeron attempted to cut off his head while he was incapacitated? Stefano had told her that decapitation was the surest way to kill an immortal permanently. Tacking on that "surest" meant there were *other* ways to kill them.

Her wild gaze locked on Aeron, who most likely still had a death grip on Reyes. The enraged warrior was unmoving now, head bowed, no sound emerging from him. Oh, God. What did that mean? "Just—just let me distract him. I'll get him away from Reyes, *then* you can shoot Aeron."

Hinges creaked as she opened the barred door.

Lucien grabbed her arm, stopping her. "The gun isn't for Aeron." He motioned to a corner of the cell with a tilt of his chin.

Danika followed the line of his vision. There, in the corner, was a thin, waist-high…thing. Her eyes widened in shock. Green scales covered its naked body. Its teeth were long like sabers, saliva dripping from them, and its ears were pointed. Bright red eyes glowed as Aeron's had glowed just before he'd attacked Reyes.

"To my knowledge, I didn't flash the creature here," Lucien said. "It is not our friend."

What *was* it? And why did she feel as though she'd seen it before? Watched it? Frowned in confusion over its antics?

"Demon," Lucien said as though she'd asked aloud. Maybe she had. Lucien aimed the gun.

"Don't shoot near Reyes," she said on a rush of air.

Lucien looked at her in surprise, as if he couldn't quite believe she was defending her captor. "I'll be careful."

Aeron's body began shaking again, nearly convulsing. He once more began growling like an animal at mealtime. What was he doing? She released the bars and her nails bit into her palms. Sweat poured down her back, even though she trembled from that shivering cold.

Standing here, doing nothing, she felt utterly helpless.

Boom.

Danika's ears rang. Underneath the ringing, however, she could make out an eerie laugh. Alarmed, she watched the creature bound around the cell walls and even crawl along the ceiling.

"Play, play. Thisss fun."

I've seen this before, she thought again. But how? Her nightmares? Her eyes widened. Yes, of course. She constantly dreamed of demons and hell, so it stood to reason she might have visualized a creature such as this.

Lucien added another bullet, fired again.

More laughter.

Aeron straightened. Blood poured from his mouth and stained his hands. Catching her first glimpse of Reyes since Aeron had begun choking him, Danika covered her gaping mouth with the back of her hand. He was slumped on the ground, motionless, his neck…flat.

Should be happy, should be happy.

But she wasn't. Tears were burning her eyes. She should hate this man for everything he'd done to her. Should, should, should. The word meant nothing to her at the moment. Bending down, she curled her fingers around one of the blades she'd stolen, not caring that her theft was now revealed.

Aeron had to die, and she had to kill him. It was as simple as that. He was a crazed murderer. He had hurt Reyes—not dead, he couldn't be dead—and he wanted to hurt her. Worse, he'd probably harmed her grandmother. It was clear her family would never be safe as long as he lived. Yes, he needed to die. *Now or never.*

Determined, she finally stepped into the cell. Lucien was too busy following the demon with the barrel of his gun to notice. She moved forward tentatively. Aeron's narrowed gaze locked on her and tracked her every movement.

"Legion," Aeron said. "Need you."

The scaled creature jumped onto his shoulders and held tight. "Me here." Bony fingers caressed Aeron's scalp. Words Danika didn't understand were whispered into Aeron's ear. Soft words, gentle.

Aeron's body relaxed, his muscles no longer clenched for attack. The red in his eyes faded.

Lucien paused outside the cell. "Danika," he said.

"Get Reyes out of here. His body can't take any more damage." Danika continued to inch forward. When she reached Reyes, she crouched beside him. Her gaze never left Aeron as she placed a finger on Reyes's neck, hoping to feel a pulse.

She didn't.

Don't panic. He was too vital, too strong to die here, like this. Wasn't he? He desperately needed medical attention. "Lucien. For God's sake, come get him."

"He's fine, and I am unwilling to lose focus with the demon unfettered."

Damn it! She couldn't leave him here. Truly, any more damage and there would be nothing left of him. Save Reyes or question/try to hurt Aeron? She didn't have to think about it. She latched on to Reyes's shoulders, knife flat—she would *not* release it—and tried to drag him. When Reyes was out of range, she could attack Aeron without fear for him. But Reyes's large body proved to be too heavy and she only made it a foot before stopping to catch her breath.

Aeron straightened, his knees bending to accept his weight, his hands curling to strike. Any minute, and he would attack.

"He was your friend," she said, pushing back to her feet to haul Reyes another few inches.

"But you are not," Aeron replied.

"No, I'm not."

He grinned, wicked, eerie. "Do you wish to hurt me, little human?"

"Yes." No reason to lie. The truth blazed in her eyes, she was sure. "I wish to destroy you."

"Try."

"So you'll feel better about what you plan to do to me? No, thanks. Not while Reyes needs help. But once he's out of the cell, you're mine."

For some reason, the conversation seemed to calm him as much as the little creature still whispering in his ear. "Do I scare you?"

"You? Scare me? Never again." Another inch. A few more, and she'd have Reyes's shoulders out the door.

"Why don't you come for me, then?"

"The difference between us is that I care about someone else more than I care about my own wishes."

He lost his grin in a hurry. "You cannot care for Reyes."

She didn't want to, knew she shouldn't. But... Footsteps suddenly echoed behind her, saving her from trying to form a reply.

"The others are coming." Finally Lucien opted to help. He approached her, gripped the base of her neck before she could protest his touch. One second she was holding Reyes, the next she was inside Reyes's bedroom.

Dizziness assaulted her. When Lucien released her, she realized she couldn't stand on her own. She toppled over, her knees hitting the floor. She cringed at the action, but was too wired to feel the jolt. "What the hell did you do to me?"

"Stay here," Lucien said.

As she fought to stand, she glared up at him. "I don't—"

Without another word, he disappeared, leaving her gaping. Bastard! She couldn't, wouldn't, leave Reyes down there with that...that...animal. *Should have killed the beast when you had the chance.* Determined to return, she lumbered toward the front door. She tripped over a pair of boots and barely managed to stay upright.

"I told you to stay put."

Spinning, experiencing another wave of dizziness, Danika released a startled gasp. Lucien had appeared once more, stoic, uncompromising. He was cradling Reyes in his arms as he strode to the bed. Gently, he laid the still-motionless warrior on the mattress. The springs creaked.

Danika rushed to Reyes's side.

"Take care of him," Lucien uttered, a warning in his tone.

"I—will." The last was said on a sigh. He had disappeared again.

Almost afraid to look, she slowly turned her head. Her eyes landed on Reyes, and her stomach twisted. There were so many sides to him: captor, savior, demon, man. But he was still such a mystery to her, this being who had both threatened her life and saved it. And here he was, defeated. His throat was smashed, his Adam's apple smooth and discolored.

His chest was utterly still.

The tears that had stung her eyes so often this day now ran freely down her cheeks. How could someone so strong have been— Through the watery haze, she thought she saw his chest move, thought she saw his decimated throat constrict. *Please! Let that be real.*

Her hand fluttered to his heart, the beat frantic against her palm. A wheeze filled her ears, and it was a glorious noise.

He was alive!

Crying out, she fell to her knees. She clutched at his hand, felt his fingers give a weak squeeze. The strength of her relief was appalling. Unwelcome. Because it meant she would never be able to betray this man. This demon. Not now, not later. Aeron, yes. Sabin, yes. But not him, never him. Not even to save her family. "I'm here, Reyes."

His eyelids cracked open.

"Don't try to talk. Just know that I'm here. I'll take care of you." Only problem was, she had no real medical training and didn't know what to do. She choked back a pained laugh. She'd been in this situation once before. Ashlyn had been sick. Bargaining for her mom, sister and grandmother's lives, she'd lied, told Reyes she was a healer, and doctored Ashlyn as best she could.

Ashlyn had come out okay. Would Reyes?

Dark irises came into full view. They weren't flooded with pain; they were glazed with…pleasure? Surely not. Their gazes collided a moment before he closed his eyes again. Her lungs deflated on a sigh.

Reyes's lips moved, but no sound emerged from them.

"You're hurting yourself," she said. "I told you not to talk. We'll—"

"Don't go back to Aeron without me," he managed to get out, the words savage. "Promise." His hand clutched at her. "Protect you."

Again, he wanted to protect her. Little wonder he'd battered down her defenses and reduced her to a devoted puppy. "I promise."

CHAPTER TEN

REYES AWOKE GRADUALLY, his senses already on alert thanks to several oddities.

One, there was a weight on his chest. Warm, so warm, and soft. He was used to waking unfettered, a little cold. Two, the scent of thunderstorms and angel-skies filled his nose, sultry and erotic. It was a scent he craved with every fiber of his being, but one that was dangerous to his peace of mind. Three, he never wanted to leave this paradise.

Pain did not agree.

Pain was prowling the cage of Reyes's mind, roaring. Roaring so loudly Reyes covered his ears. The weight on his chest shifted to the side, taking with it that delicious warmth and softness.

The roaring increased in volume, and he cringed.

"You okay?"

The voice of an angel, a perfect match for the scent. Danika. The roaring became a broken mewling, her rich timbre soothing the beast.

What was it about her? What made her so different from the other women he'd known?

Ashlyn had alleviated Maddox's torment. Anya had renewed Lucien's desire to love. Both women had accepted the warriors for who and what they were. Danika enhanced Reyes's pain *and* drove him crazy. She would never accept him. But even if a miracle happened and she could, he would never be able to bed her, thereby allowing Pain to sink its claws inside her. Change her.

As a couple, they were hopeless.

That failed to lessen his need for her. Again, he wondered why. She was pretty, intelligent and courageous, but other women were equally so. Weren't they? At the moment, he could think of no one else whose bright eyes pierced him to his soul. No one else whose silky hair caressed his skin so perfectly. No one else who faced him dead on and refused to back down.

Only Danika.

Her name whispered through his mind, and he eased open his eyelids. First thing he noticed was that morning sunlight seeped past the black curtains, painting hazy yellow dots everywhere he looked. Normal enough. Then a dazzling halo appeared in front of him, strands of pale hair tickling his chest. A soft breast meshed into his side.

"You okay?" Danika asked again. Concern burned in her sleep-rich eyes, lids at half-mast. Through the thick shield of her spiked lashes, he could see electric green, his new favorite color. "You took quite a beating last night."

"Last night?" His voice was raspy, and every word rubbed his throat raw. A delicious sensation. "Your hair." He reached up and drew several strands through his fingers. "Pale again."

"I took another shower and the semipermanent dye washed the rest of the way out."

"I like it."

Appearing uncomfortable, she nibbled on her bottom lip.

His body heated another degree. Oh, to have those teeth nibbling on *him* again. "Last night?" he prompted.

"With Aeron. In his cell."

The memories flooded him, images flashing one after another, and he jerked upright. He'd taken Danika into the dungeon. He'd entered Aeron's cell. Aeron had looked guilty at the mention of Danika's family, as if he'd already taken one—or more—out. Then Aeron had attacked him and Pain had loved it.

Mortification created a symphony inside him: the pound of

his heart, the rush of his blood, the purr of his demon. He'd reveled in it, and Danika had been there, had seen him take pleasure in so vicious an act.

Shamed to his soul, he closed his eyes, dropped his head into his waiting hands. *She doesn't know,* he assured himself. *Otherwise, she would not be sitting calmly on the bed, conversing with you. She would be hurling insults like "pervert" and "deviant."*

Some women could accept his particular brand of pleasure. Most could not. For a few years, Reyes had found his partners in BDSM clubs. They'd been secret venues back then. Private. The women had liked to be strapped down, whipped, and he'd liked delivering the pain. And when he'd commanded them to hurt him, they'd done so willingly, happily.

But after learning that the women he'd bedded had erupted in violent sprees, he'd stopped going to the clubs. For centuries, he'd relied only on his own hand, cutting himself while he fisted his cock. Then he'd had what he'd considered an epiphany. Surely those females had been predisposed to violence. Surely *that* was why they'd harmed innocents so casually after bedding him.

So he'd tried again, this time taking Paris's advice and choosing Sunday-school teachers and librarians as his bedmates. The first few times he'd asked them to wear spurs on their ankles and dig them into his back. Among other things he did not like to recall. "You're sick," a few had cried. "Get help, you pervert."

If only they had continued to resist him.

Before long, they, too, had begun to crave pain. For themselves, a thousand others. When he noticed the hungry glint burning deep in their eyes, he'd ceased all contact, hoping, praying they would morph back into the women they'd once been. They hadn't.

Soft fingers brushed his brow, smoothing his hair out of the way. Always before, that type of touch had disgusted him.

Physically, he'd felt nothing, so the gesture had merely reminded him of what he could never have. Only the hard bite of nails and the sharp sting of teeth had delighted him.

Here, now, with Danika, he still felt nothing physically, but the generous act rocked him emotionally and he found it just as tantalizing as a sting. She had never touched him like this before.

Your demon infects every woman you desire. To have Danika is to damn her soul. Do not forget.

"Reyes?"

He blinked, Danika coming into slow focus. "Yes."

"I lost you."

"I am sorry. You are well?" he asked.

"Yes."

Her hand fell away from him, and both he and the demon wanted to shout in protest. He blinked in surprise. The demon was upset? Missing a soft touch?

"There was a…creature with Aeron."

"Yes," Reyes said with a nod. "I remember."

"Had you seen it before? Do you know where it came from?"

"I had not, but I know it came from hell." Pain had recognized it for what it was—a brother in evil. Reyes turned his head, facing Danika. "Do not concern yourself with him."

She paled, color fading to snow-white. Whatever thoughts danced in her head were not pleasant. "Why didn't you fight him?"

"The little demon?"

"No. Aeron. I've seen you engage him in combat before. You weren't afraid. You were strong and…" She gulped, as though the rest of the confession pained her. "Capable. But this time, you just stood there. You let him hurt you."

Reyes straightened fully, his eyes never leaving her. Her legs curved behind her, her hip flat on the mattress. She rested her weight on one elbow, her hair a glorious silk curtain that fell over her shoulders. She still wore jeans. Jeans he had picked out for her. He felt pride and satisfaction, for he'd spent hours shopping for her, hopeful he would one day see her in what he chose.

Her features were so delicate. She could have fallen straight from the heavens and he would not have been surprised. Small, pert nose, rounded cherub cheeks. Ruby-red lips that glistened.

As always, the sight of her caused his chest to ache. Pain loved it, loved the ache and the ensuing hollow sensation in the pit of his stomach. Reyes smiled wryly. Perhaps he would simply gaze upon Danika for the rest of her too-short human life. His demon would always be sated.

At the thought of her death, the ache became a throb.

"Well?" she said.

What had she asked him? He replayed their entire conversation in his mind. Oh, yes. Aeron. Reyes's secret enjoyment. He'd had good intentions before Pain took over. "I have hurt him many times. He owed me."

"No." Danika shook her head. "That's not why you did it."

He frowned. No way in hell could she guess the truth. "Then why?"

"You wanted answers. For me. And you thought that was the only way to get them."

All right, maybe she could. Until now, she had only believed the worst about him. Was she…could she possibly be softening toward him?

"Are you and Aeron still friends?" There was a hard edge to her tone this time. So much for softening.

"Yes. We are." He hoped. He loved Aeron. He did. Danika, though… He still wasn't sure how he felt about her or what, exactly, she meant to him. Only that she did mean something she shouldn't, and he couldn't stop the emotions she pulled out of him.

Can't have her.

"Stop," she said stiffly, and turned away from him. She stared up at the ceiling.

His brows furrowed in confusion. "Stop what?"

"I don't know. That gleam in your eyes when you look at me, it…distresses me."

"I cannot help myself."

A pause. "There can be nothing between us, Reyes." There at the end, her voice cracked.

"I know."

She wrapped her arms around herself. "What am I doing here?"

"I could not leave you with the Hunters." Truth.

"Maybe you should have."

In that moment, he knew beyond any doubt the Hunters had asked her to act as Bait. His stomach rolled into several hard knots, each beating against the other. He would have to remain alert with her. Always alert. Not reveal anything that could hurt his friends. He would have to watch her, make sure she didn't try and sneak those bastards inside the fortress or tell them where the warriors were headed. And why.

But he couldn't let her go. He couldn't kill her, even though it was the smart thing to do. Even though his friends would demand it if they learned the truth. They suspected, otherwise Sabin wouldn't have entered Reyes's room to question her.

How much danger was Reyes placing them in by letting her live? Did it matter to him? *I am such a fool.* Perhaps he did love her.

Pain laughed giddily at the thought, for love brought its own brand of torment. Lots and lots of torment. In the heart, the soul. Both causing a physical ache too intense to be relieved.

Reyes scowled. "Do not mention the Hunters to my friends," he commanded tightly.

She laughed. Unlike Pain's, it was not out of giddiness. Strain echoed in the undertones of that forced amusement. "I couldn't, even if I wanted to."

"And why is that?"

"They left."

His confusion morphed into anger, and he jolted to his feet. The stone was cold against his skin. He stalked to his closet. "When?"

"This morning."

"Everyone?"

"Except the one named Torin. Maybe a few others. I can't keep your friends straight."

Pausing in the door frame, Reyes pinched the bridge of his nose. Once he would have been furious at being left behind. Now, what he felt for Danika was even stronger than his desire to find *dimOuniak*.

"They came for you. When they saw you were still recovering, they told me to deliver a message."

A muscle ticked below each of his eyes as he pivoted and faced her. "Well? Deliver it."

Danika raised her chin. It was an action of defiance and one he'd noted she performed often, ready to take on the world. "The one called Sabin said to tell you to stop acting like a pussy and do your duty. What's in Rome? Someone mentioned a temple."

Reyes ignored her question and glanced down at himself to hide the glint of fury he knew must be shining in his eyes. His weapons were no longer strapped to his ankles and thighs, but he still wore his jeans. They were unfastened. While he liked the thought of Danika undressing him, he did not like the notion that she could have taken his weapons.

He hated that he had slept like the dead. She could have done anything at all—might have done everything—and he wouldn't have known. Frowning, he hastily snapped the jeans and turned back to his closet. He withdrew the velvet-lined cache of guns and knives, saw that was in order, nothing out of place. Good. He wouldn't have to frisk her.

"I didn't steal from you," she said sharply.

"All right." Not that he believed her. He palmed one of each weapon, then checked the gun's chamber. Loaded. He'd have to be more careful now that Danika was living with him. He couldn't keep his weapons at the ready. His frown deepened as he stored the semiautomatic at his back and faced her.

She was watching him warily, her features as pale as a snow queen's might be. The ache returned to his chest, and he bit the inside of his cheek. The gods should be punished for endowing one person with so much beauty.

"Headed somewhere?" she asked.

"Maybe." His gaze roved over the walls. Two daggers were missing, though she'd taken great pains to cover her tracks by shifting the angle of the weapons that had once surrounded them.

He didn't blame her, wouldn't take them from her. He was surprisingly...aroused by the thought of this woman being armed. *Idiot.* She probably wanted his blood spilled all over the floor, pooling between the stones.

He shivered at the thought. She would have to stab him to spill his blood, and gods knew how good that would feel. *If she wanted you dead, she could have cut off your head last night.*

"Why didn't you run from me while you had the chance?" he asked.

She slapped a hand over her forehead and fell against the pillows. "I don't know. I'm a moron."

"Why didn't you hurt me?"

"Again, I don't know. Okay? You're the goddamn enemy. I should be able to cut your throat, no problem. I've trained for it, you know?"

He blinked. "For cutting my throat?"

"Yes. I've taken classes. Not just self-defense, but classes that teach you how to take down your enemy and get away with it." She brushed a piece of lint from her leg. "I will *never* be helpless again."

I helped destroy her innocence, and I didn't even have to touch her. Shameful.

Reyes leaned his shoulder against the closet's frame. "Do not be too upset with yourself. Perhaps you could not bring yourself to hurt an unconscious man. That is an honorable thing."

"Yes, but you aren't a man."

No, he wasn't. He was a demon, and the reminder stung. Enough to prompt the next words to tumble out of his mouth. "I am awake. Try now."

"Fuck you," she snapped.

"Try."

"Go to hell."

"Try, Danika. Prove to yourself that you can take me down."

Her gaze shot to him, twin laser beams that cut past skin and bone. "So you have a chance to hurt me? No, thank you."

"I will not move. You have my word."

She clicked her tongue against the roof of her mouth. "Do you *want* me to hurt you?"

She sounded incredulous, yet he realized that's exactly what he'd been pushing her toward. He wanted her to jump from the bed and attack him. He wanted her nails deep in his skin, her teeth deep in his neck again. He wanted pain. From her. Only her.

He wanted pleasure, the only way he could get it. Even though he knew better. Her innocence was already gone. What harm could there be in taking things a little further?

"If you will not attack me, kiss me," he said. He was trembling now, his need too strong to be denied. If he couldn't have the pain he craved, he would take something else. Her taste. He doubted it would sate him, but he didn't care.

She gasped, and he wasn't sure whether it was in horror… or anticipation. Then he saw her nipples harden, and he knew. Anticipation.

His chest felt as if steel bars were pressing down on it. "Kiss me," he said, and the words were so low, so quiet and needy, *he* could barely hear them.

"Go to hell," she repeated, staring at his lips. This time, however, there was no heat in her voice. Only husky desire.

"If you will not come to me, perhaps I will come to you."

She didn't offer a protest. Goose bumps broke out over her delectable skin, her breaths shallow and the pulse in her neck fluttering wildly. And yet he suspected deep down that if he kissed her, she would hate him. Hate him more than she already did. She didn't want to want him, would be ashamed for giving in to her captor, one of the men responsible for her family's current predicament.

Still, he found himself stepping toward her.

She jerked upright, panic in her eyes. "Why are you doing this?"

To gain his bearings, he paused in the center of the room. His chest had started aching again, Pain soaking it up, savoring every pang. "I have to know."

"What? What do you have to know?"

"What you taste like." Another step.

"What happens when you know?" she rasped.

"I stop wondering. Stop dreaming of you every night, thinking of you every minute of every day." Another step closer. "I think you wonder, too. I think you dream of me and wonder. You hate yourself for it. You hate me for it, but you cannot stop."

She was shaking her head, sunny hair flirting with her shoulders, caressing her elegant neck. He wanted to be the one to touch her, tickle her. He wanted to give her pleasure, even if he could feel none himself.

Finally he admitted the truth. She *was* different from the other women he'd known. While they had been living beings, they hadn't been fully alive. Danika was. She was the epitome of life and vitality. Perhaps, for one blessed moment, he could soak up that life force and find pleasure in a pleasurable act. Perhaps she could gift him with release—without pain, without suffering and agony. Just once.

"I don't want you," she choked out.

"Liar." If he didn't do this, he would be haunted by what-ifs for the rest of eternity.

Two more steps and he was at the side of the mattress. She didn't scoot away. She drew her knees to her chest and wrapped her arms around her legs. Her little white teeth nibbled once more on her bottom lip.

"As I said before, you could have left this house, this room, but you didn't."

"A moment of insanity." Her eyes darted over his face. What she searched for, he didn't know.

"Many moments. I slept for hours."

"So? That doesn't mean I want to kiss you. That doesn't mean I want your hands all over me, skin on skin."

Sweet heaven. "What does it mean, then?"

Her lush lips parted and her tongue swiped over them, leaving a sheen of moisture.

"Nothing to say?" Slowly, slowly, he leaned down.

Slowly, slowly she stretched out, lying down, putting more and more distance between their mouths. When her back hit the mattress, she had nowhere else to go. But she didn't turn away, didn't push at him.

Finally he was only a whisper away. He braced his palms at her sides. Strands of her hair caressed his skin like live wires against a switchboard. Gods, the agony. The agony of being so close physically and knowing a kiss was all they could share....

More, his demon begged. *Please, more.*

Reyes was as hard as a rock, every nerve ending alive. "What does it mean?" he insisted.

"You talk too much." Danika glared up at him, eyes as harsh as her tone. Demanding. *Wanting.* "Do it. Get it over with. End it."

He wished it were that simple. Do it, never think of it again. Never want it again. Never want her. Perhaps even forget her, so that if Aeron ever claimed her, Reyes would not care. Would not wish for death himself.

"What are you thinking about?" Danika asked, softly now.

Gods, she was lovely. Even piqued, she radiated such beauty it hurt to gaze upon her. Her lashes were long and thick, and there was a single freckle beside her right eyebrow.

"Did you—did you change your mind about the kiss?"

"No." How could he, when he craved it more than a tomorrow? "You may not give me another chance. I want to savor every moment of this."

"If we're going to be fools, we need to get it over with. Savor later." Obviously tired of waiting for him, she latched on to his cheeks and tugged him all the way down. He fell on top of her, and her breath burst out on a gasp. He inhaled deeply, taking every molecule inside his lungs, branding himself with her essence.

"This means nothing," she said.

"Less than nothing," he lied.

"I'll hate myself later."

"I hate myself now." She opened her mouth to reply, but he swooped in and swallowed the words.

CHAPTER ELEVEN

DEAR GOD. *How have I lived without this?*

Danika tangled her fingers in Reyes's silky hair and held tight, her nails scoring his scalp. His tongue was hot, spiced with passionate man. His body was hard on top of hers.

For some reason, he pressed his palms flat against the bed and lifted so that only their mouths connected. No. No, no, no. She wanted to feel his weight, his heat, his strength and his hardness.

She shouldn't. Nothing should matter but her family, her freedom. Yet from the moment she'd seen Reyes lying unconscious, near death, she'd been unable to think about anything but him. *Wrong, so wrong.* Except how could this be wrong when she felt comforted for the first time in months? How could this be wrong when she felt truly alive?

Just a little longer, she thought. Once the curiosity abated, once she knew beyond any doubt this man's taste—oh, God, his taste—didn't affect her more than any other man's, she could push him away.

Later she would act like the smart woman her wonderful mother had raised. She would act responsible, would find a way to question Aeron successfully. She would leave this fortress and never return.

"Danika," Reyes whispered. "Angel."

Angel. "Don't stop."

His lips were soft, the tiny bit of shadow beard on his jaw

scraping her cheeks. Every time he angled his head, taking her deeper with his tongue, harder, and scraping her a little more, a lance of pleasure traveled to her nipples, between her legs.

She moaned, unable to quiet herself.

"Do you like my kiss?" he asked. "I'm not hurting you?"

"I like. Not hurting." As she squeezed the knotted muscles in his shoulders, she didn't think she would have minded a little pain. She yearned to have his teeth bite at her and his body pound against her. Inside her.

"I'm glad." His tongue swept past her teeth and worked the roof of her mouth, massaging.

So good, she thought, but still, she needed more. Perhaps she needed everything he had to give. She definitely needed him rubbing against her—why wasn't he rubbing? Some of her desire waned. Why had he sounded controlled? So…unaffected?

The questions chilled the hottest flames of her ardor, and she began to notice other things, as well. She had spread her legs but he hadn't fallen into the offered cradle. She'd clutched at him, desperate for more, yet he remained detached from her, only touching her with his tongue. She'd gasped again and again, yet his breathing was completely unchanged.

Danika pressed into the pillow, pulling from Reyes's lips. She was still panting; he was still breathing normally. She glared up at him, unsure what to think.

"You started this," she said, anger rising inside her. He had started it and yet he hadn't really participated. "Why? And don't give me any bullshit about wanting the need to end. Clearly, you don't desire me." Saying it caused the anger to spike.

His eyelids flickered open. Normally they were so dark the pupils seemed to swallow up the irises. Now they flickered and swirled like a sea of churning emotion, a hint of crimson framing the black.

Demon eyes.

She gulped. It was terrifying, being reminded of his inner

evil. And yet, still her desire remained. Still, her body ached and hungered. For him, only him. Why?

Much as she'd tried to convince herself that he was the same as any other man, she'd only managed to do the opposite. He was Reyes, a combination of man and demon, drawing and repelling her at the same time. He was right and wrong wrapped in the same sensual package, with a kiss and flavor that transported her at once to the heights of heaven and the depths of hell.

He had sprung from her nightmares, yet he had become her fantasy, weaving gossamer wings of desire through her every cell. He was the only thing she wanted and everything she shouldn't have. She would have been able to pick him out of a lineup blindfolded, his woodsy scent like a tether that bound them together.

What did she truly know about him, besides the fact that he was possessed by a demon? She knew that everyone else seemed pale and weak when compared to him, wilted carnations surrounding a lone, thorny rose. She knew no one else had ever set her on fire like this. She knew that she'd been cold for a long time and only he had been able to warm her.

Surely that warmth was drugging her, luring her down this road of temptation. Not Reyes himself. Yes, she'd blame the warmth. For now. The alternative scared her too much.

"Just get off me," she said, amazed at her calm.

"I do want you," he said, and he sounded tortured, as though knives were being shoved under his fingernails.

"Liar." She echoed his earlier accusation as she pushed at his shoulders.

He didn't budge. He did frown. "Stop, angel. You do not want me to leave."

Angel. He'd called her angel again. Once, in the dungeon, he'd even called her his. She tried not to soften. Men had used endearments on her before, but none had ever uttered one with such a you-belong-to-me-and-only-me undertone.

"You don't know what I want," she snapped, "and obviously I'm not what you desire." *Be happy about that, you idiot.*

Shame coasted over his rugged features. Shame and grief. His gaze fell to her shoulder, where her T-shirt gaped and cotton fell away from skin. "I want you. Swear to the gods, I do."

As he'd spoken, his lower body had brushed hers. He wasn't hard. Her cheeks heated. When he'd first walked to her, his penis had been so hard and full it had strained past the waist of his jeans. One taste of her, and he'd gone limp. *Am I that bad a kisser?*

"Don't make me tell you to get off again," she said. "I don't know what game you're playing, but I told you this was dumb. I need—"

"No game," he interjected hotly.

She continued as if he hadn't interrupted her. "I need back inside the dungeon, pronto, and this is wasting my time. I need to talk to Aeron."

"First, you will listen to me."

"Reyes. Off. Now!"

"We *will* talk, Danika."

She glared up at him. "Force this, and I *will* hurt you."

His eyes closed again, hiding whatever emotion was banked in them. His lashes were like summoning fingers, beckoning her deeper into a world of shadows and dark seduction. "I can't— I'm not—"

"Dungeon. Aeron. Nothing else matters. Talk time is over. Kiss time is over. Like we wanted, it's over and done. I won't wonder about your taste again." Sadly, she knew she would dream of that kiss for the rest of her life. She would dream of what might have been, fantasize about what would have happened if he'd truly wanted her.

"Danika, I—"

Again he paused, and she experienced a wave of painful curiosity. "What?" Her heart pounded against her ribs. "Just say it so I can go!"

His eyelids popped open, fire blazing bright in his pupils. He got in her face, pressing his nose to hers. White-hot breath blistered her skin. "Not another word from you. I have something to tell you."

These last few months, her will had been ignored completely. Her wonderful life had been taken away, her existence stripped to the bare necessities. Everyone she loved—gone. Painting, her lifeline to sanity—gone.

She wouldn't capitulate on this.

"Not another word, huh?" *You've trained for combat. You know what to do.* Heart pounding, Danika flattened her palm on the cold mattress. Sweat beaded over her skin. Last time she'd defended herself, she'd killed. *Careful this time.* She didn't want to hurt this man beyond repair. She just wanted to wound him a little.

"I never wanted to tell you this, had hoped it would be different with you, but I cannot allow you to think I do not crave you." *Block his voice and his bittersweet words. Act!*

"I—"

Danika struck.

With all of her strength, she propelled her palm up and into his nose. *Crunch. Snap.* Warm blood poured from him, spraying her. Reyes moaned. Not a moan of pain, she realized, but of pleasure—exactly the sort she'd longed to hear while his tongue had filled her mouth.

The shock of that moan froze her in place. What. The. Hell?

Slowly Reyes turned his head and faced her again. The blood had already ceased flowing, his nose readjusting itself all on its own. Her eyes widened. He was an immortal warrior, yes, she'd known that. He healed quickly. That, too, she'd suspected after the choking last night. But how could she have predicted the explosive need that would appear in his eyes because she'd broken his nose?

His cock swelled quickly, again as she'd craved earlier, a

brand between her jean-clad thighs. What would she have felt if they'd been naked? She swallowed, and Reyes licked his lips, as if he could suddenly taste her there.

A tremor catapulted down her spine. Their bodies brushed, her nipples against his strength, her softness against his warrior-might, and electricity sparked. For a moment, only a moment, the sensation was painful and the pain was a pleasure inside her.

Reyes jolted away from her, that dark lightning gone in an instant. He stopped and stood at the far wall, the glistening head of his erection rising above the waist of his now too-tight pants.

"Reyes," she said, unsure. Needy all over again, scared and confused.

"I want you, but I cannot have you unless you hurt me." The harsh admission seemed ripped from his throat. His shame had returned. His guilt. And hope? "I can only experience pleasure with pain."

Slowly she sat up, her brain too fogged to make sense of what he was trying to tell her. "I don't understand."

"Yesterday you asked what demon possessed me. Well, my demon is Pain. It makes me crave physical agony, and the more excruciating the better. Bodily suffering is my only source of pleasure."

Just as it had been hers in that single moment.

No, not a single moment. The truth slinked through her like an ice shower in the midst of a perfect day. It *had* happened before. Yesterday, when she'd awoken in Reyes's bed. She'd bitten him, and she'd liked it. "Can your demon enter *me?*" Her stomach curled into itself. That was impossible. Right?

"No," he said, but his gaze had sharpened.

Don't think about this right now. You'll panic, lose focus. "What you're telling me is that, to be with you, I'd have to torture you?" Over and over again?

He nodded.

Her mouth dried, and she suddenly tasted cotton. If she

came to care for him—*if?*—and gave herself to him, what would be expected of her? Would she have to scratch him, pinch him, bite him? "Other women have…hurt you?"

He gave another grave nod.

Danika's hands fisted, her nails cutting into the sheet. In that moment, she had no problem summoning the will to harm someone. The thought of Reyes with another woman propelled her toward a jealous rage she'd never before experienced. "Did that work?"

"For a while. Pain is pain, no matter the reason it's meted."

"Do you still—" *Indulge with those little hookers?* she finished silently. "Do you still seek that kind of woman?"

"Not for many years."

The anger and the jealousy melted somewhat. "Do you want me to injure you?" Could she?

Surprisingly, he shook his head. Dark hair swayed at his temples. "I crave the pain, I will not lie, and I would love you to be the one giving it to me. But…" He licked his lips, looked away.

"But what?"

"I would never allow you to hurt me like that."

"Why?" The question burst from her before she could stop it. Not wanting to see pity light his features, she pulled her gaze from his face—and found herself staring at fresh cuts in his arm. He'd been slicing grooves this entire time.

Shaking, she wound her own arms around her middle. *That's* what he needed, knives in his veins. She'd always assumed he was clumsy. She gave a humorless laugh. He wasn't clumsy at all. How foolish she'd been.

"It would change you," he said, "and not for the better. You are perfect, just as you are."

Do not react. Ignore his words. The conversation was dangerous, and nothing good waited at the end. Either she would lose her mind, beg to be allowed to give him what he needed and be disgusted with herself for doing so, or he would continue to reject her, humiliating her. *Get away from him.*

"You said what you wanted to say. I—I need to speak with Aeron now. I've wasted too much time. I need to find my family."

A blank mask fluttered over Reyes's face.

Her chest ached. For him? For her? For what could have been? She didn't know. "What kind of person would I be if I continued to put myself above them? They might be in trouble, might be scared and worried about me."

"I will talk to him again and you may listen," Reyes countered.

"But—"

"You saw how Aeron erupted at the mere sound of your voice. *I* will talk to him. Understand?"

She nodded reluctantly. The information Aeron possessed was too precious to stay here squabbling over semantics. "Will you let me go after them? If he tells us where they are?"

"I'm afraid I will never be able to let you go."

It was the second time he'd said that to her, but this time the words were whispered and she had to strain to hear. When his meaning registered, she nearly leapt off the bed and attacked him. Only the knowledge that he would like it held her in place. "Try and keep me here, then," she snarled. "See what happens."

"You misunderstand. I will help you find them," he said, "and I will escort you to wherever they are." *If they are alive.* The unspoken statement echoed between them. "In return, you will not betray my friends to the Hunters. Not even Aeron."

Every drop of heat leached from her cheeks, leaving them cold. He knew. Had probably known all along. "I—I—"

"You do not have to tell me what they said to you, what they asked of you or what you promised them. It doesn't matter. My knowledge of it could get you killed." He turned, giving her his back. "Do you agree to the trade?"

The Hunters had vowed to help her find her family, protect

them. But they were mortals, humans like herself. They hated Reyes and the other Lords, wanted vengeance against them and would do anything for victory. Even mow her down if she got in their way, she suspected.

They had asked for her help, for her to enter this fortress and collect information. So far, she had not lived up to her vow to help them. There hadn't been time, and she hadn't had the inclination. Reyes had distracted her.

Now he was asking her to switch sides completely and trust the enemy.

"Do you agree?" he demanded.

"I agree," she said, but she wasn't sure she spoke truthfully. She had a phone briefing scheduled with Stefano tonight, and she would do whatever was necessary, use *anyone,* to find her family. To keep them safe, she would have every single one of Reyes's friends killed if necessary.

And ruin Ashlyn's life. Anya's, too. Her stomach churned with sickness. God, the equation worsened with every hour that passed.

She'd already proven she couldn't destroy Reyes.

And that was okay. He wouldn't hurt her family. Or would he? If she conspired against his friends, he could very easily morph from sweet protector to murderous demon. Which meant he would have to die, as well.

Damn it!

"You will not betray us, even if your loved ones are gone?" he pressed her.

Were her intentions flashing all over her face? She closed her eyes. "I agree, okay?" she said again, and this time the words were choked. The coming days might prove to be the worst of her life, dashing her hopes, ruining her family...and devastating this man she both wanted and feared.

Reyes nodded soberly. "Then let's do this."

CHAPTER TWELVE

"Haven't we done this before?"

"Didn't work out last time," Reyes said. He was standing inside the cell as he had yesterday, but Aeron noted his old friend remained a safe distance away. "I thought we'd try again."

"No. I think you've returned for more." Aeron stared at Reyes, who looked every bit the warrior primed for battle. When didn't he, though? "I think you liked my hands on you."

A muscle ticked below each of Reyes's dark eyes.

"A few years ago I asked if I could whip you, beat you. *Something.* I would have stabbed you, even. I didn't want to do it, didn't want to hurt you any more than you wanted to kill Maddox each night, but I knew you needed the pain so I was willing. I loved you enough."

"And I loved you enough to say no. Remember that?"

Aeron ignored the question, because he *did* remember. Thinking of it could deflate him. He petted Legion's bald head when the creature settled on his lap, saying, "I'm still willing to help you. If you want to hurt, give me your woman." He laughed, even as fury clouded his friend's face. "One slice, that's all it will take. She'll fall, and your heart will literally break. Pain for eternity will be yours. My gift to you. You can thank me later."

The tip of Reyes's tongue slid over his teeth. A show of aggression. Well, a *need* for aggression. Yet Reyes remained in place. Unlike Aeron and Maddox, he rarely erupted. He was a man who waited, then struck when his enemy least expected it. "You've changed. Once you were desperate to let her go. What happened?"

"I simply realized I cannot win against the bloodlust. I've given myself to it, and I've never been happier," he said.

"Liar. You hate what you are. I know you do." Reyes sighed when Aeron didn't respond. "Tell me where her family is. Please."

Aeron turned his wrist, his hand never leaving Legion as he rattled the chains that bound him. "Free me."

Reyes's expression was tortured, but not in the usual way. He appeared torn apart by pain—pain for once he did not like. "You know I can't let you go."

"I know you *won't*."

Bleak, Reyes nodded. "You're right. I won't."

"Then you have your answer. You won't, I won't."

Legion slithered around him, and two small hands were soon whispering over Aeron's back. They were scaled yet smooth. Worshipping. Massaging his muscles to loosen them. When he gained the desired results, the creature eased to a stand. His chest pressed against Aeron's shoulders, and he peeked over at Reyes. His lips smacked hungrily.

"Not yet," Aeron told him. He didn't understand why the little demon liked him and not the others, but he accepted it as fact. He didn't understand why the demon had followed him here, but he was glad. For some reason, he needed the creature. Legion calmed him as no one else had been able, quieting Wrath, muting the bloodlust, keeping him aware. Except when Lucien and Reyes had come to take him away from the cave. Then, Aeron had gone crazy.

He'd been so close to escape. Legion had been eating through flesh, about to eat through bone, when the fiend had sensed the warriors' impending arrival and disappeared. Only to reappear here later when all had settled.

"Do you know where the women are?" Reyes asked, probably unaware Legion was picturing him splayed on a silver platter, knife and fork optional. "Tell me that, at least."

Oh, Aeron knew where the women were. He knew every damned second of every damned day. The knowledge taunted him constantly, laughing at his helplessness, driving him to madness. When the women were dead, the laughter would stop. The madness would fade, and Aeron would stop craving the destruction of everyone he encountered.

"Tell me," Reyes repeated.

"Yes," he finally admitted aloud, knowing the boast would hit its target and slice deep. "I know where they are." *What have you become?* He knew he should feel guilty, but couldn't summon the energy. Locked deep in the earth, his emotions had seemed to wither away, leaving only hate. A need to cause death.

Reyes's nostrils flared and his eyes blazed with obsidian fire. Yes, contact.

"Can I sssuck hisss blood?" Legion asked, claws sinking into Aeron's shoulders. "Pleassse. Pretty pleassse."

"No," Aeron told him. He owed Reyes a quick death—too much would the warrior enjoy a long and torturous demise. Teeth shredding his veins, blood pouring from him would be pleasurable. And Reyes did not deserve pleasure. After all, Reyes was keeping the girl from him. Such a crime deserved a harsh punishment.

Crime? That is not a crime, that is a mercy. This is not you. Fight this.

His eyes narrowed. There was nothing to fight. He had been given a task, and he would fulfill it.

"What about girl?" Legion asked. "Can I drain girl?"

A low growl rang from Reyes.

"No," Aeron said. "She is mine."

Now Reyes stalked forward, silver blade glinting in his

hand. "She is *mine*." He realized what he was doing in the middle of the cell and stopped, remaining just out of range.

Too bad. "I know she's nearby," Aeron said silkily. "Her scent is strong, stirring me to battle even now."

Reyes stepped backward, guarding the only exit. Guarding *her*. Aeron closed his eyes, her screams of death suddenly ringing in his ears. *Don't hurt me. Please don't hurt me*, she would say.

He frowned as realization settled in his mind. Those screams weren't hers. They were real, a memory, and they belonged to another. Every single cry was a heady caress that pleasured his decimated senses. Clearly, whoever he'd hurt—killed?—he'd enjoyed cutting down.

The scent of blood filled his nose, sweet and sultry, a warm night after a bitterly cold day, gentle moonlight after too much time roasting in the harsh sun. He felt transported, as if he were standing over her body again, jeering at her weakness.

This isn't you. You hate this, hate what you are, what you've become.

Once—an eternity ago?—he'd watched mortals, fascinated by the contrasts between their lives and his own. He often wished for death, yet he would most likely exist forever. They died a little more every day, yet they embraced vitality as he never had. They were weak; he was strong. Yet they were not afraid to laugh and love.

Love—as if they didn't realize that everything could be taken away in a heartbeat of time.

Why? he'd always wondered. He had long craved an answer, though none had ever come. And here he was, enjoying the recollection of torturing one mortal and plotting the upcoming death of another.

Even Wrath found the concept confusing and wrong.

Aeron hadn't forgotten that he and his demon had fought these dark urges to slaughter. At first. But the gods had won, and they'd eventually succumbed. Death now flowed through his veins, thicker than blood, and had become—with an irony not lost on Aeron—his only reason for living.

"Would you like it if I begged?" Reyes asked him tightly.

Would he? Aeron smiled, feeling the first true spark of amusement he'd known in weeks. He thought perhaps he would. Proud, headstrong Reyes bowed to no one. To have him do so here and now would surely be empowering.

"I would, I would," Legion clapped, the sound booming in Aeron's ear.

Reyes didn't hesitate. He dropped to his knees. "Please." The word was nothing more than a rumble. "Tell me where they are."

As Legion cackled, Aeron lost his smile, realizing then it was not empowering to have his friend on his knees but shaming. "You love her?"

"No." Violent shake of his head. "I cannot."

Liar! He must. Why else would he debase himself this way, something he'd never done for another? Not even for a Lord.

Aeron and Reyes had been there the day their friend Baden was decapitated by Hunters. They'd watched in horror as the warrior was attacked from behind, stabbed repeatedly, throat slit. They'd run toward him, screaming, enraged, desperate, battle-hungry. But they had not begged the Hunters to stop. They had not begged for Baden's life. They had simply attacked.

Would pleading have saved the keeper of Distrust?

Probably not, he thought, but why hadn't they tried? They had loved Baden like a brother and his death had destroyed the small pieces of humanity they'd managed to save from their demons.

"What are you thinking about?" Reyes asked, still on his knees.

"The worst night of my life," he admitted.

"The opening of the box, then."

"No. Baden." Guilt had been branded inside him that terrible night. Guilt that he'd failed to protect a friend. Guilt that he had punished only a few of the men responsible before walking away from the Hunter-Lord war, hoping to find a sliver of peace in an eternity of chaos and death when he did not deserve it.

I've never loved anyone enough to fight, to war, or to beg.

"He was a good friend," Reyes said. "He would have hated to see us like this."

"He would have looked at us with disappointment in those yellow eyes of his. We would have ignored him because he'd want us to kiss and make up, and then he would have stabbed us to get our attention."

"Being ignored wasn't something he could tolerate."

"No."

They peered at each other in silence. Reyes didn't move, but remained on his knees. He would stay there until Aeron told him what he wanted to know, of that Aeron was now sure.

But if he told Reyes where the women were, and Reyes managed to hide them from him, Aeron would always be this way. He would never return to normal, would never again know anything except bloodlust.

"Please." Another rumble.

Legion slithered over his shoulder and down his chest like a snake, then propped his chin on Aeron's upraised knee. "Thisss not much fun. Why can't we play? Why can't we drink?"

"Soon," Aeron said. Then, to Reyes, he said, "Tell the girl to step up to the bars."

At last Reyes popped to his feet. He shook his head, dark hair swinging, panic flaring over his features. "No. She—"

"Is here. I'm here."

At the sound of that determined, feminine voice, Aeron angled his head. Reyes jumped in front of her, remaining in the cell while she stayed out of it, but blocking his view nonetheless. Aeron scowled. "Move. I will not hurt her." *Not right now.*

The warrior seemed to debate with himself for a long while,

rooted in place. Finally he stepped stiffly to the side, allowing Aeron a peek at the girl. She stood at the bars as ordered, clutching them, knuckles white.

Wrath exploded into a frenzy of activity, pacing the prison of Aeron's mind, drooling with anticipation. *Act.*

"No," he replied through gritted teeth.

Act! She is here, she is ours.

"No!"

Legion petted his temples, and the screaming faded to a mere whisper.

"Excuse me?" Danika said, looking from him to the little demon.

Reyes stepped in front of her again, body tense, waiting.

Delicate fingers settled over Reyes's shoulder and gently pushed him aside. The warrior could have resisted, could have held his ground this time—and his taut features proclaimed that he wanted to—but he didn't. He inched to the side.

Once again, Aeron was staring at Danika. She was small, only reaching Reyes's shoulder. Light hair framed her face and her green eyes sparkled like emeralds. Her nose was uptilted like a queen's, as if she waited for her servants to grant her every desire. She was slender, a little too slender, with a face as dainty as an angel's wing—but her expression was not soft. Harsh determination radiated from her.

"You still want to kill me," he said.

"Yes." Her lips were red and swollen. Obviously, she'd been kissed, and very recently, too.

Aeron's gaze settled on Reyes's mouth. It, too, was well used. He would not have pegged the human as Pain's type. He would not have pegged Pain as *her* type, either. But he *had* sensed the tension between them the first time she'd come to the fortress. A tension that was stronger now, more intense. Reyes had even called the woman his.

They were enemies, yet they'd become lovers. How sweet,

he mentally sneered. And yet, beneath the sneer, he could feel a tendril of…wistfulness?

Legion licked Aeron's cheek and then his tiny body was slithering around his neck, then down, where he perched his elbows on Aeron's knees. A favorite position of his, apparently. That forked tongue flicked out at Danika, a rattle sounding. "You familiar. Want to play?"

She blinked, shook her head as if dislodging a puzzling thought. "You saw me yesterday. And no."

"Oh." The little fiend's disappointment was palpable. He flattened against Aeron's chest, his green scales fading slightly.

"You hurt Legion," Aeron growled, oddly offended by the fact. With the knowledge of the demon's unhappiness, Aeron's bloodlust threatened to explode, his tenuous control slipping. "Which means this conversation is done. Leave."

"I'm sorry, I'm sorry," Danika rushed out, offering an apologetic glance to Legion. "I didn't mean to hurt your feelings. Really. It was…a game. Yes, a game."

"Love gamesss." Relaxing, color returning, the creature added, "Ssseen you before yesterday."

Aeron, too, relaxed.

Danika shook her head. "I'm sorry, but you're mistaken."

"You fly in flamesss. Watch minionsss torture dead."

The girl blinked as she had before, a mixture of horror and astonishment in her eyes. "I do, but only in my dreams. How do you know? Have you seen my paintings? Wait, that's not possible."

"Don't answer," Aeron told Legion, an idea hitting him. He could use the information as a bargaining tool. And in the process, he could, perhaps, decipher the puzzle the girl had just presented.

Flames. Minions. Had to be hell, Legion's home and the only place the creature could have seen her. Aeron wasn't sure if the girl had somehow entered hell or if Legion was playing another of his games. But for the first time since the Titans had taken over the heavens and ordered Aeron to kill Danika and her family, the terrible command began to make sense. If the girl *could* travel to the dark underworld, could she also access the world of the gods? Could she watch them? Maybe even divine their secrets?

Why not smite her down themselves, though? Surely an easy task for any god. Why force Aeron to do their dirty work?

He glanced over at Reyes, who had paled. They must have put the same pieces of the puzzle together. If Danika were to be captured by godly enemies and forced to betray heavenly secrets, the gods would never leave her alone. They would not rest until she was dead.

There would be no saving her.

"I don't— I'm not—" She scrubbed a hand over her face, as if the action could jump-start her brain into understanding. When she stilled, her expression was carved from stone. "Stop trying to distract me." Her gaze moved to Aeron and stayed. "Where is my family?"

"We will trade information, you and I."

"Okay." No hesitation.

He watched as she slowly unwound her fingers from the bars, dropped her arm and reached for Reyes. The warrior slid his hand through the bars and captured hers, intertwining their fingers. They sought comfort from each other, Aeron realized. One silently asked for it, and the other silently gave it. Did they even comprehend what they'd done?

"What do you want to know?" she asked, her voice shaking. Her eyes slitted, and she cleared her throat. She asked again, and this time her voice was clear.

"Have you seen hell? And do not lie to me. One lie, and the conversation ends."

A moment passed before she answered, as though she were weighing her options in her mind. "Like I said, I see it in my dreams," she finally replied.

"Do your sister, mother, grandmother dream of hell?"

She shook her head, blond tresses dancing. "They've never spoken of it."

There was a hitch in her voice, but he pretended not to notice. If she had lied, he had, too, for he did not want the conversation to end. "What do—"

"We're supposed to trade information," she interjected with a steely edge. "So let's trade. Where's my mother?"

"In the States. A small town in Oklahoma."

Absolute relief suddenly lit up her lovely features, and she closed her eyes. A tremor slipped through her, and several tears beaded between her eyelids before sliding down her cheeks.

He didn't, *couldn't,* allow the sight to affect him. "Have you ever dreamed of the heavens?"

"Yes."

"What do you—"

She gave another shake of her head. "No. I answered. Now it's your turn. Where's my sister?"

"Thisss boring," Legion said with a sigh, curling into Aeron's lap and closing his eyes.

"Your sister is with your mother."

"Oh, God." Another tear of joy and relief journeyed south, streaking a crystalline path to her chin.

Aeron thought her legs might have collapsed had Reyes not released her hand, arm snaking around the bars, as well as her waist, holding her up. She didn't protest. No, she sidled closer to him.

How could they trust and need each other like that?

They were fools; he was not jealous. "What do you see when you trek these spiritual planes?" he asked.

"I see great evil and unerring goodness. I see death and life. Darkness and rainbow colors. Demonlike creatures who destroy, screams all around them. Angels who repair the damage, songs of glory humming from their wings."

When she did not elaborate further, Aeron frowned. None of what she described was reason enough for the gods to mark her for death. His kind of death, at that: the sins of her past cutting through her skin and bones as though they were no more substantial than butter.

"What have you seen of the gods? What—"

"My grandmother," she interjected. "Where is my grandmother?"

He pressed his lips together, his heart rate increasing, sweat beading on his temples. If he told the truth, she would leave, and he wasn't ready for her to leave. Not yet. Thousands of questions still ran through his mind.

"I'm not satisfied with your last answer," he said. "Tell me if you've seen the gods."

Even though several feet separated them, he could hear her teeth gritting together. "I don't know if I've seen them."

"Think!" he roared.

She flinched, and Reyes growled over at him.

"How would I know? I don't believe in gods and goddesses, I don't know what they look like or sound like." Her breathing was choppy, raspy. "I could have dreamed of them a thousand times and not have known it."

"Help her figure it out," he snapped to Reyes.

Reyes looked down at her, his expression hard. Reminded Aeron of the night Reyes had asked him to fly Danika into town. She hadn't wanted to go, Reyes hadn't wanted Aeron to touch her, but he had stepped back and forced the players into action for the greater good.

He'd always been like that, placing the needs and wants of his friends above his own. He'd also always been determined, unwilling to back down when someone he loved desired something—even if they began to hate him for his methods of obtaining it for them.

"If you're withholding information, stop," Reyes said. He

released her and left the cell, locking the door behind him before turning back to her. "Aeron will not renege on his word. Tell him what he wishes to know, and he will tell you about your grandmother. What have you seen recently? Describe it—or them—to us. What have you heard? No detail is too small."

She gulped. Licked her lips. Another tremor swept through her as she tore her gaze from her man and faced Aeron. "Was there—was there a war recently? You know—up there?"

Aeron's jaw dropped.

Reyes might have gasped. He did step away and turn to see her more clearly.

So. It was true. She *could* see into the heavens. The reason for her death order was finally revealed with absolute certainty.

"Yes," Reyes croaked out. "There was."

"Greeks fighting against Titans? I think that's what they called themselves."

"Yes," Aeron answered.

Her cheeks leached of color. "The Titans won and the Greeks were locked away. Well, most of them were, at least."

"Yes." The word emerged from both of them as the faintest of whispers.

"The Titans are scrambling to find a group of weapons. The…king, I think it was, held a meeting with his new Captain of the Guard. I guess that's the leader of his army." She kept talking, the words rushing from her as if she feared stopping and being unable to start again. "They have a plan. The captain will come to earth to watch and wait, follow and steal. I don't recall everything. My painting could give the details I'm forgetting. After I dream, I try to forget. I don't want to remember."

"Painting?" Reyes asked, more a croak than a question.

She nodded, eyes shadowed with memories. "When I dream of…heaven and hell, I always paint what I see to purge it from my system."

"Where are the paintings now?" he asked, punching the

wall behind him with so much force she backed two steps away, palms up.

"A few are at my apartment in New Mexico. Most are in storage, where I'm paid up for a year."

Reyes spun from her and faced Aeron, grim, expectant.

Danika, too, eyed him. "I answered fully. Now it's your turn. Tell me about my grandmother."

After everything she'd told him, he owed her the truth. He did not try and sugarcoat it. He looked her straight in the eye. "I think I killed her."

CHAPTER THIRTEEN

ROME. A place of majesty, steeped in history and opulence, violence and pleasure. No matter where a man stood in this magnificent city, the sea would sing to him, innocent and tranquil; the sky would respond with a song of its own, a peaceful melody of fading light.

Neither calmed Paris.

He stood at the edge of the Temple of the Unspoken Ones, hidden beside his friends. Waiting. The eerie temple—sometimes he would swear he heard tortured screams on the wind, rising above the sweet melody of the waves—had risen from the sea not too long ago, shrouded from the human eye until recently. Now workers swarmed the area, buzzing back and forth, cleaning and searching the crumbling corridors for glimpses into the past. They didn't know that the gods planned to use the temple to bring mortals full circle. Once they'd worshipped and sacrificed at the altars of their heavenly creators, soon they would worship and sacrifice again.

No matter what their desires were, he was sure.

The rising of the temple, and its counterpart in Greece, was merely stage one. At least, that's what Paris surmised. He was perhaps the most human—the most earthbound—of all the Lords of the Underworld, and the others might scoff if he offered an opinion on their new sovereigns, the Titans. But Paris liked to think his immersion in humanity added to his understanding of all things spiritual. Having spent so much time among mortals, he knew their emotions well. Greed, jealousy, the desire to be loved.

Yes, there was definitely an overlap between mortal emotions and godly ones.

What were the Titans if not greedy for the power that had once been theirs; jealous that the Greeks had reaped the bountiful harvest sown by *their* hard work; and desiring the adoration and worship that had been denied them for thousands of years? Their wants and needs had not been considered during their time in prison, so now they would indulge their every whim.

And yet, this insight did not help Paris. He couldn't figure out how to fight them. They had amazing powers, could flash from one place to another with only a thought, could control the weather and observe the world and its citizens unimpeded. They could curse with one hand and bless with the other. Paris had a demon who liked to fuck. A demon who weakened without sex and wasn't much of a weapon in any game but seduction.

No question who would win a fight.

If he did nothing, however, his friends could be obliterated. Hunters, his most hated enemy, could be made into guardians of peace and prosperity. Paris wondered if the dominoes had already been set in place for just such a reality and if only a small gust of wind was needed to begin the downpour.

What could he do, though?

Find Pandora's box, yes. That way, he and his friends couldn't be separated from their demons. It would kill them, for once they'd melded, they'd become inseparable, death or insanity their only other options.

He felt so damn helpless. He felt raw, constantly angry. He felt…empty. And all of that negative emotion was wrapped in hot threads of fury. His Sienna was dead. He'd burned her body in a funeral befitting a warrior and scattered her ashes. She wasn't coming back.

Who should he blame? The Hunters? The gods?

Himself?

Who should he punish? Who should he slay in retribution?

An eye for an eye, he'd been taught the first day of his creation. If a warrior failed to mete out the proper penalty for crimes against him, his enemy would view him as weak, attacking over and over again, never ceasing, confident in victory. What was a man to do when the enemy might very well be himself?

"Ready?" Anya asked.

Paris glanced up, pulled from his musings by her excitement. The warriors surrounding the goddess nodded at her, just as eager as she was. They were bordered by shadows, easily skipped over amid the hum of animated activity inside the temple. Humans were collecting rocks and gently scraping at moss.

"Here goes." Anya smoothed her hands down her perfectly flared hips, fingers catching in the diamonds studded at her waist. She fluffed her long, pale hair. "You boys had better be properly impressed by my powers and fawn over me accordingly when I'm done."

Murmurs of "Yes, Anya," and "We will, Anya," rose among them. Even the Lords were afraid of her.

Though Anya had lost many of her powers when she had chosen Lucien over her eternal freedom, giving up her most beloved treasure to be with her man, she was still the creator of disorder and could wield a storm with only a thought.

Paris counted five Hunters among the workers, the mark of Infinity on their wrists. The mark of death, in Paris's mind. *Blame* them *for Sienna's death. They recruited her, filled her head with their lies. Hurt them as she was hurt.* His hands fisted at his sides.

"The things I do for my men," Anya murmured, then strolled into the midst of the humans.

Paris watched as their motions slowed before stilling altogether. Conversations faded to quiet, then to utter silence. Everyone turned and stared at the magnificent beauty wearing a too-short black skirt and a transparent lace-up-corset top.

"Excuse me, but who are you?" someone finally asked. A human, no tattoo on either of his wrists. Short, balding, a bit overweight. A name badge hung from around his neck. Thomas Henderson, Global Society of Mythological Studies. "Do you have clearance?"

"Absolutely, I do." Her sensual lips lifted in a grin, even as she lifted her elegant arms. "I wouldn't be here otherwise, now would I, sweetcakes."

His brow puckered in confusion. "What's your name? Everyone on the list is already here, and I don't remember adding another name."

"No need to check again. A storm's coming." Lightning suddenly lit the sky, gold in a canvas of pinks and purples. The wind kicked up, whipping Anya's hair in every direction. "You should go home."

All of the men were staring at Anya in awe and lust they couldn't hide.

"Mine," Lucien said, watching her with desire in his mismatched eyes.

Paris had to close his eyes for a moment. *I want one of those. I want a "mine."*

Maddox looked at Ashlyn that way. Reyes looked at Danika that way. It was as if the women hung the moon and stars. But what had such a thing gotten Reyes? Grief, most definitely. A death sentence followed the woman everywhere she went, and more than that, Sabin believed she had joined the Hunters and was gathering information for them about the Lords and Pandora's box.

Sabin wanted her dead, like, yesterday. Had even palmed a gun last night while Reyes slept, meaning to plant a bullet in Danika's brain and save Aeron from a fate the warrior had once considered worse than death. Lucien had stopped him. Somehow, someway, Danika's presence calmed Reyes's need for pain. Since her arrival, he hadn't jumped from the fortress roof or pursued any of his usual dangerous activities. He cut himself, yes, but the death wish was clearly gone.

A Lord could not ask for more.

It's what they all craved: peace after an eternity of war and agony and blood. How could they knowingly steal that miracle from one of their own? They couldn't. So they'd left Reyes to deal with the woman alone. Well, not alone. Torin, Kane—the keeper of Disaster and a man you could not take *anywhere* without lightbulbs shorting out and plaster falling from ceilings— and Cameo remained in the fortress, monitoring the computers, guarding the home from invaders. Oh, and William. Not that Paris had any confidence in the man's skills.

Violence, Disease, Disaster and Misery together. Now, that should be fun, Paris thought dryly. Grinning, he shook his head. Sienna would have loved to get her delicate little hands on that information. She would have—

What amusement he'd entertained died a fast death, leaving him once more barren inside and sporting a fierce frown. He had to stop thinking of her. She was dead. Burned. A hated enemy, besides.

Fat raindrops blazed from the sky like arrows, slamming into the ground, pummeling everywhere but where the warriors stood, some hitting the ground so viciously they rebounded onto Paris's freshly polished boots. Hail soon followed, beating like fists.

"Hurry!" someone called.

"The storm's getting worse," another shouted.

Footfalls echoed. Paris was reminded of hamsters running inside a wheel as the humans raced to their boats. With every second that passed, the rain increased in volume and intensity; the hail grew thicker, heavier. Golden bolts of lightning offered a frantic, electric dance. Thunder boomed; dust and debris filled the wind-churning air.

Anya's storm was alive, magnetic, the tiny hairs on Paris's

body standing at attention. He closed his eyes for a moment, only a moment, wishing that electricity would infuse his body, killing the hardened man he'd become and returning him to the carefree man he used to be.

When the last of the humans had sped away, the storm rose...until it formed a dome around the temple. No one would be able to see past it to the warriors who would soon be searching the grounds. Not even someone in the air, camera staring down.

"Clear?" Anya asked.

"Clear," Lucien told her.

Slowly she lowered her arms. The rain and hail thinned, catching on and staying outside that dome. The rumble of thunder died.

As the chaos around the temple faded, Paris scanned the area. He caught the glint of silver, the barrel of a gun peeking from behind one of the still-standing marble walls. Anticipation zinged through him as he palmed a gun of his own. *Hunter.*

For thousands of years, he'd left the battling to Sabin and his crew. He'd tried to live a good life, uneventful and repentant. After all, he'd once helped cast the world into darkness and despair by releasing Pandora's demons. He deserved nothing better.

Now, his past sins no longer mattered. He hated the Hunters more than he hated himself. And after Sienna...

"Hunter," Lucien muttered, his blades already unsheathed. "Eleven o'clock."

"Mine," Paris told him.

"I see him," Sabin said, "and I'm wondering why you get all the fun."

"Mine," Paris repeated.

Sabin rolled his eyes. "I counted six earlier, and I'm betting they're all here, waiting."

Six? "I counted five."

"You miscounted," was all his friend replied, checking the chamber of his .45.

"Every single one of them does *not* have a gun and those guns are *not* 9 mm semiautomatics," Gideon the liar said.

Excellent. A shoot-out.

Paris blocked the stream of memories trying to batter their way into his mind: deafening shots, zipping bullets, a feminine gasp of pain. "They haven't seen us or they would have started firing already."

Lucien didn't reply. He disappeared, there one moment, gone the next. He reappeared next to Anya and said something Paris couldn't hear. Anya nodded and seemed to be caught in the center of a small, whipping tornado a moment later. Then the tornado rose above her, creating a thick wall between Hunters and Lords.

The first blast sounded, the first bullet flying. But it hit the wall of wind and fell to the ground, useless.

Lucien was beside him again a second later, Anya nowhere to be seen. Her protests echoed, though. "—tricked me. The wall was to save you, not protect me so you could flash me." He must have taken her home. Or above the dome to continue wielding the storm. Another shot rang out, and one of the Hunters yelled, "Demons!"

"They came," someone said gleefully. "Must be our lucky day."

"You know the rules."

A third shot. The wind wall had fallen away. Rock exploded and dust spewed behind Paris as the bullet slammed just above his shoulder. He ducked, already crouching forward.

"We'll circle around in opposite directions," Lucien said, "and meet in the middle when every one of them is dead."

"Let the blood flow." Paris muttered, and then his gaze locked with Strider's, whose eyes were the same cerulean shade as his own. Strider was the keeper of Defeat and could not lose, no matter the circumstances, without severe consequences and excruciating pain.

"Need one alive for questioning," Strider told him.

"You're asking for a miracle."

Bullets began flying in quick succession, beating all around them. Strider grinned, a feral flash of teeth completely at odds with his pretty-boy face. He pointed to the always-silent, always-reserved Amun, a dark slash in the quickly falling night, who lifted a tranq-gun.

"You out there, cowards?" a Hunter called.

"Come and get us," Strider said. "If you can."

Paris nodded in understanding and sheathed his weapon. They were to keep one alive. If possible. With a semiautomatic in hand, Paris wasn't sure he'd remember to keep things nonlethal.

Strider leapt into motion, staying low to the ground. He disappeared around a bush. A few seconds later, a scream echoed through the island, pain-filled and shocked. One down. Only five left.

Each of his inhalations heavy in his ears, Paris jolted forward. Amun kept pace beside him, and they whipped around half walls and rocks and slid against the moss-covered floor. He saw his target, a human he might have passed on the street without glancing twice. Tall. Average face. Average build. The menacing, hate-filled gaze gave him away, however.

"Always hoped I'd get a chance to face you. Be the one to bring you in." Grinning, he aimed the barrel of his 9-mil at Paris's leg and squeezed the trigger. Aiming so low prevented Paris from ducking, which he knew had been the Hunter's purpose. Most people ducked, and if he did, the bullet would sink right into his heart, temporarily stopping him cold. So Paris leapt, flying at the shooter and intending to tackle. And when the bullet hit him, it lodged in his leg. Painful, but not debilitating.

He slammed into the Hunter and they propelled down,

smacking into hard stone, debris ripping at their exposed skin. Amun was there a second later, aiming the tranq-gun and shooting the bastard right in the neck.

At first, the struggling Hunter gave no sign he'd been hit. But when Paris punched him in the face, nose cracking under the pressure of his fist, the man couldn't even lift his hand to feel the damage. Finally, he stilled altogether and Paris rose, panting.

"Hope you…suffer…" the man managed to croak. "Deserve it." His eyes closed.

Still, the gunfire raged around them.

Strider was there a second later and gave Paris another smile. "Ready for the next one?"

"Absolutely." He didn't glance at his throbbing thigh. There would be time to patch himself up later. He'd have to remove the bullet; it hadn't gone all the way through and he could feel the little metal cylinder abrading his muscle.

Of course, he'd have to find a woman and screw her to heal.

Once, he would have laughed happily at that. More and more, he hated himself, his actions, and the women who accepted him. *Better a woman than a man.* His stomach clenched at that. As dependent on sex as he was, he *had* to be with someone. If he couldn't find a woman…

"Come on," he growled, and he, Amun and Strider joined the fray.

Blood dripped from him onto the ground, leaving a crimson trail that blended with the puddles left over from Anya's storm. His legs shook and he stumbled once.

He never found another target; the Hunters had already been defeated. All but one were dead, and that one was sleeping. Three of Paris's friends had been shot, and Lucien had to flash Gideon back to the fortress in Buda to recuperate, his stomach riddled with holes.

Suddenly tired, Paris sank to the ground. Water and blood soaked his pants, and it probably looked as if he'd wet them, but he didn't care. *I didn't get to kill anyone,* he thought with disappointment. He wanted a Hunter to jump from the bushes. He wanted to attack that Hunter. Wanted to slice a blade through the man's throat. Wanted to stab over and over and finally, hopefully, release some of the turmoil inside himself.

As he dug his fingers into his throbbing wound, Lucien flashed the living Hunter to their dungeon. A dungeon that had gone virtually unused for centuries and now seemed to welcome a new occupant every day. They might as well place a welcome mat in front of the fortress with all the traffic they were getting.

Paris didn't find the bullet until a few minutes later, when Lucien returned. The warrior was pale, shaking.

"You okay?" Paris managed to work past clenched teeth. Fuck, that hurt! The metal was slick and kept slipping from his grip.

"He awoke and stabbed himself with a little knife he'd stuffed in his pocket before I even set him down. Got me in the neck, too." Blood oozed from a perfect hole in Lucien's neck. "Now I'm being summoned to transport the others." Even as he spoke, his eyes glazed over and his body slowed its movements.

Death had called him to action. No telling how long his spirit would be gone as he and his demon escorted souls to heaven. Or hell. He could have taken his body, but probably hadn't wanted to deal with his aching neck.

Paris sympathized. What would it take to get the bullet out of his thigh?

When he finally achieved success, his shaky arm fell limply to his side, the compressed metal tumbling out of his fingers. Strider plopped beside him, unharmed, and motioned to his bleeding wound with a tilt of his chin.

"Maybe work on your reflexes for next time."

"Fuck you."

His friend grinned. "I'm flattered, but have to decline. You know I don't swing that way."

Paris's head fell back and he stared up at the lightning storm still shielding the temple. "I walked right into that one."

"Well, not everyone can be as smart *and* as beautiful as me."

Strider had to have the last word, so Paris pressed his lips together and didn't comment. To distract himself, he scanned the temple to see what the others were doing.

Amun stood off to the side, observing as usual. Blood coated his left hand. *His* bullet had gone straight through, lucky bastard. Lucien's body was still vertical, still unmoving. Sabin was polishing one of his blades.

Just like home.

He rubbed his temples in an attempt to assuage the oncoming ache, idly studying the rest of the occupants. Danika was laughing at—

Paris's eyes widened. What the hell? Danika? Here? Shock pounded through him as he lumbered to his feet. A wave of dizziness joined the shock, causing him to sway, but he managed to remain upright. In the trail of blood and water leading to his feet, shimmery images had formed a living wall.

"Do you see that?"

"See what?" Strider asked. "Lucien? Dude should've taken his body with him. Why'd he leave it, anyway?"

"No. That." Shock only intensifying, Paris pointed.

Strider arched a brow. "Sabin? Yeah. Ugly as always, but that's no reason to look ready to vomit."

"No, the woman."

There was a heavy pause. Then, "What woman?" Now Strider sounded confused.

Paris was confused. The images were in full color, different scenes playing throughout, as though separate movie screens had been erected. The only common thread, he realized, was the star of the show: the lovely Danika.

In all of them, she hovered in the shadows, merely watching those around her. Much like Amun. In some, angels frolicked happily. In others, demons laughed evilly. In the final scene, however, Danika stood front and center. Her left arm was outstretched—and Pandora's box rested in her palm.

He hadn't seen the box in thousands of years, but he remembered every corner, every embossed jewel, every facet of the object that had led to his downfall. Nothing about the box had changed. Ivory bones taken from the body of the dying goddess of oppression were fused together, forming a deceptively small square. Rubies, emeralds, diamonds and sapphires sparkled from their midst.

When Promiscuity realized what it was looking at, the demon roared, clanging through Paris's mind, desperate to destroy the very thing that had bound it so torturously for so long.

Smash the box. Smash it!

"I can't. It's not real."

The demon paid no heed to his words. *Smash!*

Despite the screams inside his head, Paris hobbled closer. In that final, living portrait, Danika stretched the box out farther, as if offering it to him. She even winked at him.

His jaw nearly hit the floor, the pain of his wound forgotten. What the hell?

CHAPTER FOURTEEN

"HOW ARE YOU FEELING, Danika?"

Danika perched on the edge of Reyes's bed, her head between her legs, her breathing shallow and rough. She couldn't seem to fill her lungs, only seemed to scratch them with what little air she dragged in. An hour had passed—an eternity, maybe—since Aeron had delivered his "I think I killed her" when speaking of Danika's grandmother.

She'd demanded every detail from Aeron, and what he'd said had meshed with what Stefano's men had seen. *I carried her into a building. She was already bleeding, already hurting. I raised my claws. She screamed. That is all I know.*

Danika's shock had worn off, and grief, sorrow and fury had taken its place, blending together inside her. She couldn't remember leaving the cell. Didn't recall walking into Reyes's bedroom. He must have carried her here. As Aeron had carried her grandmother to her death?

"I need to see them," she managed to gasp out. "I need to see my mother and my sister." Did they know about Grandma Mallory? Had they witnessed the terrible event? Oh, God. Oh, God, oh, God. Tears flooded her eyes. She would find them, tell them if they didn't know, and then she would come back here and stab Aeron in his blackened heart.

No, scratch that. She would stab Aeron first. Then she would have at least one piece of good news to pass on to her family. The thought failed to cheer her.

Warm, strong hands curled on her upper arms and slowly dragged her up. The dark that haunted her dreams was suddenly weighing down her present. But Reyes loomed in front of her, determined to save her. "I am sorry this happened, angel. I am."

Her chin trembled and her throat constricted. "You're sorry?" she said, her fury blooming ahead of all the other emotions in an effort to save herself. "You played a part in this, you fucking bastard, so you can leave me the hell alone. She was a good woman. Caring and tender. Loving. Admit it. You're happy she's gone, aren't you? Aren't you?" she screamed when he didn't reply.

"I am not happy. Your pain hurts me."

"And you love to be hurt, right?"

"Danika, I—" A pause, heavy, oppressive. "Aeron said he *thinks* he killed her. Perhaps he did not. Perhaps she survived."

"An eighty-year-old woman against a supernaturally strong demon?" She laughed without humor. "Please."

Reyes's fingers bit deeper, almost painfully, as he shook her. "Don't you dare give up hope."

"Hope." She uttered another of those humorless laughs. "Hope is a demon worse than your Pain."

Reyes released her as if she'd suddenly sprouted horns and stabbed him with them. Wait. He would have liked that, she thought darkly, and wouldn't have moved away. Guess he'd released her as if she'd tried to kiss him again.

"Answer me true. Did you make that comparison because of your hate for what might have been done or because you believe Hope truly is a demon?"

"Does it matter?"

"Yes."

She shrugged, going numb again, so numb she couldn't make herself care about the conversation anymore. "Both." What a roller coaster she'd been on these past two days. It was too much.

"How do you know Hope is a demon?" he demanded. "Humans always think of Hope as good and wonderful and right."

"So it's true?" What else was out there, stealing joy and destroying lives? "I should be surprised."

"How?"

Another shrug. "Grandma Mallory used to tell me stories. I thought they were harmless, her mind's way of coping with the chaos of her life."

"In this," he admitted reluctantly, "she was right. Hope is indeed a demon. A monster now housed inside an equally treacherous immortal warrior."

Like you, she almost said but stopped herself. Reyes had not proven himself to be evil. "You know him—it?" Her lips curled in distaste. "Again, why aren't I surprised? Grandma told me Hope purposely raises expectations, makes people believe there's a potential for a miracle, and then he crushes those expectations, leaving nothing but ash and despair." Stefano was right. The world would be a better place without a demon like that.

"We are not all like that," Reyes said, as though he'd read her mind. "Hope was given to a warrior like me, yes. Galen was his name. But he was a corrupt man possessed by a corrupt demon and combined they are more dangerous than anything in this fortress. When I knew them, they delighted in uplifting and then crushing those around them."

She wrapped her arms around her middle, cold again. So cold. From fury to nothing to *this.* A torturous gamut. She'd feared this day for two weeks, dreaded learning that her amazing grandmother had been murdered while Danika was too busy running to help her.

Reyes's gaze bored into her, piercing like a laser. "I need honesty from you, Danika. Did you hear any of what you've just told me from the Hunters?"

"No." They'd mentioned nothing about either Galen or Hope.

A moment passed in silence, she and Reyes staring at each

other. What he was thinking, she could only guess. That she had to die now and there could be no more saving her? That she would go back on her word now that she knew her grandmother was dead?

Sweet Grandma Mallory. Memories of a long-ago night played through her mind. Stars had twinkled from the sky as she and her grandmother made camp inside her tree house.

Lie back, baby girl, and Grandma will tell you another story.

Shuddering, Danika had climbed into her sleeping bag. Cool night scents floated on the breeze, but they had failed to calm her. Grandma's stories were not like the fairy tales her sister liked to read her. *"Will this one scare me?"*

"Maybe. But it's okay to be scared sometimes. I don't want you to be like me. I want you stronger, better equipped to deal."

"I don't want to deal. I don't like to be scared."

"No one does, but feeling the emotion is good. Gives you a chance to prove you're stronger than it is."

"O-okay. I'll listen to the story."

"That's my girl."

Those tales of demons had frightened her back then—and that was when she'd considered them simple fiction—but she hadn't let them keep her up at night or stop her from enjoying life. Because of her grandmother. When her parents would have coddled her because of her nightmares, Grandma Mallory had helped her find a core of strength so Danika wouldn't one day fall under the pressure as she had done. She'd taught Danika how to fight the evil inside her head. How to win.

And it had worked…until Reyes and his friends had entered her life. Now, she was that frightened little girl again. Sadly, there would be no more deluding herself into thinking those bedtime stories had been make-believe. Her grandmother had seen things. Ugly things, evil things. *Real* things.

"What other stories did she relay to you?" Reyes asked.

"If I tell you, will you help me find her…her…body? Help me give her a proper burial?"

"Yes. *If* she is dead. I still think there's a good chance she's alive."

Don't you dare start to hope. You just admitted Hope is a demon. Danika allowed the stories to occupy every available space in her mind, sorting through them, trying to pull the most important facts front and center. How much time passed, she didn't know. But when she focused, Reyes was sitting in a chair directly across from her—close enough to touch— patiently and silently waiting.

"Did you know there were more demons than there were immortal warriors?" she found herself asking softly. "Without the box, some had to be placed inside the prisoners of Tartarus. Demons like Fear. Loneliness. Greed."

Only for a moment did he appear disbelieving. He worried two fingers over his jaw. "Were any placed inside the Titans?" he asked, but the question was not for her. Clearly, he was thinking aloud. "They were prisoners at that time. Of course, there were hundreds of other immortals locked away during any given decade, so…" He shook his head. "No. No, this isn't possible. Had this happened, I would have known."

"Maybe your demon didn't know. It was locked inside a tiny, dark box. And I doubt your gods tell you everything. Besides, all I know is what I was told. Believe it or don't believe it. I don't care."

"But how could your grandmother know these things…" He stopped, sucked in a breath. "She was like you, was she not? She had visions?"

Danika nodded sadly. "We've been haunted by demons our entire lives." *She helped me deal with mine, but I failed to save her from hers. I should have stayed with her, guarded her.*

That dark skin Danika so loved to touch slowly paled. "This is…this is too much to absorb," Reyes said. "More demons?

More possessed warriors?" He shook his head, scrubbed a hand down his face. "Do you know what this means?"

"That you have to slice my throat now?" The question was devoid of sentiment.

He *tsked.* "I told you. I will not hurt you. Not now, not ever." Then, "Danika, this means we have been intertwined since the beginning."

There was awe in his tone. Reverence. His meaning, however, escaped her. "The beginning of what?" she asked, suddenly so tired she could barely hold up her head. *After all the self-defense and combat lessons I took, I couldn't save the woman who watched me every summer, played hide-and-seek with me in the woods and taught me how to ride a bike.* Was she looking down from heaven, ashamed? Was she now at peace with the angels they'd both seen in their dreams?

Reyes cleared his throat. "We have been intertwined since the beginning of my creation, I think."

That would mean fate had played a role in both their lives, and right now Danika didn't want to consider fate.

"The grandmother who told you of Hope, she is the one…" His voice trailed off, as if he feared broaching the topic again.

"Yes. She is the one Aeron—" sweet Jesus, saying it was hard "—killed." *There'll be no more stories from her.* Danika squeezed her eyelids tightly closed, blocking the tears forming there. *As soon as I get my strength back, Aeron is mine.*

Gentle fingers smoothed over her brow, along the curve of her nose.

She shivered, surprised by the warmth and comfort seeping from his skin into hers. How could she sit here, letting a demon touch her like this? Letting a demon—*Pain*—console her? "Tell me about the warrior who houses Hope." She would give the information to Stefano, no hesitation. It wouldn't be a betrayal to Reyes to feed Hunters data about a man he despised.

One of Reyes's brows arched. "Why?"

"To distract me. I don't want to think about my… I just don't want to think anymore."

Again Reyes reached out, gently hooked a strand of her hair behind her ear. "Galen and I were friends once. Soldiers in Zeus's elite army. I didn't yet know that he was the kind of man who would smile to your face but stab you the moment your back was turned."

"Where is he now?"

"I know not. After the possession, he disappeared." Reyes leaned down and kissed her cheek, the brush of his mouth soft and gentle. "Is there anything I can get you? Anything you need?"

"I'm going to destroy your friend, Reyes." The admission sprang from her, unstoppable. "Aeron. I know I told you I wouldn't, but…"

He sighed, weary. "All I ask is that you think about your actions. Aeron is stronger than you. He is immortal, you are mortal. You could probably hurt him, but most likely he will not die. *He* can hurt *you,* and you will crumble."

"He has to sleep. I don't mind taking his head while he sleeps. Or…" Slowly she faced him, lids cracking, parting. The room receded, the warrior becoming her only focus. "You're as strong as he is. You've defeated him before. He came for me, but you stopped him."

As she spoke, a curtain of unease fell over Reyes's harsh features.

"Kill him for me," she beseeched.

"Danika—"

"Kill him, and I'll do anything you want. I'll cut you as many times as you need."

"Danika," he said again. In the three syllables it had taken to utter her name, she'd heard a war being waged. He was fighting himself.

Twice she'd watched him exchange blows with Aeron, but never had she seen such a look of torture on his face. A lump formed in her throat, and she swallowed it, felt it settle deep in her stomach. Still, she didn't take back her request.

"As I said, your grandmother might be alive. Why won't you consider the possibility?"

"Aeron remembers her bloody body." What's more, the Hunters had seen Aeron carry an unconscious woman away. Not that she could admit that little tidbit.

"But Aeron did not recall rendering the deathblow. Warrior that he is, he would not forget something like that. That has to mean that when he left her, she was still breathing."

Maybe…possibility…what if…

"In the morning, I will take you to your sister and your mother and perhaps you can locate your grandmother. Tonight, I will have Torin hunt— Uh, damn. Find them. Torin will find them for you."

Danika stiffened, every muscle suddenly humming with tension. "Will he hurt them? If he hurts them, I'll—"

"No, no. You have my word. No harm shall befall them."

She believed him. Stupid of her, but she did. She had no other lifeline at the moment.

"No matter what, we *will* find your grandmother, as well. You will know, one way or another, what happened to her."

No matter what. One way or another. Ominous phrases. And yet, the second stirring of hated hope *did* spark to life. Maybe…possibility…what if…the phrases once again swept through her mind. It was human nature to wish for the best, she supposed, and too hard to believe otherwise without solid proof. She hadn't seen her grandmother's body; as Reyes had reminded her, Aeron had said he *thought* he'd killed her, not that he truly had.

Grandma Mallory *could* be alive.

The numbness encasing her began to melt, leaving flickers of relief. "I'd rather leave tonight," she said. "Aeron knows where they are. Make him tell."

"I tried. Twice. But do you really want to continually remind him that they're out there? When he craves their deaths? Torin can do this, I have no doubt. He just needs time."

She clasped his wrist and peered up at him, wanting to kiss him and push him away at the same time. To hug him and hit him. "Thank you."

"You are so lovely," he whispered. Then he shook his head, as if he couldn't believe he'd uttered those words and needed to clear his thoughts. "In the cell you said you paint to purge yourself of your nightmares. Why don't you paint tonight? Perhaps it will soothe you."

Do not soften. You are already too close to the edge. "You just want another glimpse inside my head."

"Can I not want both your comfort *and* the knowledge you possess of the gods?"

, She released him, feeling bereft, and shrugged. "I would need the proper supplies." There was a bloom of excitement in her chest at the thought of holding a brush. She'd never thought to paint again.

Twin pink circles suddenly colored Reyes's cheeks, and he cleared his throat. He straightened, looking away from her. "I—I already have everything you will need."

Danika studied his profile. His nose was a shade longer than the other warriors', very aristocratic. His lashes were thick and curled up toward his brows. His jaw jutted stubbornly. "What do you mean?"

"I visited your home. I had your purse, your address, and after you left, I could not stay away. I traveled to your home, saw your supplies and bought some for the fortress. Just in case."The admission croaked from him. "Will you use them?"

Just in case what? "I— Maybe." He'd been inside her home? What had he thought of her small and cluttered house? Loved? Hated? And why did the image of him surrounded by her things feel so…right?

Reyes didn't try to pressure her. He simply nodded as if he understood her reluctance. "I need to leave for a little while, talk with Torin. Will you be all right on your own?"

She wasn't sure she would be all right ever again, but she said, "Yes. Of course."

Reyes faced her, leaned down and placed a soft kiss on her lips. Hers parted automatically, welcoming him inside. The hot length of his tongue pressed forward, slowly, tenderly, giving comfort rather than passion. She accepted, too raw to resist.

"Angel," he breathed.

Her arms wound around his neck of their own accord, holding him close. Perhaps she would hold on forever. Here, right now, there was no pain or loss or what if, only a strong man who scared *her* demons away.

His fingers settled on her waist, and he pulled her as close to him as he could get her. Her legs parted to allow him the final contact, placing hardness to softness. A gasp left her as a jolt of pure desire speared her, chasing away her fatigue.

She remembered how he'd kissed her this morning and experienced no real pleasure. Until she'd hurt him. He'd even told her that he could not really *feel* without a sting, a bite or a scratch.

Even though this kiss represented the passing of his strength to her, she wanted him to like it. She told herself she wanted him to like it so that he would continue to protect her. That if the time came, he would choose her over Aeron and slay the man. She told herself it was because if Reyes desired her, he would not renege on his word. He would take her to her family in the morning.

Sadly, she knew she lied.

Deep down, she wanted him, desired him madly, and had from the first. She'd been a captive here and had found herself face-to-face with him after he stormed into the room she'd been locked in, demanding a healer for Ashlyn. It had seemed as though a match were being struck inside her chest, lighting everything on fire. Burning and blistering. Every man she'd ever dated, every man she'd ever kissed, and the two men she'd slept with over the years had faded from her mind as if they'd never existed.

So odd. Besides her dreams and her secret paintings, she'd never been a fanciful girl. Oh, she believed in love—her parents might have divorced when she was just starting her teens, and her dad might have taken off and begun another family, forgetting the one he already had, but she did believe. Her grandparents had loved each other madly, only parting for death.

And while Danika had never experienced the emotion herself, she'd always been content to wait, not to rush out and force it as so many of her friends had done. She had lived as if there would always be a tomorrow, as if the here and now were of no significance. As if the future meant more than the present.

Everything had changed after the kidnapping. Her entire world had crumbled and as she'd slowly rebuilt the pieces of her life, she'd realized a future was *not* guaranteed. Here and now mattered. Nothing else.

Right now, she had Reyes.

She would have to hurt him to make him like her. Before, watching him cut himself, she hadn't thought herself capable of such a deed. Now... "I want to," she said, only realizing she'd spoken aloud when the words echoed in her ears.

He nipped at her bottom lip. "What? What do you want?" His fingers tightened on her hips, digging into the bone.

"You." She had trouble catching her breath.

The fine lines around his eyes softened. "You don't know what you're asking for, angel."

"Show me, then."

"No." He meshed their lips back together and his tongue rolled over and under hers, his addicting flavor a drug to her starved senses.

An Important Message from the Editors

Dear Reader,

Because you've chosen to read one of our fine novels, we'd like to say "thank you!" And, as a **special** way to thank you, we're offering to send you a choice of <u>two more</u> of the books you love so well **plus** two exciting Mystery Gifts — absolutely <u>FREE</u>!

Please enjoy them with our compliments...

Pam Powers

Peel off seal and place inside...

The Editor's "Thank You" Free Gifts Include:

- *2 Romance OR 2 Suspense books!*
- *2 exciting mystery gifts!*

Yes!

I have placed my Editor's "Thank You" seal in the space provided at right. Please send me 2 free books, which I have selected, and 2 fabulous mystery gifts. I understand I am under no obligation to purchase any books, as explained on the back of this card.

PLACE FREE GIFT SEAL HERE

☐ **ROMANCE**
    193 MDL ERQS 393 MDL ERRG

☐ **SUSPENSE**
    192 MDL ERYS 392 MDL ERQ4

FIRST NAME	LAST NAME

ADDRESS

APT.#	CITY

STATE/PROV.	ZIP/POSTAL CODE

Thank You!

The Reader Service — Here's How It Works:

Accepting your 2 free books and 2 free gifts places you under no obligation to buy anything. You may keep the books and gifts and return the shipping statement marked "cancel." If you do not cancel, about a month later we'll send you 3 additional books and bill you just $5.49 each in the U.S. or $5.99 each in Canada, plus 25¢ shipping & handling per book and applicable taxes if any.* That's the complete price and — compared to cover prices starting from $6.99 each in the U.S. and $8.50 each in Canada — it's quite a bargain! You may cancel at any time, but if you choose to continue, every month we'll send you 3 more books, which you may either purchase at the discount price or return to us and cancel your subscription.

*Terms and prices subject to change without notice. Sales tax applicable in N.Y. Canadian residents will be charged applicable provincial taxes and GST. All orders subject to approval. Books received may vary. Credit or debit balances in a customer's account(s) may be offset by any other outstanding balance owed by or to the customer. Please allow 4 to 6 weeks for delivery. Offer available while quantities last.

If offer card is missing write to: The Reader Service, 3010 Walden Ave., P.O. Box 1867, Buffalo, NY 14240-1867

BUSINESS REPLY MAIL
FIRST-CLASS MAIL   PERMIT NO. 717   BUFFALO, NY

POSTAGE WILL BE PAID BY ADDRESSEE

THE READER SERVICE
3010 WALDEN AVE
PO BOX 1341
BUFFALO NY 14240-8571

NO POSTAGE
NECESSARY
IF MAILED
IN THE
UNITED STATES

How long since she'd been held like this? How long since she'd stopped running and simply *experienced?*

"We have to stop soon."

"What?" Her arms tightened around him. "No!"

"Must." His fingers wrapped around her wrists, gripping firmly, branding her. He moved her arms away from his body, and then he dared to release her.

Her eyelids flickered open. He was sweating, his lips compressed in a thin slash. His breathing was uneven. Lines of tension bracketed his beautiful dark eyes—eyes alive with a thousand different needs, needs he would not allow her to meet.

He wanted her this time, it seemed, but she hadn't hurt him. He'd said such a thing was impossible. What did that mean?

"You don't need a man pawing you right now." One step, two, he backed away.

She flattened her palms against her thighs, nails digging deep. "You weren't pawing me."

"But I wanted to."

Would she have cared? Surprisingly, she didn't think so. He'd given her hope, hated hope, but she was grateful. Or had his demon overtaken her mind again?

Reaching out, he smoothed several strands of hair from her brow. His arm shook. "Rest, angel. Tomorrow we travel, and we will have to move quickly and remain in the shadows."

Because of the Hunters, she silently finished for him. The people she should have been helping. Feeling hollow, she nodded.

"If you change your mind about painting, the supplies are through that door." He pointed.

She sighed, watching as he turned on his booted heels and strode from the room. There was a knife in his hand.

WHEN REYES REACHED the bathroom in the empty bedroom across the hall, he collapsed onto the cold, hard floor. He'd done his best to keep his beast hidden from Danika. He hadn't wanted her to know how close he'd been to ripping off her clothing and stabbing himself over and over again while he pounded into her soft body—how close he'd been to begging *her* to stab him.

He was surprised by the depths of his desire for her. She hadn't hurt him, yet he'd been ready, eager. A first, and too shocking to believe.

He needed to contact Lucien and tell him about the other demons, the other possessed warriors. He needed to find Torin and have the warrior start tracking Danika's mother, sister and possibly her grandmother. But not like this. Reyes was too on edge, the demon too loud inside his head, clamoring for pain. The need hadn't been this wild in weeks, so it had taken him by surprise. How he'd maintained his control, how he'd kept from hurting Danika, he didn't know. Why it had happened, he didn't know, either.

With a shaky hand, he tore at the waist of his pants. His nails were claws and cut the skin, skin on fire and too tight for his bones. He was smiling as his cock jumped free, but there was no relief. He ached, oh, gods, he ached from the pleasure of Danika's scent, her lovely eyes feasting on him, her lips pressing against his.

His fingers wrapped around the thick base of his shaft, so taut his knuckles instantly blanched, and he hissed in a breath. *Not my hand,* he pretended, *but Danika's.* Yes, he could easily imagine her soft, sweet hand holding him, squeezing him to this razor edge of pleasure-pain.

Reyes moaned, holding himself all the tighter as he pumped up, then down. With his other hand, he clutched the knife he'd already palmed and pressed the cold tip against his thigh. *Do it. Cut.* On an upward glide, he sank the blade hard, so hard. The skin broke and blood trickled. On a downward slide, he dug the tip deeper, nicking a vein.

Not enough. Not nearly enough.

There were sharp grooves on the hilt, and those grooves bit at his hand, drawing even more blood. Self-loathing rose inside him as he slicked the knife's apex through muscle, not stopping until he hit the bone.

Why can I not be normal? Why can I not take a beautiful woman with the gentleness she deserves?

He twisted his wrist, digging a hole into his femur. His head fell back and he roared at the exquisite headiness, pleasure zooming from one corner of his body to the other, a drug, a demon all its own.

Just a little more.

Up and down he continued to pump, the path slick because of his blood. His hips writhed as he continued to twist the knife. There was another sharp lance of pain, another sultry wave of pleasure.

What if he had no need for pain? What if Danika were here, sucking him deep into her mouth?

"Yes, yes," he chanted. Her sunshine hair would spill over his legs; perhaps he would see the pink tip of her tongue laving the thick head of his penis. He might feel the light scrape of her teeth every time she descended, taking him to the back of her throat.

Would she like the taste of him?

Maybe she would take him in her mouth while he licked and sucked *her.* Another moan escaped him. She would be wet, wet for him and him alone. Her taste would be like the ambrosia he blended into his wine.

She would drip with desire. *For me, only me.*

For us, the demon snapped, raging inside his mind.

Reyes clenched his teeth. *For me. Never us.* You *are the reason I cannot have her.*

I *didn't open the box, now did I?*

Reyes gave the knife yet another twist, and the tip sliced the bone in two, driving straight into another muscle. At the moment of penetration, a climax ripped through him. He roared loud and long, his muscles contracting, hot seed jetting from him and blending with his blood. Both scalded his skin, like battery acid on silk.

Only when the last surge ended did he lose his last bit of strength and sag, completely depleted. His arms fell to his sides, lifeless. He was panting, could taste metal in his mouth. During orgasm, he'd bitten the inside of his cheek.

Can't stay here. Have to clean up before someone finds me. Slowly his eyelids cracked open, golden light seeping into his consciousness. He needed to find Torin and— His thoughts skidded to a sickened halt.

Danika stood in the bathroom's doorway, staring down at him in horror.

CHAPTER FIFTEEN

DANIKA DIDN'T KNOW HOW to assimilate what she'd just witnessed. *That* was what Reyes needed to experience pleasure? Before, part of her had thought she could maybe give him what he craved. But he hadn't just cut skin. He'd cut veins, muscle and even bone. There was so much blood, a seemingly never-ending river pooling and congealing around him.

Now he was looking at her through hooded eyes, lips grim, a crimson splatter on his chin. "What are you doing here?" Cold, no emotion.

"I fo-followed you," she managed to get out. "I—I—" She was shaking so badly, and her throat kept trying to close around a surge of bile.

Had other women hurt him like this? Pleasured him like that? The thought disturbed her, but not as it should have. She didn't like the thought of other women meeting his needs. She didn't like the thought of other women doing something to him that she had not done—or perhaps could not do.

Reyes lumbered to his feet, swayed. His thigh gushed. She thought she saw the severed bone underneath the muscle and couldn't glance away. Her gaze was held captive and tracked every drop that spilled. His penis rose proudly, still thick and full, smeared with desire and blood, the heavy weight of his testicles drawn tight underneath.

Even possessed as he was by the demon of Pain, she didn't understand how he could find release in so brutal a deed.

"Look at me," he barked.

"I am." A broken whisper.

"At my face." He jerked up his pants and fastened them.

The action released her from the trancelike state. Gradually she dragged her gaze up his body. His navel was surrounded by the faintest dusting of hair—how had she missed it before?—and his stomach was roped with hard lines of muscle, a testament to his inhuman strength.

Her tremors increased the closer she got to his face. A shadow beard dusted his jaw, hardening the angles of his face, making him appear all the more dangerous.

He was scowling at her, his lips peeled back from his teeth. His nostrils flared as he inhaled. "I told you to stay in my room."

His eyes, normally polished onyx, were tinted red. Glowing. Pulsing. She gulped. "I couldn't, I didn't—"

"Go!"

"Don't talk to me like that. Got it?"

"Leave. Please." A whisper.

As he stood there, panting, angry, bloody as if he'd just returned from a war, she lost her…whatever it was she'd been feeling. Disgust? Confusion? Shock? *I want to paint him like this,* she thought. He was a thing of beauty. Dark, a combination of cinnamon and honey, with eyes like an eclipsed sun—a person didn't know whether to stare, blind to all else, or look quickly away.

What intrigued her most, however, was his tattoo. That butterfly, with its wings spread in midflight, half consuming his chest and neck, seemed to be watching her, beckoning her closer. It had always been ominous and harsh, almost evil, and yet it now appeared…gentle. The colored skin was glittering, a mix of ruby, onyx and sapphire. The usually sharp-tipped, forged-of-steel wings were somehow softened.

I've seen this before, she thought. *I've* painted *this before.*

Hadn't she? There was something unerringly familiar about it, though not enough to jog her mind completely. Maybe it was the fact that she'd seen a few of the other warriors' tattoos. Each man had worn the mark in a different location and each had been a different color. Maddox was branded on his back, Lucien on his chest. Aeron, she thought with a shudder, all over.

Danika found herself reaching out, arm shaking, desperate to feel Reyes's brand, to know the texture and the temperature. Hot and raised? Or cold and smooth?

He jolted backward, slamming into the wall, his arms spread to hold himself up. The sink jostled, the soap slipping and falling to the floor. *Thump.* "Do not touch me, Danika."

Her cheeks heated with mortification as her hand dropped to her side. "Sorry," she muttered. "I'm sorry." *You knew better. He's feral right now, so you have to be careful.*

"Don't apologize." Motions clipped, he swiped a towel from beside the sink and bent down. Back and forth he mopped the blood. "*I* am sorry you witnessed that. Please, just…return to my room. Please. I will join you shortly." The request was disjointed, proving how rattled he really was.

"I'll help you clean up. I—"

"No!"

He shouted so loudly, she cringed. Damn it! Where was her courage? Where was her vow to never back down from another fight?

Immediately after the echo quieted, Reyes stiffened, ceased moving and rushed out, "I *am* sorry. Again. You did nothing wrong, only offered to help. But I always clean up my mess, and I will not allow you to dirty your precious hands."

Precious? Her? There wasn't a drop of sarcasm in his tone, only absolute sincerity.

He pivoted, keeping his back to her as he skidded into motion. "Please, Danika. Go."

He was embarrassed by what he'd done, she realized. He

was ashamed. She didn't know what to say to soothe him. Didn't know what to *think* to soothe herself.

Danika backed out of the bathroom. She didn't look away from Reyes, who was still cleaning, still avoiding her, until her shoulder rammed into the door frame and she had no other choice. When she reached the hallway, she pressed herself against the wall. Tremors racked her.

She wanted to find Ashlyn, discuss this with someone who just might be able to understand, but her friend had left with Maddox and the others early this morning. Ashlyn had conversations to listen to, she'd said, and it had surprised Danika that the ever-protective Maddox had agreed to the journey. Should she go back as Reyes had ordered? Or stay and wait for him? Both appealed to her, but for different reasons. Leaving would give her time to calm down, to think. Staying would provide an opportunity to go with Reyes when he spoke with Torin about her family.

Admit it. You're worried about Reyes. You want *to see him again.*

She stayed.

Fifteen minutes passed, the sounds of shuffling feet, running water and curses filling her ears. Strangely, impatience kept its distance as her mind rolled and churned like a storm about to break.

She had some major decisions to make.

She was due to contact Stefano later tonight and the tiny cell phone he'd given her was burning a hole in her pocket. What would he do if she failed to call? What did she want him to do? With Reyes seeing to her every need, things were…complicated.

Oh, she still wanted revenge. If she discovered that Aeron truly had killed her grandmother, she would return to his cell and she would not hesitate to cut off his head. But what if he hadn't killed Grandma Mallory?

Don't you dare give up hope. Reyes's voice whispered through her mind, even though they both knew how evil hope could be.

Could she allow the Hunters to storm into his home, capture the residents, hurt them, lock them away and ultimately slaughter them? Reyes would not be excluded from that. They wanted him, hated him. And she would not be able to warn him because he would warn the others—which totally defeated the goal of keeping Reyes intact, the only true decision she'd made.

She'd thought herself in deep. Now... What should she do? She felt torn between two sides, straddling a fence with no freaking clue as to which way to fall. Something would happen and she'd lean one way. Then something else would happen and she'd lean the other.

"Danika."

At the sound of Reyes's voice, she blinked open her eyelids. When had she closed them? He loomed in front of her, this warrior who so conflicted her. He'd cleaned himself up, had seemingly scrubbed away his emotions as surely as he'd scrubbed away the blood. His expression was blank, and yet her heart fluttered as it always did when he was near.

"You waited," he said.

If that pleased or angered him, she couldn't tell. "Yes," she said, breathing deeply of his fresh pine scent. He wore a black T-shirt and new pants. "I'd like to go with you to speak with Torin."

His head tilted to the side, his gaze boring into her. "You are not...scared of me?"

"No." Truth. She was just more confused than ever.

A sigh slipped from him, and beneath the casual resonance was a rushing river of relief. "I find I am once again helpless against you."

As helpless as she was against him? "I don't understand this." Not the connection between them, and not their mutual unwillingness to hurt each other when they were both supposed to do so.

"Neither do I." He held out his hand. "I will take you to see

Torin, but you are not to touch him. You are not even to get within reaching distance of him."

"O-kay."

"This is serious. Do you remember the plague that blasted through Buda when you were here?"

She nodded, twining their fingers together. At first contact, warmth speared her.

"One brush of his skin against yours and there will be another one."

REYES LOVED THE FEEL of his fingers intertwined with Danika's. Every time she'd been alone and he'd come upon her, touched her, her skin had been as cold as ice. Seconds after touching her, that ice always melted into him, a deliciously painful prickling.

Painful.

He tried not to think about what Danika had witnessed. The thoughts flowed, anyway. What a monster he must have appeared, taking pleasure in so gory an act. Had he cried out her name? He could not be certain.

He rounded a corner, wanting to look back at her but not allowing himself to do so. She had seen him at his worst, but she hadn't run screaming. He took what little comfort he could in that. Having seen her shocked expression, however, he'd known—he knew—soul-deep that he could never bring Pain into their relationship. Which meant he could not make love to her. Ever. *You already knew that.*

He thought perhaps he'd subconsciously entertained a ray of hope that one day he *could* make Danika his, totally and completely, without worrying that he would hurt her, need her to hurt him or that she would become a killer afterward. Foolish hope. Hated hope. Truly a demon.

It's for the best, he assured himself. His angel deserved only goodness. She deserved a gentle man, someone who would make her laugh. Someone who would not fill her with disgust. With herself, with him.

Just like that, jealousy awoke inside him, a beast far more ferocious than Pain, screaming inside his head, scratching at his skull.

"You're squeezing my hand," Danika said on a pained gasp.

Instantly he relaxed his grip. "I am sorry." Would he ever be able to let her go?

"I'm tougher than you think," she said. "I'd just rather not face one of your friends with my bitch-slap hand broken."

She meant the words as a joke, probably hoping to lighten his mood, but he took them to heart. Here, in the fortress, she needed every ounce of her strength. His friends were a threat to her well-being, and she would never be welcomed as Ashlyn and Anya ultimately had been. Fighting to bury a swell of emotions, he lifted her palm and placed a gentle kiss on the inside of her wrist. "I will be more careful with you, I swear it."

A shiver moved through her.

They reached the end of the hall and stopped. Torin's door was closed. Muffled voices carried through the wood. Laughing voices? Reyes's brows drew together as he knocked. The voices ceased abruptly.

Cameo opened the door and Reyes was momentarily rendered speechless with shock. Beautiful as always, petite and dark headed and a vicious warrior only a rare few had been privileged enough to witness in battle—and live to tell the tale—she usually remained alone or in the shadows while at the fortress. Not by choice, he thought, but because the men could not be around her without wanting to kill her. She carried all of the world's misery in her silver eyes and tormented voice.

He'd never heard her laugh before, had never seen her smile. Or not since those long-ago days before they'd opened *dimOu-*

niak. That he'd now witnessed both here, and with Torin, who could not touch another living thing skin to skin—even an immortal—was shocking. Torin usually avoided women like the very plague he harbored inside his deceptively healthy-looking body. He could not have one, so did not usually tempt himself with the presence of one.

What the hell was going on?

"What do you want?" Cameo asked.

Dear gods, the agony. Listening to her was like sinking into a nightmare.

"Why am I suddenly eyeing the hilt of your dagger and hoping to plunge it into my chest?" Danika whispered, confused and a little dazed as she gazed at the female warrior.

To his knowledge, she had not crossed paths with the female warrior last time she'd been here. Which meant this was her first encounter with Misery. The first was always the hardest. "Cover your ears and close your eyes."

For once, she didn't question him and rushed to obey.

"I need to speak with Torin," he told Cameo.

She propped her hip against the door frame. "Well, you can come back later. I was here first. This your woman?"

"Yes," he said, adding without pause, "*You* can come back later." He had to glance away. His chest was hurting, and not in a good way. Was a...romance brewing between Cameo and Torin? Stranger things had happened, he supposed. Like Danika, staying here with him when she could have run again.

"She's pretty."

Exquisite, if you asked him. "Leave, and I will give you the black dagger you admired. The one hanging on my bedroom wall."

Anticipation instantly showered her features. Damn, he'd been looking at her again. The ache returned to his chest. He rubbed the spot just above his heart as Cameo flicked a glance over her shoulder, paused, then faced him once more.

"Fine. I'll go," she said, and stepped around him. As she disappeared down the hall, she called, "But I'm coming back in a few, so make it quick."

Reyes reclaimed Danika's hand—he couldn't go long without touching her in *some* way—her icy skin heating again. She opened her eyes, those magnificent green angel eyes that both cut him and soothed him.

"What happened?" she asked, still a bit dazed.

"Cameo is the keeper of Misery."

"Ah. That explains a lot. Poor woman."

Lips twitching, Reyes led her into Torin's bedroom. A sophisticated computer system consumed the far wall. Monitors flashed different colors and scenes, some displaying the steep hill their fortress rested upon, some the city and its people.

Torin rested in a swivel chair, facing them, arms locked over his chest. He had white hair and green eyes, a shade darker than Danika's, that gleamed wickedly. "What?" he said in the same put-out tone Cameo had used.

"Is there something you want to tell me?" Reyes asked him.

Torin's gaze swept over Danika, intent, before returning to Reyes. "Something you want to tell me?"

"No."

"Well, there's your answer. Why are you here?"

"My family," Danika said, urgency now humming from her. She stepped forward, caught herself and inched back. "Do you know where they are? Aeron mentioned a small town in Oklahoma."

"That info could have been useful a few hours ago." Torin turned and faced his computers. His skill with them was the reason the warriors were so well moneyed. "The guys and I had a chat this morning before they left. Lucien asked me to look for that very same information. See, when you and your family were last here, I placed dye in your food."

Reyes caressed her arm, hoping to relax her. Thankfully she did not erupt at the admission.

"Yours wore off a lot quicker than it was supposed to," Torin continued. "Don't know if it was because you were scared and sweating more or what. The dye was supposed to remain in your system for months. Still, your sister dropped off next, then your grandmother and then your mother. I haven't seen a glimpse of any of you in weeks. Don't worry, I know what you're thinking. I should have placed a tracking chip in your shoes, but didn't think of it until now. Live and learn."

Reyes doubted that was what Danika had been thinking, but he remained quiet.

"Anyway, I've been at the computers for hours, searching for even the slightest glimmer. Nothing."

Danika had stiffened in expectation—and hope?—only to sag in disappointment. He released her hand and wound his arm around her waist, willing his strength into her body. She sank against him. For comfort?

"Until," Torin added, fingers tapping over the keyboard, "this."

Danika stiffened again. "What?" Excitement dripped from the word, saturating the air.

Without glancing up from his monitor, Torin waved a hand in the air. "You've seen Paris bake cookies, right? His skills are pathetic, I know, but that's beside the point. When you eat those cookies, they break down and seem to disappear into your system. Only, they don't disappear. There are lasting effects. Fat, cholesterol and so on.

"Our dye is a special blend of ingredients that modifies a human's body chemistry so each individual gives off a signal all her own. The lasting effects are far stronger than that of a cookie. Better, I remembered they're still traceable even when the dye itself has worn off."

Now Reyes was the one to stiffen. Ashlyn had almost died when she'd ingested an "ingredient" meant only for immortals.

Realizing the path his mind traveled, Torin added, "I wouldn't have used it on the women if Sabin hadn't already tested it on a few Hunters."

Slowly Reyes relaxed. Danika, he realized, was breathing heavily. He squeezed her tight.

"Five minutes," Torin said, "and I'll have a printed map of their current location. You can call me later when you're close to them, and I'll tell you if they've moved."

Now a tremor swept through Danika's slight frame. "My grandmother, do you know where she is, as well?"

A pause. A stiff nod. "I've already backtracked the program to see where she's been, but there's been little activity from her signal this week."

Hope lit Danika's angel face, brightening the entire room. "She's alive, then. She's really alive! Aeron was wrong. If she was dead, she wouldn't be trackable. Right?"

Torin answered without hesitation, his expression deadpan. "Right."

Eyes widening, she tented her hands over her mouth. "Oh, my God. This is…this is…this is the best day of my life!"

With a brilliant laugh, she threw herself at Reyes, her cheek burrowing into the hollow of his neck. Her skin was petal-soft, fragrant with the scent of night skies. "I'm so happy right now I could burst."

Reyes held her, but kept his gaze on Torin. His friend gave a clipped nod in response to Reyes's unspoken question. A dead body, it seemed, could still give off a signal.

Inhaling deeply, Reyes closed his eyes. He held her, loving the feel of her, every muscle he possessed straining toward her. He shook with the effort to remain still, though he could not stop his nails from elongating, his teeth from sharpening. The two only happened when the demon's hunger spiked.

I've already fed you. Just…enjoy her.

They might not have her much longer.

When she learned that a dead body could indeed be tracked… Dread consumed him, and he closed his eyes. She had been offered hope, such evil hope. The same he'd tried to give her earlier. He would not take it away. Yet.

CHAPTER SIXTEEN

"THIS TIME, stay here," Reyes said.

He deposited Danika inside his bedroom and left to do God knew what, shutting the door firmly behind him. She waited several long, agonizing moments before sitting on the edge of the mattress, her gaze never leaving the entrance. When he failed to reappear, she relaxed and tugged the tiny cell phone from her jeans pocket.

Stefano had figured the Lords would search her and take it, maybe use it to try and track him, but he had thought giving her a phone worth the risk. So had she. Everyone carried phones nowadays and she hadn't thought the Lords would automatically assume she'd gotten it from the Hunters. Now, she almost wished Stefano hadn't tucked it into her pocket before drugging her, or that the warriors *had* found it. Then she wouldn't have had a choice to make: to check in or not to check in?

In theory, it was an easy decision. Family won. Always. Things were not always that simple, as she was coming to realize. The Lords had known her family's location but had never struck. A point in their favor. Then again, the Hunters had never tried to hurt her family—but what if she chose to help the Hunters, and they failed to stop the Lords? After all, they had failed all these centuries. The warriors would—perhaps—learn she helped their enemy and they would—definitely—come after her with more fervor.

If she failed to check in, though, the Hunters might try to

sneak inside the fortress and save her. There might be a fight. If Ashlyn returned, she could be hurt, and thereby the baby. Anya, too. Reyes.

Her gaze lowered to her hands. The cell's keypad blurred. Reyes had taken such good care of her. Tomorrow, he was escorting her to her family. Oh, God, her family. All of her conflicting thoughts melted away, her mind focusing completely on her loved ones.

Danika's lips curved in a happy grin. They were alive, and they were together. She didn't know why Grandma Mallory had left her friend's house without word yet had remained in Oklahoma, and she didn't care. She didn't know why the three women had decided to risk capture and stay together; she didn't care. They were alive! That was all that mattered.

She would have to call Stefano and buy herself a little more time to figure this out. And she would have to do it now, before Reyes returned. Tamping down a wave of dread, she dialed the number. Her hand shook as she placed the phone at her ear.

"Happy House," a deep voice said.

"It's…me."

There was an energizing pause, and the faux overworked-employee persona faded. "You're still alive."

"Yes. They've been good to me," she admitted.

"The devil always smiles before rendering the final blow." Static crackled over the line. "What have you learned?"

"There's another demon out there, Hope, and he's their enemy. Other than that, nothing. They've kept me isolated, asking questions about you and your group."

"Another demon?" The sound of a pen sliding against paper echoed. "What have you told them?"

"That you guys asked me questions about them, but I didn't have any answers for you." That, at least, was the truth.

"Is it possible to search the fortress for journals, pictures, information about anything they've been up to?"

"No. I've been locked inside a bedroom."

"No good with locks?"

"No." Another lie.

"Have you considered…" His voice trailed off.

Seducing one for answers, she finished for him. "I—I—" She couldn't force an answer to form.

"Just think about it." There was a pause. "Everything you do is for the greater good. Remember what I told you. Peace, harmony. No more adultery, no more suicide. The welfare of your family."

In his fanatical way, he really did care about the world and its people and was willing to do anything to save them. Not altogether altruistic, but he did believe perfection waited just around the corner, the Lords the only thing blocking the way.

Danika wasn't sure what to believe anymore. Reyes had said there would always be evil in the world as long as people had free will, demons roaming the land or not. "I'll think about it." But she knew she wouldn't. She wouldn't whore for him, no matter the cause. If she slept with Reyes, it would be because she desired him.

"We've been watching the fortress," Stefano said, "yet there's been no activity inside. Any idea what they're doing?"

If she admitted most of the Lords were in Rome, the Hunters might view the fortress as fair game and sneak inside. Torin and Cameo and anyone else who'd stayed behind couldn't fight them all.

"I don't know," she finally said. *God, am I possessed by the demon of Lies?* "I'll try to find out."

"Have you heard—"

"Wait. Someone's coming. I have to go." Yet another lie, but she hung up and shoved the phone back into her pocket. For a long moment, she simply sat there, shaking. Then her shoulders slumped, and she covered her eyes with her hand. She had trouble drawing in a breath.

What's wrong with me?

She'd asked herself that very question a thousand times, it seemed. For once, she thought she might know the answer. Infatuation. She was infatuated with Reyes, and had been since the beginning.

There. She'd admitted it. No excuses this time, no talking herself out of it. He drew her; she wanted him, and she needed to *not* want him. Her desire had begun to color her every action, her every thought and what little common sense she had left.

Danika jumped to her feet. Her knees nearly buckled, but she latched on to the bedpost and held tightly. Being with Reyes wouldn't be pleasurable. It *couldn't* be. She'd have to *stab* him. But maybe she needed to experience it firsthand. Maybe that would finally drive him from her mind and her fantasies.

She could purge him from her thoughts as surely as she purged her nightmares when she painted.

Just the idea caused goose bumps to form on her skin and shivers to trek the length of her spine vibrating through her so that the shaking in her limbs increased. Her mouth dried. Desire and nervousness swam through her bloodstream, a balance of good and evil. The thought made her laugh, but it emerged as a croak.

Licking her lips, she released the post and stumbled forward. No telling how long Reyes would be gone. She'd have to keep herself busy, distracted, or she would be a bundle of anxious energy and sickness when he returned, unable to crawl into bed for anything more than sleep.

There was only one thing she knew of that would absorb her concentration completely. Painting.

Her hands were itching with anticipation before she reached the closed door. The metal was cold against her skin as she twisted the knob. As she stepped inside, she expected a closet full of supplies. Instead, she found another bedroom, spacious, airy—and converted into an artist's studio.

She drank in the luxury, a shocked gasp escaping her. Canvas after blank canvas awaited her, each propped on an easel. Against the far wall was a table lined with multisized brushes and tubes of color.

He did this for me. Not because he'd wanted to see into her dreams. He hadn't known about them when he'd done this. But simply because he wanted her to be happy. The realization was as shocking as the studio itself, and she found herself softening all the more toward him.

"What am I going to do with you, Reyes," she whispered.

How many times would Reyes surprise her like this? First the clothing, then his attempts at soothing her fears, and now this dream studio. Everything he did, everything he said, battered against her sense of self-preservation. Danika's hand fluttered over her racing heart. Even at home, she hadn't had such an elaborate setup. She'd made a livable wage painting portraits, but spare cash had been a rarity.

Before she became aware she'd taken a step, she was standing in front of the table, lifting the brushes, testing their weight and feeling their bristles. Reyes wanted to see the images from her dreams, the angels and the demons, the gods and goddesses. Suddenly she wanted to give him anything, everything.

But as she studied the palette of colors, both oils and acrylics, she knew her dreams would not be the focus of her first painting tonight. He would.

REYES PREPARED ANOTHER MEAL for Danika. Thankfully Paris had gone shopping before leaving for Rome, so there was plenty to choose from.

He carried the tray of fresh fish and salad to his bedroom, experiencing a slight twinge of panic when he didn't spot Danika right away. A quick search, and he found her in the studio, serene as she sketched something on one of the canvases. So absorbed was she that she didn't hear him enter. Did not even look at him when he called her name.

Her eyes were glazed, as if she were in some sort of trance. Her wrist flicked up and down the blank board gracefully, her body swaying from side to side in a fluid dance. His chest ached, his cock swelled. Pain battered against his skull to get to her. *None of that.*

Not wanting to distract her, he left. Breathed in and out, trying to still his raging heartbeat. He didn't think her lovely image would ever leave his mind. Hair hastily tied back, several strands escaping. Black smudges on her cheek and jaw. Lips red and glistening from the sharp nibble of her teeth.

He was rock hard and shaking uncontrollably by the time he reached the entertainment room. He hadn't realized he'd done it, but he'd already palmed his blades. Desperate for pain, he plopped onto the dark red couch; the men refused to buy any other color upholstery because of him, a fact that sometimes embarrassed him.

At least he didn't feel the need to jump from the fortress roof again.

"So what's a guy have to do to get some action around here?"

Reyes's head whipped to the side at the sound of that unknown voice. One of his daggers was soaring through the air a second later.

An unfamiliar warrior lounged in the plush red recliner, legs extended, the very picture of tranquility. He captured Reyes's weapon without a blink and studied the hilt. "Nice work. You make it yourself?"

Recognition suddenly dawned. "William." Anya's friend. Not many people could make it up the hill and into the fortress without setting off Torin's traps and sensors. But Torin had turned them off for this man, and Anya had warned everyone in the house to leave him alone or suffer the consequences.

"Yep, that's me. I know, I know. You're humbled I'm here,

feel like throwing rose petals at my feet, blah, blah, blah. No need, though. Just try and think of me as a normal guy."

Reyes rolled his eyes. Anya had failed to mention the immortal was an arrogant ass. "Yes, I made the blade. Why are you here?"

Frowning, William tangled a strong hand through his black-as-night hair. "Boredom, my friend. Boredom. Everyone just took off, no welcome party for me or anything. I decided to watch some TV, but the only movies you've got are porn and as I've been without a female for the past few weeks, they're just making me jealous."

"The movies belong to Paris," he said.

A laugh. A shake of William's head. "Say no more. I met the man."

"I did not mean, why are you in this room. Why are you in Budapest? Why are you in this fortress?"

William shrugged those big shoulders. "Answer doesn't change. Boredom. Well," he added after a moment's thought, "maybe it changes a little. Anya came to visit me not too long ago and put me in a tight spot with the new god king. I failed him, so he burned my home to the ground—even though he got what he wanted anyway. I've got nowhere else to go and Anya owes me big-time."

Reyes stiffened, every muscle in his body going on alert. "If you came to hurt her, I will—"

"Relax." The warrior held up one hand, palm out. His blue eyes twinkled as he raised his shirt with the other. "I couldn't hurt her even if I wanted to, and believe me, I've wanted to. She stabbed me right here."

His gaze lowered to the man's stomach. A long, thick scar slashed through his navel. "Nice."

"Girl always has been good with knives." William dropped the shirt and grinned.

Except for the scar, looking at William was like beholding the most perfect being ever created. Perfect skin, tanned and smooth. Perfect nose, sloped and straight. Perfect teeth, perfect cheekbones, perfect jaw. He was leanly muscled and exuded confidence. Reyes did not want the man anywhere near Danika.

Thinking of Danika caused his stomach to knot. "You said you desired a woman?" Reyes asked him.

William sat up, his features practically glowing with anticipation. "Have one in mind?"

"Meet me at the front door. Fifteen minutes."

Without another word, Reyes marched from the room and into his chamber. Danika stood in the exact same spot he'd left her, still lost in her painting. She hadn't even begun adding colors yet, but was still sketching the outline.

He didn't know much about the process, but suspected she would be at the task for hours more. His body was on fire, more so than before, and he needed pain. Taking matters into his own hands had not helped, had only managed to shock Danika and embarrass him.

Tomorrow they would be traveling and in close proximity. He would smell her sweet scent constantly. He would hunger for her desperately. And he might not be able to cut himself as he would need. If he didn't completely sate himself tonight, he could end up hurting or scaring Danika. Pain might try and force her to do things she wouldn't want to do. Things that would haunt her for the rest of her life. *That,* Reyes would not tolerate.

Perhaps he would take another woman.

The idea plagued him as he showered. Clean and dry, he strapped weapons all over his body, pulled on a fresh shirt and leather duster. As he tied his boots, he watched Danika work. Bedding a woman was dangerous, and could quite possibly be disastrous. How many lives had he already destroyed?

Maybe it won't be like that anymore. Maybe enough time had passed to dilute the demon's power so it would no longer affect his partner. Maybe. Besides, Reyes had better control now. But the thought of being with another woman sickened him. He wanted *this* one. He wanted *her* body underneath him, *her* legs wrapped around his waist, squeezing him, *her* pleasure moans in his ears.

But he couldn't have her, and he knew it. Not now. Not yet. If the woman he bedded tonight showed no signs of bloodlust…maybe. All he could do was breathe Danika in deeply—gods, that sea-storm scent drove him wild—and stalk from the room.

William was already at the front door, pacing. When he spotted Reyes, he stopped and grinned. "Where we going?"

"Club Destiny." Before Reyes could talk himself into staying home, he strode past him, out the door and into the daylight. The air was slightly chilled, rain clouds in the muted sky. Several rays of sunlight seeped from the canopy of trees.

"Anyone going to be there?" William asked, keeping pace beside him. "It's only midday."

"Someone will be there." Many someones. "Paris visits the club at all hours of the day and night, so women stay there, waiting for him."

William rubbed his hands together. "Humans, right?"

"Yes." He maneuvered around the thick base of a tree, careful of its limbs. One touch, and poisoned darts would be released, slamming into his chest.

"Not into human females?"

He flicked the warrior a glance. "What do you mean?"

"There was disgust in your voice just now."

Oh, yes. He was disgusted. With himself. "I like human females. Be careful of that rock," he added without pause. "A pit waits on the other side of it."

They steered clear, already halfway down. Wind rustled the leaves and whistled through the stones. "Why all the traps up here?" William asked, clearly intrigued. "I mean, I noticed the trip wires, the poisoned darts and the hanging stones on my way up."

"Hunters once came knocking."

"Ah. Say no more. Let's get back to the blonde."

Reyes's hands fisted at his sides, bereft without his blades. He felt as though unseen gazes were boring into him, spotlighting his flaws, his mistakes. Judging. Condemning. This might be the wrong decision, leaving her, but he didn't know what else to do. He wanted her so badly, had to have her, but couldn't until he'd proven she was safe from his demon. Which meant being with another woman.

But would she want him if he first took someone else?

"She's feisty. I like that."

"She is not up for discussion," Reyes snapped.

"Ouch. Touchy subject. I see your little demon awakens when she's mentioned. Your eyes glowed neon-red, just like Lucien's tend to do when he looks at me." Chuckling, unafraid, William held up his hands in surrender. "I'll never bring your girl up again, swear."

"You are odd," Reyes told him. "Most would tremble at the thought of my demon. You laugh."

"You forget. I fought Anya, and she's fiercer than all of your demons put together." William slung an arm around Reyes's shoulder. "Ten minutes with me, and I can help you forget the person I'm not supposed to talk about. You'll see."

They strode in silence for several minutes and soon hit the bottom of the hill. The sensation of being watched increased, and Reyes studied the surrounding area, gaze cutting through the shadows. Nothing seemed out of place, no one lurked nearby, but he didn't relax his guard.

"Let's get this over with," he said, and moved forward.

CHAPTER SEVENTEEN

"YOUR REPORT, Stefano?"

"Gladly. I spoke with the girl. She mentioned another demon. Hope. Said this one's the Lords' enemy. Clearly they lied to her. Hope is not evil. Besides, we've seen and heard nothing of him. As for movement, at fifteen hundred hours, the one called Reyes left the fortress with a warrior we haven't yet been able to identify. The girl just left the premises, as well."

"Was she bound?"

Dean Stefano sat at his desk and held a phone to his ear, sweat pouring from him. After talking with Danika, he'd spent a little time in front of the punching bag, hammering away. Then a call had come in from a trusted source, one who had relayed unexpected news. News that could destroy everything he'd worked for these past ten years.

Then he'd had to make a call of his own. *This* call. His heart would not stop pounding.

"No," he said. "She didn't appear subdued in any way. She was with the female demon Cameo and seemed willing to follow her. I'd say she acted of her own accord. Might even be working with the demons now." It would be a shame if that were true; he'd had high hopes for young Danika.

His boss remained silent for several seconds. They had worked together for a decade now, and he knew Galen to be single-minded in his pursuit of a life without Lords. Fierce, ruthless in his quest. Righteous.

That's as it should be. Galen was an angel, sent from the heavens. A living, breathing angel who flew through the skies on the wings of glory. Stefano hadn't believed him, not at first. Then he'd seen the wings. *Then* he'd looked deep into the man's eyes—eyes as fathomless as the sky, eyes that offered hope in a world of despair. Stefano had grabbed on to that hope for all he was worth.

Galen had assured Stefano that when the demons were gone, the world would become a peaceful place. Pain and misery, pestilence and disease would be things of the past, a distant memory. Ten years he'd been fighting this battle, and he'd never regretted it. His wife would be avenged, and never again would a happy couple be hurt as they'd been.

"Keep a close eye on them. Do not trust the girl and do not let them take her anywhere. If they try to move her, kill her."

"You can count on me." In war, there were always casualties. "There's something else." He gulped. "The girl…she's not simply a human. My source claims she's some type of living weapon. Supernatural, like the demons. What she is exactly, he didn't know. But if she *is* working with the Lords and if she *does* have special powers…"

There was a pause. "Why did you let her go then? Not only let her go, but gift wrap her and deliver her to the enemy?"

Because you told me to, he thought, but didn't say it. They had the same objective, and discord would only distract them. "My apologies. How shall I proceed?"

"Retrieve her. And if you can't—kill her. Better she dies than helps them."

DANIKA GAZED AROUND the nightclub. A silver strobe hung from the ceiling and tossed glistening pinpricks of light in every direction. They gleamed like stars in a black velvet sky, made for wishing and dreaming.

Hungarian rock blasted from the speakers. People danced,

their bodies undulating together in a heady rhythm. Hands roved, caressing, kneading…seeking. The scent of sex practically coated the air. Waitresses hustled drinks from the bar to tables, then raced back to grab a few more.

Where was Reyes?

On the dance floor? Grinding his erection into another woman? Asking that other woman to scratch him, bite him, *hurt* him?

Danika's hands curled into fists. She'd finished the preliminary sketches on two paintings and had even added a little color. One, she'd hidden. It was for her eyes alone. The other she'd propped in the studio before going in search of Reyes, knowing he would want to see it. She hadn't found him. Instead, she'd found Cameo, the beautiful woman who made her want to pluck out her eyes and jam sticks into her ears.

Cameo had escorted her here and now stood at her side. "Look. I probably shouldn't have brought you here, or let you leave the fortress at all. Try to run, and you won't like me when I catch you. But I'm a sucker for romance, so here we are. See him?"

"I won't run." The emotional pain caused by the woman's voice was almost too much, and she nearly covered her ears to block it. "And no, I don't see him."

"When you do, just remember he is a warrior with a tortured past you cannot even imagine. If you want him, you'll have to fight him."

Maybe it was their topic, but the more Cameo spoke, the more the sensation of misery eased. "Don't you mean *for* him? Fight *for* him?"

"Oh, no. You'll have to fight him. He won't surrender to his feelings easily. Good luck. Remember, no running or you'll regret it." With that, the female warrior disappeared into the shadows, leaving Danika alone in the doorway.

Well, as alone as a woman could be when surrounded by people. Were any Hunters among them? The suspicion chilled her. What if they *were* here? Stefano had told her several of his men would be in the area. What if they saw her? Tried to talk to her? Sweet Jesus. She and Stefano hadn't covered what to do in this type of situation because neither of them had thought she would be leaving the fortress. Despite the ice in her blood, sweat instantly beaded over her skin.

Where the hell was Reyes?

As she barreled her way through the crowd, her gaze scanned every face. No one familiar jumped out at her. By the time she reached the bar, she didn't know whether to be relieved or terrified.

"What'll it be?" the bartender asked in Hungarian.

She'd spent a month studying the language before she and her family had first flown here, so she knew enough to get by. "Coke," she replied, not wanting to risk alcohol. Though numbness would have been welcome, all of her wits were needed.

A few seconds later, the drink was sliding toward her. She slid one of the multicolored bills Cameo had reluctantly given her to the man and faced the dance floor again. Again, no Reyes. Shaking now, she moved forward, trying not to slosh her drink over the rim of the glass.

A man latched on to her free arm, grinning and pulling her closer. Scowling, she ripped herself free. Her expression must have been murderous because he paled and held up both hands in surrender.

She sipped the soda and moved forward, gaze continuing to search, blood pressure rising. There was a wall of windows at the far end of the club, elevated to overlook the floor. Another room? Probably. Probably VIP, too, with a guard at the door. Yep, she saw two seconds later. There was indeed a guard.

You're smart. Sometimes. You can find a way inside.

Determined, she raised her chin and marched. The tall, muscled man standing in front of a staircase frowned over at her, and that frown deepened the closer she came. He crossed his arms over his middle.

"I'm looking for Reyes," she said, first in English, then in fumbling Hungarian.

His brown eyes gave no flicker of recognition either time. "Back off, lady. It's a private room." English. At least he was polite enough to be rude to her in a language she could understand.

She persevered. "If you'll just tell him—"

"Back off, or I'll have you thrown out."

"I have information he needs, and he'll be—"

The guard reached out, intending to shove her. But strong fingers wrapped around his wrist, squeezing, and he howled.

"No touching the girl." A large figure stepped from the shadows. "What are you doing here?" that figure growled, releasing the man.

Danika's eyes widened, and her mouth fell open. Her heart instantly sped into a frantic tango, mimicking the dancers behind her. Reyes towered in front of her, cut and bleeding. Blood was dried and splattered on his neck. His black shirt was ripped, gaping around his navel and revealing a small patch of tanned skin.

"I asked you a question, Danika."

He'd been with a woman. The knowledge was like being hit in the chest by a dozen arrows, all laced with poison. She thought of the last time she'd slept with a man. Sadly, she had to go back years. Even more sad, it hadn't been that good. Something had been missing. Reyes's kiss had promised that something. Or so she'd thought. The urge to slam her palm into his nose, shoving cartilage into brain, filled her, but she managed to stop herself in time. He'd like it.

And there'd be no more pleasure for Reyes. Not from her.

"I just came to tell you that your enemy could be here, watching you. I didn't realize you'd be doing a little hunting of your own." She placed her drink on the nearest table, spun and stalked away. Where she was going, she didn't know. *I will not cry.*

Now strong fingers curled around her shoulder, halting her getaway.

This time, she couldn't stop herself. She swung around and planted her fist straight into his eye. His head whipped to the side.

When he righted himself, she saw that his nostrils were flared with…desire? Oh, yes. It was in his eyes, too, his pupils dilated and consumed the brown irises. He reached for her.

"Don't touch me," she shouted over the music, jolting back.

His arm fell to his side. "Hit me like that again and you'll regret it."

"You plan to hit me back?"

"No, but I will be all over you, unable to keep my lips off you."

"Oh, yeah," a male voice called from above them. "Fight it out, baby. Fight it out."

Her gaze lifted. A gorgeous man had opened the windows in the VIP room and now hung halfway out of one. There were two women beside him, caressing his bare shoulders and back, licking and nipping at him.

Was that what had been happening to Reyes before she'd arrived? She saw red. He, at least, still had his shirt on.

"Bring her up here, my man," the stranger commanded with a grin. "Let her join the party."

"Shut up, William," Reyes growled. "You are not helping."

While she'd been aiding him and his cause with her painting, Reyes had been scoring babes and making friends. How sweet.

"Come on. Bring the blonde. There's plenty of room, and I'll be bored without you."

"I don't want her up there."

Because she'd spoil his good time. No reason to say it out loud. Danika had heard enough. She had a good ten feet between them in less than a blink. If only she could stop her trembling. *Why do I care who he's been with? He's a demon. They're evil.* Sometimes. *And I'm working for their mortal enemies.* Kind of.

Someone backed into her path, laughing at something someone else said, and she shouldered her way past him, uttering a quick, "Sorry."

"Hey," he shouted. Whatever he thought to say next died on his lips as Reyes caught up with her and punted the man out of the way.

His arm banded around her waist in an iron lock. She glared up at him but didn't struggle. There was no reason to. Physically, he was stronger than she was. *Where's your training?* He led her through the crowd. People gasped as he approached and jumped out of his way. If they weren't fast enough, they were sent flying to the ground. None of them demanded an apology or even seemed to mind, she noticed. Some actually *smiled* when they touched him, as if he were a god, their savior.

"I know Hunters were watching," he said. "In turn, Torin was watching them and called me when there was a problem. He'll call me if there's another. How did you know they were here? Did you see your captor?"

Were, he'd said. *Another problem.* "What happened?"

"We'll discuss that later."

"I'm not going back to the fortress with you," she told him, ignoring his question.

"No, you're not."

So…what? Where was he taking her? Was he getting rid of her? Kicking her out? "You're a bastard, you know that? But fine. Whatever! Throw me out on the streets. I don't care. I'm leaving tomorrow, anyway, and the journey will be much easier without you."

They reached the side wall, three doors greeting them. Two were marked bathroom—one a man's, one a woman's—and one said *Keep Out* in big red letters. Reyes didn't slow as he shouldered that door open, shattering the lock and ushering her inside.

There was a desk, several chairs, filing cabinets and a computer. Oh, and four men. All four jumped to their feet, gaping at Reyes.

"Out," he barked.

There was a slight hesitation, but they didn't protest. Once they gathered their wits, they nodded and raced out of the office as if their feet were on fire.

Danika stalked to the desk and whirled. "How dare you!"

His eyes narrowed, homing in on her. "How dare I what? Claim this room? The club was destroyed by Hunters nearly two months ago, and I rebuilt it in three days. Believe me, they are happy to let me use anything I want."

Even the female patrons? she almost shouted, barely managing to contain the words. "No, how dare you force me in here? I'm done with you!" And what did he mean, Hunters had destroyed it? She remembered the aftermath of the explosion, but hadn't realized Hunters were responsible.

He closed what little distance there was between them. His warm breath trekked over her face, and she tried to hold her own breath. She really did. But that lasted only a minute before she was sucking in his scent, her lungs desperate.

"No, you aren't," he said softly, menacingly.

Though she wanted to tear her gaze from his harsh and beautifully angry face, she didn't look away. *I'm strong now. I do not back down. Ever.*

"Are you angry because I left without you?"

"Please." She raised her chin, squared her shoulders, just like she'd learned in one of her classes. Sometimes appearing confident was enough to send your opponent running. "I'm not angry."

"Liar," he lashed out. His top lashes intertwined with the bottom, blocking even a minute view of his pupils. "Why? Tell me."

"Go to hell."

"How many times must we establish that I'm already there?" He leaned down, a little closer to her.

Another tremor shook her. "There's nothing for us to discuss. I came to warn you about the Hunters, and I've done that."

"I believe I asked how you knew."

"I believe I refused to answer."

His head tilted to the side, his gaze raking her body, lingering in all the right spots. "Are you going to betray me, Danika?"

"I should," she said, practically spitting the words.

"But you haven't." A demand for the truth.

Her lips thinned into a mulish line.

He massaged the back of his neck, looking tired all of a sudden. "What am I going to do with you?" The question was clearly meant more for himself than her.

"Nothing. I'm leaving, and you're going back to your girlfriend. Don't worry. I won't return to the fortress." Cameo's words chose that moment to invade her mind. *You want him, you'll have to fight him.*

I've already lost, she thought. Keeping her nose in the air, she pushed past him. Or tried to.

His arm snaked out, an unmovable blockade.

Automatically, she gripped that arm, her nails sinking deep in warning. But he closed his eyes and moaned in ecstasy. Her eyes began to close, too; she began to moan, just as ecstatic. Touching him always warmed her, and now was no different. The chill left her blood. Her nipples hardened and her stomach quivered. *How can I still desire him?*

Danika forced her arms to fall to her sides. She couldn't control the wild thump of her pulse, though. Couldn't stop the dark flood of regret washing through her. Fight him… "Who were you with? You came here to fuck, didn't you? Don't try to deny it. I've had boyfriends and know how you guys are. Well, who'd you pick?"

Reyes bared his teeth, resembling a feral animal as he leaned the rest of the way in to her. Their noses brushed and he snarled, "I do not want to hear about any boyfriends you've had. Understand?"

"Y-yes." God, his anger… Exciting when it should have been frightening.

"And as to who I picked, are you sure you want to know?"

"Yes." This time, at least, she managed to sound somewhat confident.

"Why?"

Because I want to kill her for daring to put her hands on you. Because you're mine and I do not share. "Because," was all she said, her chin trembling. Damn it! *Do not cry.*

"I did come here to find a woman," he said.

Danika bit the inside of her cheek, blood filling her mouth.

"I found one," he added.

Motherfucker! The curse echoed through her mind, white-hot, searing. "I'm so glad," she gritted out. "I hope the two of you had a fun time." *I hope she gave you an STD and you both die from it!*

God, when had she become so bitter? So vindictive?

"Fun?" He laughed, but it was an ugly sound. "When I could not bring myself to touch her?"

"When you—what?" The hottest flames of her fury sizzled and crackled before finally dying. "You didn't?"

"No."

"Oh." Danika's shoulders slumped, and her eyes closed. Relief poured through her like—

"So I found another."

Her gaze snapped back up, locked on him. From relief and hope—hated hope—to fury. "And?"

"I could not bring myself to touch her, either. Both would have given me the beating I so desperately needed when I left the fortress. They were eager to tie me up and whip me. They would have hurt me, and we all would have loved it."

"Would have?" Her glare landed on his still-wounded neck. She arched a brow. "That's funny. Looks as if you already did."

He grabbed her arms and shook her hard enough to give her whiplash. "Would have. All I could think about was you. All I wanted was you. And they were not you, so I could not force myself to take them."

She licked her lips. "So you…did this to yourself?" *Please. Please, please, please.*

"No. When I first arrived, there were four Hunters in the club."

Now she gulped. Her fury, gone. Her hope, renewed. And yet, she had no relief. Not this time. He hadn't been with another woman, and that delighted her. But he had killed. Killed the very men she was supposed to be helping. "*Were* here? You keep saying that."

He nodded, grim.

"You fought them?" She didn't need to ask; she knew the answer, but perhaps she needed confirmation. Perhaps she needed time to halt the desire intensifying inside her. This man still belonged to her, wanted her as fiercely as she wanted him. "Who were they?" She hadn't meant to ask the question aloud, and gulped when she realized what she'd done. Had Stefano been among them?

Frowning, Reyes dug in his pocket, withdrew a stack of IDs, and handed them to Danika. She flipped through them with shaky hands. No Stefano. But the men looked like any other average Joes and it saddened her that they might have been hurt.

"They didn't see us until it was too late. William and I had already dragged them outside. We…took care of them." His anger seemed to melt from him. "I've battled, angel, and I'm hurting. I need you, and this time, I'm going to let myself have you. Will you let me?"

She'd already decided to be with him. If only to wipe him from her mind, get him out of her system and stop the fantasies plaguing her. If only to prove to herself that being with him would *not* be pleasurable for her.

"Will you? I'll go slow. I'll be tender. I'll be careful with you. I won't let my demon out. You won't have to hurt me."

He'd ticked off all the reasons she should give herself to him, as if he'd thought of every argument she could raise. "I—I—" She'd expected to stab him. That would have disgusted her. Wouldn't it have? Now, he wanted slow and tender? No pain? "What will you want me to do to you?" Would she be able to give him what he needed this way? Would *he* be able to forget *her* afterward?

"Love me, just for a little while."

She groaned quietly. What if, when the loving was over, she wanted more? Craved him more? Couldn't live without him? Slow and tender could only be bad for her, endearing him to her all the more.

"Why slow? Why tender?" she found herself asking.

"In the past, women have grown to…like what they do to me a little too much," he said. "They then begin to hurt those around them. I do not want that for you. I thought to take another today and ensure no harm would come to the woman. If she remained as she was, I would have been free to take you without worry. If she changed, I would have known to stay away from you. But I can't stay away from you."

Frightened, she slowly backed away from him. His arms fell to his sides, his expression tormented. She stopped, opening her mouth to say…what? She knew what she should say. No. They should wait until he needed pain again, because it was the best way to get him out of her fantasies. That she would never long to hurt someone. But she recalled the time—was it only a day ago?—that she had bitten him. She'd liked it.

You know what you're up against now. You're prepared.

Already her nipples were hard, her limbs trembling. Moisture was pooling between her legs; warm flutters consumed her belly, stretching and awakening every cell, every organ.

"Tonight," she said. "Only tonight. Tomorrow…"

He released a breath she hadn't known he'd been holding. "Tomorrow you can hate me again."

CHAPTER EIGHTEEN

PARIS HAD TOLD THE OTHERS about the images he'd seen at the temple, and everyone believed he'd been the one to see them because it had been *his* blood to first mix with the rain. Lucien had flashed back to the fortress, but he hadn't returned. Sabin had tried to call Reyes a thousand times—no answer—and had finally given up and contacted Torin, who informed them that the warrior was out dancing.

Dancing? Wasn't like the usually somber Reyes, Paris thought, and wondered if Danika had anything to do with it. How would Reyes respond to the news that his woman was going to play an integral role in finding Pandora's box?

Pacing the floor of his temporary bedroom, Paris tangled a hand through his hair. The others were seeing to their rented home's defenses. He should be with them, should be helping. He had more reason than most to guard against Hunters. Yet his friends had realized he wasn't watching the monitors as ordered but was lost in thought, so they'd disgustedly sent him away.

He'd left the busy living room without protest, happy to grab some time for himself. His mind was chaotic, churning and struggling with a single thought. *What if.* What if Sienna could be brought back? What if he simply had to ask the gods?

Since the Titans had escaped Tartarus and overthrown the Greeks, reclaiming the heavens, they had caused him and his friends nothing but grief. They had commanded Aeron to kill human women, and then cursed the warrior with a crazed bloodlust when he'd refused. They'd chased Anya relentlessly and marked her for death. They'd allowed Sienna to die.

No, you *allowed her to die.*

There was no denying that, but damn, he hated the reminder. Most likely, the new gods didn't have his best interests at heart any more than their predecessors had. But unlike the aloof Greeks, the Titans yearned for worship and adoration. And Paris could give it to them. For a price.

Stop pacing. Act.

Heart pounding with urgency and excitement, he fell to his knees. The shag carpet abraded his bare legs. He'd removed all his clothing, wanting nothing to offend the fickle gods. If one—or two or three—did indeed come to him, and he offended in some way, he could be punished. *More than I already am.* He could be banished to hell, killed or asked to do something he didn't want to do.

"Worth the risk," he muttered to remind himself of his goal. He gripped a dagger in his left hand, his knuckles so tight around it they were in danger of snapping apart. *Now or never.*

He raised the dagger as high as possible. The silver metal glistened as the candle on the nightstand burned. *Who shall I try and summon?* His mind whirled with possibilities, flashing the names of the beings he'd studied and learned this past week in preparation for searching the temple.

Cronus, the warrior king? Cronus would understand power and respect it. But he seemed to hate the Lords, and he'd been the one to order Anya's death.

Rhea—wife to Cronus? Paris knew nothing about her. Geae, mother of the earth? She would, perhaps, show the most concern for his plight. Oceanus, the god of the water? Tethys, who loved Oceanus? Mnemosyne, goddess of memory? Hyperion, god of light and father of the sun? Themis, goddess of justice?

No, Themis was in prison, he recalled Anya mentioning. She had aided the Greeks all those thousands of years ago, helping them defeat the Titans. Immediately upon regaining the throne, Cronus had locked her up.

Who else could he approach?

There was Phoebe, goddess of the moon. Atlas, who had once held the entire world on his back. Epimetheus, the god of afterthought. He was supposedly the stupidest of all the gods. Prometheus, god of forethought. Now there was a god who'd understand unrelenting torment. He'd spent thousands of years having his liver eaten every night, only to regrow so that it could be eaten again.

Mythology was tricky. What humans knew was bits and pieces of the truth twisted together with falsehoods. Paris, exiled from Olympus all those centuries ago, didn't know what to believe. Didn't know who was strongest, who was loved and who was hated. If he called the wrong name…summoned an enemy… He might be wise to summon a female, for hardly anyone could resist the demon of Promiscuity. But if he tried to seduce the wife of a god… Anya had told him William had slept with Hera, and as punishment Zeus stripped William of his ability to flash or be flashed. That way, William could never again escape from a bedroom he was not supposed to be in. He would have to remain—and deal with the enraged husband.

No females, then.

He pushed out a sigh, his mind turning once more to Cronus. Might as well go for the gold. The god king was the most enigmatic of the bunch, hard and embittered. But he had brought Lucien back to life recently, and that was the type of ability Paris needed.

If the temple did not have humans swarming all over it, he would have returned and performed the coming ritual there. As it was, he would have to make do. Closing his eyes, he called, "Cronus, king of gods. I summon you."

Several seconds ticked by and nothing happened. Paris hadn't expected the god to appear right away, had known a sacrifice would need to be offered to even tempt such a being to his presence. So he lowered his arm, slowly, deliberately, and slashed the blade's tip across his chest. The flesh ripped open inch by inch and warm blood flowed down his stomach, pooling in his navel.

Still, the seconds passed with no result.

"God King, I need you. I beg an audience."

The crimson continued to flow…and flow… He'd set a glass of water on the floor before deciding to continue the ritual. Just in case. It was Anya's rainwater, the tears of the earth.

Paris soaked one of his hands inside, then wiped the droplets across his wound. Blood and water mixed, the crimson fading to pink as it slid along the ropes of his stomach and onto the floor.

"I beg for a glimpse of you. I humbly wait on my knees." He raised his hand again, the dagger still clutched there, before slashing another wound on his chest, a direct crisscross. Pleading was more difficult than he'd imagined. Last time he'd fallen to his knees like this, his cries had been ignored and a demon shoved inside his body. "I will wait forever if you so deem."

"Is that so?" The quiet voice echoed throughout the bedroom, wry, a little angry.

Paris's eyelids popped open. The murky light hadn't brightened, a halo didn't surround the god king's thin form, but there he was. Cronus. Shock nearly felled Paris, and he was immensely glad he was already on his knees.

The god had thick silver hair and a regal beard. His eyes were dark, fathomless pools. Clean white linen draped one of his shoulders and cascaded down his body. He clutched a staff in one hand. The Scythe of Death—a weapon not even Lucien possessed.

He was tall and lean, aged, but power radiated from him.

Paris didn't dare stand. He bowed his hand, heart racing all the faster. Cronus had come. He'd truly come. "Thank you for deigning to appear."

"I did not do it for you. I am…curious."

Tread carefully. "If that pleases you, it pleases me."

"It does not please me. I do not like puzzles."

Not a good start. "I offer my sincerest apologies for disturbing you, my king."

Cronus chuckled, the sound still wry but no longer laced with anger. "You have learned something of control and diplomacy in all your thousands of years, I see."

"No thanks to the Greeks," Paris said. One thing he and Cronus shared was a common enemy. A common hatred.

As he'd expected, the words delighted the new king. "Zeus was never my equal." Cronus stepped forward, the scent of stars and sky radiating from him. "I am pleased you realize this."

Paris noted the king's toes peeked out from under the long chimation he wore. They were framed by pristine sandals and tipped by clawlike nails completely at odds with the dignified appearance the god presented.

Perhaps they were not so different, god and demon.

Cronus walked around him but never touched him. "You are Paris, unwilling keeper of Promiscuity. My sympathies to your demon, for I know what it is like, being imprisoned."

Oh, yes. They were alike. "Then you also know what it is to suffer."

"Yes." Another pause. Fingers sifted through Paris's hair. "Did you summon me because you wish to be free of your demon?"

With one wave of his hand, Cronus *could* separate man and beast. If he did so, Paris would die.

Paris could barely remember his life without the demon. Yes, he wanted peace. Yes, he wanted freedom inside his own mind, wanted his thoughts to always be his own, but Promiscuity was the other half of him. "No, my king," he finally said.

"A wise choice. That pleases me."

"As your servant, I pride myself on pleasing you."

A soft chuckle. "Well said."

Paris kept his head bowed and watched as his blood coated

the bottom of the god's linen. The stain seemed to take the shape of a heart. "I must admit, I expected…"

"A monster?"

"Yes." He didn't dare lie. This was too important. "I thought you would be happy to end the Lords."

There was a rustle of clothing, the god no longer in front of him, then warm breath was caressing Paris's ear. "You expected correctly," the king whispered. Another rustle, and the warm breath disappeared. "I am a monster. I am what prison made me."

"Now you crave the worship of your people. I will worship you all the days of my life if only you will—"

A gust of wind slammed into Paris's back, knocking him face-first into the floor. His blood had clotted and now splattered his cheek, too thick to fall.

"Face me, demon."

Slowly Paris raised his head. There was Cronus, in front of him once again. He wasn't used to obeying anyone but himself and the demon. Instinct demanded he refuse simply on principle. To obey was to invite more demands.

For Sienna, anything.

Without further hesitation, his eyes latched on to the god's face. The room's shadows had seemed to grow arms, reaching out and wrapping Cronus in their midst, shielding him. But his gaze, dark as it was, glowed.

"You cannot begin to know my wants."

"My apologies."

An eternity ticked by in silence, but the tension in the room never eased.

"I must admit I have been unsure what to do about you and the other Lords," the god finally said. "You are abominations, that much I know, and yet you do serve a purpose."

Abominations? Spoken like a Hunter. Truthfully, Paris had once thought the very same thing. He and the others had done terrible wrongs. To the world, to mortals. Even to the Greeks by betraying their trust. But they had spent centuries trying to absolve their sins. "Purpose?"

"As if I need explain myself to you," Cronus scoffed.

There was nothing to say to that. Nothing that would help him, that is.

"I know what you desire, demon. The woman, Sienna. You want her returned to you."

It was difficult, hearing his most private desire spoken aloud. For him, for the demon currently slamming from one side of his brain to another in a desperate frenzy. While Paris loved the thought of being with only one woman, his companion did not.

"Yes."

"She is dead."

"As you once proved with Lucien, you are more powerful than death."

A whisper-soft chuckle. "Flattery, oh, sweet flattery. But I will not grant you this wish. What's done is done. She's gone."

Giving in to the crushing weight of disappointment now pressing into his shoulders was not an option. A warrior did not give up until the last breath was taken—and even then Paris suspected there might be opportunity to negotiate. "I will bargain for her."

"Yes, with your *worship*," Cronus said drolly. "You, demon, have nothing of value."

For once Promiscuity seemed more concerned with doling out pain than taking pleasure, because both Paris and the demon roared at that, ready to lash out. "Surely there is something," he replied tightly.

"No. Nothing. I have no need of more warriors. I have riches, freedom, power beyond imagining. You have my cage, but I cannot bargain for that because I gave my word and my word is law. Should you find my other weapons…perhaps."

"Please," he rushed out, afraid the god would vanish at any moment. "You are my last hope. I will do anything you ask, if only you will grant me this one request. I am lost without her. I need her, for she is the calm in my storm. My anchor. Without her, I am just the shell of a man. Have you never felt that way about anyone? Have you never wanted something so badly, you would give your own life for it?"

A pause. A sigh. "Your desperation intrigues me. Since Anya gave away her greatest treasure to save her man, I have wondered at exactly what the depths of love will drive a heart to do."

At his words, every cell in Paris's body lit up.

The god's head tilted to the side, his expression pensive. "Tell me why you choose this woman above everything you could ask me for. Why not risk all and beg me to release the warrior Aeron from his quest?"

"I—I—" Fuck. What kind of friend was he? That should have been his request, and it should have been his request weeks ago. "I am ashamed to say I have no answer for you."

Fingers again ran through his hair, gentle, almost tender. "That does not clear my confusion. She was your enemy, and yet you have placed her above your lifelong friend. He would save you. She would kill you. You love him. You do not love her."

No, he didn't, and his guilt ratcheted up another notch. "Can't I have both?"

"I am still not convinced I will grant you even one."

Paris closed his eyes in a futile attempt to shut out that terrible, ever-growing guilt. "My body was able to respond to Sienna as it has never responded to another since I was cursed. I thought, hoped, she could save me from myself."

"Very selfish of you. I thought you had learned control in your years on earth, yet still, you are a slave to Promiscuity?"

Thanks for digging the knife deeper. "Yes."

"If I gave her back to you, she would ultimately betray you. You know that, do you not? Your friend would continue to suffer, and yet he would love you even though you chose a woman over him."

The words were too much, too real, and Paris sagged forward, clutching his stomach, fighting tears from his eyes.

"That is enough for now. Think about what I have said, demon, and we will talk again." Cronus was gone in the next instant.

"WHAT ARE YOU DOING, Sabin?"

"Preparing for war," he answered, eyeing the warriors surrounding him. They were propped in every corner of their rented house in Rome, watching him intently. "You know that."

A little while ago, Lucien had returned to Buda and flashed the now-healed Gideon and Kane here. The ceiling's plaster was already crumbling on top of Disaster's head.

Lucien had brought them to "talk some sense into" Sabin. Sabin thought the others needed sense talked into *them*.

"What? Why?" Maddox demanded.

"That's what I do, what I'm good at." He returned his attention to his Sig Sauer, loading bullets into the magazine. "The Hunters we killed at the temple aren't the only ones here. There are more, and they're most likely searching for us. More than that, Paris saw Reyes's woman holding our box in that damned vision of his. Was she holding it for us? Or *them?*"

The ominous question cast a dark silence over the living room. No one knew the answer. "She saved Ashlyn once. I like her," Maddox said, and not for Ashlyn's benefit. Currently his woman was resting in another room. He meant what he said.

But Sabin wasn't done. "We know Danika spent time with them. We know she doesn't like us. Hunters could still be here, following us, meaning to snatch the box from us the moment we find it."

"We have *not* known that since the beginning," Gideon said in a show of agreement. He rubbed his temples, blue hair momentarily shielding his fingers from view.

Strider patted his waist and nodded when he encountered his blades. "I'm with you."

Sabin glanced at Amun. The man rarely spoke. As keeper of Secrets, he *couldn't* speak without revealing things everyone in the room was probably better off not knowing about each other. But he, too, nodded.

Anya planted her hands on her waist. "I'm not going anywhere without Lucien."

Love, Sabin scoffed. He'd fallen a few times over the centuries, and each time had been a mistake. Eleven years ago, Dean Stefano's wife, Darla, had been the last to win his heart. After her death, he'd vowed not to allow himself such emotions again. Always he drove women into depression because they couldn't stop doubting themselves and their actions; in extreme cases, like Darla's, that depression drove them to suicide. Love was not worth the hardships it wrought.

Gideon shrugged. "You know how I hate to fight Hunters."

Good. He was in, as well.

"You want to war? Just like that?" Maddox snapped his fingers. "Without preparation? We did that in Buda, and you know what happened there. A bomb, Torin nearly killed. A plague unleashed on the city. *You* were partly responsible for bringing the Hunters to our door. Obviously, you haven't changed."

When they'd split up those few thousand years ago, Maddox had sided with Lucien, hoping for peace, and Sabin had mourned the loss of a great soldier. He did not want to split again. But...

"You haven't, either," Sabin growled. "There cannot be harmony without war. History—history we have *lived*—has proven that time and time again. We must fight for what we want or it will be taken from us."

"I want the Hunters dead," Maddox said tightly. "I do." He was Violence, as tempestuous as human females could often be. The storm inside him drove him to constantly seek calm around him, Sabin knew, but he also knew Maddox now controlled his demon just by thinking of his woman. "I just want my friends alive more. You are rushing out there. You do not know how many Hunters there are, what weapons they have and can use against our females. You—"

Beautiful Ashlyn stepped into the room.

Maddox hadn't seen her, Sabin didn't think, but the man pressed his lips together, cutting off his words. The warrior always seemed to know when the human girl approached, though Sabin wasn't sure whether he could smell her lovely scent or simply sensed her.

His violet eyes scanned the living room and when they landed on her, his expression softened. Sabin studied her, as well. She was the color of honey and just as sweet, as lovely as a cameo. She always appeared so…fragile, which made it difficult for him to understand how she had tamed such a wicked beast as Maddox. No doubt she'd even be able to convince him to change diapers once the baby was born.

Maddox motioned her to him. Smiling, she obeyed. The moment she was within reaching distance, the warrior enfolded her in his arms.

There would be no more talk of war. Maddox would kill anyone who scared his woman, and that was as it should be.

"Hey, everyone," she said.

A chorus of "heys" rang out.

Maddox frowned down at her. "You are pale. You need more rest. Let me carry you back to our—"

"No, not yet. I, well…I heard something," she said, features somber now.

Everyone, including Maddox, stiffened. Ashlyn had the unique ability of hearing every conversation that had ever transpired in whatever spot she stood in, no matter how much time had passed, no matter what language was spoken. Those voices were quiet only when Maddox was near her. None of them were sure why that was the case, but Ashlyn liked to say that it was a sign she and Maddox were meant to be together.

Sabin had wanted to make use of her gift on several occasions; Maddox had told him the voices tormented her and had forbidden it. But the warrior would not turn his wrath on Ashlyn for walking away from him and listening on her own. A fact Sabin had mentioned to her on several occasions.

"Did you leave the house?" Maddox asked her, the question tight with only the slightest hint of anger.

"Maybe," she hedged. "I know you were worried I'm not getting enough rest and wanted me to nap before going out again to listen for past conversations about the box with Anya—who, by the way, would not stop talking about being ejected from the battle at the temple, so I didn't hear much. But any more rest and I might as well dig a grave. I just went for a walk. That's all."

Good girl, Sabin thought. He didn't mention that knowing Maddox, Anya had not been the girl's only protector earlier. The warrior had most likely been in the shadows, watching her from a safe distance while she worked.

"Ashlyn," Maddox uttered, the name a warning. "These are dangerous times. No telling who could have been out there, waiting, watching."

"I didn't mean to get started again, it just happened. But as you can see, no harm befell me."

"This time," he growled. "No harm befell you this time. I cannot believe you left without at least informing me. Do you *want* to be captured by our enemy? They would not hesitate to use you, hurt you." With every word, his anger became more pronounced.

"I was careful. Besides, I want to do my part. I want you safe and if I have to take a risk now and then to ensure that you are, I will."

"Yes, but now you risk our baby."

Abject hurt contorted her features. "I love this child and would never place her in unnecessary jeopardy. But just so you know, you're as important to me as our baby. Your safety is vital. And in case you've forgotten, we're connected. You die, I die."

He shuddered at the reminder.

"I disguised myself before I took my walk just in case, but I didn't actually see anyone who looked like a Hunter. No visible wrist tattoos, anyway. And if it makes you feel any better, the chatter I heard was from a few hours ago."

Maddox buried his head in her hair. "I cannot lose you. I would die a more painful death than any that has come before."

"I will not lose you, either. That's why I'm doing this."

"Tell us what you heard," Sabin commanded, then added, "Please," when Maddox snarled at him. Temper, temper. Politeness was not a natural inclination for Sabin, and he had to work for it.

Her fingers curled around Maddox's wrists, holding on to him as if he were a precious treasure. "You were right," she told Sabin. "There are indeed Hunters. They're looking for you. Or rather, they *were* looking for you."

She'd heard that, too, had she? He tried not to smirk at Maddox, but he failed. *See,* he projected. *Something needs to be done about them. War is the only way.*

You were wrong, Doubt added, the words slithering into Maddox's mind, Sabin knew. *You're always wrong.*

"Sabin," Maddox barked.

"Sorry." The demon couldn't help itself, and Sabin could not always stop it from inflicting doubts on others. When an opportunity presented itself, the demon took it. Every damn time. *This is why I can't have a woman of my own.*

"I was able to isolate around twelve different voices. They're swarming into Buda," Ashlyn said, "because they just learned where the second artifact is. They're on their way to get it."

CHAPTER NINETEEN

DANIKA AND REYES FINALLY reached the fortress, leaving dusk behind. They hadn't kissed or even touched since departing from the club. They hadn't spoken, either. Reyes wasn't sure if that was a blessing or a curse. What was she thinking?

Silence continued to cloak them, even when they strode inside his bedroom. Never turning his back on Danika, he closed and locked the door. She didn't face him. He leaned against it, the wood's coolness seeping past his torn shirt and into his skin. Thankfully Pain had receded to the back of his mind, temporarily sated from his battle with the Hunters, and was making no demands.

Danika stood in front of the bed, staring down at the black sheets. With trepidation? With anticipation?

Reyes hoped the latter. The Hunters had cut him so deeply and in so many places, he probably needed stitches on every limb. He'd chosen not to doctor himself, however. The pain was sublime, throbbing through him, making him quake with pleasurable sensations. He could finally be with this woman, and she wouldn't have to hurt him. He would be so gentle with her, he wouldn't allow himself to worry about corrupting her.

"Nervous?" he asked.

A moment passed before she responded. "No."

Liar. He didn't grin, though his lips twitched upward. "Shall we talk first?" Even offering a reprieve was difficult for him. He craved her in his bed, naked and straining against him.

"No. No talking."

His brow furrowed, and he frowned. She'd sounded so…determined. Why did she not want to talk with him? *Does it matter? You did not wish to talk with her, either.*

Slowly she turned, finally facing him. As always, the sight of her angel face stole the air from his lungs. Such beauty in such a small package, he thought. A gift for her, perhaps, but most definitely a curse for him. He couldn't look away. Would happily have died then and there, just to have her image be the last to grace his sight.

Her cheeks were flushed, her eyes glittering brightly, emerald framed by black lashes. Up and down her chest moved, faster and faster, as if she couldn't quite catch her breath.

"We are to make love in silence?" he asked her. His hands itched to touch her. To cup her breasts, thumb her hard little nipples. His mouth watered for a taste of her. He'd bite her, this time. He'd—no. He would be gentle, he reminded himself.

Her eyes stretched wide. "We aren't making love."

"Then what are we doing?" he demanded, folding his arms across his chest.

"We're having sex." She raised her chin and braced her feet apart, the very picture of a warrior before battle. "And yes, silence will be…good."

Again, his brow wrinkled in confusion. "Why?"

"I want your body, not your life story," was all she said, but *I want to forget you afterward* hung in the air like the sword of Damocles, ready to fall and cut him into a thousand pieces.

He scowled. Once she had told him she knew nothing about him; she had *wanted* to know more. What had changed?

A trick, perhaps, to manipulate him into talking about his friends?

No. No, he didn't think so. His head tilted to the side as he studied her more closely. Her jaw was set in stone, her shoulders squared. The pinkish hue in her cheeks was fading.

She reached up, hands shaking, and gripped the hem of her T-shirt. She began to raise it, revealing inch after inch of creamy skin. Her stomach was flat, her navel delicate and made for his tongue.

He was in front of her a second later, his hands covering hers and stopping her progress. The shirt's material covered her face, blocking her features from his greedy view. She gasped as his stomach brushed hers.

"You do not want to want me," he breathed into her ear. The shirt prevented his breath from caressing her, but she shivered anyway. "You want to keep me at a distance, I think."

"Can you blame me?" she asked, the words spoken on a trembling sigh. "Now, let me undress."

"No, I can't blame you." He dragged the shirt the rest of the way over her head and tossed it aside.

The shoulder-length mass of her sunshine hair tumbled down, framing her face. She wore a black lace bra—one he'd purchased for her—and her breasts swelled from the top. He swallowed, wondering if she wore the matching panties.

Gaze glued to his, she gripped the hem of his tattered shirt and began to lift. He raised his arms. Ultimately, she had to stand on her tiptoes and he had to lean over to remove it. When he straightened, she uttered another of those heated gasps.

"So strong." She reached out with a shaky hand and traced her fingers over one of his wounds.

At the first brush, he closed his eyes in surrender. There was such sweet, sweet pain in having an injury stroked.

"When did you get this?" she asked.

"I thought you craved silence?"

She sighed.

"A little while ago," he said.

"From the Hunters?"

"Yes."

Her lips compressed into a thin line. "At least it's healing."

Healing? Damn. If any of his injuries decided to repair themselves before he'd taken Danika, he would pour salt into them or reopen them himself. Nothing would stop him from having this woman. Gently. Sweetly. The way he'd always dreamed of taking a woman but had never been able.

"Am I hurting you?" she asked, and then she laughed without humor. "Never mind. Just…kiss me. Take me to bed."

Bed. Yes, oh, yes. He opened his eyes and stared down at her. One step forward. Two. He backed her into the mattress. Her legs hit, and she tumbled down. Licking her lips, watching him, she scooted backward.

"Take off your jeans," he commanded hoarsely.

She eased to her back and raised her hips. Unfasten. Unzip. Down, down the denim shimmied. Oh, sweet gods, she'd worn the matching panties. They were like a violent storm cloud against her creamy skin. Hopefully wet.

His cock strained, desperate for her. Suddenly Pain seemed to stretch awake in his mind, yawning, purring. He gnashed his molars.

"Your turn," Danika said, propping her weight onto her elbows.

Had he thought her lovely before? His chest actually hurt as he looked at her just then. She was Aphrodite in the flesh. She was seduction incarnate. She was…his.

Not yet… Not just yet… She wanted him to bed her, she didn't want to get to know him. He would not allow one without the other.

"You mentioned my life story. Well, I spent several years locked inside a cell," he said, "a willing prisoner. Not because of the Hunters but because I could not control my intense need to give and receive pain."

"I don't think—"

"Back then, in ancient Greece, I battled Hunters and I destroyed cities. Screams were my sustenance. After one of my friends was killed, a man I had once laughed with and fought beside, the truth of what I was began to sink in."

"I don't want to hear this." She shook her head, those silky locks dancing at her temples.

"I knew I could not learn to control my beast when temptation lurked in every corner. Everyone who smiled, everyone who enjoyed, I wanted to eradicate. In my demon-soaked mind, they had no reason to experience joy."

"Reyes."

"So I asked Lucien to lock me up. Of all of us, he was the one who first gained control of his demon. He did not want to, but he agreed. During those months of confinement, I learned to cut myself whenever the need for pain arose. Eventually, I trained myself to crave only that, my own pain. My demon craved it, too, the rest nearly forgotten." If only confinement worked on Aeron….

"Stop. Please, just stop."

"Why? Because knowing I suffered makes me seem more human? Because you do not want to think of me as anything more than a demon? Because one day, when we've parted, you hope to forget I ever existed?" The last was uttered in a feral snarl.

"Yes!" she shouted, jolting upright. Her chest rose and fell, fast and shallow. "Yes, okay. Yes. I shouldn't desire you, but I do. I can't get you out of my mind, even though I should be thinking about a thousand other things. We have no future. I mean, really. One of your friends wants to kill me and everyone I love. You live a life of war and all I crave is peace."

True. All that she'd said was true. "Yet here you are, in my bed." *And here I am, unable to let you go.*

"Yes." Both her voice and her expression softened. "I'm trusting you. With my family. My body. Don't make our eventual parting any worse for me. Please."

Please. The word echoed in his mind. Reyes met her heated gaze with his own. For the briefest of moments, he was transported to the heavens. To the past. In his mind, he saw himself standing beside Aeron, Torin, Paris and Galen.

Galen. Until Danika, Reyes had not thought of Galen in centuries. Galen had pulsed with life; his mere presence somehow made them feel stronger, better. Reyes hadn't known the warrior plotted against them every time their backs were turned.

And seeing the image of his carefree friends, so unburdened then by life and sins and suffering, he had to fight the urge to shout a warning he knew they would not hear.

They'd been celebrating that day, he recalled. The night before, a horde of Gorgons had sneaked inside Zeus's chamber, intending to awaken the god and turn him to stone. A single glance would have done it, and the king would have been unprepared, too surprised to cast his gaze downward in time.

Paris, ever the ladies' man, had been sleeping with one of the females—blindfolded, of course, to prevent turning to stone. The besotted female had blurted out her sisters' plans, and Paris had immediately alerted the Guard. Together, they'd ambushed the Gorgons, defeating them in minutes and with hardly any bloodshed.

We are unbeatable, Galen said proudly.

Torin nodded in agreement. *Is it wrong that I wanted to take one of those snake-headed females as my prisoner?*

Reyes rolled his eyes. *You are as bad as Paris. The thought of being bitten and clawed during sex...* He shuddered.

You just haven't been bitten the right way, Paris said with a grin.

I prefer my women sweet and tender, thanks, Aeron countered.

"Reyes," Danika said, drawing him back to the present.

He shook his head to clear his thoughts. *If I had only known what awaited me.* "I want to give you anything and everything you ask for, Danika."

Relieved, she sagged against the mattress. "Thank you."

"But making myself forgettable for you," he finished, "I

cannot do. You're going to haunt my dreams for all of eternity. I have to know I meant something to you."

"You do," she said, tortured. Her gaze dropped to her legs as she drew up her knees. "And that's the problem."

"Resist me if you must, but do it later. After. I'll even help you. Here, now, give me everything." He unsnapped his jeans, pushed them down and kicked them off. Except for his weapons, he was bare underneath. "Look at me."

She did, her eyes going straight to his erection...staying. A tremor slithered down her spine.

"I am cruel and I am selfish, but this need I have inside me, this need for you and no other, is stronger than anything else I've ever encountered. I doubt two years of lockup would dull it in the slightest."

"I—I don't know how to respond to that."

"Then don't." He didn't need to hear her confirm that he'd made an impact on her and that her defenses were crumbling. The rosy flush darkening and spreading over her entire body told him plenty. "Just give. Take."

One by one, he discarded his blades. Only when he was stripped to his skin, nothing between them, did he climb onto the bed. Her pupils dilated as she watched him, and goose bumps spread over her, joining the flush.

He trapped her feet between his knees and reached up, his fingers curling around the waist of her panties. Slowly, so slowly, he dragged them down, revealing the paradise between her legs.

She didn't try to stop him. No, she encouraged him, raising her hips to allow an easier glide. He fisted the material, its dampness teasing his palm as his gaze drank her in. Her thighs were lean, the small patch of hair guarding her femininity as sunny as the hair on her head. Tiny as she was, her legs seemed to stretch for miles.

"Exquisite," he told her.

"Th-thank you."

He leaned down and braced his palms beside her hips. "Shall I continue?"

"Yes." A plea, desperate and needy.

His cock jerked in reaction. "I've dreamed of this moment, of having you." He lifted one of her legs and placed a soft kiss upon her ankle. The skin was smooth, cold chased away by heat at the moment of contact.

Another tremor moved through her.

With his free hand, he gently pushed her other leg into the mattress, parting her thighs. Wider…wider…

He growled low in his throat, the sound primal and wild. Pain pawed from one side of his mind to the other, eager but content for the moment. Already Danika glistened with arousal. He kissed her calf, and she gripped the sheets.

"Do you want me to… Should I…"

"Hurt me?" he asked.

A tentative, "Yes."

"No." Holding her like this and not being buried deep inside her was a physical agony all on its own. "Not you."

She frowned. "Will you find pleasure without it?"

"Oh, yes." He hoped. This time, he kissed the inside of her thigh. His tongue flicked out, tasting, gliding over the smooth skin.

A moan escaped her as she raised her hips.

His fingers trekked up her other leg and stopped a whisper away from her curls. "Continue?"

"Reyes," she breathed.

"Continue?" he insisted.

"Yes. Please."

He brushed past those moist folds—sweet heaven—and buried a finger inside her. She was hot, tight, deliciously wet. "I knew you would feel this way." In. Out.

"Yes! Like that."

Taste.

He didn't know if the urging came from deep inside his

mind or from the demon and he didn't care. Shaking, he leaned down and traced his hot tongue over her center. Heaven, he'd thought before. Ambrosia, he realized now. Her sweetness coated his tongue, filled his mouth. She tangled her hands in his hair, nails digging into his scalp.

Yes, he nearly shouted.

He licked and laved her, worked another finger inside, and began pumping in and out again. In and out. So good. So damned good. The pleasure of having her underneath him, spread for him, was intense, undeniable, and a moment passed before he realized his wounds *had* begun to close and his enjoyment…had not diminished. It was shocking. Something he didn't understand. Why?

If he did nothing, would the pleasure fade? Would his demon spring up and demand he hurt his lover? Would his demon begin to influence Danika, making her into something she did not want to be?

Reyes was unwilling to wait to learn the truth. Too much was at risk.

He reached behind him and dug his nails—claws now— into the scabbed flesh on his back. Yes, yes. The pain, the trickle of blood. As expected, heat roared through him, his pleasure intensifying.

"Who is here with you?"

"Don't stop," she begged.

"Who is here with you?" he repeated, harshly this time.

"You are."

"What is my name?"

"Reyes."

"Who do you desire?"

"Reyes."

His strokes against Danika's clitoris became frenzied. She moaned over and over, the sounds a symphony to his battered soul. She begged for more; she begged him to stop. He gave the first, refused the last, inserting a third finger inside her and stretching the tightness of her sheath.

A climax slammed into her.

She tensed around his fingers and tongue, inner walls holding him captive. He swallowed every drop of her satisfaction.

When she quieted, he rose above her. Their gazes met and held. She was trembling, sated, her eyelids at half-mast, and yet desire still shone in those emerald orbs. "You didn't…"

"No."

She licked her lips. "Will you?"

"Oh, yes."

"Do you need—"

He shook his head, the motion clipped. His body burned with unsatisfied passion. Which hurt, wonderfully so. He closed his eyes and enjoyed the sensation. Other partners had whipped his flesh to ribbons, stabbed him, bitten him, but none had tormented him like this. The pleasure-pain sang through him, a discordant melody that offered the sweetest kind of solace. The kind he'd always dreamed of but had despaired of ever experiencing.

How had she given it to him?

"You're so beautiful," Danika whispered. "I want to paint you, just like this."

"I would like that." Reyes opened his eyes and crawled up her soft body. He removed her bra, the clasp in front easily giving way to his fingers. Her full breasts sprang free. Her nipples were still hard, but now he could see how pink and perfect they were.

He licked and sucked one, then the other, and soon she was writhing again. Soon she was begging again. Soon he was lost in the essence of her, the demon urging him on, craving more.

"Condom," she panted. "I need you inside me. Now."

He nodded, grabbed one of the foil packets he'd stolen from Paris and stored in his nightstand and covered himself. He would not risk impregnating her, even though part of him embraced the idea—craved it. He would never do such a thing to her, never force her to bear the spawn of a demon.

In this, at least, he would not be selfish.

"Ready?" she asked him. She rubbed herself against his erection, slick. Wonderfully wanton. Her nipples abraded his chest, creating a delicious friction. For once, he didn't wish razor blades were scraping over him instead. "Ready?" she asked again.

Gods, yes.

He didn't have to guide his shaft inside her. The tip was already nestled at the brink, ready...drawn to her by an invisible wire. "Savoring," he said. "Need to savor."

She nibbled on her bottom lip. "Waiting is torture. I thought you didn't torture people anymore."

His mouth edged into a strained smile.

"Now. Please, Reyes."

Unable to resist any longer, he cupped her face and pushed all the way to the hilt, groaning in abandon as he did so. Her arms and legs wrapped around him, not just holding him captive but surrounding him with all that she was.

And just like that, she climaxed again.

Her moans spurred him on. In and out, like his fingers. In and out, like he'd fantasized. His thoughts fuzzed, Danika his only focus. Her perfect body, her thunderstorm fragrance. Her sweet moans and her hands, even now petting his back. Nothing else mattered. No one else mattered. Oh, the exquisite agony.

More. Need more.

His lips claimed hers in a scorching kiss, his tongue plundering. Her desire melded with his, heating, branding. Perhaps her goodness even seeped into him, because lights seemed to blink throughout the darkness of his soul, scattering shadows in every direction.

More!

She writhed, and her nipples continued to abrade his chest. The sweet scent of her satisfaction enveloped him.

"How can I want more?" she panted. "Can't get enough. Need…need…"

The pleasure became too much, stinging, and Reyes exploded. He hadn't had to stab himself. A little clawing, but that was hardly significant. Mostly, he'd enjoyed. A shocked, blissful roar burst from his lips, hot seed jetting from him. His spirit might even have left his body.

He didn't know what happened, how it happened. All he knew was the pounding of his heart, the clenching of his muscles, the throbbing in his bones. All he saw was heaven. Clouds, the glide of white-feathered wings, the glisten of gold, the rainbow shine of gemstones. Cool air caressed him. He was floating, soaring, weightless.

But then the last spurt of desire left him, and he collapsed atop Danika. His strength, gone. The clouds faded completely, the wings, the gold and gems, gone. He saw utter darkness and couldn't quite catch his breath. Sweat clung to his skin.

Danika was hot underneath him, panting, trembling.

"What happened?" she gasped.

"Climax." A climax unlike any he'd experienced before.

"No. Reyes, you disappeared."

CHAPTER TWENTY

DANIKA SNUGGLED into the warmth of Reyes's body. For several hours she'd dozed on and off, lulled by the drugging satisfaction humming through her. Reyes slept like the dead and had not awakened once. Had not shifted, had not made a sound. Twice she'd pressed her ear against his chest to ensure his heart still beat.

Now she remained awake, warm and sated. Except her mind churned, refusing to settle down. Being with Reyes had been…everything she had not wanted. Perfect, wonderful, amazing, sublime. No man had ever pleased her like that.

Every heated touch had sparked a tidal wave of desire. The waves had been never-ending, hurtling her from one plateau to another. And that he hadn't allowed her to keep emotional distance between them…even now, she shivered. They had connected, body and soul, and she had secretly loved it.

One question tormented her, though. Well, besides the fact that he'd disappeared but thought she had imagined it. Maybe she had. Her climax had been so intense, she could have blacked out, dreamed he was gone and then woken up underneath him. What she wanted to know more than anything was whether or not he'd enjoyed being with her.

Unless he'd faked it, he'd come. But he hadn't let her hurt him. *That's* what he needed to feel pleasure. She'd wanted to do it, too. Not only so that she might have been able to purge him from her system, remembering him as the worst bed partner ever, but also because she'd wanted to give him anything and everything. Even pain. She'd wanted him to remember her as she would forever remember him.

He claimed he didn't want her tainted by the violence of his life. She'd thought she didn't want to be tainted, either. But as he'd caressed her, as his mouth had devoured her, she'd wanted to meet every single one of his needs.

Other women had hurt him as he craved. Why couldn't she?

Danika twisted her head and gazed at Reyes's sleeping face. Soft and relaxed, the harsh lines of stress were no longer visible. His lips were lush and pink, something she hadn't noticed while his intense eyes watched her.

Carefully she reached up and brushed a lock of hair from his forehead. He inhaled more deeply, but gave no other reaction. Her heart seemed to expand, to grow so big it swallowed her ribs.

I care for him. Though she'd fought against it, there was no denying it.

He'd taken care of her, given her food and shelter and clothing. Never once, even when ordered, had he hurt her. He'd purchased paint supplies for her and created a studio just for her amusement. He'd made love to her as if she were more important to him than breathing.

His strength and courage constantly amazed her; his past fascinated her. He hadn't wanted to hurt others anymore, so he'd locked himself away. Talk about discipline. Compassion. Determination. He was possessed by a demon, and yet he had the heart of an angel. The contradiction delighted her, and she suspected she could happily spend the rest of her life learning his nuances—and there would still be more to learn.

Oh, yes. She cared. And what the hell was that buzzing noise?

Her gaze circled the bedroom, her cheek brushing Reyes's white-hot skin. His heartbeat picked up speed. The buzzing continued sporadically, but she finally pinpointed its location: her pants. That meant...

Dread cascaded through her. She was getting a call on the cell phone. Only one person had the number. Stefano. She gulped. For a moment, only a moment, she wished he *had* been at the club tonight. That he'd faced Reyes, that her struggle with what to do, who to help, was over. When that moment passed, however, guilt scraped at her.

Danika gingerly slid from the bed, watching Reyes for any sign of wakefulness. Still, he remained at peace, unmoving. Part of her longed for him to open his eyes, see the phone and save her from herself. The other part of her prayed he stayed just as he was. She was naked, nipples now hard from the cool air, and one look at those intense black eyes and she would melt, Hunters forgotten. She would beg for Reyes's mouth on her, his heat flicking away the chill.

Her legs were shaky as she stumbled to her pants and she almost toppled as she crouched to pull the phone from their pocket.

The buzzing continued.

Another glance at Reyes—still sleeping. *What are you doing? Don't do this.*

I have to. There's no other way to save Reyes.

She padded to the bathroom and quietly shut the door. Alone, she flipped the phone open. Her mouth dried as she whispered, "Hello."

Once again, Stefano didn't bother with pleasantries. "You left the fortress." A statement, not a question.

Yesterday, she'd been happy to know he was out there somewhere, watching her. Now… "Yes."

"Obviously they've released you."

"Yes," she repeated, recalling that she'd lied to him the last time they'd spoken, told him she was locked in a bedroom.

"Where are you?"

"In a bathroom."

"Alone?"

"Yes."

"Are you working for us, Danika? Or them? Have you forgotten everything I told you? For God's sake, they want to kill your family!"

The harsh question hung inside her mind like a noose, ready to hang her no matter how she replied. "You know that I—" What?

"If given a chance, they'll rape and mutilate your mother. Then your sister. They've already killed your grandmother."

She was shaking her head in denial.

"We're extracting you," he said flatly. "It's for your protection. My sources tell me the one called Aeron is nearly insane with bloodlust for you. We don't want you hurt. Unlike the Lords, we want to protect you."

Extracting her? "Wait. You want to take me out of the fortress?"

"As soon as possible."

No. In the morning, she and Reyes were traveling to Oklahoma. "No, I can't. *You* can't. I—"

"You have no choice, Danika. We're gearing to enter even now. While *they* place no value on human life, we do. We want you safe."

What? They were going to break into the fortress? There would undoubtedly be a battle, blood and death. She tried not to panic, though ice began to crystallize in her veins and a loud ringing blasted in her ears. "If you think I'm working for them, why did you call? Why are you warning me? Wanting to help me?"

"Anyone can make a mistake. They probably lied to you, convinced you they would leave your family alone if you would only stay with them, maybe help them with something. Maybe even help take us down."

Her mouth opened and closed, but no sound emerged. Everything he said made sense.

"Will you be ready?" he asked.

There could be no more stalling, no more straddling the fence, unsure of who to help and who to bring down. To her surprise, she didn't have to think about it. What he said made sense, but it didn't feel right. Sometime in the past few days, her anger toward Reyes had faded completely. Hate had been replaced by…something else. She didn't know what emotion lurked inside her, just that it was somehow at once both soft and almost violent. She would trust him to help her find her family, which meant cutting her safety net, the Hunters.

"Yes," she lied.

"Smart girl." Stefano's relief was almost palpable. "How many Lords are inside the fortress?"

"All of them," she said, lying again. This morning, most of the men had taken off. Had Stefano seen them leave? Or had the warriors simply disappeared as Lucien had done on several occasions?

If Stefano knew the truth, he'd see the seizing of the fortress as easy. *Keep lying. He might not know.* She plopped onto the toilet lid, legs suddenly too weak to hold her up. She leaned forward, elbows digging into her knees. One hand continued to hold the phone to her ear, the other rubbed her temple to ward off the sudden ache. "They're heavily armed. You shouldn't risk entering the fortress. Why don't I sneak out and come to you?" She could tell Reyes where they would be waiting, and he could…take care of things.

"You aren't trained for that sort of thing. It's better if *we* handle this."

What could she do? What could she say to stop this?

"Think you can reach the roof without detection?"

"I—I—" Shit! "Maybe. What time should I be there?"

"One hour."

Dear God. One hour. Could Reyes contact Lucien in time? Could Lucien bring the others here? Sickness rolled through her. "I'll do my best," she said, trying desperately not to tip him off. Her voice was weak, barely audible.

"Don't disappoint me, Danika. Need I remind you what's at stake?" Stefano disconnected, and Danika closed the phone.

She didn't straighten, couldn't; she was too busy trying to breathe. God, there was so much to do, and failure could cost Reyes his freedom—or his life.

"Interesting conversation."

The harsh statement assaulted her ears, and she jolted. All the blood drained from her face. Reyes stood in the now-open doorway, his expression unreadable. He leaned against the frame, one arm behind his back in a deceptively casual pose. He wore a pair of jeans he hadn't bothered to fasten. His chest was bare, the injuries and scabs gone.

"It isn't what you think. I swear."

One of his brows shot into his hairline. "So you weren't talking to a Hunter?"

She jumped up, mouth floundering open and closed.

Reyes's gaze immediately jerked from her. The arm behind his back shot forward and a second later a T-shirt was flying toward her. "Dress. Lucien is here. He wants to talk with you."

She caught the material and hastily tugged it over her head, shielding her nakedness. Her vision was blocked for less than a second, but by the time she refocused, Reyes was no longer standing in the doorway.

The shirt ended at her knees, but she still felt exposed as she raced into the bedroom. Cool air kissed her legs. "Reyes, I was *helping* you! You have to believe me."

She stopped short when she spied Lucien. The warrior was fully dressed, and his clothing was stained with blood. Reyes now stood beside him. Both men were staring at her expectantly.

"Look," she rushed out. "I'm supposed to learn everything I can about you. I've been trying. I admit it. The Hunters who captured me and asked me to spy for them are led by a man named Stefano. Dean Stefano. He was going to help me find and protect my family. To do that, I thought you had to be destroyed. But when I got here, I just couldn't do it. I've spoken to Stefano only twice since I've been here, but I've never given him any useful information."

"Is that all?" Reyes asked, surprisingly calm.

She nodded.

"Very well. Let's move on to another subject, then. I told Lucien what you told me, that there are other beings possessed as we are. Is there anything else you know about them?"

She held up a hand and gave a shake of her head. Why wasn't he accusing her of lying about knowing nothing more? "What are you talking about?"

"The men in prison, the ones housing the demons we released."

"Like that matters now! Will you just let me finish? Please. This is important. Life or death."

His eyes narrowed, but he said no more.

"Hunters are about to attack the fortress. You have an hour, probably less, until they arrive."

"You were painting earlier," Reyes said as if she hadn't spoken. Still, his expression gave nothing away. "Where is the canvas?"

Her gaze flicked to Lucien, then back to Reyes. What the hell? She'd laid everything on the line, admitted her crime, and *that* was all Reyes had to say to her? She'd told him men were about to storm his home, weapons blazing, and he only cared about her paintings?

"I would have been here sooner," Lucien said, "but souls were calling and I could not resist them. I *was* able to flash here for a moment, but you didn't see me. As Reyes said, you were painting. I must see that canvas, Danika."

"I'm not telling you where it is! Not until someone explains why you don't seem to care about the Hunters. They plan to capture you and suck your demons out. They're even looking for the box."

Something glistened in Reyes's eyes. What, she didn't know. It was dark and dangerous, both exciting and perilous. "Torin has the entire hillside monitored. He knew the moment they stepped onto the property, and he's already taken several out."

Taken several out. Aka killed them. Danika rubbed her stomach in a vain attempt to calm its sudden turmoil. "So Stefano lied to me? They're not waiting an hour but have already begun attacking?"

"Yes, he lied. He didn't trust you," Lucien said. "My guess is he told you to go to the…roof?"

Dazed, she nodded.

"He told you to go there because he expected you to do the opposite. They have troops on the ground and they could have snapped you up. Now, what do you know about the box? Any small detail could be useful, but tell me quickly for I am needed outside."

Her gaze settled on him. Looking at him was easier than looking at Reyes. Gave her heart time to slow and her lungs time to expand. "I've already told Reyes everything I know about it, and that's very little."

"Do you know where it is? Where the other demon-keepers are? If they're still imprisoned?"

"No to both questions. I don't know."

"Would your grandmother?"

"You'll have to ask her." She prayed he got the chance.

Lucien's head tilted to the side. "Paris had a vision of you." His oddly colored eyes seemed to swirl, beckoning her. The scent of roses suddenly filled the room. "In it, you were cupping the box in your hands. You were smiling."

Incredulity tumbled through her, and she laughed. "That's impossible."

"If you know something…" Closer and closer Lucien stepped.

She wanted to run, but her feet were rooted in place, holding her captive. And then she didn't want to run anymore. The warrior stood right in front of her, a whisper away, and that rose-scent invaded her every cell. Her mind floated to the clouds.

Utter relaxation softened all of her muscles. *Whatever he says, I'll do. Happily.*

"What do you know, Danika? Tell me."

"Nothing," she said, head lolling forward. She was going to fall and couldn't stop herself. Part of her didn't want to stop.

Reyes was suddenly there, his arm around her waist keeping her upright. He was strength and heat and chased away the cold. "That is enough, Lucien."

"Reyes," Lucien snapped, and it was the most callous she had ever heard the man.

"No," Reyes replied, equally harsh.

"I didn't betray you," she said. She rested her cheek against his chest, praying he believed her. She'd allowed herself to care for him. She couldn't lose him. Not now.

"I know." His fingers rubbed her hip, up and down.

"Wait. What? You know?"

"Yes."

She tossed up her arms. "Well, why were you angry with me?"

"Angry? I was not angry."

"You stormed away from me. You barely even looked at me."

"Angel," he said on a sigh. His hand lifted and he cupped her jaw, angling her to face him. "I am new to this sense of…caring. I hated that you were speaking to a Hunter, I worried for your safety and I did not want to scare you away with my fervency. Also, I knew you were trying to protect me when you lied to the Hunter about the number of warriors here. But I also knew you had created problems for us that you didn't intend."

"I don't understand."

"Now they think we are all here, when there are only a few. They will send more men, bring more weapons."

The heat drained, totally and completely. "I'm sorry. I didn't think… I just thought… Like Lucien said, Stefano doesn't trust me," she said. "He might assume I was lying. He might think only a few of you are here."

"I can bring the others here," Lucien said. "We'll be prepared for the worst."

Oh, God. There was going to be a fight, after all.

"Don't worry," Reyes said. "All will be well. Now. The painting," he reminded her. "Get it for us. Please. We need to see if what you created means anything or can help us."

She nodded just as a phone rang, the sound echoing off the walls.

Frowning, Lucien dug inside his pocket. He barked a quick, "Yes," when the phone was next to his ear.

A moment passed.

His frown deepened as he hung up. "Sabin is impatient."

"I'll be right back." Danika rushed into the studio and lifted the second painting she'd done from its place against the wall. She studied it, taking in first the bright colors and then the complex cast of characters. At the top of the canvas, two men and one woman, all garbed in white robes, sat upon thrones and stared regally down. At the bottom, a breathtakingly beautiful man with angel wings *and* devil horns led a human army across a sea of blood.

There was a butterfly tattoo on his lower stomach, the same type of menacing brand Reyes and the other warriors possessed.

The colors had yet to dry completely, so she was careful as she carted it into the bedroom. There, she propped the canvas on her legs. "Here."

Both men gaped when they saw it.

"What?" she said.

"Do you have any idea who those beings are?" Lucien asked her, his voice strained.

"No." And she didn't. Other than what she'd painted, she knew nothing about them. "But I've seen them in my nightmares," she admitted. "Many, many times."

"Cronus, the king of gods, sits in the center throne. Atlas and Rhea are beside him. At the bottom, those men are Hunters."

"And at the head of the army," Reyes said, sounding choked, "is Galen. Keeper of Hope."

The two men shared a heavy look.

"I cannot believe this. If this painting tells us true, he is leading the Hunters." Lucien gave a shake of his head. "I never suspected...never thought... Why would Hunters willingly follow him? A demon?"

Reyes reached out to trace a fingertip over the winged man's face, realized the paint was still wet and dropped his arm. "Danika and I spoke of him earlier, yet I still cannot wrap my mind around this."

"We will have to deal with it later. There is no time to do so now. I must transport the rest of the warriors here." Lucien's gaze flicked briefly to Danika. "Tell her. She needs to know." With that, he disappeared.

"Tell me what?" Dismay thickened her blood, and her fingers tightened on the canvas.

Grim determination suddenly radiated from Reyes. "Ashlyn heard something. About certain artifacts we are searching for. We knew the second had the power of sight," he said, "something that could see into heaven and hell."

Her brow wrinkled in confusion. "What are you talking about?"

"It's you." His gaze collided with hers and held, a black pit beckoning her to fall. "*You* are the artifact, Danika. You are the All-Seeing Eye. That is why the gods want you dead. That is why Hunters are even now on their way. Everyone wants a piece of you. And I fear no one will rest until they get it."

CHAPTER TWENTY-ONE

BY THE TIME Sabin arrived in the fortress, Hunters were already scaling the mountain. Lucien had flashed him inside Torin's bedroom, a wall-to-wall computer system consuming most of the space. All of the other warriors but the still-imprisoned Aeron surrounded the technological genius, staring at the many screens. No, not true, he realized. Pain was also absent. Again.

"Explosion?" Torin asked, glee in his tone.

"Yes. Blow them to hell," Maddox growled, fingers clenched around a serrated blade. "The only good Hunter is a dead one."

"No." Lucien tugged at his earlobe. "If they manage to bypass the pits, nets and arrows, let them inside. An explosion will draw innocent humans to the hill, and that we cannot allow."

Maddox's nostrils flared. "Ashlyn—"

Lucien gave another of those tugs. "I've already flashed the women to safety, though neither went peacefully. With Anya as her guard, your female will be fine."

The heat of Maddox's anger died, his shoulders slumping. "Very well."

"We let them inside and our home will be painted red," Paris said. "I, for one, will not enjoy cleaning. And with Aeron locked up, I know that duty will fall on my shoulders."

"I've fought Hunters a lot longer than you have," Sabin piped up. "Believe me, it's better to kill them here than to fight them in the city where innocents can be harmed and used against us. And they *will* use innocents. Women and children make wonderful shields."

"All for the greater good," Cameo mocked sorrowfully, and he cringed. Someone needed to put a muzzle on her. No matter how much time they spent together, he would never get used to her voice.

"This is fun," the immortal named William said, rubbing his hands together.

Sabin stared over at him, wondering who the hell had invited him. Making new friends wasn't on his agenda. "What are you doing here?"

Lucien pinched the bridge of his nose. "The warrior is our welcome guest and might be an asset in the coming battle." His tone was anything but happy, though Sabin was willing to bet he hoped the "welcome guest" was maimed in the fray. "We are dealing with more than we ever imagined."

"What are you talking about?" Sabin demanded.

"I am talking about our old friend Galen. I have just learned the Hunters are led by him."

"Galen?" Sabin laughed. "Surely you're joking."

The other warriors laughed, as well, but there was unease beneath their mirth.

Sabin slapped Lucien's shoulder. "We haven't heard from him in thousands of years."

A shake of Lucien's head, those mismatched eyes intense. "This is not a joke. As Ashlyn informed us, Danika is the All-Seeing Eye. One of her paintings has revealed it as so. They asked her to go to the roof. They want to steal her from us."

The words, spoken so calmly, were lethal to Sabin's disbelief. Galen. Responsible for all of his torment. His greatest enemy. Once a trusted friend.

Galen had been the one to suggest they distract Pandora and open that cursed box. Galen had been the one to laud the merits

of showing the gods their mistake. Galen had been their ally—
or so they'd thought.

The gods did not trust us with the safekeeping of the box,
Galen had said. *Have we not proven our strength, over and over
again? Have we not bled for them? Have we not protected
them, all these many centuries? And yet they choose a female
over us. She has not half our strength!*

Cameo had taken offense at that and clawed Galen's face.
The demented man had laughed. Cameo had also taken offense
that Pandora had been the female chosen, rather than herself.
So the warriors had rallied together, confident in their success.

But Galen had planned to betray them all along, jealous for a
reason that had nothing to do with the box. Lucien had been
chosen by the gods as Captain of the Guard; he had not. Only later
had they learned that Galen had used them to do his dirty work,
the actual opening of the box. While they were carrying out his
brilliant idea, he was mobilizing Pandora's army to help him cut
down his "friends" so he could capture the demons himself, take
credit for saving the world—and usurp Lucien's role.

At first, everything had gone smoothly. Paris had managed
to lure Pandora away, for even then females had not been able
to resist him. The others had stealthily approached the box. But
when they reached it, a cadre of soldiers rushed them—Galen
among them.

A battle quickly ensued. Bloody, violent. In the end, the box
was indeed opened, the demons released—all those demons,
finally free. But despite Galen's best efforts—despite *their*
efforts—there'd been no catching them. The demons were
stronger than any of them had assumed. Worse, the box had
vanished like a phantom of the night as the demons devoured
the flesh of Pandora's guards, piranhas who'd been starved and
desperate. The screams…they haunted Sabin still.

Though Galen had turned on them and "helped" Pandora,
he *had* played a role in the box's opening, and so the gods pun-

ished him alongside the others. Hosting the demon of Hope didn't seem like a harsh enough punishment to Sabin, but Sabin had been unable to deliver his own brand of justice. In the turbulent aftermath of their demon-curse, Galen had disappeared and Sabin had been both glad and furious. Vengeance would have been nice. Perhaps now he'd have his chance.

"How dare he do this?" Strider snapped. "Wasn't one betrayal enough for him?"

"If he's controlling the Hunters, could he also be pulling the strings at that Hunter-infested Institute Ashlyn used to work for? She once mentioned that no one had ever seen its president because he never went out in public." Maddox glanced around the room. "Galen, do you think?"

"Maybe." Sabin shrugged. "Ironic that a facility that prides itself on human superiority could be secretly run by a half demon, half immortal. How do you think he manages to keep the Hunters from knowing the truth about him? They cannot know or they would revolt. And why would Galen want us dead, anyway?"

"Why did he convince us to open the box, and then turn on us?" Strider asked. "He had to win, always, no matter the price."

"Look who's talking, Defeat," Maddox said.

"Perhaps he always planned to try to crush us, to rise above us—even the gods—and win the heavens."

Sabin gripped the dagger sheathed in his weapon belt. "Whatever his reasons, if you're right and we're about to have a cozy little family reunion, I'm going to take his head. His skull will look nice on my nightstand. Save me from having to get up to use the bathroom at night."

Paris flicked him a wry glance. "I tell the jokes here. Anyway, I wouldn't get my hopes up that he'll make an appearance."

Grinning like the insane freak that he was, Torin clapped excitedly. "Hopes up. Galen is Hope. Funny. Too bad I think you're right. For whatever reason, Galen hasn't yet revealed himself to us. He doesn't know that we know he's the leader of the Hunters."

"Then let's send him a warm fuzzy card and invite him over. And by *card* I mean all of his Hunters in body bags," Strider said.

"Oh, that's so wrong." Meaning, it was right. Gleeful, Gideon rubbed his hands together. "This is going to be absolutely yawn inducing."

"So," Torin said, fingers flying over the keyboard. "Did we decide to let the Hunters inside or not? They want Danika, the All-Seeing Eye, and they'll be desperate because they think she'll be able to help them find the box, ending us. Letting them inside will place them closer to her."

Sabin shook his head. "Nope, not closer. Reyes is escaping with her. She'll be moving farther away, while the Hunters close in on us."

"How's she an artifact, anyway?" Cameo grumbled.

"Gods, woman," William said. "Your voice is like death. Can you shut it until I leave the room? Please. Seriously, you're like the one woman in the world I *want* to resist."

She glowered over at him.

"*You* had better 'shut it,'" Torin snapped at the warrior, no longer grinning, "or you'll find yourself in one of Strider's body bags."

Cameo's glare became the closest thing to a grin Sabin had seen on her face in centuries. "Ashlyn said the artifacts are guarded by the monster Hydra, and Anya later confirmed it. No one has been guarding the girl."

"Perhaps Hydra *used* to guard her," Sabin said. "Danika's had to be around since ancient times, but obviously isn't immortal so has had to be reborn. Maybe reincarnated. Or maybe the ability is passed through her bloodline, which is why, according to the gods, the entire family has be annihilated. Or perhaps Hydra simply lost her. Hell, maybe *Reyes* is Hydra. You've seen how he is with her."

There was a beat of silence, then someone chortled, "Reyes

is Hydra," then Lucien said, "Let them in. We'll fight them here. Safest that way."

Torin nodded, his fingers never slowing on the keyboard.

Itching with the desire to fight and fight now, Sabin studied the monitors, eight screens that spanned the entire hillside. Nighttime had long since fallen, moonlight allowing only the barest hint of light past the canopy of trees.

All of the Hunters were wearing black and had even painted their faces. But they couldn't hide from the heat sensors or even Sabin's trained eye. Besides the red blur, every rustle of leaves, every scattering of dirt gave them away.

"Shit. They're like locusts," William said. "I mean, seriously. Bugs. There's probably a hundred of them out there."

"Scared?" Sabin asked.

"Hell, no. I think I just came."

Sabin's kind of man.

"How long till they hit?" Strider asked. He shifted from one booted foot to the other, anticipation humming from him.

Torin shrugged, his long white hair shifting on his wide shoulders. "Four minutes. Maybe three. Depends on how smart they are. Some already fell in our pits, and some were killed by the hidden arrows."

As long as I get some, I'm happy, Sabin thought. "They won't storm through the front door all at once. They'll split up. They know *we* know they're out there, so they're not going to try to be quiet much longer. Some will stay at ground level. Some will climb through windows. Some will probably come down from helis, just in case Danika obeyed orders and went to the roof."

"Then we'll split up, as well," Lucien said. "My men and William will take the hill. Yours can have our leftovers."

Sabin grinned. "What you mean, is we'll fight the bulk of Hunters. I knew I loved you for a reason."

A chorus of chuckles rang out, just as he'd intended. Lucien and his men took off then, grinning as they headed outside. They had lived here for hundreds of years. They knew the best places to lie in wait, knew every secret passage to secure.

Unfortunately, Sabin did not. "Should we free Aeron? Let him join the fight? He's a good man to have at your side."

"Hell, no," Torin said. "He'll go for our heads, as well as the Hunters. What's the matter? You scared? Well, don't be. I'll have a monitor trained on every floor of the fortress. Program your cells to vibrate and I'll alert you as the Hunters enter, telling you where they are."

"How did I ever let you go?" Sabin asked him.

"You didn't," Torin said dryly. "I left you to follow Lucien."

"Semantics." He turned to his warriors and motioned to the hall with a tilt of his chin. "Let's do this."

Each of them nodded and stalked from the bedroom, withdrawing their phones as they walked. Sabin was behind them but quickly pulled ahead, his stride long and purposeful.

"Good day to die," Kane said.

For Hunters, it certainly was. Sabin shoved his phone back into his pocket and filled a hand with his 9 mm. He stretched the fingers of his free hand, popping his knuckles.

"Which faction do you think we're dealing with?" Strider asked. "Stefano, still?"

"It so matters," Gideon replied at the same time Kane said, "Any. All. Who cares?"

"Stefano, beyond any doubt. Late-night attack, overeager army and semiautomatics. Besides, he's the one who first captured Danika. He didn't yet know she was the Eye or he wouldn't have let her go," Sabin said, adding tightly, "He's mine. You see him, you leave him alive."

The man wanted to punish Sabin for the part he'd played in his wife's suicide. That was fine, understandable even. But Stefano kept coming after his men, would never leave them alone, and that wasn't. Sabin might have turned his back on love, but he valued his men over himself and he would not allow them to be hunted like this. "Gideon, entertainment room. You know what to do."

"Nope. I don't." Gideon branched off from the group.

"Kane, north hallway."

With a nod, Kane swerved at the next corner. One of the lightbulbs in the chandelier shattered the moment he did so, spraying glass in every direction. There was a hiss, a muttered curse. Then, of course, another bulb exploded.

Disaster. Couldn't take him anywhere, and gods knew there was no way to avoid explosions with him around. Poor Lucien.

"Cameo—" Sabin had tossed a glance over his shoulder. Cameo wasn't among his remaining warriors. Where the hell was she? Irritated, he ran his tongue over his teeth. The woman had been disappearing more and more lately. "Amun, south hallway."

No response. Not even a nod, but Amun changed directions.

"Two minutes more," Strider said, "and then the real fun begins. I doubt Lucien and his crew can kill them all outside."

Sabin flicked him a glance. "Why two minutes? How do you know?"

"Internal radar."

Before the last word left Strider's mouth, the sound of glass breaking echoed through the house. Sabin and Strider shared a grin. "Your radar sucks. Begins now, I'm thinking." He palmed his other gun, the metal a welcome weight in his hand. "West hallway for you, my friend. I'll take east."

Strider nodded, turned on his heel.

"Be careful." Sabin rushed forward, steps eating up the distance. Another window shattered, this one just ahead of him. His cell phone vibrated in his pocket. *Little late, Torin,* he thought. A moment later, three men swinging from rappel wires sailed through the now paneless window on a gust of wind.

His hands whipped up, wrists crisscrossed, his fingers hammering at the triggers as his arms moved, left going right, right going left. *Boom, boom, boom.* The men jerked, screamed and then sagged onto the floor.

Seeing their dying bodies, a sense of satisfaction filled him. Yet blended with it was the impatient rumble of his demon. Doubt wanted in on the action.

"Have fun," he mumbled, and could almost picture the demon rubbing its gnarled hands together in glee.

His mind was ripped open as the spirit reached across the mental plane, searching for weak thoughts to pounce upon. Well used to the experience, Sabin didn't even grimace. Good thing. The distraction could have cost him.

Two other Hunters flew through the window. He shot them as quickly and as effortlessly as he had the others. This was his life—this had always been his life. Fighting, warring, killing. From his earliest memory, he'd known enemies were not to be tolerated. That's why he'd been created, after all: fighting, warring, killing. And that's damn sure how he would take his last breath when he finally reached the end of the line. Fighting, warring, killing.

A rustle sounded behind him.

Spinning, he fired in quick succession. Two more Hunters fell, collapsing forward, shouting in pain. One of their hands reached out and touched his boot. A grenade rolled from those now-lifeless fingers. The pin had already been pulled. Shit. Quick as a blink, Sabin grabbed it and hurled it out the window, praying he didn't hurt his friends. But better it detonate outside than in.

"Fire in the hole," he shouted.

Boom.

So much for preventing explosions. The foundation of the fortress shook. Fire and smoke, screams and the pound of footsteps erupted. A wave of heat billowed into the hallway, blistering his skin. Debris whipped inside, too, and a detached tree limb slapped his face before hitting the floor.

Sabin made to spring over the bodies, only then realizing that one of the Hunters hadn't yet died. The man managed to raise his gun, smiling as he muttered, "No mercy. Isn't that your creed?" He squeezed off a shot.

The bullet slammed into Sabin's thigh, stinging. "Mother-fucker!" Close-range shots were a bitch, and he knew immediately the muscle was blown to pieces. Grimacing, he unloaded a round into the Hunter's already broken body, the sound so loud Sabin's ears rang. "Yes," he spat. "That's my creed."

The man gasped his last breath a second later as blood trickled from his mouth.

You're too weak, Sabin heard Doubt whisper to one of the Hunters outside. *The Lords will kill you. Most likely you won't survive to see another sunrise.*

As clearly as if the Hunter were standing next to him, Sabin heard the man's reply. *No. No. I'm strong. I'll kill* them.

You're practically pissing your pants in fear. Fear they can sense. They'll attack you like an animal. What if they cut you up and mail your bones to your family?

Used to the stream of doubts, Sabin tuned out the whispers. His head turned left and right, left and right as he backed into the corner beside the broken window. A quick peek out the window—no Hunters about to swing inside. A glance down the hallway—no sign of Hunters there, either.

Sucking in a breath, he gazed down at his wound, his pants already glued to his skin, a bloody hole staring up at him. Fucking great. He reached down, probed the entrance and nearly screamed. It was worse than he'd thought. Twisting his wrist, reaching behind, he felt the back of his leg. There was another hole. Thankfully, the bullet had left him. Okay. Maybe not so bad, after all.

He ripped a strip of cloth from the hem of his shirt and tied it around his thigh, stanching the blood flow.

How are your men doing? Lucien's? You should hope no one dies. The Hunters outnumber you so it's possible—

"Shut up," he commanded the demon who was trying to turn the doubts on him.

Most of them have trained to keep their minds blank, Doubt whined. *Only a few were open to me and they're now dead.*

The demon needed to hear the thoughts of its victims before it could attack. "Poor baby," Sabin muttered. "But if you get me killed, you'll lose everything. Become crazed. Eventually be sucked back into the box."

The back of his skull rattled as the demon jolted in horror. *No box. No box!*

"Quiet down, then." Blessedly, the creature obeyed.

Outside, Sabin could hear the pop and whiz of gunfire, the pained gasps of humans. The slide of steel through skin and bone. He glanced into the night, remaining in the shadows as much as possible. He saw the glint of silver—blades, throwing stars—in the moonlight, arcing through the air before connecting with a target.

His gaze caught on one of his friends. Maddox was rushing forward, leapt in the air and fell upon a cluster of Hunters. For several seconds, there was a tangle of arms and legs. A blade moved quickly, fluidly, a dance of feral motion. Then there was utter stillness. Had Maddox—

The warrior pushed to his feet, dislodging lifeless bodies. Maddox turned and motioned to someone with a wave of his fingers. Reyes, who had his arm wrapped around a human female's waist, stepped into the light, but they were gone a moment later.

The All-Seeing Eye. Thank the gods I didn't kill her when I had the chance.

His cell phone vibrated in his pocket. Shit. The patter of footsteps suddenly sounded again, catching Sabin's attention. Too late. He whipped around. Four Hunters had entered the hallway. "Found one!" he heard as they trained their weapons on him and raced forward.

"He's mine. When he recovers from my blows, he's yours."

"I *will* hurt him. Now, later. This is for my son, demon!"

A barrage of bullets slammed into him: shoulder, stomach, next to the fresh wound in his thigh. He'd known better than to allow himself to be distracted. Pushing past the pain, he launched forward with a roar. He fired his semiautomatics until the magazines were emptied, dropped them and spread his arms, bullets continuing to hit him.

He and the Hunters met in the middle of the hall.

They crashed together and tumbled to the floor. One of the Hunters cracked his skull into the marble so hard he didn't move again. The other three withdrew blades and tried to slice at various places on Sabin's body. But he'd expected the attack and had palmed his own during the fall.

Humans, no matter how smart, were no match for an immortal's strength and speed.

He had their necks gushing before they managed more than a few incisions. Panting, Sabin lumbered to his feet. Dizziness battered against his brain like a drum, and he swayed. This rate, and he might not live to fight Stefano. Much less Galen, if the coward ever showed his face.

He closed his eyes for a moment, fatigued, weak.

He must have blacked out, because when he refocused, a human was standing just in front of him—though out of striking distance, he noted. Not just any human, either. Stefano.

Hate rose like a tidal wave in his chest, but he didn't have the strength to rise.

"Knew it was you," Sabin said. His throat felt raw, as if blood and acid had played Search-and-Destroy with his voice box.

Stefano *tsked* under his tongue. "Look at you, Doubt. You must be in pain. How sad."

Sabin slowly moved his good arm behind his back, where a dagger dangled from a chain. He could feel the cold metal against his skin.

"Oh, I wouldn't do that if I were you," Stefano said, lifting his own arm and aiming a gun at Sabin's face.

Sabin stilled. "We both know you're not going to kill me."

"Perhaps we do. But I have no problem hurting you, taking you to the brink of death. My team includes doctors who know how to save a man who's only a heartbeat away from extinction."

"Aren't you a sweetie?" Damn, but his head was filled with a sickening fog. A fog that had nothing to do with weakness but everything to do with…drugs? Had Stefano injected him with something while he was unconscious? Sabin wouldn't put it past the fucker.

"Yes. Yes, I am. I didn't slice off your limbs as I wanted. I didn't carve Darla's name in your chest."

Hearing his lover's name from this man's lips was foul. "She hated you, you know? You think I lured her away from you, but the truth is, she ran willingly into my arms."

Stefano's nostrils flared. "Liar! She loved me! She would never have betrayed me. But you and your demon messed with her mind, changed her." His breath was sawing in and out with the force of his fury. "The last eleven years I've prayed and hoped you would take a lover so I could take her from you, but you never did and I'm through waiting. I'll take your friends, your dignity instead. And ultimately, I'll take your life."

"And such violence will make the world a better place?" he asked dryly. "What of peace and harmony?"

A tongue over teeth. A change of expression, from anger to composure, as if Sabin's questions reminded him of his purpose. "Where's the girl?"

"Maybe we sold her." Sabin straightened his fingers, and they brushed the tip of the knife. "Maybe cut her up and had her for breakfast." Sabin envied Gideon just then, hating that he himself passed out cold every time he tried to lie. Hated that the only way around it was speaking in terms of "maybe" and "probably." Anyone who knew him knew his tricks.

Stefano knew him. "Where is she, demon? She has to be nearby. You knew she'd been with us, and wouldn't want her far from your side."

Another wave of dizziness swept the corridors of his mind. *Don't lose control of yourself. Don't give Stefano the upper hand.*

You're wounded. He already has the upper hand.

His jaw clenched. *Didn't we talk about this? If you want to live, demon, you had better turn the waterworks on the Hunter.*

He's closed his mind. Needs a distraction. Make him think.

A distraction. "This brings back memories, doesn't it?" Sabin asked. "We've been in this position before, only you were the one wounded. You and your men raided my home in New York, thought to sneak in and take us while we slept. You soon learned the error of your ways. Won yourself a personal introduction to my favorite blade. Got you in the stomach, yes?"

Stefano's nostrils flared. "Yes, and you assumed I was dead. Packed up your stuff and moved on, leaving me there to heal, my hatred only growing."

Got him, Doubt crowed, then whispered into the Hunter's mind, *All this planning, the loss of men, the expense of fire-power, but what if it's not enough? What if the Lords escape unscathed once again?*

"Tell me about the girl. The truth this time," Stefano barked. "You wouldn't have killed her. She is the Eye."

"The what now?" He'd known the Hunters had learned of Danika's ability, but now he wondered just who had told them. "Did you just say she was an eye? Her peepers were nice, but I wouldn't define the girl by them."

Even as he spoke, Doubt continued to fill Stefano's head. *She could be leading the Lords to the third artifact even now. If they find the box first, there will be no way to contain the demons. Sabin will live, and you will one day die.*

Stefano's eyes narrowed, the hand holding the gun shaking. "Stop that!"

Sabin blinked innocently, fingers secretly wrapping around his blade. "Stop what?"

"Stop filling my head with those poisoned thoughts. Is that what you did to Darla? Is that how you killed her?"

"She killed herself." He had to be careful. He didn't want to strike Stefano and cause the man to shoot him in the face. That kind of wound could maim him for eternity. Maybe even kill him. "You look as if your head is about to explode. Anything I can do to help? Like tell you you're working for a demon?"

Stefano's lips pulled back from his teeth in a snarl. "Play dumb if you desire. In the end, it won't save you and it won't save the girl. And don't try to sway me with your filthy lies. My leader is an angel and our cause ordained by the heavens."

Sabin saw the muscles in the man's finger twitch and knew the Hunter was only a heartbeat away from pinching the trigger. Angry as he was, he probably didn't care about keeping Sabin alive any longer.

His next words confirmed it. "I don't care what happens to your demon when you're dead. I want you gone. Punished. Once and for all."

Nope, he didn't care.

Sabin summoned a reservoir of might, twisted and rolled—and none too soon. A pop echoed, a bullet whizzing past his shoulder, burning, cutting, but thankfully not lodging. Before his opponent had time to squeeze another shot, he jumped up, kicked out his leg and connected with Stefano's ankles. When the man stumbled to the floor, landing with a thud, Sabin booted the gun out of his hand.

Somewhere in the background, he could hear the scuff of shoes against marble. Enemy? Or ally?

Stefano scrambled backward. So badly Sabin wanted to stride forward, slam his palm into the bastard's nose, cut his neck, *something*. But the last of his strength had all but deserted him. He was panting, still dizzy, and his muscles were clamping down on his bones, holding him immobile. He could only wait, praying it was his friends who would round the corner.

"We aren't finished," Stefano spat, standing. He looked down the hallway and paled.

Thank the gods. That meant it was Sabin's friends who were headed their way. Or one of them, at least. From his periphery he saw Gideon, who was in the process of raising a gun.

"Sabin," Gideon called. "Shit! I'm not here for you, man."

Obviously seeing no other exit, Stefano raced for the window and dove out. Unless there was a mat waiting for him on the ground, he would die when he hit. He was giving up? That easily?

Gideon didn't stop and check on Sabin. He leapt past him and rushed to the window. Sabin grinned weakly. *Trained him well,* he thought, black falling over his vision. His knees finally gave out and he slid to the ground.

"I totally believe what I'm seeing. Fucker was *not* caught by our favorite friend and his feathered wings." *Pop. Pop.* Gideon emptied his gun until there was a *click, click, click.* "Great! Nailed him."

Sabin blinked until his eyes cleared, the immortal responsible for his torment coming into view. There Galen was, long white wings outstretched and flapping delicately as he hovered just outside the window. He was tall, strong and as handsome as ever—as if thousands of years hadn't passed.

He was grinning.

Sabin thought he'd been prepared to see the warrior. Or as ready as he could be, given the shock of Lucien's revelation tonight. He wasn't.

"Now you know," Galen called, his voice as charismatic and empowering as Sabin remembered. "Now the real fun begins."

They were the last words Sabin heard before crumpling into oblivion.

CHAPTER TWENTY-TWO

THREE DAYS. Three damn days since Danika and Reyes had left the fortress. They'd traveled on and off, going from plane to stolen car to train, never remaining in one place for long. Just in case. Neither of them wanted to lead Hunters to her family. And as much as it stunk to be on the run again, it was a thousand times better because Reyes was at her side. Surly as he was.

They hadn't spoken much. He barked an order every now and then—duck, run, be quiet—but that was the crux of their few conversations. She hadn't seen any Hunters, but that didn't mean anything and she lived in constant fear and dread. As usual.

They slept in cheap motels, always in the same room but never in the same bed. Sometimes, at night, after he'd fortified every exit of their motel room with extra locks, Reyes would barricade himself inside the bathroom. Like now.

Eyes narrowed, Danika peered at the closed door. She lay on a full-sized bed, the small, dingy room cast in shadows that were interrupted every so often by car lights streaming through the stained red curtains. She'd kicked off the stiff, starchy comforter and had propped herself against the headboard. Waiting. Reyes had been inside that bathroom for half an hour.

Oh, she knew exactly what he was doing. The knowledge didn't disgust her, it…saddened her. Why did he no longer desire *her?* Why did he not come to *her* for relief from his demon?

Because he thought she was some silly artifact?

"Dummy," she muttered.

He and his friends kept in close contact. From the one-sided conversations she'd managed to "accidentally" overhear as he whispered into his cell phone—would have helped if she'd possessed Ashlyn's ability to listen to any conversation—she knew Hunters had indeed attacked the fortress. Stefano had escaped unscathed. A few Lords had been seriously injured but were thankfully healing. Oh, yeah. And they wanted her to paint. Breathe, eat and paint. That's all they wanted her to do.

A few months ago, that might have made her happy.

Reyes had given her a sketchbook, which she'd used every morning to purge herself of her riotous dreams. Dreams more violent than ever as demons clawed at the jagged, flame-drenched walls of hell. When she finished, Reyes would tear the pages and have her fax them to Lucien. She didn't know if the drawings had helped their cause. No one would tell her a damn thing.

"'Cause I'm just the lowly painter girl," she grumbled.

The bathroom door creaked open. Reyes had turned off the lights, so she saw only his shadow as he strode out. The scent of sandalwood was laced with the metallic tang of blood, and both wafted to her. While she couldn't see his features, *she* was bathed in moonlight and his to peruse. She felt the intensity of his gaze boring into her, sliding over her.

His heat—oh, she missed his heat. Since being with him, she hadn't experienced any more of that mind-numbing cold. Still. Was it too much to ask of him to keep her well supplied in his mega hotness? Apparently.

"Worried about your family?" he asked, settling on the pallet he'd made on the floor.

She'd called her grandmother's friends. They still denied seeing the woman, and she believed them. "No. They're fine. Maybe I'm crazy, but I've convinced myself they're fine. I *am* excited about seeing them tomorrow. Thank you for finally re-lenting, by the way."

"I did not relent for you. I relented because I have seen no sign of Hunters."

"Whatever. I'm still grateful."

One minute after another passed. He didn't move. No sound—not even the whisper of his breath—rose from that floor. She hated the silence. It allowed her mind to wonder and churn, worry about what Reyes was thinking, fret about what would happen in the coming days, lament the fact that she'd once wanted only one night with Reyes but would now beg for another. And another.

The more she smelled Reyes, the more she desired him. The more her blood rushed and the core of her throbbed. "Distract me," she said, scooting down the mattress to lie flat. She pulled the sheet up and it rasped against her hardening nipples. She barely stifled a moan. "Please."

"How?"

"I don't know. Tell me something about you." Had she asked that of him before? She couldn't remember.

"I thought you did not wish to know anything about me."

Oh, yeah. "I changed my mind. I'm a girl, I can do that."

Another minute of silence, then, "I do not want to play this game, Danika."

Something she'd noticed about him. He called her Danika when he wanted to keep distance between them. He called her angel when he wanted to draw her closer. She missed being called angel.

They'd had sex all those days ago, and it had been wonderful. She wanted, needed, more. Of him. Only him. He was an addiction. He'd believed her about not helping the Hunters when other men might have thought her disloyal. He'd rushed her to safety, covering her body with his own when gunshots blasted. He'd given her a taste of the paradise she sometimes painted, gently rocking her to orgasm.

Now, she wanted wild. Hard and rough. Yes, she'd once

thought she would be too disgusted to participate in such an act. Thought she would not be able to hurt another being like that. Right here, right now, she knew better. There was nothing more satisfying than meeting a man's—your man's—needs. Being the one to please him completely, give him utter relief.

A few times on their journey, she'd tried to broach the subject of sex with Reyes. She'd even reached out and brushed her fingers through his hair, over his jaw and down his chest. The first time he'd stopped her by walking away. The second he'd snapped a terse warning.

"I can't sleep," she said. "Talk to me about *something*. You've obviously been around a long—long—time." Okay. Now her frustration was showing. She'd basically called him an old man. "Surely you can regale me with some type of history lesson."

She thought she heard him snort.

Her lips twitched. "Not up for the challenge?"

"Tell me something about yourself first. How did you support yourself? In your old life."

Old life. Seemed an eternity ago. "I did portraits and murals. I was never rich, but it paid the bills. My mom was disappointed at first. Painting is how my grandmother earned a living for most of her life, and they wanted something different for me. Medical school, law school. Something more…important, I guess."

"Painting is important. It adds beauty to the world."

"Thank you." His words endeared him to her all the more. "My grandmother tried to kill herself once. Said her paintings were driving her insane. But then, after the unsuccessful attempt, her creative well dried up and she never painted again. That well must have sprung inside me, because I began having the dreams a few weeks later. Her life became peaceful and mine, though I was only a child, turbulent. I guess that's why I always understood my mother's reluctance to let me pursue the arts."

"What happened to your father? Did he stay home when you traveled to Budapest or is he…had he…"

"Died? No. He walked out on us a while ago. Started another family." The loss had devastated her. She'd considered him a god. At the very least, a good man with a kind heart. But he'd abandoned her as if she'd meant nothing to him. "My mom told me his midlife crisis kicked in."

"I am sorry."

"After that, my grandparents—my mom's parents—stepped in and helped my mom raise us. My grandpa became a second father to me, which is why his death nearly destroyed me."

"You have known much loss in your short life."

"Yes." And she didn't want to lose Reyes, too. She'd tried to prevent it, had fought against it, but somehow he'd come to mean the world to her. "Your turn to tell me something."

A pause. Then, "Give me a moment to think."

She rotated to her side. Again the sheet rasped against her, reminding her that a very handsome, sensual man was mere inches away. *Still. I'm wearing a T-shirt and surrounded by cotton. My body shouldn't react as though I'm naked and being draped by silk.* But the heat was spreading, infusing her every cell.

"Tell me about your other girlfriends." That ought to put a damper on her arousal. Then she realized exactly what she'd said. "By other," she rushed to say, "I don't mean that I'm your current girlfriend or that I've ever been your girlfriend." God, could this conversation get any more embarrassing?

A sigh pushed from him, and Danika would have sworn she felt that minty breath all over her sensitive body.

"I tried to keep females. Two of them."

Two? The whores! *Whoa, girl. Bring it down a notch.* "Keep them? What do you mean?"

"Have a relationship," he clarified.

"What happened?" *Did they fall down a flight of stairs and break their ugly faces?* Jealousy was so not a good look for her, she decided.

"After a few weeks in my bed, they began to lash out at everyone they encountered. I mentioned that before, but did I tell you they laughed while doing it? Tripping people—innocents. Pushing, scratching, punching. Even cutting."

She detected a note of guilt in his voice. "And you still think you made them that way?"

"I know I did."

"Maybe that was their nature. Maybe you just helped them unleash their true desires. Maybe you were subconsciously drawn to that type of woman, knowing they would not find your tastes...unappealing."

More silence. Then, "Maybe," he said, and there was hope in his voice this time, the guilt completely overshadowed.

Hope. She wouldn't ponder the merits of it. Not tonight.

"Your nature is gentle," he added as an afterthought, "yet the very day we were reunited after months apart, you bit me."

"I was furious with you and scared for my family."

"Or Pain influenced you, luring you to attack me."

"Or I was furious and scared," she said again.

"As I said, your nature is gentle."

"Nope, sorry. I hate to disillusion you, but I've always had a volatile temper."

"I do not believe you."

"No," she said. "You believe me, you just don't *want* to believe me. Why is that? Don't want to admit we might be more alike than you're comfortable with? Don't think you'll like who I really am?" Ouch. Just the thought sparked an ache in her chest.

"I like who you are. I am just scared of who you are. Sweet, passionate, giving, caring. And yes, a little wild. I want you more than I've ever wanted another."

Sweet Jesus. Words to melt the coldest of hearts.

"Tell me of your boyfriends," he commanded. The words lashed at her.

"You told me you never wanted me to discuss them."

"I changed my mind. I am a man, I'm allowed to do that."

She laughed. Gold star for Reyes for throwing her words back at her.

"Have you ever…loved a man?"

"No." Did she love Reyes? What she felt for him was so much more intense than anything she'd ever felt before. The fervent wanting and the craving and the softness inside her…. Shit, shit, shit. "But I've dated," she forced out. "A lot."

"What do you mean by *a lot?*" Some of the fierceness had left him. At least he no longer sounded ready to kill anyone who even glanced in his direction.

"A girl has to kiss a thousand frogs before she finds her prince, my sister used to tell me. I took that to heart and used to go out with anyone who would ask me. And just so you know, I was *not* easy."

"Easy?"

"You know, doing the naked tango with anyone who expresses interest."

Another almost snort. "Rest assured, I know you are far from easy." Then, "Did someone *call* you easy? If so, I will—"

"Reyes, stop," she said, unable to keep the laughter from her voice. His fierceness had returned full force. "No one called me easy." She loved that he was willing to destroy anyone who might have, though. "I just wanted to make sure *you* knew. I've only dated a few guys seriously."

"Shall I kill them?"

"Why, Reyes, I think that's the nicest thing you've ever said to me."

Danika thought she heard him chuckle.

"I have never been in love," he said, surprising her.

Suddenly she felt like singing and dancing. He was hers, had always been hers. "Not even before you were possessed?"

"Not even before."

She tried to picture him as he must have been hundreds,

thousands, of years ago but couldn't. "What were you like? Back then?"

"I was like I am now, only…more relaxed, I suppose." He chuckled, a memory probably playing through his mind. That chuckle slid over her like a caress. "I did have a teasing side and used to torment Aeron relentlessly, hiding his weapons, cutting his hair while he slept. Finally, he started shaving it."

"I wish I could've known you."

"Perhaps it's good you didn't. We were like children back then. We were born fully formed of body, but our minds were new and we constantly marveled at the world around us. We trained to be warriors, yet had only the gods and their amusements as our role models."

Even with his description in her mind, she couldn't picture him so childlike, laughing and running and teasing. "How is it possible you were born a fully grown man?"

"You mix the blood of a god, earth, fire, water…" His voice trailed off. "At least, that's what we were told. And you? What were you like as a child?"

"Typical, I suppose. Tantrums and whining to get what I wanted. My mother used to call me her Tasmanian devil."

"You probably looked like an angel, even then."

Angel. Her heart skipped a beat. "Reyes," she said breathlessly.

"Yes," he replied with resignation.

"I want to be with you again."

The silence returned, a snake that slithered around its prey and choked. Had he truly stopped wanting her? Despite everything he'd just said? He'd had a taste of her, and that had been enough? Or had he just not liked what he'd tasted?

"Danika—"

She growled in frustration. *Danika* again. "Never mind. Just…shut up and go to sleep." She flipped angrily to her stomach and pounded her fist into the pillow to flatten it.

There was no sound to alert her of any movement on Reyes's

part, but suddenly he was on top of her, his heavy body pinning her down and smashing her face into the mattress. She gasped.

His fingers gripped her neck tightly, turning her face and allowing her to breathe. He didn't shift, though, didn't roll off and free her. He kept her pinned. He hovered over her, warm breath lashing out like a whip. From the corner of her eye, she could see his face in profile. His eyes glowed with fire, and his teeth were bared.

Moonlight finally found him, casting a golden glow over his dark, honey-colored skin. He was panting, sweat was glistening. His long, thick erection pressed against her bottom, and she shivered.

"I will not taint you," he snarled. "Do you understand? If that means I cannot have you again, then I will not have you."

"Then you're dumb! You've said that before, and I'm tired of hearing it."

"You have no idea what could happen to you. You have no concept of—"

"You're afraid I'll become pain hungry like those women. Well, guess what? That isn't my nature! I killed a man, Reyes. A human. A Hunter. I hurt him and then I killed him. Have I since attacked everyone I've encountered? Did I attack you and your friends when I had every reason to do so?"

"No." Reyes arched into her. "No."

She couldn't stop her moan. "I made love to you, yet I didn't then start plotting the deaths of your friends, wanting to hurt them. In fact, immediately afterward I tried to *protect* you." Made love, she'd said. Before, she'd insisted it was only sex.

"Because I was gentle. Because I kept my demon away from you."

He wanted her to demand gentleness again. He wanted her to demand he keep his demon away from her again. She knew it, felt it, but wasn't going to do it. "Give me everything you've got this time. Let me prove I'm not going to change."

"No. I am not willing to risk it." But he didn't stop moving against her, rubbing that erection between her cheeks. His hands slid down her arms and latched on to her wrists. He moved them over her head and gripped them with one hand while tracing the other along her side, stopping at the curve of her breast.

Her teeth had long since sunk into her bottom lip. She nibbled, drawing blood. "Yes," she groaned. "Keep going. Touch."

His fingers dug around her, between her body and the mattress, and then he was cupping her breast fully, the nipple locked between two fingers.

A spear of pleasure shot through her. She raised her hips, meeting his erection, silently begging for a more intimate touch. "Remove my shirt. Touch my skin."

"Too dangerous."

"We're doing this."

"You plan to force me?" he asked with amusement.

"If need be. Now remove my shirt."

Growling as if in pain—sweet pain—he released her only long enough to drag the material over her head and toss the shirt aside. "Gods," he growled. "You're not wearing any panties."

"I was hopeful." She could feel his jeans against her lower body, rough, like calluses. "Done resisting me?"

How many minutes passed before he spoke, she didn't know. Finally, he said, "We'll be gentle." The words were so low, so rough she had trouble understanding them. "We'll be slow. Like before."

Danika shook her head, hair batting against her temple. "Hard. Fast."

"No. I've already cut myself and have no more need for pain."

He'd already cut himself? Since leaving the bathroom? As for the other, she knew he was lying. He'd sounded too reluctant; he would need more. "But—"

His hand once again dug and cupped and she forgot her protest.

"Oh, God," she shouted. "Yes. More."

"Are you wet, little angel?"

She felt as if she'd been waiting for him, for his touch, forever. Desperate and eager. "Find out for yourself."

A moment later, she was flipped over and peering up at him. He was a god, strong and fierce, all of his intense sexuality focused solely on her. His gaze glided over her breasts, and he licked his lips. Then that gaze moved to her stomach, and her muscles quivered.

He stopped and lingered at the fine patch of curls between her legs. Lines of tension branched around his eyes as his hands gripped her knees and spread them wide. His gaze heated, flames actually crackling inside the black-as-night, starless depths.

"Grip the headboard," he commanded.

She'd been reaching for him, meaning to scrape her nails over his chest. Perhaps draw blood. "But—"

Once again he stopped her from finishing a sentence. "Grip. The. Headboard. Now. Or I'll return to my pallet."

Was he close to losing control? If so, he needed her to hurt him. Right? She could finally prove to him—and herself—that she was capable of doing this. "Let me, Reyes. Please."

"No. I will not tell you again. Grip the headboard or this ends now."

"Fine. But I am not always going to be so accommodating. Understand?" Eyes narrowed, she slowly reached behind her and clutched the iron rails. They were cold, drawing goose bumps from her flesh. "Happy?"

"Not yet. Not until I taste you."

God, yes. "I want to taste *you* this time, too."

A moan separated his lips. He liked the idea, but she suspected he wouldn't cave. He probably assumed she'd explore his body, trying to hurt him while doing so. He assumed correctly.

What would she have to do to prove to him that she wouldn't be tainted by the violence he needed?

"So pretty," he cooed, all of his anger gone. Two of his fingers played between her damp folds, circling her clitoris.

Her hips arched of their own accord, her body desperate for more of him. "Reyes," she breathed.

"More?"

"Please."

Those two fingers pushed inside her, pumped once, twice, ratcheting up her desire to an uncontrollable degree.

"You're soaking my hand," he said, pride in his tone.

"Lick me. Please." She had to have his fingers, had to have his tongue. All of him she could get, she craved. And yet, she suspected it might never be enough.

Rather than grant her plea, he pulled from her and severed contact.

"No!" she cried. "What are you doing?"

"Getting naked." He shed his jeans, tossed them aside.

Oh. "Hurry!"

But he didn't return to her right away. She couldn't stop writhing as he leaned down toward the floor.

"Reyes?"

"Condom." He straightened, a silver packet glinting in the moonlight.

"Not so indifferent, after all, hmm?"

"Bought them this morning. Knew my resolve was weak." The packet disappeared from her view, and there was a rustle of sheets.

Then his fingers were back inside her. Three this time. "God, yes. Yes."

And then his mouth was on hers, hot tongue stroking inside her.

So good. Felt so good. His cock rubbed against her, smooth and hot. There was another flash of silver, he moaned in bliss, and she thought, *Another condom?* Surely not. He didn't need two. What…why… Oh, God. He kissed down her body, knew just where to lick, just where to suck and lave.

"Stop for a minute," she gasped out. She needed to think, and she couldn't do it with his mouth on her.

"Why?" he asked, sucking on her clitoris as he pulled back. She nearly came, the pleasure was so intense.

Silver. What had that second flash of silver been? What would cause him to moan like that?

"Danika?"

A knife, she suddenly realized. He'd cut himself. She knew it, and she didn't like it. Her eyes closed briefly, blocking the sight of him. Her arousal had glistened on his lips, and he'd been in the process of licking it away.

"Hand over the blade," she commanded. "Now."

REYES WAS SHOCKED by Danika's order, aroused to the point of that delicious pain. He marveled that he hadn't needed to cut himself to sustain his erection, but he'd done it because he hadn't wanted Pain to rear its ugly head. He hadn't wanted his resolve to weaken, giving Danika an opportunity to pounce.

Like now.

Even still, less and less did he want to stop her. More and more, he liked the thought of being hurt by her.

Won't taint her, can't taint her. Too precious. Too mine. Too long without her.

He tossed the blade so that it embedded in the far wall, the hilt swaying mockingly.

"No," he said, glaring down at this woman who so consumed his thoughts.

He'd had her once and shouldn't have desired her so fiercely again. But he needed her. Craved her like air. And he could have her, if he remained gentle.

"The knife," she said tightly. "Get it for me."

Scowling, he leaned down until they were nose to nose. She hadn't released the headboard, so her back was arched. Her hard nipples pressed into his chest, a temptation he wanted in his mouth.

Soon.

He gripped his swollen shaft with one hand and her chin with the other. "Do you want me?"

Her pupils, already dilated, swallowed the rest of that lush jade. "Yes. You know I do."

"You'll take me, then, without hurting me. And I'll give it, without hurting you. That is the only way this can work."

He waited for her response, the tip of his erection pressing into her. When a minute dragged by without a word from her, he leaned down and sucked her nipple into his mouth.

Another gasp from her, this one layered with need.

"Tell me I'm right," he insisted. He sucked on the other nipple, hard, then licked the sting away.

"Yes. Yes."

All he needed to hear.

He shoved to the hilt, and they cried out in unison. Her inner walls were hot and wet, silk forged by liquid fire. All of his muscles strained for release, for the exquisite pleasure he had never really experienced with anyone else.

From the beginning, his heart had recognized this woman as his. Like the demon, she was part of him, a part needed to make him whole. Her courage delighted him. Her teasing way, now that he'd experienced it, tempted him. Her willingness to help him despite everything that had happened touched him.

Right here, right now, she was his. A ticket out of hell and into heaven.

He did not know if he would ever be able to let her go, but he knew that he needed to try. For her safety. As she had once pointed out, his life was one of war and torment and that would not change. She deserved better.

He'd tried to distance himself from her, but had failed. Tomorrow, he thought, pumping and gliding in and out of her.

She writhed, her head thrashing. She moaned and chanted his name. "How is it so good?"

"Angel," he panted. "Don't know."

She climaxed a second later, knees squeezing him. She finally released the headboard and grabbed his face, jerking him down for a wild kiss.

Their tongues rolled together in a bid for dominance, their teeth clashing. Her nails dug into him, and he followed her right over the edge, roaring her name, seed jetting in a hot flow. He didn't know how it was possible, how he could feel pleasure without intense pain. Didn't understand why Pain was so quiet when he was with Danika, as if the demon was content to allow Reyes these moments. Didn't understand how he felt almost...normal with her.

He didn't have time to ponder it, either. Like the last time, his spirit seemed to leave his body, floating, soaring, stopping only when reaching the golden gates of heaven. He'd given no real thought to this before, assuming he'd simply been drunk with pleasure. Now, he watched wide-eyed as angels flew beside him, feathers brushing his skin in delicate strokes. Clouds hovered all around, the sun shining brightly, the sky painted azure.

One angel looked at him, smiling slowly. "Light and dark," the heavenly creature said in a voice more song than human. "Pretty."

In that instant, Reyes realized something frightening. Danika was indeed the All-Seeing Eye, and that Eye was more complex than anyone had realized. For she somehow opened a portal between earth and the hereafter. A portal many would probably kill to possess.

DREAMS PLAGUED DANIKA all night. Dark dreams, turbulent and bloody. The fires of hell licked at her, smoke billowing, putrid, filling her nose and making her gag. She'd been here a thousand times before, but the evil never failed to creep her out.

Scaled demons of every color crawled all around the rocky cavern. Screams, such screams, echoed off the blood-soaked walls. No one seemed to notice her, for they were too busy racing between the souls chained all around.

Her gaze landed on one human soul in particular, his features suddenly clear. Her jaw dropped. Somehow, someway, she was staring at the Hunter she'd killed. How was that…how could…no, not possible. *Just a dream,* she reminded herself.

"Tell me what you know about the Eye," a demon purred at his side.

The Hunter trembled, remaining silent.

Laughing, the demon began clawing at his skin, ripping it to ribbons. He screamed over and over, the demon continuing to laugh, and soon *her* screams joined the chorus.

"I'm here, angel. I'm here."

Reyes's voice pierced her mind and jerked her from the dream. Sweat poured from her body. She couldn't quite catch her breath. Reyes held her, and she burrowed against him, his strength trickling into her.

"What happened?" he asked, stroking her back.

"I saw a demon torturing the man I killed, and demanding to know about *me.* Just hold me," she pleaded. In the morning, she would sketch what she had seen. Right now, she simply needed her man. *Maybe I* am *the Eye. Maybe I can see directly into the afterlife.* The nightmares had always *felt* real. Made sense, she supposed, that they would be.

God, the thought of that…sickened her.

Reyes's arms tightened around her. His fingers traced patterns along her spine. Several minutes passed, and she began to relax. Her sense of rightness returned, the bad stuff giving way to good.

Funny that it had taken a demon to chase her nightmares away, she mused as she drifted to a peaceful sleep.

CHAPTER TWENTY-THREE

MORNING ARRIVED, but the motel room showed no sign of it. Sunlight didn't seep past the taped-together curtains covering the only window and Reyes must have unplugged the clock, because there were no bright red numbers alerting her to the time.

Danika's eyelids opened slowly. The scent of coffee wafted to her, a summoning finger she couldn't resist, and she eased up. The cotton sheet fell to her waist, baring her breasts to the cool air.

Shivering, she gripped the material and snatched it up to her chin. All the while her gaze circled the small area. Reyes was no longer in bed. His clothes were gone from the floor.

Where had he—

The door opened before she could work up a good steam, finally allowing a flood of bright light inside.

Danika blinked against it, even held up a hand to cover her now-watering eyes.

"Good. You're awake," Reyes said, shutting the door.

Since the light had been successfully chased away by shadows, she allowed her hand to fall to her side, her hungry gaze seeking the man who had given her so much pleasure last night—the man who had not let her give him the same.

He stopped beside the table, and she noticed he held a small sack in his hand. "Breakfast is on the table. I am sorry the selection is poor, but I shopped here, at the motel, so that I could watch our door and ensure your safety."

She tore her gaze from him—hardest thing ever—and looked

at the table. A cup of coffee, three candy bars and a bag of chips awaited her. "That's perfect," she said, and she meant it. Not because she liked those items but because he'd gone to so much trouble for her. Her stomach rumbled. "What's in the bag?"

"A shirt," he said, offering no more.

What was with him? He was acting distant again, as if last night hadn't happened. Lids narrowed, she swung her attention back to him. Over the past few days, she'd noticed he changed T-shirts at least three times a day. She thought she knew why. He didn't want her to see dried blood on the material.

To have bought one this morning meant he must have cut himself. Again.

"Take off your shirt," she told him.

A muscle ticked in his jaw. He strode to the bathroom, throwing over his shoulder, "Eat, shower, dress. We see your family today."

Her heart leapt at the thought, betraying the nervousness she'd denied last night, as well as excitement. Were they happy? Did they miss her as intensely as she missed them? Why had they gotten together and not included her?

Shoving those questions aside for the moment, Danika catapulted off the bed and raced for the bathroom. Naked, she twisted, spread her arms and clutched the frame, blocking Reyes just as he tried to enter.

He stopped a whisper away from her. Her nipples instantly hardened, reaching for him. His mouth, his touch. That fragrance of sandalwood that seemed to follow him no matter the time of day or what he'd been doing, enveloped her.

She licked her lips. "Take off your shirt."

His dark gaze locked on her, hot as it slid down...down... Her skin erupted in those delicious goose bumps, and her legs trembled.

"You have the most delectable little body I've ever seen," he said hotly.

"Th-thank you. Now the shirt. You won't be able to distract me."

His free hand latched on to the frame, just under hers, as if he needed to hold on to *something*. The wood cracked beneath his grip, though he tried to maintain a casual expression. "I know why you are so cold all the time."

"I said you can't distract me. Besides, I'm not cold *all* the time. I can recall two instances when I was nearly burned alive."

His lips twitched, even while the heat in his gaze intensified. "No, not all the time."

"Why, then? Because the air is cold?"

At her dry tone, the twitching became a full grin. Every nerve ending in her body sparked, shooting her full of electricity and warmth. That smile, oh, that smile. As heady as his caresses.

"You are a portal to both the heavens and the underworld." He leaned down…down…his lips brushed her ear.

She shivered.

"At times, your spirit connects with the hereafter, pulling images into your mind."

She shook her head in disbelief. "If that were true, I would have been cold my entire life. But I didn't experience that bone-numbing sensation until after I met you."

"I must be a—" he closed his eyes for a moment, obviously searching for the correct word "—conduit for you, then. Every time I'm with you, I fly to the heavens."

Now she grinned. "That just means I'm a better lover than I ever realized." First they thought she was some All-Seeing Eye. Now a portal? *Hello, I'm just a normal—albeit somewhat insane—girl.*

At least, that was her prayer. She didn't want to be anything more. She didn't want people chasing her for the rest of her— short?—life. She deserved rest and relaxation, damn it. With Reyes. They could travel to a beach, laze on the white sand, and he could pretend to be her massage therapist.

"With training, you could probably learn to control your visions. Decide where to visit, heaven or hell. Decide how long to stay, who to watch."

By the middle of his speech, she was shaking her head. Sweat had broken out over her body, yet the chill had returned to her blood. "I don't want to talk about this anymore. I want you to take off your goddamn shirt!"

His head tilted to the side, but he didn't obey her.

Fine. He wanted to avoid the subject of his self-inflicted torture, then she'd give him something worse to ponder. Maybe then he'd beg to talk about his newest wounds. "Listen up. You come when you're with me, but from what I can tell you only hurt yourself a little. Nothing close to what the other women had to do to you. That has to mean your demon is tamer when you're with me. True?"

He hesitated, his eyes suspicious, nodding stiffly.

Surprise filled her, because she'd merely been guessing. If the demon calmed for her and no other, that had to mean *something* was going on. *Was* she a portal? "If I am the Eye and I am a portal, it stands to reason I would send your demon somewhere when you're inside me."

His mouth fell open.

"I wonder where the demon goes. Who knows, maybe it travels to hell to visit its buddies. Want to test the theory?"

As if he were in a daze, he staggered backward. "I—I—"

"This is good news." She stepped toward him. "Right? You can be with me without fear of destroying me."

"I do not dare hope," he whispered brokenly. "You know what happens when people hope."

Shit. She didn't have a ready reply to that.

"You wanted to see my wounds." There was a heavy pause in which he remained absolutely still. Then he dropped the bag he'd been holding and gripped the end of his shirt. He jerked the material over his head, baring his chest to her view. "Look."

Her plan had worked. And yet, she realized she would have liked to continue the discussion. She'd made some excellent points. But then her gaze moved over him and she saw the scabs that covered the entire muscled expanse of his chest, some even marring the butterfly tattoo. They were long slashes and short slices, and all intertwined in a mess of pain.

"You did this to yourself?" she asked tightly.

"Yes."

Would he ever trust her to help him? Probably not, she thought next, disappointment flooding her. Unless…

One day soon, she would have to surprise him. If she was able to send his demon away, he would not need the pain. What he needed was peace of mind. Only stabbing him would prove that she *could* hurt him, *could* meet his needs and not mutate into a pain-hungry little hooker.

With that in mind, she flattened her palm on his chest and pushed. Though she was strong, he was stronger, and the movement wouldn't have budged him unless he allowed it.

He allowed it.

"We're done here," she said, and slammed the bathroom door in his face.

WOMEN. Would Reyes ever understand them?

He was doing Danika a favor, keeping her from the dark side of his life, yet she'd looked at him with absolute betrayal in her eyes. Even now, two hours later, that expression haunted him.

What if she's right? What if Pain leaves you when you're with her?

Did he dare try and confirm such a fantastical thought? Could irreparable damage be done if she was wrong? He just didn't know.

"Are you all right?" he asked her.

She nodded. She was unusually quiet as they navigated the Oklahoma sidewalks, doing their best to remain in the shadows of the tall, redbrick buildings and out of the sights of other pedestrians. Cars and trucks buzzed along the road. He hadn't spotted any Hunters, or even anyone watching them too intently.

"Just a little farther," he said, reaching for her hand. Earlier, Torin had e-mailed him the women's location. They hadn't moved, and they were still together.

Danika nodded again, her ponytail bouncing. Her features were pale and drawn and she pretended not to notice his hand.

Reyes hated seeing her like this.

He dreaded what would happen if—when?—she found that her grandmother had been killed and buried, and that was why the woman hadn't moved. Would Danika rediscover her hatred for him? Would she rail at him or seek comfort from him?

Would she wish she had aligned herself with the Hunters?

Dread coursed through him. He should warn her, prepare her. But he opened and closed his mouth, and the words never left him. And then they were standing in front of the targeted building, a dilapidated structure with boarded windows and spray paint marring the brick.

"I'll go in first," he said.

"No." A tremor of…dread? excitement? rocked her. "They'll freak when they see you."

Reyes cupped her cheeks. Clouds shifted, turning the bright sky to murky gloom. When they shifted again, sunlight tossed a beam directly at her, paying her smooth, flawless skin the homage it deserved. Just then, she practically glowed. She didn't look part of the earth, but something more powerful, something beyond.

I've had this woman, tasted her.

His body tightened, preparing to have her and taste her again. *Not yet… Perhaps not ever again.* The demon purred happily, and Reyes didn't know if it was because he wasn't going to allow himself to have her or because there was a chance he would ultimately cave.

Where had that purr been the last time he'd made love to her?

Where do you go when I'm with her? he couldn't help but ask the creature.

Fires.

Fires. Hell?

Sometime soon, I have to let her go. It's for the best, safer. For all the reasons he'd named before and a thousand more. Being with her opened that portal into heaven—which meant he might very well cause her to open the one into hell, as well. Also stood to reason that, if he traveled to heaven, she would be the one to travel to hell. Already her nights were plagued with terrors. She did not need more evil in her life.

Letting her go, though… His hands tightened into fists. One day, would she fall in love with a human who would not hurt her, destroy her or ruin her? A man who would give her children and—

Roaring sounded in his head. His. The demon's. No man but him would touch her. Not without dying.

"Reyes, you're hurting me."

Instantly his arms fell away from her. He jerked a hand through his hair, no longer having to wonder how the demon felt about her. "I am sorry, so very sorry."

She gave him a weak smile, reaching up and tracing a finger down his nose. "Hey, don't worry about it. I'm fine."

She seeks to comfort me. I am not worthy of this woman. Though he wanted to push her against the wall, claim her lips with his own, drown in her scent and her flavor, he motioned to the door. "Are you ready to go inside?"

Indecision played over her lovely features. She lowered her lids, spiky shadows tumbling down her cheeks.

"What is the matter?"

"Why didn't they want *me* here?"

"They—"

Reyes caught a glint of movement in the window just above them. Two boards covered two windows yet they didn't quite meet in the middle, allowing a crack of visibility.

The form he'd glimpsed had been too big to be a woman.

He'd thought that if the women were still alive, they were merely in hiding. He had not considered the fact that they might have been captured by Hunters. He'd assumed the Hunters would have contacted him and the other Lords if that had been the case, suggesting a trade. *So foolish.*

"Danika," he said, gaze searching the surrounding area with new intent. He had to hide her, had to keep her safe.

Too late.

The door swung open, revealing three men. Each had a weapon, and all three were pointed at Danika, as if they knew training a gun on Reyes would not have mattered.

Fury surged inside him, intensifying when Danika gasped in horror. "Oh, my God."

"Hands at your sides, demon," one of the men told him, "and step inside. Try anything, and I'll hurt the girl."

Hurt Danika? He chewed on the inside of his cheek, purposefully shredding his flesh. The demon stalked and prowled, growling. *Ready, Pain?*

Oh, yes. Evil laugh.

"Danika," Reyes said. "Close your eyes."

He didn't look to see if she had obeyed. He simply unleashed his demon.

THE BLOOD, the carnage, the screams.

At one point, Danika had to cover her ears with her hands. She couldn't stop trembling. Stupid girl that she was, she hadn't closed her eyes as Reyes had demanded; she'd wanted to help. War was something she'd prepared for—or thought she had.

Then Reyes had seemed to change from warrior to crazed skeleton in a blink. She'd no longer seen the skin she so loved to touch. She'd seen gnarled bones and teeth so long, sharp and thick they could have belonged to a shark.

The Hunters had fired their guns at Reyes, but he hadn't

seemed to notice. He certainly hadn't slowed. He'd simply devoured them. Even now, he propelled from one Hunter to the other, claws ripping into flesh. Snarls and snaps sounded, eerie, like something out of a horror movie.

Wide-eyed, she continued to watch, afraid to get in his way. Afraid he wouldn't care who she was and would attack her, too. So badly she wanted to run and hide. Blood already splattered Reyes from head to boot, slicking his hair to his scalp and his clothes to his body. So badly—but she didn't. Her family was inside this building. Were they okay?

I should have come for them sooner.

Amid the terrible chaos, she grabbed a fallen gun and rushed past Reyes and through the building. Where were they? She checked the nearest room—empty. The next room—four Hunters were inside, cursing, loading bullets into weapons.

One of them saw her and aimed his gun at her, shouting, "Filthy demon whore! I don't care what they say you are." She raised hers, too. They fired at the same time. But the next thing she knew, she was being shoved to the ground, eating dirt, and Reyes was racing past her, a mere blur. A second later, the men were screaming.

Oh, God. Danika lumbered to her feet, legs nearly giving out. She stumbled forward, determined to continue her search. Reyes hadn't hurt her, had still managed to protect her. She rounded a corner, saw a flight of stairs. Weapon trained ahead, arm shaking, she climbed them two at a time. Another corner.

Three Hunters, all of them trembling and pale, waited at the end of the hall. They saw her and fired. Just like before, Reyes was there, shoving her down and taking the blows himself. Was he hurt? Oh, God, oh, God.

He likes pain, remember? He's fine. Her ears rang and her heart raced.

When she looked up, the men were already on the floor, unmoving. Reyes was nowhere to be seen. Danika scrambled up yet again, racing forward, tripping and falling twice. She knew she scraped her knees, but her adrenaline was so high she didn't feel a thing.

Down the hall, a woman screamed.

"Mom!" she shouted, recognizing the voice. "I'm here."

"Danika?"

Another scream.

"Danika, baby, run. Get out of here!"

She ran, not away but forward. A moment later she was standing inside a bedroom, panting, sweating. Her mother and sister were chained to the heating unit. Her grandmother was chained to a bed, both of her legs in a cast.

Reyes was in the process of breaking those chains, his face still skeletal. He was shaking, bleeding. She should not have doubted him and would not again. Even in this form, he wanted her happy. The women were trembling and kicking at him, but still he persisted. Finally, all three were free.

Danika rushed to them and fell to her knees, gathering her mother and sister in her arms. Hot tears were flowing down her cheeks, blending with theirs.

"Danika, he's—he's—" her sister stuttered.

"I know, I know. Don't worry. He's not going to hurt you. He's a good guy." Her family was alive. She was with them again, holding them. Shock and pleasure and relief all tumbled through her.

"I thought you were dead," her mother said through her sobs. "They told me you were dead."

"I'm here now. I'm here." Wiping her face, she let go of them and pushed to her feet. "We will not be parted again. I swear it. I'm just sorry it took me so long to get here."

They stood weakly, and together they walked to the bed where her grandmother lay. Tears were falling down her weathered cheeks, as well. Danika clutched the woman's trembling hand in her own.

"What happened to you?" she whispered, using her free hand to run her fingers over one of the casts.

"The monster with wings." Grandma Mallory sniffled. "He found me, threw me down and…and…" Her chin quaked.

Danika almost made her granny stop, but she had to know. She covered her mouth, cutting off any words that might try and escape. She nodded to prove she was listening.

"He could have killed me after I fell, but he didn't. He picked me up and carried me to this building. I think I used to dream of him. I've tried to block those dreams so long they're only mist in a storm now, but I think maybe he saw me during those dark terrors, because he looked at me as if he knew me. I don't know why, but I told him not to relive his past mistakes. He backed away and then he left me."

Tears splashed down her face. Dear God. They'd always dreamed for a reason. What could she have avoided if she'd studied her dreams rather than feared them? Didn't matter, she supposed. In the end, Grandma Mallory's dreams had saved her. And there was still time for Danika's to save Reyes, once and for all.

"I'm sorry, I'm sorry," her grandmother said. "Now isn't the time for that. You want to know how I got here. I couldn't move, was stuck in this building. The bastards with guns had been following me, I guess, because they found me later that day. They already had your mother and sister."

Her hand fell, her gaze circling the still crying group. They were pale, with bruises under their eyes. "Were any of you—"

"No," Ginger, her sister, said. "No, we're fine. For the most part, they left us alone. They fed us, kept us healthy. Apparently they planned to use us to draw out our former kidnappers."

Like they tried to use me, she thought angrily. Thank God Reyes had—her gaze circled the room again, not seeing him. *Give him a moment to calm down. Enjoy your family.* Because in that moment Danika knew, all the way to her bones, that she was going to help Reyes bring down the Hunters once and for all.

No one threatened her family and lived. And Reyes was her family.

CHAPTER TWENTY-FOUR

REYES HAD ALREADY COME DOWN from his demon-high, had caged the beast even now drenched in agonizing physical pain and sated bloodlust. A beast currently purring with satisfaction. Now, Reyes feared the thoughts that must be running through Danika's mind. He trembled, weakened from his injuries, knowing he couldn't reassure her yet.

She was currently wrapped in the loving arms of her family—gods, how she glowed. If she knew he was in the room, she gave no indication. Quietly, he stepped into the hall and withdrew his cell phone.

He'd wanted to do this all night, all day, but hadn't wanted Danika to overhear and hadn't been able to reach Lucien when he'd been collecting their haphazard breakfast. With Danika preoccupied with her family, there was no better time.

As he dialed Lucien's cell, his knees gave out and he sank to the ground. Once again, his friend failed to answer. This time, however, the keeper of Death simply appeared in front of him, mismatched eyes bright, face tight with fatigue. The fragrance of roses drifted from him, stronger than Reyes had ever smelled it.

Reyes wiped at his face with one hand and used the other to pocket the phone. He didn't bother standing. "Here to collect souls?"

"Not yet, but I feel the tug." Lucien's gaze slid past him, past the cracked open door. "What happened to you, my friend? You have more holes than a slice of Swiss cheese."

"Hunters happened. They were here, waiting, holding Danika's family hostage to use against us later."

Those unusual eyes jerked back to Reyes, shock in their depths, before once again peering past the doorway. "Bastards. And they call themselves the good guys."

The sound of feminine laughter, then silence, then urgent female warnings drifted to them.

"You have to kill him, Dani."

"No, no. You don't understand."

"There's nothing to understand."

Reyes didn't hear Danika's response. Their voices became whispers. Was *he* the "him" who needed killing? Probably. After this latest battle, he was surprised and humbled to find that Danika hadn't rushed to agree.

Lucien arched a brow. "The reunion, I take it."

He nodded and lumbered to his feet, hand immediately going to his temple and rubbing, as if the motion could shove the dizziness away.

"The building is probably wired and monitored," Lucien muttered. "We need to remove the women as soon as possible."

"Let's see what we're dealing with first."

"Very well."

They searched the entire structure and did indeed find a room very much like Torin's in Budapest. There were computers and screens of the surrounding area, as well as one monitor that seemed to be showing another compound—where a large group of Hunters were gathering weapons.

"They were probably alerted, might even have watched the battle," Lucien said. "I imagine they're coming here."

Reyes hunched over, trying to catch his breath. "Is the fortress secure?"

"Yes."

"Take us back, then," Reyes said. "All of us. Me last."

Lucien nodded, began to mist a second later, when Reyes grabbed his arm, stopping him. "How is Sabin?"

"Better. He'll recover."

Good. Lucien disappeared completely then. Reyes couldn't allow the Hunters to see what was going on, so he used the last of his strength to disable the wires. As he worked, he heard several of the women screaming and knew Lucien had just materialized in front of them. He wanted Danika unafraid, but he wanted her safe more.

Several minutes later, Lucien reappeared. "You're the last. Ready?"

He gave a single nod. It was all he could manage.

Lucien touched his arm. Next thing Reyes knew, he was standing inside his bedroom in the fortress. His knees gave out again and he collapsed on the edge of his bed, remaining upright by clutching the nearest post. "Where are the women?"

"Locked next door. I will help you deal with them, I just need…the souls are calling to me." Lucien disappeared. When he returned a long while later, he reeked of sulfur. Reyes, who hadn't moved an inch, wasn't surprised the Hunters' final resting place was hell.

Reyes's head lolled forward, chin hitting his chest heavily. "Listen. I need you to go to Aeron's cell."

"Why?"

"Please. Take your phone and call me when you get there. If I had the strength, I would go myself."

Expression confused, Lucien once more disappeared. In a heartbeat of time, Reyes's phone was ringing. He flipped it open, fingers fumbling, and barked a quick, "You there?"

"Yes," Lucien said.

In the background, beyond his door, Reyes could hear mumbling. He would have given his left arm—literally—to walk to it and press his ear to the wood. But in the end, he didn't have to. He could hear Danika soothe her family, her voice gentle yet determined. A grin curled the corners of his lips. *My little soldier.*

He had to see her.

The overwhelming need gave him strength, a surging heat that swarmed through him and lifted him to his feet. One unsteady foot in front of the other and he was flipping the door's lock and winding his fingers around the knob.

"Reyes, are you there?"

Lucien.

"I'm here. Listen, last night Danika told me about a dream she'd had," he whispered so the women wouldn't hear him. "In it, she visited hell. Heard and saw the demons there, heard and saw their victims. But Lucien, I don't think it was a dream."

Crackling static. Reception in the dungeon was spotty at best. "I don't understand."

"When I'm…with her, I'm somehow propelled out of my body and into the heavens. I think she's a portal into the hereafter."

"Are you sure? Perhaps you—"

"I'm sure. Last time, an angel actually spoke to me."

"Dear gods."

"I know."

"But what does this have to do with Aeron?"

"Not Aeron. His friend."

"The little demon?" Shock rang in Lucien's voice. "Reyes, break this down for me as though I were a child. Why?"

"Do you remember the Hunter Danika killed? Well, she saw him in hell and a demon was questioning him, demanding to know about the All-Seeing Eye."

There was more crackling static, tense and heavy. "The repercussions of this could be devastating."

Reyes knew that well. "Ask the demon why his friends would want information on Danika."

Bars rattled. Dark curses arose. Both so loud they managed

to blast through the weakened phone signal. Lucien sighed. "I only see Aeron."

"Damn. Try to draw him out. I'll compose myself and be there in a moment." He closed the cell and once more pushed it into his pocket—or rather, missed his pocket. The phone clanked to the ground. Scowling, he bent over and swiped it up. He swayed as he straightened, but managed to slide it in place and enter the women's bedroom without falling.

All four were on the bed and clamped their lips together as they turned to gape at him. Three of them paled. He was still covered in blood, he realized, and probably looked every bit the monster they imagined him to be. He'd been shot. A lot. Stabbed, too. His clothing was tattered, his wounds still seeping. Still, his hungry gaze sought Danika.

"Reyes!" She grinned when their gazes met, but that grin quickly faded. "You're hurt!" She moved from her family, rushing toward him...soon so close he could smell her stormy fragrance.

Heart pounding in his chest, he shut the door in her face. Turned the lock.

He heard her gasp. Her fists banged against the wood. "Reyes!" she growled.

He'd seen her, knew she was unharmed. It was time to walk away from her. For good. Last night she'd wanted to hurt him during sex. Had been eager to do so. Being gentle hadn't stopped the dark cravings as he'd hoped. And even though he hadn't allowed her to hurt him, his demon must have affected her already, propelling her toward the life Reyes had endured for too long. Pain, always pain.

What if she wanted to hurt her family next? She'd fought so diligently to save them. He wouldn't jeopardize that.

"Reyes! Let me out."

"Dani," the grandmother called unexpectedly. "Leave him be." The pounding continued.

Reyes ran a fingertip along the wood. Then, slowly, he

stepped away from the door. Only when he reached the end of the hallway did he pivot. Some of the home's furnishings were missing, he realized as he limped. A few tables, all of the knick-knacks Ashlyn had added. There was no blood on the walls, so the warriors must have been hard at work, cleaning. Thankfully, he didn't see any of the warriors in question. He wasn't sure how he would have reacted if they'd asked him about Danika.

Danika, Pain suddenly shouted.

"Hush," he replied.

But the more distance he put between him and Danika, the more the demon growled inside his mind.

Danika, Pain shouted again.

"I'm riddled with bullet holes. What more do you want?" Reyes growled back.

Her.

"Why?" She was the epitome of pleasure. "She is not for us."

Mine.

"No!" Down the stairs he pounded, his steps long and furious, eating up the distance to the dungeon. He found Lucien in front of Aeron's cell, gripping the bars, silent.

Reyes stopped beside him and looked into the holding. Aeron was still chained to the wall, his eyes bright red, his fangs long and sharp. His nails were elongated into claws. The demon, Legion, slithered around his neck, down his arms and then across his ankles.

"It is able to flash," Lucien said. "It popped itself into the middle of the cell and now is refusing to talk to me."

"I talk," the demon said.

"Then tell me where you went."

"Hell."

"Why?"

"You get why, my friend get free," Legion said, forked tongue flicking out. "He isss sssad. Me not like sssad. Ssso we trade."

Actually Aeron appeared enraged, his gaze tracking Reyes's

every move, but Reyes wasn't going to argue the point. "I'm afraid I can't trade with you. If Aeron goes free, he will try and kill my woman. And Aeron," he said to the warrior, "I thought you'd like to know you didn't kill Danika's grandmother. You walked away before rendering that final blow."

There was a hitch in the warrior's breath, a slight tensing of his large form. "I failed."

"Reason to rejoice."

"I failed," Aeron repeated stiffly.

Reyes sighed.

"Uh-oh. You make him mad." Legion crouched, moving into an attack stance. "You pay."

Would no one cooperate with him?

"Settle down, boy," Lucien told the little demon. "We only want the best for Aeron."

Legion hissed like a startled cat, the noise scraping at Reyes's skin. "Me no boy. You think me a boy?"

Everyone stopped, stared. Even Aeron.

Reyes was the first to find his voice. "You're a…girl?"

A nod. "Me pretty."

"Yes, you are." Reyes exchanged a glance with Lucien. "Beautiful."

Aeron had yet to recover from the shock.

"I need your help…sweetheart. There is a demon in hell who was asking a damned soul about a woman," Reyes said to the she-demon, getting them back on track. "*My* woman. I think he means to hurt her. Is there anything you can tell me?"

"Oh, oh. Big newsss in hell," Legion said, lips lifting in a proud, happy smile. He—*she*—turned to Aeron. "Everyone talking 'bout it. Visssiting demon told them. Can I tell, can I, can I?"

Still silent, Aeron nodded.

"Ssshe ticket to heaven. Whichever demonsss find her, get to ussse her to essscape."

SABIN LIMPED TO THE CENTER of the entertainment room and turned—swayed, damn it—to face the people who were scattered throughout. Some were playing pool, others watching TV. Some were drinking. Ashlyn was sitting in Maddox's lap.

"What are we going to do with the girl?" he rasped. His throat was still raw, still healing from the bomb smoke he'd inhaled.

All eyes anchored on him.

"Study her paintings," Lucien said, cue in hand. "That's all we can do."

"That, and treat her well," Ashlyn interjected.

Softhearted women were the bane of the universe. "Now that they know what she is, Hunters will come after us more fervently now."

"I'd think that would delight you," Paris said, glancing up from the flesh-fest playing out on the television screen.

It would, just as soon as he healed fully. Even now he wanted to prop himself against the wall. "We need to lock her up, put her somewhere they won't think to look."

Ashlyn gave a firm shake of her head. "No way."

"Yeah, good luck getting past Reyes." William slapped Lucien on the shoulder, though his amused gaze never left Sabin. "Man is wicked good with knives."

"Who invited you into this conversation?" Sabin grumbled.

"Anya," the immortal replied with a grin. "She said I could stay as long as I wanted. Now, will you let us finish our game or what?"

More and more, Sabin couldn't help but like the irreverent bastard. "Anya, put a leash on your friend."

"Why? I'm winning."

The two returned to their game of pool, Lucien watching Anya bend over to take a shot. "I'd rather we kill the girl than allow her to fall into our enemies' hands. She's too powerful, could perpetrate too much damage to our cause."

No one responded. They'd already tuned him out.

Kane picked up a wine bottle, and the glass shattered. "Damn it!"

Rolling his eyes, Sabin strode to him, grabbed another bottle and filled a glass. "Here. So?" he demanded of the others.

Torin, who stood off in the corner, alone and out of reach, finally acknowledged him. "Touch her, and our groups will split again. Reyes would rather die than lose her, and I would rather lose you than hurt him."

Sabin sighed, scoured a tired palm down his bruised face. He valued these men and didn't want to lose them again. Perhaps one day they would prize him as much as they used to.

Perhaps not.

Doubt, you stupid motherfucker. I hate you!

"Then we're gonna have to push her to find the third and fourth artifacts for us," he said, "so that the score remains in our favor. Hunters find the other two, and the war might never end."

HOW AM I TO KEEP HER SAFE when the king of gods, every demon in hell and all the Hunters want a piece of her?

Reyes had trouble sleeping that night. Not only because Legion's words continued to echo through his mind, but also because Danika was mere feet away. All he had to do was roll from bed, open the door separating them, and he could sweep her into his arms.

He tried not to think of the first and could not help but wallow in the second. His wounds had mostly healed, so he had the strength to claim her.

One more time.

Too dangerous, he'd already decided.

Worth a chance. She's worth a chance.

If you're gentle, you minimize the risk.

Gods, he didn't know where the thoughts originated. With himself or the demon. And did he care? Having Danika one last time, holding her, feeling her warm breath, luxuriating in her soft body, glutting himself on her sweet taste…

Fisting the sheets, he ground his teeth together. These were hazardous thoughts. Hated thoughts.

Welcome thoughts.

She was so much a part of him, he didn't like being without her. He needed her. Wasn't complete otherwise. *For her own good. Better this way. Be selfless for the first time in your life.* How many times would he have to tell himself that? Her family hated him and had every right to do so. They would castigate her for staying with him. Guilt would bloom inside her, and hate would soon follow on its heels.

Distracted as he was, he didn't sense the intruder until it was too late. A cold blade pressed into his neck.

He stiffened. His lashes lifted and his gaze landed on Danika. Had she been an enemy, he would have reacted less violently. As it was, his entire body shuddered and jolted. Moonlight bathed her, shining around her pale head like a halo. Her hair was loose and tumbling around her shoulders. She wore an oversize white T-shirt. His. A sense of possessiveness awoke every cell in his body.

He was rock hard.

Fight this.

"How did you escape?" he demanded.

"I've learned to pick locks since the last time I was here."

Her stormy scent wafted to him and he couldn't help but inhale deeply. "Go back to your family."

"Nope. Sorry. I'm going to prove I can hurt you without suffering myself."

He didn't give her time to cut. Quick as a snap, he grabbed her wrist and held tight, preventing her from moving. With his other hand, he claimed the knife and tossed it to the floor. Her eyes widened as he next jerked her forward, right on top of him.

He rolled them over and pinned her into the mattress. *Fight this. Fight*—her breath fanned over his cheek. Her breasts meshed into his chest. Her legs wound around his waist, placing her wet, bare core against his erection. She was liquid fire.

All thoughts of resisting her vanished. *One last time,* he found himself thinking again, the urge tempting him. Winning the battle. Not that he'd put up much of a battle. "You should have stayed with your family, tucked safely in bed."

Her chin jutted stubbornly. "I missed you," she admitted grudgingly.

He rubbed his erection against her sweet spot, unable to stop his hips from moving. She gasped, he moaned. So good. Always this good.

"You're naked," she said on a raspy breath. "Hmm, I'm glad." Her arms wound around his neck and pulled him down for a white-hot kiss.

His tongue dueled with hers, wild, untamed. He arched back only long enough to rip her shirt over her head and toss it aside before diving back into her immediately. Her nipples stabbed at him, her hands clutched at his back, and her legs fell open, pressing them as close as they could be without penetration.

His cock throbbed, ready, so ready. "Once again, you're not wearing any panties," he managed to croak as he kneaded her breast.

She bit his lower lip. "Glad?"

"Dying from the pleasure."

Smiling, she pushed him, rolling him over and straddling his waist. "Don't enter. Not yet."

"I won't." She rose above him, a siren he would have died to possess. Once, twice, she glided up and down his length, still without penetration. Her head fell back, hair a sunny halo around her.

"I want to suck you," she said.

"You're all over me."

"I know." Slowly she edged down him, not stopping until her

mouth hovered over his swollen shaft. Her teeth flashed white in the moonlight a split second before her mouth swallowed him.

His hips shot forward of their own accord, pushing his length all the way down her throat. He didn't mean to, didn't want to hurt her, but couldn't stop the action. *More. Need more.* He and the demon were chanting the words together, and in the back of his mind, he realize that meant the demon was still with him, that Pain hadn't been transported anywhere. *More, more, more.*

His fingers tangled in her hair as her mouth rode him up and down, tongue licking at the head, sucking, then flicking against the base. He bit the inside of his cheek, drawing blood.

"Danika," he panted.

She slammed down hard at the same time she reached behind her, fingers scrambling over the sheet…she paused…he moaned…she lifted her arm, mouth moving again…he writhed…then she sank a dagger right into his shoulder.

Shouting, he came on an explosion, spurting into her mouth over and over again. His entire body shook. Another roar parted his lips, the pleasure and pain an intoxicating blend he couldn't fight. Didn't want to fight.

She swallowed every drop he gave her. And when he finally quieted, when he finally stilled, she rose from his length, licking her lips and grinning like a contented cat. Blood poured from his shoulder, stinging so beautifully.

"You stabbed me," he managed to work past the lump in his throat. He studied her intently, unsure what he would find in her expression. She didn't appear drunk with bloodlust or even ready to hurt him again.

She appeared satisfied with herself.

"I thought you might take the first knife, so I strapped a second one to my ankle, hoping you would be too preoccupied with the north region to concern yourself with the far south."

His lips twitched. "Tricky."

"Necessary." Still on her hands and knees, chin hovering over his navel, she glared over at him.

Gods, he loved this woman. He could see the desire swimming in the emerald depths of her eyes. His own desire returned, a blazing fire in his blood. His cock hardened anew, filling…filling…desperate for her all over again.

"You will not deny me my right anymore," she said. "Hurting you will not change me, I swear it. I *like* knowing I'm doing something for you. I like knowing I'm pleasing you. I know you wanted gentle, I suspect that's what you've dreamed about since being paired with your demon, but you had to know—*I* had to know—I could give you hard and painful if the need ever came upon you."

"What right?" he demanded, those words snagging the bulk of his attention.

"I am yours and you are mine. I will see to *all* your needs. You will not turn to another woman. Ever."

Her words echoed in his mind, the answer to a thousand prayers. "Danika—angel." He grabbed her forearms and tugged her atop him. His hands settled on her waist and positioned her for penetration. So hot, so wet. "Wait. I need a condom."

"I want to feel you this time. All of you."

He went very still, his heart racing. "What if there's a…baby?"

"Would you mind?" she asked softly.

"I once thought so. But now, with you…" He liked the idea. Craved it. Would love to watch Danika's stomach swell with his child. "Would *you* mind?"

"I think—I think I would like it."

"You do not think I would be a terrible father?"

"Are you kidding? No child would be more loved, more protected."

He moaned, and it was a sound of pleasure. True pleasure, deep and inexorable.

"No more pushing me away. Ever." Her eyes closed as she, too, uttered a pleasure-filled moan.

He was helpless to deny her. He would watch her, make sure she never developed bloodlust or if she did, that she never sated it with anyone but him. He would do anything necessary to win over her family. He would keep Aeron from her always, protect her from Hunters, demons—the gods themselves. Somehow. Someway.

"Are you sure you want me? Be very sure. After this, I will not let you go."

Her features softened. "The future might be uncertain, but I'm sure about you. About us."

More beautiful words had never been spoken. "No more pushing you away," he vowed. "Mine. You are mine."

"Yours."

With a single arch, he was embedded deep, all the way in. His mind instantly quieted, the demon silent. *Gone?* he wondered. Was penetration, physical joining, needed to send the spirit away?

Reyes stopped thinking when Danika's hands anchored on his chest, her nails digging, stinging. In all his life, he'd never imagined a moment so perfect. A moment where his heart beat for love rather than pain. She was his. He was hers.

He couldn't give her up; he simply could not do it. She was more important to him than his lungs or his limbs. He was nothing without her. He would keep her. She'd inflicted pain, yet she was still his Danika, still his angel. Good and pure and right. Oh, yes, he would keep her.

The decision unleashed a torrent of joy inside him, so sweet he surged into her, his thumb finding and flicking against her clitoris. That's all she needed to hurtle over the edge.

"Reyes!"

"Angel, my angel." He came just as powerfully as before, rolling her over and fusing their mouths, his tongue thrusting deep. He stayed with her this time, and he suspected the bond between them was too strong to allow him through any portal.

Suddenly a blade sank into his back. Not put there by Danika, whose hands were tangled in his hair. He shouted in shock and jerked from the kiss, his head turning.

Aeron stood beside the bed, his wings spread, his eyes glowing crimson. That knife had been meant for Danika.

CHAPTER TWENTY-FIVE

PARIS DROPPED TO HIS KNEES. He'd left the warriors in the entertainment room when a sense of urgency had filled him, the god king's whisper of "Now" echoing in his mind. He'd strode to his bedroom, knowing he had to at last make a decision.

It was time. He couldn't wait any longer. He felt torn apart, raw.

Now he raised his blade high in the air, shouting, "Cronus, Lord Titan, I am here as you bade me." As he spoke, he slashed the knife over his chest. Deep, as deep as he could get it. Skin ripped, organs tore and blood gushed.

The pain was severe, and he nearly doubled over. But he had to prove his determination. He'd already slept with two women today. Two women he couldn't even recall, and one he had bedded only an hour before. He was sick of it. So sick.

He had spent these last few days thinking. It's all he ever did anymore. What a novelty that was for a man who had spent too many centuries to count giving in to his body and shutting down his mind. Now his mind was a constant swirl of questions and possibilities. Aeron or Sienna.

"Cronus, I beg you. Appear. One more audience, that's all I need. I—"

"Am shouting unnecessarily," the god king said behind him. The scent of stars instantly filled the room. A hum of power charged the air, raising the fine hairs on Paris's arms.

Though he wanted to, he didn't turn and look at his guest. He bowed his head reverently, assuming the position of a servant. He hadn't decided if this sovereign truly meant him ill or if Cronus was as confused about the Lords of the Underworld as they were about the gods.

He was unsure, tentative, but he planned to proceed as if the latter were true.

"Before I make my decision, I have questions for you," he said. "If it would please you, I would ask them."

"I have wondered about you many times, demon. You and your desires have presented a mystery I am determined to solve." The thump of sandals, the swish of cloth, and then Cronus was standing in front of him. "Ask."

"If I chose Sienna, would I merely receive her rotting corpse?"

A warm chuckle of true amusement echoed. "So suspicious. That is something the Greeks would have done, I am sure, wily bastards that they were. But I am a more generous soul. From me, you would receive her just as she once was. For you, she will look the same, speak the same. She will not simply be a talking dead body. She will have a heart, and it will beat."

For you.

The words echoed through his mind and he frowned. Did those two little words have significance or was he simply looking for hidden meaning where there was none? The gods had been known throughout the ages for their tricky natures. *Wily bastards,* Cronus had said about the Greeks, but Paris would bet the Titans were no different.

Still, he pressed on. "Would she hate me as she did before?"

Another chuckle filled his ears as fingers stroked the back of his neck. They were gentle, yet emitted a strong pulse of energy that sped his heart into an erratic rumble. "Of course she would hate you. She is a Hunter. You are a Lord. But I am sure, Promiscuity, that you can charm her into love."

Could he?

And was having her back worth the guilt he would feel at

not saving Aeron when he had the chance? Reyes seemed to think so, for he couldn't keep his hands off the woman Aeron was desperate to destroy.

Paris slowly lifted his head, and his gaze met Cronus's. The king's expression was blank, seemingly uncaring. Damn it! What should he do?

DANIKA SCREAMED as Reyes leapt away from her and tackled— Aeron, she realized, wide-eyed. Terror sprouted inside her and quickly spread its limbs. She scrambled backward on the bed, the cold headboard soon pressing into her back. *What the hell should I do?*

The two men rolled on the floor, punching, tearing at each other's skin, biting and snarling like animals. Aeron repeatedly slashed at Reyes's neck, screaming that Reyes's head would soon roll. Twice he made contact, causing the side of Reyes's throat to bleed profusely.

Reyes was already weak. She'd stabbed him only minutes before, for God's sake. Her knife. Yes. That's what she needed. Where the hell was her knife?

Her gaze scanned…there, on the floor. So close, so far. Last time this had happened, Aeron had knocked her down and she'd stayed down. Reyes had saved her, but he'd taken a beating for his efforts. This time, she wouldn't passively watch, wouldn't run away. She would help. She'd *trained* to help.

She inched off the mattress as the two men sprang apart, circling each other, panting.

"She's mine," Reyes growled.

"Belongs to the gods," Aeron snarled. He swung around, and the razor-sharp tip of his wing sliced Reyes's cheek.

Reyes's head whipped to the side. As he straightened, he smiled. "Not anymore. How did you escape the cell?"

"Cronus. Now was the time to act, he said. And when the gods speak, I obey."

Legion peeked out from underneath the shadow of Aeron's wing. "Don't hurt."

Aeron reached up to pet the top of the little demon's head. The creature purred, much as Danika had heard Reyes do when he was hurting. Just a little more, she thought, closing in on the weapon and doing her best to stay out of the warriors' way. The silver blade continued to wink up at her, taunting.

"Pays to have friends," Aeron said darkly.

"I'm your friend."

"No."

"Aeron, I love you."

"Not Aeron. Wrath."

"You're Aeron. My brother of the box."

"And yet you locked me away, even knowing how terrible such confinement is."

"You begged it of me!"

"You should not have listened!"

Down she leaned. As her fingers curled around the hilt, she saw Reyes pale. Aeron's words must have hit their target— Reyes's guilt—and they must have cut as deeply as any sword. She straightened.

Reyes had chosen her over his friend, she realized, under-standing for the first time how hard that must have been for him. These men had overcome the fires of hell together. Literally!

"I did what I had to do to protect you from yourself," Reyes growled.

"No, you did what you had to do to protect *her!*" Aeron shouted, pounding a fist against his thigh. His nostrils flared, his hands clenched as he geared for another attack. "My enemy."

Reyes was naked, weaponless, probably afraid to approach the bed, where the other dagger lay. Most likely he didn't wish to draw attention to Danika. Again he was protecting her, no matter the danger to himself.

She licked her lips, watching as he slowly inched backward.

Tremors raked her. She wanted to call out, to toss the blade she held to Reyes so he had *something* to use. What if her voice broke his concentration? What if Aeron used that distraction to pounce on him and cut his throat?

She'd seen firsthand how Reyes recovered from his wounds, but she knew he wouldn't be able to recover from decapitation.

Legion propped her scaled elbows on Aeron's shoulders and gazed imploringly at Danika. "Ssstop them. No hurt Aeron." Scaled hands stroked the warrior's hair. "Calm, friend. Calm."

"I'm trying," Danika whispered. She inched forward, remaining in the shadows, blade poised and ready. *Go for his throat.*

"I am the demon of Wrath." The more Aeron spoke, the more his voice became multilayered, deep and raspy, lilting yet harsh. "You have harmed me grievously and you will suffer."

His glowing red gaze finally turned to Danika. She stilled, unable to catch her breath.

Reyes roared and leapt forward, slamming into Aeron's chest. The two men propelled backward, Aeron's wings beating against the wall. Thump. Crack. They hit the door with so much force the hinges snapped and the wood toppled. Legion squealed and scampered from the men, hiding under the bed.

They rolled, their arms and legs slapping together. Danika could hear the chomp of teeth, the sound of cloth ripping as claws swiped through it. Bones snapping and grunts of pain. So many grunts.

If they would just part… Unconcerned by her nakedness, she kicked back into motion, closing in on the pair. *Come on. Separate, goddamn it!* She might never get close enough to them to slice, but she could still throw.

"You seek to lock me up forever," Aeron growled. Punch.

Reyes's head whipped to the side. "And if the bloodlust ever leaves you, you will thank me for it!"

Aeron jerked his wings into his back, where they folded underneath two slits. "Thank you? For burying me next to hell?"

"You met Legion, didn't you? The new love of your life?"

Finally they stopped rolling, Aeron on top. He punched Reyes yet again. Having a clear shot, Danika tossed the dagger, end over end. Target: Aeron's carotid artery. But when the tip reached the warrior, it embedded in his arm. He'd been in the process of reaching up, meaning to plunge his own dagger into Reyes's throat.

Aeron paused, glanced in confusion at his arm. Frowned. From under the bed Legion cried out in alarm, drawing Aeron's attention further from the fight. The distraction cost him. Reyes bucked and worked his legs between their bodies. His feet shoved Aeron backward in a powerful thrust. The warrior slammed into the wall. The impact didn't slow him, though. Didn't even rattle him.

He uncurled himself. Reyes rushed toward him, menace in every step. But Aeron didn't seem to care. Grinning, he launched a dagger of his own. A dagger Legion had swiped up and rushed to him. As Reyes barreled into him—only then seeming to realize what had happened, a scream of denial ripping from him—that dagger found its target: *Danika.*

"I WILL NOT WAIT much longer," Cronus said, sounding bored. "Soon I will lose my curiosity over your choice and allow you neither Aeron nor Sienna."

Paris began to sweat. *Do it. Just say a name.*

But as he opened his mouth, Cronus's head tilted to the side, his ears twitching as if he could hear something beyond the quiet of Paris's bedroom. "Oh, yes," the king said, and there was delight in his tone. "You must choose soon."

Had something happened?

The pound of footsteps hit Paris's ears a moment later. Then, a knock on his door. "Paris, are you in there?"

Sabin.

Paris glanced at Cronus—no, at empty space. The king of

gods was gone. Had he lost his chance? Scowling, he jack-knifed to his feet and strode to the door. "Not now," he said as the wood swung open.

Sabin eyed his bleeding chest with confusion. "You okay, man?"

"Fine. What's going on?"

"Aeron escaped. He and Reyes are fighting." As though to prove the words were true, a roar of agony sounded, followed quickly by an eerie laugh.

Cronus's eagerness for an answer suddenly made sense. With the realization, there was dread. There was no more time to ponder or consider the ramifications of his choice.

Perhaps he should have left well enough alone.

Behind Sabin, Gideon and Cameo raced down the hall. Both were clutching guns. Sabin shot a look over his shoulder. "We don't have a lot of time."

"What's the plan?" Paris demanded.

Sabin faced him again, already backing away. His gaze was grim. "Whatever's necessary to finally end this."

FROM THE CORNER OF HIS EYE, Reyes had seen the glint of silver. But only when he heard Danika gasp, only when he saw the crimson stain spreading over her chest, did he realize what had happened.

Danika was hurt. Bleeding. She collapsed, now silent, barely breathing, unmoving.

No, no, no. Despite his vows, he had failed to protect her. She might…she might… No! He refused to believe anything other than that she would recover, totally, completely. And yet, fury rose inside him. Fury and hate, desperation and so much emotional pain that it radiated into his bones, hurting, strength-ening him.

He was on his feet a moment later, rushing toward her. Aeron grabbed his arm, stopping him. Panic rushed him as he toppled to the ground. His friend jumped on top of him and straddled his waist.

A fist flew at him. Contact. His nose cracked in the center.

Reyes bared his teeth in a snarl, twisted and grabbed Aeron by the forearms. He had his friend beneath him a moment later. Satisfaction burned in Aeron's now-violet eyes, the red gone. Was that…surely that was not guilt blended with the satisfaction.

He hurt her. I must finish this, get to her. Help her.

He stared down at Aeron, hands already wrapped around his throat. Strong as Reyes was just then, Aeron could do nothing to buck him off or pry the shacklelike fingers from his neck.

Behind him, he could hear his friends gathering. Muttering.

"Don't do this, Reyes."

"Let him go."

"There's another way."

He didn't know who said what and he didn't care. He squeezed harder, claws digging past skin, past veins. Warm blood was pooling between his fingers.

Legion suddenly slithered forward and jumped atop Aeron's chest. Teardrops that looked very much like diamonds streamed down her ugly little face. "Ssstop, sstop. He mine."

Reyes squeezed all the harder. Once Aeron was dead, Danika would be safe. From one threat, at least. She could be patched up. Healed.

With a cry of despair, Legion launched herself at Reyes. Biting him, scratching him. The creature's saliva must have been laced with poison, because it stung like acid, rushing through Reyes's veins, burning in a way that made his demon moan. Still, he didn't let up.

"My warrior," the demon cried. "Mine. No hurt."

Aeron's eyes were wide, blood vessels popping. His body was shaking, his skin becoming pale. Almost blue. His struggles were growing weaker and weaker. Soon he would still completely and Reyes would release him, pick up one of the swords hanging on his wall and remove his head. Soon—

"Reyes," a voice said weakly.

It was the only voice that managed to penetrate his rage and his hate, overshadowing them entirely. Reyes's attention lashed to the side, to the floor where Danika lay, staring over at him.

She needed him. He released Aeron instantly and rose to shaky legs. Aeron's body went limp, but he remained awake, watching Reyes. Legion began kissing Aeron's face and chest, cooing to the warrior.

A gun cocked. "No one moves until we figure this out."

Reyes paid the command no heed, nor did he acknowledge whoever had issued it. He rushed to Danika and crouched beside her. The stones around her were soaked. She'd pulled the knife from her side, opening the wounds. She was pale, too pale, and tears burned in her eyes.

"I tried…to help," she said with a weak smile. "For once."

"You did, angel. You did help me." Gently as possible, trying not to cry himself, he gathered her in his arms. Her muscles were so frail, she was unable to move on her own. "Lucien, I need you!"

Footsteps. "I'm here." Lucien stood beside the bed, mismatched eyes concerned.

"Don't take her soul," Reyes choked out. "Just…don't. I need time to fix her."

"You know if I'm summoned to do so, I cannot stop myself," was the guarded reply.

Reyes smoothed a shaky hand over Danika's brow. "Stay with me, angel." Never had he felt so helpless.

"Always," she said with another of those weak smiles. "Love you."

Oh, gods. The words, delivered now, nearly slayed him. "I love you. So much. I cannot live without you." He didn't turn away from her as he begged, "Lucien, find a healer. Bring him here. Please."

Lucien nodded and disappeared.

There were multiple fists against the door next to his, and then feminine commands could be heard. "Open this door! You didn't have to lock us back in. We wouldn't have interrupted you. What's going on?"

"Danika. Danika, are you okay?"

"Let them in," Reyes shouted, praying she would be strengthened by her family.

Someone opened the door, and two of the women rushed inside Reyes's bedroom. They spotted Danika in his arms, bleeding, and gasped. They were rushing to her side a moment later. The third, the grandmother, was in casts and had to be carried.

One of the warriors shouted, "No, Aeron. No!"

Another growled, "I don't want to shoot you!"

That's when Reyes saw that Aeron had stood. Having all four women in the same room must have heightened his blood-lust to another degree, giving him all the vigor he needed.

Danika's sister screamed as the warrior reached for her, missed as she scrambled away.

Her mother turned, splaying her arms to block Danika. "Leave my babies alone, you animal!"

Hearing this, Danika struggled to sit up.

"No," Reyes commanded. "Don't move."

Aeron strode forward. The warriors were jumping in front of him, trying to knock him down. No one shot at Aeron, though, as they'd threatened. Reyes couldn't blame them. In the end, he hadn't been able to kill his friend, either.

Aeron batted the seasoned warriors away like flies, getting closer and closer to the women. Legion was flying between the warriors, as well, biting them as she'd done Reyes. "No hurt my friend."

Unlike Reyes, they didn't remain standing and didn't grow stronger from the pain.

They fell, unmoving, the creature's saliva poison to them.

And soon there was no one standing in the way of Aeron as he bore down on his targets.

THIS IS IT. There's no more time.

Paris dropped to his knees for a third time in the center of his room. He didn't have to cut himself, didn't have to summon Cronus, for the god king appeared of his own accord the moment Paris hit the floor.

"I have already raised Sienna from the dead," the king said. "She waits in my throne room and can be here in seconds. She can be yours, if only you'll say the words."

Oh, to hold her again. To touch her soft skin, to gaze into her lovely eyes. To have her delicate hands tracing his body with reverence. She hadn't liked him, but she had been attracted to him. She had allowed him inside her body, and it had been the greatest moment of his endless life.

"If you do not choose her, perhaps I will keep her for myself. It's been quite a while since I allowed myself a mortal." Cronus shrugged, lifting the hem of his white robe.

Paris bit the inside of his mouth. He should have known better than to summon this god and beg a favor. The thought of Cronus touching her, kissing her, sickened him. *She is mine!* "Why do you hate us so much?"

"Hate you?" Cronus laughed, but there was no humor to the sound. "Hate is too simple an explanation. You could say I'm prone to dislike anyone who once served my enemies. And yet I admit I am still intrigued by you Lords of the Underworld. There is more humanity in you than I would have expected to see in men who are part demon. Even now, as the one called Aeron stalks toward his prey, he screams inside his mind to stop, to turn away."

Paris stilled.

A sigh. "He has surprised me, I must say. He had the grand-mother in his grasp, had only to cut her throat. Yet he managed to suppress his bloodlust long enough to escape her. He even managed to wipe the memory from his own mind. The will-power required for such a thing… I marvel."

But Aeron would not be able to make himself forget the slaughter of those four innocent women, Paris knew. From the beginning, the tormented warrior had known the act would change his life forever. And not for the better. Aeron would be eternally haunted.

So would Paris, knowing he could have done something to prevent it.

"I see the way your mind is churning," Cronus said, crouching in front of him. Their gazes locked, blue against fathomless brown. "Know that if you choose Aeron, you will never again see Sienna. I will make sure of it. Just because I can."

"And if I choose Sienna?"

"Aeron will slay the Ford women. All but Danika. Her, I have decided to keep. The others are useless to me, so are of no consequence."

"Why, then, did you damn Aeron's soul with the killing of them?" Paris asked, incredulous.

Cronus shrugged. "I knew one of them was my Eye, my seer into the spiritual realms, but I did not know which one until recently. I thought to destroy the entire bloodline so it could not be used against me again. Therefore, all had to die. Yet now, having watched the youngest girl, I am reminded of all the Eye once did for me—before Zeus seduced her from my side and used her against me. Unlike her ancestor, Danika's heart has been given. She will not be swayed by other gods."

"Why not simply free Aeron, then, if you no longer have need to destroy Danika and her family? If you *want* Danika alive? Why put his freedom in my hands?"

"Because you presented me with a question I have come to realize my humans face daily. Who is of greater import, a lover or a friend? And now, demon, I am through waiting for your answer."

Paris gulped. The ultimate choice. He'd known he would have to make it, but here and now, in the moment of truth, he knew he would hate himself, no matter his decision.

"Choose," Cronus said, his voice booming angrily. "While Sienna paces the heavens, Aeron is even now upon the women. He is raising his dagger. Sienna is crying, uncertain of her future. Aeron is—"

"Aeron," he said, falling forward, already mourning all over again the only woman he ever could have loved. "I choose Aeron."

WITHOUT WARNING, Aeron collapsed beside the bed. Legion curled into his side, stroking his face. Reyes watched, blinking in shock as a smile lifted the now-sleeping warrior's lips, and peace, such peace, smoothed the lines around his eyes.

What the hell had just happened? Aeron had been poised for the deathblow, Reyes unable to act. And then everything had stopped, frozen, no one able to breathe, to move. Then the sleeping, poisoned warriors awoke as if nothing had ever been wrong. And *then* Aeron had fallen.

Everyone turned and looked at everyone else, confusion scenting the air. Lucien arrived a moment later with the healer, a sputtering human who almost soiled himself when he spied the huge crowd of hulking warriors.

"Reyes," Danika whispered.

Bending down, Reyes kissed her temple. "No talking, love. Save your strength. The healer will—"

"I'm having a vision."

He did not care about a vision; he cared about her. "Try to push it to the back of your mind. Just stay with me while the healer patches you up, all right?" He turned to the man in question, commanding, "Fix her. Give her Tylenol. Whatever you have to do, fix her."

The human kicked into gear, rushing forward. "Of course, of course."

"I'm in heaven, lying on a marble dais." Danika smiled, her eyes glassy. "I'm covered in white and the angels are singing."

"What? No, no." He shook his head in violent denial as he realized what she was saying. "Hold on, just hold on."

The healer crouched beside her, already removing tools from a black case.

"Hurry," he ordered the human. But he needn't have bothered. Danika's eyes closed and her head lolled to the side. She disappeared a moment later, and he was clasping only air.

His scream echoed through the heavens and earth, finally resounding in hell.

CHAPTER TWENTY-SIX

"WHERE IS SHE?"

"What the hell did you do with her?"

Reyes was slumped in a chair in the entertainment room, a glass of ambrosia-laced brandy in his hand. Danika's mother and sister stood in front of the television where homemade movies of Danika as a child played. Her grandmother sat beside him, her cast-clad legs outstretched.

He'd had Lucien fetch the movies three days ago and had not left the chair since. Right now, they were his only link to Danika and, hopefully, his key to finding her. *Danika. I miss you, my love.* He didn't care that Hunters were most likely gearing for another attack. Didn't care that his friends were preparing for war.

Footsteps. A slap across his cheek. He fingered his jaw, but for once he was too numb to enjoy the pain.

"Talk to us!" the sister demanded.

"Please," the mother begged. "Fight your evil side and help us."

"Leave him alone," the grandmother told them, patting his hand. "I used to see demons in my dreams, and this man is no demon. He loves our girl and is doing everything in his power to bring her back."

Was he? He felt as if he should be doing more. But what, he didn't know. "If I knew where she was, she would have been rescued by now," he finally answered. "I failed her. There. Does that make you feel better?"

Silence.

"Well, get her back!" Tinka, the mother, shouted.

"I don't know how." The admission was painful, so painful, and not in a good way.

Five days had passed since Danika had vanished. In those five days, Aeron had regained consciousness, his need to kill completely gone, as if it had never been a part of him. He'd apologized—*forgive me. Please forgive me, for I doubt I will ever be able to forgive myself. I love you, would never purposely... Gods, Reyes, I'm so sorry*—and Reyes had done the same: begged for forgiveness. *I love you, too, my friend. I should have taken better care of you. Can you ever forgive me?*

They'd embraced, and Legion, who was never far from Aeron's side, had cheered. But Reyes's sense of loss had not faded. He had summoned the gods over and over, praying, begging, all to no avail.

He didn't know what else to do.

Tinka and Ginger, the sister, began pacing and muttering in front of him. Every so often, he could see the TV. He thought he heard a young Danika laughing.

"Who took her?" one asked.

"I heard one of the monsters—uh, *warriors*—say it was the work of the gods," the other replied. "And we all heard Danika say that she saw herself in the heavens."

"If Danika saw the heavens, she's in the heavens," the grandmother said. "Trust me. I know."

"Okay, then. Let's pretend the warrior was right and the gods took her. *Why* was she taken by them?"

"Probably because she is a portal." He refused to use the word *was*. That would mean Danika was...dead. Gone. No longer reachable.

All three women stopped and eyed him sharply. "What are you talking about? What kind of portal?"

He explained, trying to hold back his tears. Pain was close

to whimpering inside his head. On the screen, Danika laughed again. What was she doing? He leaned to the side. She was blowing out birthday candles. He imagined a child of hers— of *theirs*—would look just as sweet, and he would have smiled at the image if he hadn't been so miserable.

"My baby was a portal between—"

"Is," he and the demon growled in unison. "*Is* a portal. She's still alive."

"That's just not possible," Tinka said. Then she held up her hands. "She's alive, that's not what I meant. I just… It's too hard to believe she was some kind of gateway between heaven and hell."

"You've seen wings pop out of a man's back, daughter," the grandmother said staunchly. "Believe it."

"But how could I not have known?" Tinka whispered brokenly. "How could I have missed something like that?"

"Her dreams," Reyes said. "It was always her dreams."

"I was once just like her." Mallory uttered a sad little sigh. "First time I saw one of her paintings, I nearly fainted. I was frightened for her, I admit, and didn't know what to do. Had I not fought my own visions so terribly, I might have realized what was going on and might have been able to help her cope."

"You did help her. The stories you told her gave her the strength and courage to face her nightmares rather than run from them." His eyes burned and he rubbed them with the back of his wrist. *My Danika, sweet Danika.*

Mallory squeezed his hand.

Tinka's pacing renewed. Again, Reyes was given a momentary glimpse of the TV screen. There was a blur as the camera stopped rolling and picked up on another date. In this one, Danika was probably eleven years old and painting. She was covered in the stuff, a living rainbow.

He felt closer to her like this. He could not, would not, give her up. Had begged Anya for a miracle, like the one she'd performed for Maddox and Ashlyn. She'd tried to help him, but had failed. He'd even asked his friends to take his head and end this torment. They'd refused. In the end, he'd been a bit relieved, knowing his soul would go to hell, placing him only farther away from Danika.

Somehow, someway, she was in heaven. Alive—he would not believe otherwise, ever—but there all the same.

If he had to earn his way there, he would do it. They *would* be together again.

Ginger and Tinka seemed to have forgotten his presence as they continued to pace and talk.

"The man does seem to love her."

"*Seem* is the key word. I don't care what my mother says; I can't forget what he is. What *all* of them are."

"Demons."

"Yes. The very demons Danika used to paint."

Still does, he thought, but remained silent. Damn them. He wanted them out of his way so he could see the screen fully and without interruption.

"But he cried when she disappeared."

"He sobbed, actually."

Still want to. Pain curled into a ball in the corner of his mind, licking at its emotional wounds. The creature had fallen in love with Danika just as Reyes had. Was lost without her. They were two halves of the same whole, so Reyes supposed it stood to reason they would love the same woman.

"If anyone can bring her home, it's him."

He listened vaguely, still drinking in those flickering visions of little Danika. Even then she'd been an angel, full of light and hope for the future. *I'm nothing without her.*

"Are you listening to me?" Ginger stood in front of him, hands anchored on her hips. She was taller than Danika, even thinner. Pretty, but she was not his angel.

"No," he said. "Move."

Tinka joined her daughter, linking their arms. "There has to be something else you can try."

"Bring her back," Ginger said, "and we'll stop trying to convince her to leave you."

"Not that it did any good. She wanted you in her...in her..." Tinka sobbed. "In her life."

The two women embraced. Reyes's chest ached.

Pain took no notice. *Want my angel.*

Me, too.

Need her.

Ginger and Tinka released each other and clomped off to the corner to whisper. Finally Reyes was able to see the screen in full detail. There was Danika, proudly waving her hand in front of the finished painting.

"They mean well," Mallory said.

"I know."

"Maybe, if I concentrate hard enough, my visions will come back. Maybe I can discover a way to fix this."

Maybe. But he would not get his hopes up. Reyes noticed the design of Danika's painting for the first time. He frowned, grabbed the remote control. The camera panned away from the painting, showing a frowning woman—a younger version of the grandmother, who was studying the colors and the lines.

Reyes pressed Rewind. When the painting reappeared, he pressed Pause. Ginger strode back in front of him, determination radiating from her.

"Move," he told her.

"Uh, excuse me. You—"

"Move!"

Gasping, she raced out of the way. "Fine. No need to shout."

His gaze locked on the painting once more. Could it be— was it...? It was. It really was. He shot to his feet, numbness giving way to anticipation. "Mallory. Look at the painting and tell me what you see."

She obeyed, wide-eyed. "Oh, my God. Is that…is that…?"

"I think so." He might just have found the way to save Danika.

DANIKA FLOATED on a sea of black, surrounded by winter's chill.

Every so often she could feel the brush of fingertips across her face and neck, and knew a cloth draped her naked body because the cool silk somehow kept her from drifting away into absolute nothingness. Too, she periodically heard a voice inside her head.

Tell me what you see.

She knew what the speaker wanted: to know what the demons in hell and angels in heaven were doing and saying. She also knew the speaker couldn't invade her mind without an invitation, for he had tried, over and over again, to scan her visions and had failed.

Purposefully, she projected an image of Reyes. Her shadow warrior. Her love. Oh, how she missed him. Craved him. He had held her tenderly while she'd bled, his body offering her strength, his eyes begging her to heal. She'd wanted so badly to stay with him but ghostly hands had grabbed her and jerked her away.

She hated the owner of those hands and knew it was the man even now shouting, *Enough of this. Do not show me the demon again.*

I will show you nothing else. Return me to him.

Silence.

How much time passed while the hands continued to touch her, the cloth continued to hold her, she didn't know. Time was endless here…immeasurable. There was no more denying who and what she was.

I just want to go home.

The speaker once again approached her. *Tell me what you see.*

Everything inside her stilled. For a moment that had sounded like—

Tell me what you see.

Reyes! The voice belonged to Reyes. Her heart sped up, her blood rushing hot and fast in her veins. *My love,* she said.

I'm here, sweet Danika. I'm here. Two fingers traced her lips.

But the chill didn't leave her. No, the cold remained. The scent of sandalwood didn't fill her nose. She smelled only the sweetness of the clouds and the drift of baby powder.

In that moment, she knew it wasn't Reyes who had spoken and her joy plummeted, fury taking its place. *Reyes doesn't call me his sweet Danika, you sick bastard!*

There was a rumble of anger. *Reyes will die by my hand if you do not tell me what you see!* The voice had returned to normal.

In her mind, she screamed and screamed and screamed. The sound was one of anguish and pain, agony and anger, and she projected it into the mind of her tormentor.

Stop. Enough.

Will you hurt him?

No.

She didn't know whether she could trust him or not, but she quieted. *Who are you? Why are you doing this to me?*

You can help me rule this world. Together, we will ensure the safety and prosperity of the heavens. No harm shall befall us.

Who are you? she insisted.

Let me show you. A moment later, an image of a tall, lean man floated into her head. He had a kind but formidable face, with a head of thick silver hair. He was wearing a white toga and sitting upon a bejeweled throne.

She recognized him from the painting she'd made for Reyes. Cronus.

The image in her mind shifted and she saw a woman reclining in a chaise beside the king's throne. A beautiful woman with long pale hair and wide green eyes. Like Danika, but not. The pair smiled at each other, happy, unimaginable peace radiating from them.

You helped me once. You can help me again. With your vision and my might, we can make the world all that it once was: sublime, serene, beautiful.

Not me. I didn't help you.

The image faded. *No, not you precisely. But the power of the Eye passes through your bloodline. At one time, your ancestors guided my path, kept me informed. Helped me to rule. Why won't you do the same? Once you agree, you will be free to roam the heavens. Your only job will be to observe my allies and enemies and report to me their activities. The rest of the time will be yours to use freely.*

I want Reyes. Again she projected an image of the warrior. Where was he? What was he doing? In her mind, she heard herself sob. Tears began to fall. They didn't stay inside her mind, however, but began to rain over her entire body, the cold causing her skin to ice over.

You cannot have him. He belongs to the Underworld and you belong to me.

No!

Arguing with me does not change anything.

Then know this. I belong to Reyes, and he belongs to me. You will have no answers from me as long as I'm parted from him.

She felt the god move toward her, anger in every step.

"CRONUS!" Reyes shouted from the rooftop of the fortress. "Cronus, show yourself!"

The wind whipped, hostile, as if it wanted to pound him to a bloody pulp. At one time, he had been glad for that, had welcomed the sensation. Danika had changed him for the better. She had given him something to live for.

"Cronus!"

"I am here, Pain."

Surprised, Reyes spun. The king of gods stood on the other side of the roof, his white robe swirling fiercely at his ankles. He appeared as old and frail as any human, but strength radiated from him. Strength and power the god would never be able to hide.

"Where is she?"

"Safe," was all the god said, inclining his head.

Still, that one word comforted Reyes as nothing else could have. She was safe. Which meant she was alive. Which meant she could be sent back to him. "Show her to me. Please. I beg you."

Every muscle in his body tensed as he waited. Finally Cronus nodded, waved a hand through the air, and a vision of Danika shimmered into focus. She was exactly as she'd described in the moments before she'd vanished. She lay on a marble dais, a golden, glowing vision. White draped her from neck to toes.

She was Sleeping Beauty.

"Is she…is she hurting?"

"Not even a little. I opted to keep her and so I healed her."

"Thank you."

"I did not do it for you."

Didn't matter. He'd done it, and for that Reyes would be forever grateful. "I want her back," he managed to croak past the lump in his throat. He reached out, meaning to trace his fingertip over Danika's soft red lips.

Another wave of Cronus's hand and the vision faded.

Reyes felt the demon howl. "Please. I want her," he said again.

"And she wants you." Eyes narrowed, Cronus walked forward. No, he did not walk. He floated. His feet never touched the gravel-laden slats. "But now that I have her I plan to use her. My decision to have her killed was…hasty."

"Why do you need her?"

"My reasons are my own. All you need know is that you would distract her."

"I won't. I swear it."

"You will not be able to help yourself."

"I love her."

"Yes, I know, but that knowledge does not sway me," the god said mercilessly. Then they were standing nose to nose.

Reyes smelled the sun, the stars and the moon, all in one inhalation. He hated the scent.

"The demon hordes want her, your mortal enemies want her. Even your friends seek to use her for their own gain. You cannot protect her on every front."

"I can. I would die for her. I love her. I will let no harm befall her."

Cronus arched a dark brow. "As you proved when you let Wrath stab her?"

Guilt swam through him anew. "Knowing she experienced pain nearly destroys me every time I think of it. I will not allow such a thing to happen again." His hands fisted at his sides. "I saw something today, one of Danika's earliest paintings. You…you were in it."

The god's head tilted to the side, his expression becoming pensive. "I am listening."

"In the painting one of your enemies had taken your head."

With every word Reyes had spoken, rage had further darkened the god's face. "How dare you utter such blasphemy! No one is strong enough to do such a thing. I should strike you down for the mere suggestion."

He knew he trod on dangerous ground, but he said, "It is true. I would hardly lie when so much is at stake."

"Where is this painting? You will show it to me. *Now.*" The entire fortress trembled, stones rubbing together, some crumbling.

Reyes shook his head. "I will trade it for Danika."

"The painting. Now!"

"First agree to my trade."

Cronus drew in a breath, held it, slowly released it. It was as hot as a poker and smoke billowed from his nostrils. "She is my property, and unlike you, I do not barter what's mine."

His property? Hardly. "Then you may kiss your head good-bye. I doubt your Eye is ever wrong."

Though Reyes had half feared the god would smite him for his impudence, silence reigned for a long while. Then, "When you can prove you're strong enough to protect her, summon me again. We will talk." With that, the god disappeared.

"YOU USED TO BE A GODDESS. Tell me how to prove to Cronus I can protect Danika."

Anya had been in the process of flipping through her wardrobe while William sat on her bed, begging for the precious book of prophecies she'd stolen from him, when Reyes burst into her bedroom. Without knocking, she might add. Bastard. He was lucky she wore more than a smile and a pink boa. And the only reason she did wear actual clothing was because Lucien was on the hillside, checking traps. Well, that and William was here, and the man was too much like a brother to show off her favorite boa.

"First thing first, Turd Ferguson. I *am* a goddess," she said to Reyes. To William, she added, "Begging is not a good look for you." She continued flicking outfits out of the way.

"You promised me the book," the warrior said.

"Yeah, but I didn't say exactly when."

"I'm staying here until I get it."

"That's just reason for me to keep it. You're fun to have around."

William dropped his head into his upraised hands.

"I do not mean to interrupt," Reyes said, "but—"

"Second thing second, I wasn't done. William, what do you think of this dress?" She held up a strand of beads.

"I love it," the warrior said with a grin.

"Anya, please," Reyes pleaded.

"Fine. I just hope you're ready for my irritation." Turning, she ticked off a finger and walked toward him as she spoke. "Look here, sugar plum. I helped break the death-curse that bound you to Maddox yet you bad-mouthed me to Lucien a few weeks later. That was very naughty of you."

He opened his mouth to speak.

She held up another finger and arched a brow, daring him to utter a single word. He pressed his lips together.

William laughed, his own woes clearly forgotten. "You're in trouble," he sang.

"Then," she continued, nodding with satisfaction, "you made Lucien wait *days* before telling him about Aeron. Plus, I already tried to help you with Danika. You didn't say thank-you. Next, I don't know the Titans all that well. They were already imprisoned by the time I was born. And last but definitely not least, you really smell. Ever heard of a shower, Painie?"

"I am sorry for every way I've ever wronged you, Anya," he rushed out. "You have only to tell me what to do to atone for my sins, and I'll do it. But please, help me first. Cronus demands I prove I can protect Danika before he'll give her back to me."

Gods, I'm a sucker for love. Anya studied the warrior in front of her. He'd lost weight, maybe because he'd stopped eating and only poured ambrosia-enhanced alcoholic beverages down his throat, and hadn't showered or changed in what seemed like forever. He was pale, his unwashed hair standing on end from the many times he'd plowed his fingers through.

Frankly, he was a mess.

What drew her attention most, however, was the fact that for the first time since she'd met him, he was not riddled with cuts. "Hey, why aren't you hurting yourself?"

He looked down at his arms, turning them in the light to study them, as if he hadn't realized he'd stopped. "I hurt every minute of every day. There has been no need to cut myself."

"But what if, when she returns, your pain leaves and you have to cut yourself again? Would you still want her?"

"I will happily cut myself to ribbons if only I can have her."

"Interesting." She propped her hip against the vanity beside her, tapping her nails on the marble top. *Click, click, click.* "Obviously you've spoken with King Craphead. What exactly did he say to you?"

William leaned forward, listening.

Reyes relayed the conversation, word for word, unconcerned by his rapt audience.

"And how did he take the news of Danika's paintings?"

"With fury. Fear, I think. What if he never gives her back to me?" Suddenly his knees gave out, and he crumpled to the floor. He stayed there, waiting. "Damn. I don't think I've ever been this weak."

"Well, you're not going to prove anything but weakness in this sorry condition." She raised her hand and tapped her nails against her chin. "He said demon hordes are after her. Maybe you should, like, battle them. Kill them."

"To war with them would require centuries," William pointed out.

"Yeah, but he's got nothing but time. Jeez." She rolled her eyes. "Rain on my parade of smartness, why don't you? If you don't want to go that route…" she added to Reyes.

"I don't."

"Fine. Whatever. Let's see, let's see. There has to be something else. Think, Anya, think. You, too, Willy. Put that fat head of yours to work."

Silence. Hours of silence.

"Maybe slap Cronus around a bit," William finally suggested. "That would convince me of your strength."

Anya clapped happily. "That's it! Defeat Cronus, and you'll end this little game right now, as well as rid the world once and for all of his nastiness."

Reyes's eyes widened. "You're kidding. Defeat Cronus?"

Hearing him say it dimmed her excitement. "You're right. Probably not possible. Sadly, he's the most powerful being living and you're, well, not."

"What I am is a man in love." A crazed gleam entered Reyes's eyes, a glint that scared her. If he went after the god king, Lucien would be upset. And she didn't like when Lucien was upset.

"Uh, Reyes, baby, let's put our heads together and come up with something else. Something—"

If he heard her, he gave no notice. He'd lumbered to his feet and limped from the room. Anya wished like hell she'd kept her big mouth shut.

AFTER STUFFING HIMSELF with more food than his stomach should have been able to hold, Reyes had Lucien flash him to the storage facility where Danika kept all of her paintings. Her mother, sister and grandmother had come along for the ride, a comfort to him. He was grateful Hunters hadn't beaten him to it.

Every hour he sorted through the stacks of canvas, his determination to win Danika increased. Though Cronus had never reappeared, Reyes could always feel the god's eyes on him, boring, watching, waiting for a glimpse of the mysterious painting.

But Reyes didn't offer it to him. Not yet. Since that night upon the roof, he had ceased playing the tapes of Danika's childhood. And though he longed to see them again, he knew it was for the best.

"Just a little more time, angel, then we'll be together again. I swear it." He'd already uttered the words at least a hundred times. For her. For him. Her family had stopped shaking their heads in surprise when he did so.

Ginger dusted her hands together. "I can't believe the nightmares my little sister has had to deal with."

Tinka wrapped an arm around the girl's waist. They made a beautiful pair, sandy hair gleaming, cheeks glowing rosily. *Danika should be here, enjoying them.*

Pain grunted an agreement.

"She's stronger than I ever knew," Ginger continued, glancing at the stacks of art. "A better painter, too. I mean, I knew she was good, but I had no idea."

Tears poured from Tinka's green eyes, eyes so very much like Danika's his heart wanted to explode every time he looked into them. "I can't believe I shamed my daughter into hiding these in storage. They should be in a gallery. They're hauntingly lovely, aren't they?"

Like Danika herself. "Yes. They are."

Mallory pulled a plastic bag from her purse, opened it and offered half of a peanut-butter sandwich to him. "Before we left, your friend Anya told us we had to help you keep your strength up."

He accepted it gratefully and had it consumed in two bites, liking the thoughtfulness of the woman's gesture. Danika's family—not to mention Anya herself—seemed to have forgiven him for his crimes against them. "When Danika is returned to us, she will find joy in her paintings. This I swear to you."

"I so wanted to hate you," Ginger said on a sigh.

His lips twitched. Her tart tongue amused him, reminding him of Danika.

Would everything remind him of Danika? he wondered then. He didn't mind the reminders, he loved them, but many more and he might break down, give in to the misery of being without his woman.

"What exactly are we looking for?" Tinka asked, suddenly beside him.

"Ask Mallory," was all he said, unwilling to cease his search to explain. He would *not* give up. If necessary, his last breath would be expended finding Danika.

"Look for anything involving Cronus, King of the Titans, and set it aside for Reyes to study. And before you ask, Cronus is tall, with thick silver hair and a beard, and always wears a white toga."

One of the portraits caught his eye, a colorful depiction of angels and demons, life and death, blood and smiles. Like Ginger, he was amazed by what she had seen in her young life. Amazed even more that she had thrived despite her burden, emerging as the determined yet gentle warrioress he knew.

A few more flips, and he found four paintings of Cronus. His heart rate sped up. In some, the god paced the corridors of a prison cell, flames licking the walls, smoke filling the air. In others, he fought his way free, killing with expert precision, using his scythe, which stretched and stretched and stretched miles past its usual length to take the heads of his enemies.

Why had Cronus not carried the scythe when he'd visited Reyes? Afraid he would use it and regret it? If that were the case—which Reyes seriously doubted—it would mean Cronus needed him alive. Perhaps the king had traded it for something. Danika's life? Anya had once mentioned that even the gods were bound by the laws of give-and-take, sow-and-reap.

Reyes frowned, pushing the thoughts from his mind. For now. They weren't as important as saving his woman. He moved to another stack of canvases, the first of Cronus cornering a group of trembling gods and backing them into the very cell he himself had occupied. Gods Reyes had once guarded. Seeing them now, he felt a pang of forgotten loyalty. Cronus's expression was one of cold determination. It was obvious he wanted to kill them, but wanted them to suffer the same fate he had even more.

For hours more, Reyes pored over the artwork. The women supplied him with water and snacks but remained silent, as if sensing his need to focus. Finally, he had examined every single canvas.

He hadn't found the one he wanted—had Danika destroyed it? Hidden it elsewhere?—but he had learned some valuable information and began ticking each fact off in his mind.

Cronus hated confinement. Would do anything to avoid it.

He preferred revenge over absolute safety, for never again

could the Greek gods challenge him for the heavenly throne if Cronus had killed them. Instead, he'd locked them away, taking Anya's greatest treasure to ensure they stayed where they belonged.

His scythe could elongate as surely as Reyes's nails.

All of that, on top of the first painting Reyes had seen…his mouth fell open as the answer finally, blessedly shifted into place. He jumped to his feet, having trouble catching his breath. Grinning for the first time in days.

"What?" the women asked in unison.

"I know what I have to do." Close, he was so close. All he had to do now was find a way into heaven.

CHAPTER TWENTY-SEVEN

"I MISS YOU SO MUCH, angel."

A long while passed, but there was no response.

Reyes lay on top of his bed. He had been there for hours, perhaps an entire day. He'd lost track of time. Over and over, he'd attempted to connect with Danika on the mental plane. She was up there, in heaven. She was a portal, and she'd propelled him there twice. It was reasonable to think she could do so again. The problem was that this time there could be no penetration to pave the way. Reyes could only hope their joinings had forged an emotional and spiritual bond strong enough to substitute for a physical coupling.

"I'm lost without you."

We're lost, the demon piped up.

"*We're* lost without you. Your family wants you back as desperately as I do. I've come to love them, for they helped shape you into the woman you are. One with such strength and courage."

Still nothing.

"Do you carry our child, Danika? If not, I want nothing more than to give you my baby, watch your belly grow."

Clearly, impending motherhood wasn't the key, either. He swallowed. "Danika," he growled. "Talk to me. Now. I'm angry, Danika." *Not with you, never you.* But he continued darkly, "Soon I'll be forced to cut myself. I'll bleed. And you won't be here to patch me up and make me feel better. I—"

Reyes?

Reyes blinked open his eyes. That had been Danika's voice, whispering through his mind. It had worked. It had really worked! Sweat beaded all over his skin, relief and joy spearing him. Pain lit up inside his mind like a demonic Christmas tree. "Danika? Talk to me again."

Oh, my God. Is that you? Really you? I've dreamed of you and prayed for you and begged for you.

"I'm here, I'm here." Tears burned in his eyes, scalding his irises. "I need you to pull me to you, angel."

How? The word rushed from her, as desperate as he felt.

"Picture me in your mind. Picture your hands reaching for me, wrapping around me. You can do it. I know you can." *This has to work. Please let this work.* "You're a portal. You can—"

Something cold pushed inside him. Ice crystallized in his veins, but he didn't move. Pain was grasping for her, but couldn't seem to latch on. "I can feel you."

And I you, but…

The sound of her frustration echoed in his mind. "What's wrong, angel?"

I can't get to your spirit. I'm grasping air, nothing but air.

"Grab hold of my physical body, then." He didn't even have to finish the sentence before fingers, ghostly but firm, clutched his arms—just as cold, but solid—and jerked so powerfully he was lifted off the bed and through the ceiling. The plaster cracked and gave way, falling beneath him like rain.

He slammed into another ceiling, thought he saw Maddox rolling from his bed and reaching for a blade, a naked Ashlyn gasping. Reyes was unable to hold back a grimace.

Stop? Danika asked, his journey already slowing.

"No, no! Keep going, angel. Keep pulling. No matter what sounds I make, keeping tugging me to you."

He broke through the roof and was suddenly surrounded by night sky. Stars whizzed past him like blasts of lightning. He was weightless…soaring…then clouds engulfed him, zooming past, brushing his skin and leaving a moist sheen.

The moon seemed to grow bigger, more golden, so close he thought he could see a crater. And then, suddenly, he broke through some sort of invisible shield, the air around him warming, turning from black to shining azure in a heartbeat. The clouds became clusters of diamonds and Reyes could see golden columns flanking a winding emerald road.

His breath caught in his throat. Heaven, he realized. He was actually in heaven, albeit as a man rather than a spirit.

Angels ascended in every direction, their wings gliding prettily. Several looked at him and gasped. Others frowned and hurried away. To warn someone? Who? Angels didn't answer to either the Titans or the Greeks. That much Reyes had learned from Danika's paintings. Reyes hadn't found a depiction of who they did answer to, though. He would have liked to have spoken to the…man? Woman? Would have requested the use of the heavenly army. Maybe one day…

He broke through another invisible wall, and then, finally, he was there, hovering beside Danika's dais. His knees gave out, and he crumpled beside her, one hand already in her hair, the other cupping her jaw. Her sunny hair was spread around her. Her skin was tinted slightly blue from the cold. She was draped in white like a winter queen. His queen.

"Gods, I missed you." How he had longed for this day, this moment. "I will never let you go again."

Reyes! You're really here. I can feel you. Feel your warmth.

"Cold, angel?"

Very.

"Let me warm you." He snuggled next to her, wrapping her body with his own and soaking up her chill. "I love you so much."

I love you, too. I want to see you, but I can't break free of this…sleep. I can't jolt my body awake.

He placed a soft kiss on her lips, inhaling her sweetness. Part of him had despaired of ever doing this again. Ever holding her, breathing her in. "Do you know where Cronus is?"

Oh, yes. I always know somehow. He's with his counsel.

"Can you hear what they're discussing?"

I already know. It's what they always discuss. What to do about you. What to do about me. Where to look for his other artifacts.

"Can you bring him to us?"

Maybe. But why? I hate him. I hate dealing with him.

"Which makes me sorry to ask you to do so, but I am. Trust me, angel. Please." He pressed another kiss against her lips, then along her jaw. "You are able to control a physical form with your mind. When Cronus arrives, wrap your mind around him and hold him as still as you can. We will not have long. He possesses a key inside his body that allows him to break free of any prison."

A pause. Then, *All right. I'll try.*

"If you can and if he has it, pry his scythe out of his hands. And know that whatever happens, I love you." If they failed in this, Reyes knew Cronus would kill him. This was a direct challenge and no king would take it lightly or without issuing severe punishment.

"I've got him." A moment passed. Another. Danika's small body stiffened underneath his hands. *He's angry. He doesn't have a scythe; he gave that to Chaos, who he put in charge of the Underworld when he imprisoned Hades, in exchange for a human soul. A female. Hunter. I think. He has Zeus's lightning bolt.*

"Keep a firm grip on the bolt, angel. Take it from him if you can."

He's almost here. Just a few seconds more…

Cronus stopped abruptly at the end of the dais. When he spotted Reyes, he growled low in his throat. Sparks exploded in his irises as the golden bolt was ripped from his grip and tossed aside.

From this moment on, Reyes knew every word out of his

mouth, every emotion that colored his features, was critical. Everything counted. Forcing a casualness he didn't feel, he eased to one of his elbows. "So nice of you to join us."

The god king's body shook, as if he were attempting to move. He had no luck. His arms stayed glued to his sides, his legs to the floor. "You will die for this, warrior."

Slowly, Reyes kicked his legs over the dais and stood. "You're probably wondering what's going on."

"I possess the All-key, demon. It destroys any shackle, opens any lock. You will not be able to hold me long."

"I know." His heart pounded like a war drum, but he smiled. "But you are not chained. You are simply being…momentarily embraced."

The sound of teeth gnashing together echoed between them.

"You told me to summon you when I could prove my strength." He paused, expression pointed. "Cronus, I summon you."

"Do you think I will help you after this?" The king uttered a cruel laugh. "You are very foolish, Pain."

How are you doing? he projected to Danika.

I'm not sure how much longer I can hold him. He's very strong.

Fighting a rush of urgency, he walked to Cronus, stride unhurried. Expression still pointed. "You will free Danika and return her to earth. To me. Together, she and I will destroy any foe who thinks to take or use her."

"You—"

Reyes cut him off. "In return, if she agrees, she will tell you of her dreams and the things she sees."

"She will do that anyway," Cronus snarled.

"Has she so far?" Reyes tried not to panic. "If you feel she is in danger, protect her. But do it from here, while she is with me." He strode around Cronus, slid a dagger from the holder at his wrist, and placed the blade at the god's neck. The pulse fluttered wildly. "I could take your head, like in the painting. There is nothing you can do about it—but die."

Utter stillness came over them. Such stillness Reyes could not even form the will to breathe. He waited…waited…

"I commend you, warrior," Cronus said. "You have proven your strength." It was more than a statement, it was a promise, a vow. A treaty between them.

At least, Reyes prayed it was so.

Shaking, scared to his bones, he lowered the blade. He strode back to Danika's side and clasped her hand. "Release him, angel." *And we will see what happens.*

A moment later, Cronus splayed his fingers. His bolt flew back into his hand, his eyes narrowing as he stepped toward Reyes. Part of Reyes expected him to attack. But he never did.

Suddenly Danika gasped out a breath and jerked upright. He turned his attention from the god king to his woman. She was blinking open her eyes, as if the light hurt them. When she saw him, she gasped again. "You're real."

Her arms wound around his neck, his arms snaked around her waist and they embraced with shattering joy.

"You did it!" She laughed.

"*We* did it. Angel, I never want to be parted from you again."

"Don't worry. I'm not going anywhere."

"My life is one of war, as you once reminded me. Can you live with that?" He pulled back, watery gaze locked with hers. He would leave the Lords if necessary, find a peaceful place to live, untainted by Hunters or vengeful gods.

"Are you kidding? War-happy older brothers are on my Christmas list. And hey. Demons—and I don't mean you!— now apparently want me as their pet. Not to mention that gods and Hunters are watching my every move. I'm a popular girl. Can you live with *that?*"

His lips lifted in a smile. "For you, anything."

She returned the smile with one of her own. "Good."

"You and me. Now. Always."

"Save this touching reunion for later. What did you see in

that painting?" Cronus asked, drawing their attention. "Who tried to take my head?"

Not tried to. Did. Reyes closed his eyes, gathered his strength. He'd hoped to avoid this topic for a while longer. Danika buried her head in the hollow of his neck, and he drew strength from her. "Do not strike at us in anger. Please."

"You have my word," the god replied impatiently. "Now tell me who took my head."

"A decapitation?" Danika's arms tightened around Reyes. "I remember that painting. It was my only decapitation. And the culprit was the one they call Galen. Hope."

Again, the patient stillness of a predator came over Cronus. The silence was so thick and heavy not even the flap of an angel's wing dared break it. "A demon. One of you," he growled to Reyes.

"Our enemy, as well, I hasten to add."

A long pause, finally a nod. "I wish to see it for myself." The god's gaze shifted to Danika. "I have given you back to your man. All I ask in return is that you come to me if ever you learn of a threat against me."

She nodded. "As long as I'm with Reyes, I'll tell you anything you want to know."

"Warning received." Though the god had paled, his lips curled into the semblance of a real smile. "I'll have to ensure you live forever and that you are never parted from the warrior. Won't I?"

"REYES! REYES! You won't believe it." Danika rushed into Reyes's bedroom—no, *their* bedroom now—and stopped at the edge of the bed.

Reyes was lying on his back, totally naked, the covers kicked away from him. His lids were at half-mast in that sexy way of his she so adored. His dark hair was rumpled, his lips soft and red from her latest biting. Just then—hell, as always—he was the epitome of satisfaction.

Never had she been happier.

So many things had happened in the last few weeks. Aeron had come to her, head bowed, sorrow in his eyes and apologized for the pain and worry he'd caused her. She'd forgiven him without hesitation. His bloodlust had brought Reyes in her life, and Reyes was the best thing that had ever happened to her, so there was no way she could hold a grudge.

She even liked Legion. The little fiend had moved in and was Aeron's constant companion, helping to draw him out of the dark emotional mire he still seemed stuck in. One was not seen without the other.

When Reyes had told her Legion was a girl, well, Danika had to admit she'd been surprised. But now she could see the possessive gleam in the demon's eyes whenever Aeron was nearby, and could only smile. If Aeron ever fell in love with another woman, Legion would probably eat the poor girl.

And Paris, sweet Paris. Like many of the others, he spent most of his time traveling between Buda and Rome, where he continued searching for clues to the remaining artifacts. But he was quiet now, never played his games or watched his movies. Danika hated seeing him like that and had tried to tell him that whatever the problem, everything would work out. He'd hugged her and left the room.

On the other hand, two people who seemed to be in great spirits were Torin and Cameo. They'd become best buddies and were always closeted away together. Or, when out and about, whispering and laughing. Not that they could whisper quietly. They had to remain a good distance away from each other to prevent Torin from infecting her with his disease, so their whispers were actually normal conversation, but it was clear that in their minds, they were the only people in the room. Danika wasn't sure if a romance was brewing, but liked the thought. Both of them deserved happiness in their lives.

Another happy camper was William—which made Anya happy, which in turn made Lucien happy. William had moved in indefinitely and liked to flirt with Ginger, who pretended indifference but blushed every time he neared her. Neither was serious about the other, Danika could tell, but it was nice to see them so at ease.

Danika's family was only staying another week before heading home. She knew they'd stayed this long because they didn't trust Aeron and had wanted to watch her back, just in case. No wonder she loved them! She would miss them terribly, visit often, but her life was here now, with Reyes.

Gilly, her young friend from L.A., had moved into the fortress, too. Danika had made sure of it. She and Reyes had placed her in the bedroom next to theirs, hoping to ease her transition from normal life to life among demons. The men seemed to like her, treating her as they would a kid sister even as they continued to complain about the upheaval in their once orderly lives. Gilly was leery, but Danika knew firsthand that would ease in time.

Ashlyn had taken the girl under her wing, a fierce protector not even the warriors would challenge. Danika loved her all the more for it. The woman was going to make an amazing mother, whether she had a boy, a girl, a demon, or a half human, half demon. A chuckle escaped her. Maybe one day Danika would face the same dilemma. She liked to tease Ashlyn about making Legion the child's nanny. That always made Maddox look ready to vomit, which always made Ashlyn laugh.

As for Danika and Reyes, they had spent most of the past few weeks in bed together, loving each other to utter contented pleasure. She hadn't smiled like this since, well, ever. Morning, noon and night, this man loved to rock her world. Sometimes it was sweet and gentle, other times it was wild and naughty.

No matter how he took her, she loved it. She just loved him!

She still had nightmares, but she didn't fear them any longer. She actually welcomed them. Reyes always held her afterward, something she looked forward to every time she opened her eyes.

In return, she liked to think she comforted him, too. His need for physical pain had returned somewhat, so he had to cut himself a few times a day—sometimes, she even helped. But less and less would he get that crazed look in his eye when she came at him with a weapon, and instead would sit back and simply enjoy. The amazing thing, however, was that he didn't have to be cut during their lovemaking. Then, the demon was transported to another plane, just as she'd suspected.

"Come back to bed, angel, and I will believe anything you tell me." Even as he spoke, his penis lengthened and hardened. He reminded her of the secret painting she'd done of him when he'd first asked her to paint her visions—the one now hanging over their bed. "I expect your family to burst inside at any moment. Ever since your grandmother had the casts taken off, she's been dogging your every step, wanting to help you with your paintings. Let's not waste any of this time together."

Her mouth watered at the sight of him—would she ever get enough of him?—but she clutched his shoulders and shook him. "Come see, come see, come see."

Catching her urgency, he jerked upright. Though she hadn't seen him reach for one, a dagger was in his hand. "Is something wrong? Has something happened?"

"Nothing's wrong. You just have to see this."

He pushed to his feet, still unabashed by his nakedness. She grabbed his free hand and tugged him into the studio. As always, his touch filled her with warmth.

"Did you have a nightmare, angel?"

"Kind of."

They passed the threshold, a bright canvas coming into view. She stopped in front of it and Reyes moved behind her, wrapping his arms around her waist. His erection pressed between the curves of her ass, and she smiled.

God, she loved this man. If only she hadn't pulled on a pair of jeans when she'd gotten out of bed to paint.

"Pretty," he said, leaning down and propping his chin on her shoulder.

She could feel his heart beating against her back, steady and sure. She rubbed her hands up and down his arms, unsure how he would take what she was about to tell him. "Look closely. I, uh, think I found the third artifact."

"What?" He spun her around, expression shocked.

"Look at the bottom of the pyramid. See those men?"

His gaze moved around her and latched on to the canvas. "Yes. Galen and Stefano."

She studied it, too. The pyramids of Egypt stared back at her, humans marching inside them. "In my dream, they were walking the corridors of this particular pyramid and muttering about a cloak of invisibility. They kept saying that when they had it, they were going to use it to sneak inside the fortress undetected."

Reyes gathered her close and kissed the top of her head. "You are brilliant. We must tell Lucien."

"Uh, you must dress first."

He laughed, and the sound warmed her as surely as his touch. "I love you, angel."

"I love you, too."

"I have a feeling we will soon be traveling to Egypt. Can you handle another adventure?"

"I can handle anything as long as I'm with you."

He leaned down and kissed her, a tender brush of lips. "How did I ever live without you?"

"You didn't," she quipped. "Not really."

He kissed her again, lingering this time. "No, I didn't. Until you, I was dead inside. You've given me everything. Love, life, happiness."

"Just like you've given me. Who would have thought it, you know? You, me and that sweet little demon." Slowly she grinned. She just couldn't help herself, she was so blessed. "We're a ménage of bliss."

"Now and always," he said.

"Now and always."

Lords of the Underworld
Glossary of Characters and Terms

Aeron—Keeper of Wrath

All-Seeing Eye—Godly artifact with the power to see into heaven and hell

Amun—Keeper of Secrets

Anya—(Minor) Goddess of Anarchy

Ashlyn Darrow—Human female with supernatural ability

Baden—Keeper of Distrust (deceased)

Bait—Human females, Hunters' accomplices

Cage of Compulsion—Godly artifact with the power to enslave anyone trapped inside

Cameo—Keeper of Misery; Only female warrior

Cloak of Invisibility—Godly artifact with the power to shield its wearer from prying eyes

Cronus—King of the Titans

Danika Ford—Human female, target of the Titans

Dean Stefano—Hunter; Right-hand man of Galen

dimOuniak—Pandora's box

Dr. Frederick McIntosh—Vice President of the World Institute of Parapsychology

Dysnomia—Greek, goddess of Lawlessness

Galen—Keeper of Hope

Gideon—Keeper of Lies

Gilly—Human female, friend of Danika

Ginger Ford—Sister of Danika

Greeks—Former rulers of Olympus, now imprisoned in Tartarus

Hera—Queen of the Greeks

Hunters—Mortal enemies of the Lords of the Underworld

Hydra—Multiheaded serpent with poisonous fangs

Kane—Keeper of Disaster

Legion—Demon minion, friend of Aeron

Lords of the Underworld—Exiled warriors for the Greek gods who now house demons inside themselves

Lucien—Keeper of Death; Leader of the Budapest warriors

Maddox—Keeper of Violence

Mallory—Grandmother of Danika

Pandora—Immortal warrior, once guardian of *dimOuniak* (deceased)

Paring Rod—Godly artifact, power unknown

Paris—Keeper of Promiscuity

Reyes—Keeper of Pain

Sabin—Keeper of Doubt; Leader of the Greece warriors

Sienna Blackstone—Female Hunter

Strider—Keeper of Defeat

Tartarus—Greek, god of Confinement; Also the immortal prison on Mount Olympus

Themis—Titan, goddess of Justice

Tinka Ford—Mother of Danika

Titans—Current rulers of Olympus

Torin—Keeper of Disease

William—Immortal, friend of Anya

Zeus—King of the Greeks

* * * * *

You asked for Layel's story...

And now the wait is over.
In March 2009,
Return to Atlantis in
Gena Showalter's
THE VAMPIRE'S BRIDE.
Turn the page for your sneak preview!

NIGHT HAD LONG SINCE FALLEN.

The air was warm, fragrant and fraught with danger. The insects were eerily silent, not a chirp or whistle to be heard. Only the wind seemed impervious to the surrounding menace, swishing leaves and clicking branches together.

Delilah's every survival instinct remained on high alert. No telling where the other creatures were. She'd spied a few here and there as she'd gathered stones and sticks. And then they had disappeared, hiding amongst the shadows. She could have hunted them down, could have challenged them, but she hadn't.

The god's warning refused to leave her mind. What if she killed one of her own team members? To begin at a disadvantage would be the epitome of foolish. She'd been foolish a little too often lately.

She and Nola had opted to sleep in the trees, making them harder to find, harder to reach. Right now she was strewn atop a thick branch, legs swinging over the side, handmade spear clutched tightly in her palms. Wooden daggers were strapped to her legs, waist and back.

Sharp bark dug into her ribs, helping keep her awake, alert. What were the other creatures doing just then?

What was *Layel* doing?

Layel…beautiful Layel. She'd only interacted with him twice, yet that had been enough to utterly, foolishly fascinate her. He was like no one she had ever encountered. Constantly she found herself wondering what his body looked like underneath his clothes, what his face would look like lost in passion, what he would feel like, pumping and sliding inside of her.

He despises you. He is best forgotten.

Forget that his skin was as pale and smooth as silk? Forget that his eyes were blue like sapphires and fringed by black lashes that were a striking contrast to his snow-white hair? Forget that he was tall with wide shoulders and radiated a dark sensuality women probably salivated over? Impossible.

What kind of females did he enjoy? What type of females had he allowed into his bed?

Sparks of something...dark flickered in her chest. Jealousy, perhaps. She wanted to deny the emotion, but couldn't. *Mine,* she thought. He might want nothing more to do with her, but no way in Hades would he be allowed to have another woman. Not while they inhabited this island.

What's come over you? Men were no longer something she prized. To her, they were something to destroy, a threat to her loved ones. Since her one and only mating had ended so disastrously, she had not thought to find herself possessive of a male. How many times had she watched her sisters fight over a particular slave? *He's mine,* they would shout. *It's my bed he will warm this night.* A clash of daggers always followed, as well as cut and bleeding warrioresses. How many times had she watched those "prized" men leave when the loving was over? Without a backward glance at the broken-hearted they were leaving behind?

Delilah had thought herself immune. Until now. She'd straddled the vampire's shoulders and he'd looked between her legs with undiluted heat. A shiver followed the thought, drowning her in another wave of that deep and inexorable desire. What would it be like to be bedded by Layel? Would he be gentle, taking her slowly? Or would his passion be as ferocious as his wild blue eyes promised? Perhaps even a little wicked?

"You're aroused, Amazon. Why?"

Layel's whispered entreaty was so close, so husky, she wasn't sure if she'd imagined it. She stiffened, fingers tight on the spear, as she searched the darkness for him. Only treetops and night birds came into focus. Not even where thin slivers of golden moonlight seeped through the canopy of leaves overhead did she make out the form of a man. Slowly her muscles released their vise-hold on her bones.

Why am I aroused? Because of you, she wished she could tell this fantasy.

"Well?"

She gasped. Too real, too real, too real…

Before she had time to react, however, a hard hand settled over her mouth while another shoved her to her back. A heavy, muscled weight slammed into her body. She lost her breath, barely managing to remain on the branch.

In seconds, Layel had her stretched out and her legs restrained. Her eyes widened as her spear was torn from her grip and thrown to the ground. A mocking *thump* echoed in her ears. She balled her hand and moved to strike him, but he released her mouth to catch the action. Next he caged her arms between their bodies.

"You will not hurt me," he said.

"I'll do anything I want."

"Try."

One word, but it was so smug she longed to slap and kiss him at the same time. She didn't panic. Yet. Nola was nearby. Probably sneaking up on Layel…now. But no. A moment ticked by, then another.

Nola never arrived.

Delilah's heart began to drum erratically in her chest. Her blood rushed through her veins with dizzying speed, and need quivered in her belly. Here was her fantasy, in the flesh. Hers for the taking.

You are an Amazon. Act like one. Forcing herself into action, she raised her head and sank her teeth into his neck until she tasted the metallic tang of blood. He hissed in her ear, the sound one of pleasure and pain. *You are biting him to escape, yes? So why are you writhing?*

Mmm, so good… Her tongue flicked against his racing pulse.

His hands now free, he fisted her hair and jerked her away. He was panting, anger and arousal bright in his eyes. "Think yourself a vampire, do you? Or are you half vampire? I know your kind consorts with all races and your father could belong to any of them."

She opened her mouth to respond but he shook his head, stopping her. "Scream and you'll regret it."

"As if I would scream," she muttered, offended that he thought so little of her abilities. *You did allow him to sneak up on you.*

Oh, shut up.

He blinked in surprise, as if he'd expected her to scream despite his threat.

Her irritation intensified, and she glared at him. "Did you hurt my sister?"

"She was gone when I reached you. I did not touch her."

"Then I will allow you to live. For now. But very soon I'm going to grow tired of letting you overpower me."

He snorted.

"Be thankful I haven't already killed you."

"Do not fool yourself, Amazon. You would be dead right now had I not stayed my hand."

There was fury in his voice and hate in his expression. Stayed his hand? So he *had* come here to kill her? Bastard! Except, despite everything he had said, despite the genuine loathing directed at her, his legs were between hers and she could feel the length of his shaft hardening, growing, filling.

Just like that, her blood sizzled another degree. Blistered her veins. *I am callous, and I care for no one but my sisters. If they* were in Atlantis, she might agree to take him as her slave. If only for the month males were allowed inside the Amazon camp. But here on this island, with a dangerous competition in the works, they might very well be enemies.

"Afraid, Delilah?" he asked silkily.

Her name, spoken on those red lips…a hot ache bloomed between her legs, moisture pooling there.

"Of what?" The words emerged breathless, wine-rich.

"Dying. Pain."

"No," she answered honestly. Dying didn't scare her. Pain didn't scare her. But her reaction to this man petrified her. He made her feel vulnerable, as if she couldn't rely on herself. As if she needed him to survive. He'd already overtaken her thoughts.

"You should be very afraid," he said….

REQUEST YOUR FREE BOOKS!

2 FREE NOVELS FROM THE ROMANCE/SUSPENSE COLLECTION PLUS 2 FREE GIFTS!

YES! Please send me 2 FREE novels from the Romance/Suspense Collection and my 2 FREE gifts (gifts are worth about $10). After receiving them, if I don't wish to receive any more books, I can return the shipping statement marked "cancel." If I don't cancel, I will receive 4 brand-new novels every month and be billed just $5.49 per book in the U.S. or $5.99 per book in Canada, plus 25¢ shipping and handling per book plus applicable taxes, if any*. That's a savings of at least 20% off the cover price! I understand that accepting the 2 free books and gifts places me under no obligation to buy anything. I can always return a shipment and cancel at any time. Even if I never buy another book from the Reader Service, the two free books and gifts are mine to keep forever.

185 MDN EF5Y 385 MDN EF6C

Name _____ (PLEASE PRINT) _____

Address _____ Apt. # _____

City _____ State/Prov. _____ Zip/Postal Code _____

Signature (if under 18, a parent or guardian must sign)

Mail to **The Reader Service:**
IN U.S.A.: P.O. Box 1867, Buffalo, NY 14240-1867
IN CANADA: P.O. Box 609, Fort Erie, Ontario L2A 5X3

Not valid to current subscribers to the Romance Collection,
the Suspense Collection or the Romance/Suspense Collection.

Want to try two free books from another line?
Call 1-800-873-8635 or visit www.morefreebooks.com.

* Terms and prices subject to change without notice. N.Y. residents add applicable sales tax. Canadian residents will be charged applicable provincial taxes and GST. Offer not valid in Quebec. This offer is limited to one order per household. All orders subject to approval. Credit or debit balances in a customer's account(s) may be offset by any other outstanding balance owed by or to the customer. Please allow 4 to 6 weeks for delivery. Offer available while quantities last.

Your Privacy: Harlequin is committed to protecting your privacy. Our Privacy Policy is available online at www.eHarlequin.com or upon request from the Reader Service. From time to time we make our lists of customers available to reputable third parties who may have a product or service of interest to you. If you would prefer we not share your name and address, please check here. ☐

BOB08R

Silhouette®

nocturne™

MICHELE HAUF

HIS FORGOTTEN FOREVER

Truvin's past was one story nurse Lucy Morgan couldn't stop chasing, even after she discovered he was a vampire. Drawn in by his dark side, Lucy was one bite away from feeling the true power of his embrace, and his eternal curse. Standing at the crux of a new war, Truvin was the key to tipping the balance between vampire and witch. Yet returning to his old, evil ways would destroy Lucy... and deliver to him a fate worse than death.

Available July 2008 wherever books are sold.

www.silhouettenocturne.com
www.paranormalromanceblog.wordpress.com   SN61791